KU-620-791

SABRINA JEFFRIES

THE SECRET OF FLIRTING

HEADLINE
ETERNAL

Published by arrangement with Pocket Books,
a division of Simon & Schuster, Inc.

First published in Great Britain in 2018
by HEADLINE ETERNAL
An imprint of HEADLINE PUBLISHING GROUP

1

Cataloguing in Publication Data is available from the British Library

ISBN 978 1 4722 4546 5

Offset in 12.18/15.18 pt Berling LT Std by Jouve (UK)

Printed and bound in Great Britain by CPI Group (UK) Ltd, Croydon, CR0 4YY

MIX
Paper from
responsible sources
FSC® C104740

Headline's policy is to use papers that are natural, renewable and recyclable
products and made from wood grown in well-managed forests and other
controlled sources. The logging and manufacturing processes are expected
to conform to the environmental regulations of the country of origin.

HEADLINE PUBLISHING GROUP
An Hachette UK Company
Carmelite House
50 Victoria Embankment
London EC4Y 0DZ

www.headlineeternal.com
www.headline.co.uk
www.hachette.co.uk

Sabrina Jeffries is the *New York Times* bestselling author of 41 novels and 10 works of short fiction (some written under the pseudonyms Deborah Martin and Deborah Nicholas). Whatever time not spent writing in a coffee-fueled haze of dreams and madness is spent traveling with her husband and adult autistic son or indulging in one of her passions – jigsaw puzzles, chocolate, and music. With over 7 million books in print in 18 different languages, the North Carolina author never regrets tossing aside a budding career in academics for the sheer joy of writing fun fiction, and hopes that one day a book of hers will end up saving the world. She always dreams big.

For more information, visit her at www.sabrinajeffries.com, on Facebook at www.facebook.com/SabrinaJeffriesAuthor or on Twitter @SabrinaJeffries.

Praise for Sabrina Jeffries, queen of the sexy regency romance:

'Anyone who loves romance must read Sabrina Jeffries!' Lisa Kleypas, *New York Times* bestselling author

'Irresistible . . . Larger-than-life characters, sprightly dialogue, and a steamy romance will draw you into this delicious captive/captor tale' *Romantic Times* (top pick)

'Another excellent series of books which will alternatively have you laughing, crying and running the gamut of emotions . . . I guarantee you will have a tear in your eye' *Romance Reviews Today*

'The sexual tension crackles across the pages of this witty, deliciously sensual, secret-laden story' *Library Journal*

'Exceptionally entertaining and splendidly sexy' *Booklist*

'An enchanting story brimming with sincere emotions and compelling scenarios . . . an outstanding love story of emotional discoveries and soaring passions, with a delightful touch of humor plus suspense' *Single Titles*

'Scorching . . . From cover to cover, it sizzles' *Reader to Reader*

'Full c   nd witty
dialog   *ublishers
Week*

527 000 55 7

By Sabrina Jeffries

Sinful Suitors Series

The Art Of Sinning
The Study Of Seduction
The Danger Of Desire
The Pleasures Of Passion
A Talent For Temptation (e-novella)
The Secret Of Flirting

Hellions Of Halstead Hall Series

The Truth About Lord Stoneville
A Hellion In Her Bed
How To Woo A Reluctant Lady
To Wed A Wild Lord
A Lady Never Surrenders

To Louise Burke, who championed my career for all my years at Pocket. I wouldn't be where I am today without you, so thank you. And enjoy your well-deserved retirement!

And to Micki Nuding, who taught me so much about writing. Enjoy that new house and those grandchildren. You've earned it!

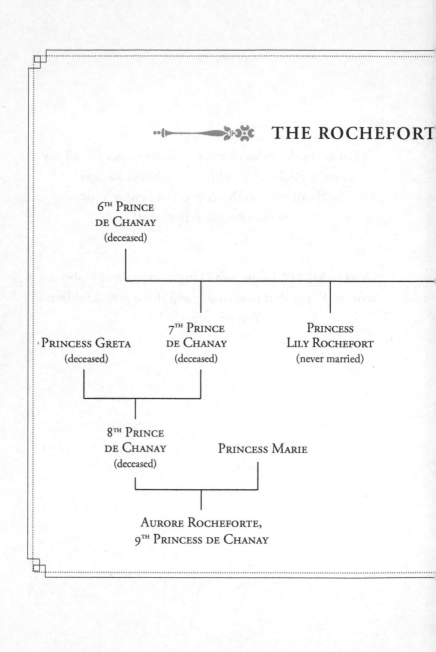

THE ROCHEFORT

6TH PRINCE
DE CHANAY
(deceased)

PRINCESS GRETA
(deceased)

7TH PRINCE
DE CHANAY
(deceased)

PRINCESS
LILY ROCHEFORT
(never married)

8TH PRINCE
DE CHANAY
(deceased)

PRINCESS MARIE

AURORE ROCHEFORTE,
9TH PRINCESS DE CHANAY

FAMILY TREE

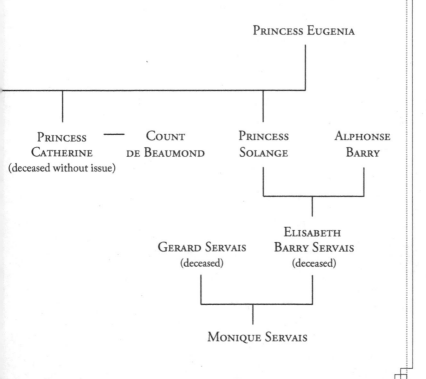

PRINCESS EUGENIA

PRINCESS CATHERINE — COUNT DE BEAUMOND
(deceased without issue)

PRINCESS SOLANGE

ALPHONSE BARRY

GERARD SERVAIS
(deceased)

ELISABETH BARRY SERVAIS
(deceased)

MONIQUE SERVAIS

THE SECRET
OF FLIRTING

Prologue

Dieppe, France
1827

Gregory Vyse, Baron of Fulkham, sipped a glass of fine brandy, savoring its smoky bite. Drinking decent spirits was one advantage of passing through France on his travels. And the taproom of this particular Dieppe inn provided the best, even if he had to pay far too much for his room to get it.

Not that his companion, Captain Lord Hartley Corry, seemed to appreciate the liquor. Hart knocked the brandy back as if it were cheap ale. As if he were nervous, actually.

Hmm. What was that about? This was supposed to be a simple delivery.

Hart pushed a package wrapped in string across the table. "Here are the letters, Fulkham. You *will* be able to get them to my cousin soon, won't you?"

Gregory slipped them into his greatcoat pocket. "It shouldn't take more than a few days if the weather holds. Corunna isn't far by boat. And Niall is expecting me."

When Hart said nothing more, Gregory asked, "Have you no messages for me from Gibraltar? From John?"

Hart blinked. "Were you expecting any?"

"I suppose not."

Though he'd rather hoped . . . His younger brother, John, and Hart were best friends, and had both been posted to Gibraltar with their respective regiments until recently, when Hart's regiment was sent home briefly in anticipation of their new posting. John could at least have sent him an update; Gregory should have received a report days ago. The next time he saw John, he'd give his feckless brother another lecture about the importance of reports.

Hart called for another brandy, and Gregory raised an eyebrow. He'd never heard that the marquess's son was a heavy drinker, soldier or no. Clearly something was on the man's mind. Gregory could tell by the tense line of Hart's lips, the drumming of his fingers . . . his darting gaze.

So Gregory waited him out. Because that was the best way to elicit the truth, something at which he excelled.

It didn't take long. Hart drank some brandy, then settled back in his chair. "Speaking of John, he told me that you sometimes . . . er . . . pay for information."

Damn John and his big mouth. "Did he?"

Hart's gaze shot to him. "John says you like having eyes everywhere."

"I do when they belong to someone I can trust. Which is clearly not the case with my little brother."

John ought to know better. But despite his marriage a year ago, the bloody fool was apparently as reckless as ever. That was precisely why Gregory hadn't wanted to use him in this work. Gregory had only agreed when it became clear that if he didn't dictate his brother's actions to some degree, John would get himself killed on his own.

Hart leaned forward. "Don't blame John for speaking of it. When he offered to get you to deliver letters to Niall in Spain, I badgered him until he explained your connection to my cousin. I mean, given that Niall . . . well . . ."

"Killed a man?"

"Yes. I was worried you wanted to capture him and carry him back to England. You *are* with the government, after all."

"True." The foreign office, to be exact. But although officially Gregory served as undersecretary of state for war and the colonies, his unofficial position was a trifle . . . murkier.

With another glance about the taproom, Hart lowered his voice. "But John explained that Niall sometimes provides you with information from Corunna, which is why you overlook that he's in exile for dueling, and I was thinking—"

"That you could do the same, now that you'll be posted elsewhere than Gibraltar."

"Exactly."

Gregory didn't answer right away. He took his time sipping his brandy, letting the silence stretch out and gauging Hart's reaction.

To his credit, Hart didn't fidget or frown. Most people would.

"Why exactly would that be an advantage to me?" Gregory finally asked.

"Because you don't have eyes at Fort Bullen on James Island." Hart paused. "Wait, do you?"

"No. But then, there's little reason for that. The soldiers are posted there to keep slave ships from operating. Not much political intrigue."

A sigh escaped Hart. Apparently, he'd been banking on the alternative source of income he'd hoped to get from spying. As a second son to a marquess, Hart probably found that his allowance and army pay didn't go quite far enough to support such lordly entertainments as gambling and wenching.

Bloody hell. Undoubtedly Gregory would regret this, but the man *was* John's friend, after all. "I tell you what," he said. "I'm planning on attending *Le mariage de Figaro* at the new theater after this. Why don't we go together? Afterward, I'll ask you questions and see how much you noticed. If you answer to my satisfaction, I'll consider you the next time you're in a position to help me."

It never hurt to have more spies. If Hart was as observant as John claimed he was sharp-witted, the man might prove useful one day.

Hart brightened. "Excellent! I'm told that Mademoiselle Servais is in tonight's performance, so you'll be glad you went. I swear she's as good as Mrs. Siddons ever was."

"I somehow doubt that. I had the privilege of seeing Sarah Siddons in her last role on the stage. Very impressive. And I'd be shocked if a theater in a town the size of Dieppe has an actress of any great ability in its employ."

The sudden twinkle in Hart's eye gave him pause. "Then prepare to be shocked, old man."

~⁂~

The theater in Dieppe had two rows of boxes. Thanks to his position, Gregory had been offered the finest one for his own use on this visit, a fact that overjoyed Hart. Gregory had to admit that the small but new venue had a certain charm, as did the performance. He'd always preferred the original play by Beaumarchais to the opera by Mozart.

As for Mademoiselle Monique Servais, Gregory had to stifle his irritation at discovering how magnificent she really was. He hated being proved wrong.

Well, not *wrong*, exactly. A comedic role like that of Suzanne lacked the gravitas of any of

Mrs. Siddons's great dramatic personae, so comparisons between them would be apples versus oranges. But still . . .

"What did I tell you?" Hart said as the music came up for the interlude. "She's astounding."

Gregory disliked exaggeration. "If by 'astounding' you mean that she's a particularly pretty French chit with a superior speaking voice and an unaffected manner that enhances her credibility as Suzanne, you'd be right. But other than that—"

"Other than that, what? Admit it, man. She has the curves of Aphrodite, the face of Helen of Troy, the voice of . . . of—"

"A siren? As long as you're making comparisons with mythical beings, you might as well throw that one in. And you speak only of her physical attributes."

Which *were* uncommonly attractive. Despite wearing a massive powdered wig, she managed to walk with a sensual grace that made him wonder what she looked like beneath that ridiculous costume from his grandmother's era.

Then again, even Frenchwomen with modest features had a talent for projecting beauty to the world. And Mademoiselle Servais's features, as best he could tell from this distance, weren't remotely modest. What's more, her voice was melodic without being singsong, and she enunciated every word of dialogue. She captivated the audience—and him—each time she stepped onstage.

"You're just a sore loser," Hart said in a moment of keen perception. "Tell the truth—she's better than you imagined."

"I will concede that. But then, my expectations were low." When Hart scowled, he added, "And you're supposed to be paying attention to more than just the actress, remember? This is a test, after all."

"Right." Hart crossed his arms over his chest. "Ask me anything."

"What was the name of the porter who took our tickets?"

"Mr. Duval," Hart said readily enough.

Not bad. No one generally noticed such people. "His given name?"

Hart thrust out his chin. "He didn't say."

"Actually, someone else did when they greeted him, but you may not have heard." Gregory settled back in his seat. "Describe him, starting with his hair and ending with his shoes." When Hart did a creditable job of that, Gregory nodded. "Now tell me what you think his life at home is like."

That seemed to startle Hart. "His life at home?"

"One can tell a great deal about a man's circumstances from how he behaves, dresses, speaks. But for now, just give me your impressions."

Before Hart could begin, a knock came at the door to the box. When Gregory bade the person enter, it was none other than the porter himself.

"Is everything to your satisfaction this evening, gentlemen?" Duval asked in French.

"It is, thank you," Gregory said dismissively.

Then Hart chimed in, obviously trying to keep the man there longer so he could better answer Gregory's question. "Could you arrange for us to meet Mademoiselle Servais after the play?"

As Gregory stifled a groan, the porter's face clouded. "I'm afraid not, sir. She usually hurries home."

"She has a husband and children to attend to, I suppose," Gregory said.

"An aging grandmother, sir. Mademoiselle Servais is unmarried."

Interesting. And unexpected. Since the French always referred to their actresses as *mademoiselle*, one could never know for certain if they had husbands. But he'd assumed that a woman of such unparalleled attractions would. So he felt an oddly powerful satisfaction at hearing that she didn't.

He could easily imagine her in his bed. She was exactly his sort—sensuous but graceful, an elegant siren.

Siren, bah. He was as bad as Hart. He had no time for women right now, certainly no time to dally with a French actress. That would hardly be wise for his career. And his career trumped everything.

Hart stood. "You may not know this, but I am a marquess's son and my companion is a baron of high rank in the British government. If you can manage a meeting, we'll make it well worth your while. We won't keep her long."

Gregory lifted an eyebrow at Hart. What was the man up to?

The porter nodded. "I will see what I can do, gentlemen."

After he left, Gregory said, "If you're hoping that your maneuver will distract me from my questions—"

"Actually, I've been wanting to make the 'French chit's' acquaintance, and I figure two men of consequence are more likely to interest her than one."

Ah, yes. John *had* described Hart as a bit of a lothario. "And *we* will make it 'well worth' the porter's while?"

"You can take my part out of my first payment as a spy."

Gregory snorted. "You certainly are sure of yourself."

"A useful ability for a spy, don't you think?" Hart said with a grin.

It was. But that didn't mean Gregory would let the fellow lead him about like a mule. "For tonight, you can practice those skills without me. I intend to return to my room after the play is over. I've got reports to write."

"Surely those can wait until later. How often do you get to meet a woman of such stellar talent as Mademoiselle Servais?"

"Often enough for me to be cynical about it. Performers belong in the golden light of the stage. In my experience, once they climb down from their lofty perch to become ordinary people, they prove either boring or flighty or both."

Hart laughed. "Come now, I doubt she'll be boring, and if she's flighty, who cares? A little flirting never hurt anyone."

In an instant, the voice of Gregory's late unlamented father leapt into his head. *Come now, boy, who cares if I tipple? A little drinking never hurt anyone.*

Except when it was followed by the back of a hand. Or a fist.

He pushed that thought down into the well of secrets it had come from. "I prefer my flirting to be with a woman who can further my interests, frankly."

Hart shook his head. "Good God, for a fellow in his thirties you act like an old man. Live a little. You're too focused on work, you know."

His brother and mother often made that accusation. Gregory found it ludicrous. Work kept him sane. Work drove out the memories and banished the cold sweats at night. Work was a godsend.

Hart slanted a glance at him. "Unless you're afraid that the 'French chit' won't take to you."

"Don't attempt to manipulate me with insults, old chap. It won't work. I perfected the strategy when you were still a cornet."

A heavy breath escaped Hart. "Damn it, Fulkham. Just half an hour to spend with an actress. I might not get even that if you don't come along. She'll be nervous if it's just one of us."

The man was like a dog with a bone. Which would actually make him very good as an informer. And it never hurt to stay on the good side of a marquess's son. "Fine. If she'll see us." Not that Gregory doubted she would. His own rank and the promise of money generally got him whatever he wanted, and Hart's rank alone would do that.

But after the last act ended and a servant brought them backstage, he began to think he'd been proved wrong in that, too. For as they wended their way through a warren of dressing rooms, they could hear the porter arguing with a woman in French. There was no mistaking the dulcet tones of Mademoiselle Servais, who was clearly annoyed.

"I don't care how important these men are," she said. "Cursed Englishmen, always expecting to get their way. I have to get back to my grandmother. If she should wake and become confused—"

The porter said something Gregory couldn't make out, and the woman released a drawn-out sigh. "Oh, very well, then. If you must. I know you need the funds." Her voice hardened. "But don't expect me to fawn over them. I have no patience for men who are arrogant, usually with no reason."

No reason? Apparently my lady actress had her own delusions of grandeur. And he didn't have time for such nonsense, damn it.

But before the porter could even answer her, the servant who'd fetched them from the box showed them into a room little bigger than the coat closet in Gregory's London town house, with scarcely space enough for her and the porter, much less him and Hart.

With a nod at Gregory, the porter slid past them into the hall, leaving them alone with the actress. Too late to escape now. She stared them down unrepentantly, though she had to know they'd overheard her insults.

She was still in costume, but he noticed things about her that his distance from the stage had obscured—like her voluptuous bosom and surprising height. Her prominent chin gave her the look of a woman of purpose. And up close, she looked younger than she had onstage. Even the heavy theatrical makeup couldn't disguise the tight skin of her neck, her youthful hands, and the lack of lines about her mouth and eyes.

Her *gorgeous* mouth and eyes. Her scarlet-painted lips were unexpectedly full, the kind that made a man want to taste and tongue and suck. Her stunning green eyes shone iridescent in the lamplight from between long, lustrous lashes. They enticed him, and that put him on his guard.

Those eyes seemed to be assessing him, too—weighing his worth, character, and proclivities in the same way he often did those of other people. It disturbed him to be on the receiving end. Who *was* this chit, anyway?

"Good evening, gentlemen," she said in excellent English. "What may I do for you?"

Hart offered her a courtly bow. "We came to express our admiration for the performance."

"Did you?" She met Gregory's gaze coolly. "I don't think your companion has the same purpose."

Had he been scowling at her? Probably. The woman had thrown him off his game. He'd spent years schooling his emotions into calm, and it vexed him that she had managed to ruffle it.

Forcing a smile, he dipped his head. "On the contrary, I found your acting quite proficient."

"What effusive praise," she said dryly, surprising him with her knowledge of English vocabulary. "I shall try not to let it go to my head."

"What he meant to say was—" Hart began.

"I can speak for myself." Gregory wasn't going to be chided by some French actress. Nor was he going to "fawn over her," to use *her* words. "You're clearly an adept performer, mademoiselle, at least in a comedic role."

"What exactly does that mean? What's wrong with a comedic role?" she asked in a voice smooth as butter. But her gaze sliced into him like a blade of carved jade.

It unsettled him, made him impatient to be done with this. "Surely you will admit that such roles lack the deep feeling of dramatic ones. So of course they are easier to perform."

To his surprise, that garnered him a light, tinkling laugh that thrummed along his every nerve. "If you think that, sir, you have never been on the stage."

Hart stepped forward. "He didn't mean to insult—"

"Of course not." The gleam in her eyes mocked Gregory. "He is merely stating the usual opinion of an English lord—that great literature should always be *très tragique*."

The word *usual* arrested him. "It isn't merely English lords who hold that opinion, but arbiters of culture of every rank." Damn it, he sounded as arrogant as she'd assumed, the opposite of what he wanted.

That seemed to sober her. "*Every* rank? Truly? Because I generally find that such opinions come from those who have never lived with tragedy, whose moated castles protect them from poverty and violence."

"Poverty? Yes." The image of his mother's battered features swam into his memory. "But no one escapes violence in this age, regardless of their rank."

"Come now, sir," she said coldly, "if that were true, men of your sort wouldn't find tragedy entertaining. But those of us who toil daily in the darkness prefer to be taken away from it, if only for a short while. We prefer to laugh. And I truly believe that making people laugh is a noble endeavor far superior to making people cry."

Impossible woman. What did *she* know? "You are, of course, entitled to your opinion. But I would point out that Shakespeare is lauded for his tragedies more than his comedies."

"By whom? I like his comedies very well. Though I confess I prefer Beaumarchais's farces. Or, in your language, the excellent work of Oliver Goldsmith. *She Stoops to Conquer* comes to mind."

She was beautiful *and* well read. He began to regret his caustic words earlier, which had put her on her guard.

"That's my favorite of Goldsmith's, too," Hart put in, clearly determined to be part of the conversation.

"I have never seen or read it," Gregory said bluntly.

Humor lit her face. "Of course not. But you should. You would approve of the hero, I daresay."

Hart laughed. "Touché."

Not knowing anything of the play put him at a disadvantage. Gregory hated that. "And I assume that *you*, mademoiselle, approve of the title, since the woman gets to 'conquer.'"

"I do indeed enjoy that, but mostly because of *how* she conquers—by revealing to the hero his little snobberies and hypocrisies."

Gregory stiffened. "An intriguing assessment coming from a woman who's—"

"A mere *comédienne?*" she said archly.

"So young." Damn, he'd really put her back up with his ill-considered remarks earlier. "How old are you, anyway? Twenty-one? Twenty-two?"

When she blinked, he knew he'd guessed correctly. Then she attempted to mask her surprise by fluttering a fan before her face. "You should know by now, monsieur, that a woman never tells her age. It dulls her *mystique.*"

The coy remark made him scoff. "Only if she's old and losing her attractions. Clearly you are neither. I would say you have *mystique* to spare."

Amusement sparkled in her eyes. "Ah, so the haughty English gentleman *can* exert himself to be charming when he wishes."

In that moment, he glimpsed the real Mademoiselle Servais—flirtatious and full of joie de vivre beneath the prickliness he'd brought on with his condescending remarks. He wished to see more of *that* Mademoiselle Servais.

Allowing his gaze to skim down her lush form, he drawled, "It is no exertion at all with you, mademoiselle. Forgive me if I gave you the idea that it was."

When the faintest tinge of color pinkened her pretty cheeks, Hart cut in to say, "To be fair, my companion spends his days in the somber profession of politics. He has little opportunity to perfect his ability to charm women."

Just as Gregory bristled at that characterization of him as some sort of bumbler in the art of flirtation, she added lightly, "And probably little inclination, either. He relies on his rank and riches to charm them."

Gregory fixed her with a steady look. "I would never be so foolish. Women of any worth generally see past such trappings."

She met his gaze with an unnerving intensity. "Ah, but I suspect that you find few women of such worth in *your* circles, eh, monsieur?"

"I certainly don't find them very often in theaters."

He'd meant the words as a compliment to her—an implication that *she* was the exception to the rule.

But his tone must have resisted translation, because she blanched, then nodded regally to them both. "In that case, you will not mind if I excuse myself. It is long past time I returned home."

Devil take it. What was it about her that made him speak so clumsily?

"I'm sure his lordship didn't mean—" Hart began.

"I know what he meant," she said. "I have more experience with his kind than he thinks."

This was the point where he should apologize, should explain what he'd been trying to say. But he'd be damned if he'd curry the favor of some French actress who thought him beneath contempt. He was the bloody undersecretary of the foreign office, for God's sake. He didn't cower before anyone.

Hart glared at him, but Gregory ignored the man. "Well then, mademoiselle, perhaps we shall see you when you are more at your leisure."

Her green eyes glittered. "Oh, I don't think I shall ever be at my leisure for *you*, sir." As Gregory tensed, she turned to cast a dazzling smile at Hart. "Though your charming companion is always welcome."

Hart started to return the smile, then caught himself with a nervous glance at Gregory, and an unfamiliar sensation tightened the muscles of Gregory's belly. Jealousy? No, that was ridiculous. He'd just met the woman. What did he care if Hart got the benefit of her smiles? She was playing them off against each other. That was all.

Though Gregory knew that game, he'd never been the loser in it. "Good. Then he can stay and entertain you with his charm."

Turning on his heel, he left the dressing room, angry at her and angry at himself. She'd made him lose control, and he *never* lost control. But the damned chit had essentially given *him* the cut direct! No one ever dared.

Footsteps sounded behind him. "That went well," Hart grumbled.

Gregory bit back the impulse to say something snide. He'd already revealed too much of himself to Mademoiselle Servais in front of Hart as it was; he damned well wasn't going to add insult to injury.

He fought to make his voice sound bored.

"You were the one who wanted to dally with an actress. You should have stayed."

"She didn't want me there." Hart's tone sharpened. "She ignored me completely, except when she was trying to goad you. She was only interested in you."

Was the man mad? "If she *was* interested in me, it was merely as a razor strop for her sharp tongue. Nothing more."

"Didn't seem that way to me."

Gregory was in no mood to argue with him.

"I suppose this means I've failed the test," Hart added.

What test? Gregory nearly asked before he remembered what Hart meant. "Don't be ridiculous." He wasn't about to reveal how she'd rattled him. "Some actress's poor attempts at insult have naught to do with whether I can use you as an informant. So if you come across anything you think I might use, let me know."

It was an idle promise, after all. What could the man possibly learn out on James Island?

"Oh! Well. Thank you, then," Hart said jovially. "Good of you to offer."

They walked out of the theater together.

Hart cleared his throat. "The night is still young. Would you want to—"

"Sorry, old chap, but as I said before, I have reports to write. Have a good trip."

He left Hart gaping after him. Gregory didn't care. Much as he liked the fellow, he'd had enough of company for one night. He had work to do.

So why was he still seething about the actress's responses as he entered the inn? She was no less impudent than any other Frenchwoman to an Englishman. He ought not be annoyed, but he was.

Because she was sharp. Observant. Quick-witted. All things he admired in a woman. He wasn't used to having such a woman not admire those things in *him*.

Except that there had been the one moment when she'd blushed and he'd thought perhaps she . . .

God, he didn't care! Absurd that he should even think he might.

He stalked up the stairs, so lost in replaying their conversation that he didn't at first hear the innkeeper hail him, and when he did, he rounded on the fellow, snapping, "What is it?" in French.

The man paled. With a shaky hand, he held out a small envelope. "Th-this message just came for you, my lord. I was told to put it right in your hand."

Gregory spotted the seal belonging to one of his informants from Gibraltar and muttered, "It's about damned time." At last, word from someone concerning John's mission. He would rather it had come from John, of course, but . . .

That gave him pause. Why *hadn't* it come from John? As he hastily opened the letter and scanned its contents, his stomach began to roil.

My lord, our mission was compromised. You were right to advise caution, but I'm afraid it did no good. I regret to inform you that your brother is dead. He decided to . . .

A description of what had gone wrong followed, but the words swam before his eyes. His knees buckled beneath him and he sat down hard on the stairs.

His brother was dead? It couldn't be. How could it be? Impossible.

But clearly it was true. There was no reason for the man to lie.

Gregory stared sightlessly past the innkeeper to the taproom below, crowded with men drinking and carousing. And to think that only a few hours ago, he too had been . . .

Grief clogged his throat with tears he couldn't shed. How was he to go on without John? How was Mother?

Oh, God, *Mother.* This would destroy her.

"John, you reckless fool," Gregory hissed.

Despite his cautions, the lad had gone and gotten himself killed. And it was all Gregory's fault—for using him in the first place, for not reining him in. For not being more of a father to him once their own father was gone.

Gregory stiffened. Not *gone.* Murdered. Best never to forget that, or he would truly lose his soul. Or at least the part of it that still had a conscience.

What had that actress said? *I generally find that*

*such opinions come from those who have never lived
with tragedy, whose moated castles protect them
from poverty and violence.*

Anger flashed through him, tangled up in his
sorrow and guilt and pain. Damn her to hell.
She had no idea what she was talking about. A
moated castle kept things in as well as out. It
could hide shame and heartache, neglect and
abuse, blood and gore and death.

Especially death. And now John was dead.
Dead. Gregory must get that through his head or
how was he to continue?

So as he let his grief overtake him, let himself sink into its madness, he put all thoughts of
Mademoiselle Monique Servais from his head for
good.

One

Dieppe, France
October 1830

Monique Servais sat alone in her dressing room, reapplying face paint between acts. Once again, the Dieppe theater was performing *Le mariage de Figaro*, but this time she was playing the Countess and not Suzanne.

She grimaced. Of *course* she was playing the older woman these days. Some ingénue had the role of Suzanne now that Monique had reached the advanced age of twenty-four.

No, that wasn't fair. It was her peaked appearance and her lapses in remembering her lines that had relegated her to the lesser role. She got little sleep anymore, with her grandmother Solange wandering outside the apartment at all hours.

So it was just as well that Monique had an easier part. She would soon have to hire a servant to keep watch even at night. And how was she to pay for that? It wasn't as if the theater would give her more money, especially in her current state.

A knock came at the door, and Mr. Duval poked his head inside. "There is a gentleman who wishes to meet you after the performance."

"Another?" She waved her hand dismissively. "You know I don't do that."

"I think you may want to speak to this particular man, my dear. He says—"

"I don't care what he says or how much he pays you." She swiveled on her chair to look at Mr. Duval. "I can't linger after the performance these days—you *know* that. Grand-maman is getting worse. Besides, I hate all those leering fellows. There was that merchant who thought he could convince me to become his mistress by giving me a fur tippet. And that . . . that vile Dutchman who wanted to suck my toes."

So far she'd avoided taking a protector. But if Grand-maman got worse, she might have no choice.

She shuddered. "Not to mention the baker with the admittedly delicious cakes who also stank of fish. Even *you* said it wasn't worth the money he paid you for an audience with me."

"And let's not forget that British lord, the one who annoyed you so thoroughly."

Gregory Vyse, Baron Fulkham. Even after three years, she remembered his name. And his faintly accented French and the way the room had seemed to shrink to fit him when he walked in. Not to mention his eyes, so starkly blue in his handsome face, and his wealth of wavy hair, black as a starless night.

Curse him. Turning back to her mirror, she resumed touching up her face paint. "British lord?" she said with forced nonchalance. "I don't remember any British lord."

Mr. Duval chuckled. "You rage about him every time anyone mentions the virtues of tragedy over comedy."

"He was arrogant and insufferable in his opinions," she snapped. "Of course I rage about him."

"So you *do* remember him," Mr. Duval said smugly.

She glared at Mr. Duval in the mirror. "I remember that you forced the man on me and that I regretted it. Just as, no doubt, I will regret the one you are trying to make me see tonight."

"This one is different."

"You always say that," she muttered.

"He's from Chanay."

She paused with her powder brush in midair. Grand-maman was also from Chanay, in Belgium. "What's his name?"

"The Count de Beaumonde. He says he's your great-uncle. Your grandmother's brother-in-law."

She recognized the name. Grand-maman had spoken of the count many times, and with great affection, too.

Monique's hand began to shake so much she dropped the brush. "He's here. In the theater."

"Yes."

"Who's with him?"

"Only a servant. But the count says he traveled from Calais today to speak with you and your grandmother."

She could scarcely believe it. After all these years of Grand-maman's exile from her family, one of them had finally come to see her. Before this, not a single person from the Chanay branch had bothered.

What was she to think? What did it mean? "Did he say why he'd come?"

"No. But he said it was most important. Shall I tell him he can meet with you?"

She had to say yes. These days Grand-maman spoke of nothing but her childhood in Chanay. The count might be able to cheer her. Besides, Monique was curious to meet one of the relatives her grandmother had seemed so amazingly fond of.

"Set it up," she said, "but not here. At the apartment. Tell him to come at eleven."

That would give her an hour after the play to make herself presentable. To make Grand-maman presentable and prepare her for seeing her long-lost relation. They must both make a good impression. Monique didn't know why the man was here or what he wanted, but she was not going to let him see her looking like an overpainted harlot in this cramped dressing room. Or pitying Grand-maman for having such a granddaughter.

After all, it wasn't every day that one got an

audience with a member of the royal family of Chanay.

⌒‿⌒

Unable to sit still, Monique paced the small parlor of their comfy apartment as her grandmother sat on the sofa doing embroidery. Ever since Grand-maman's mind had begun to fail her, she'd reverted to old habits from her girlhood—embroidering reticules, speaking like a royal, and expecting luxuries that Monique could never afford.

"Who is this visitor we are expecting?" Grand-maman asked.

Having already answered the question twice, Monique said, a trifle impatiently, "Your brother-in-law, the count. You remember."

Her grandmother lit up, just as she had twice before. "Oh yes! A lovely man. How kind of him to visit! I shall be very happy to see him." She rose. "Shall I call for wine?"

Monique hastened to her side. "No need." Especially since their one servant had left long ago. She gestured to the bottle of red Burgundy sitting on the tea table with three glasses and a little pile of petits fours. "We are all ready for him."

"Good, good. He must have the best."

A knock came at the door.

Wiping her clammy hands on the skirt of her best gown, Monique stiffened her spine and walked calmly to the door.

She opened it to find a white-haired gentleman who looked even older than her sixty-five-year-old grandmother. Dressed in a costly opera cloak of black satin, a suit of black silk, an ivory cravat, and a subtly patterned waistcoat, the darkly attractive fellow was the very picture of discreet elegance. Oddly enough, he reminded her of her late grandfather, who was of no relation to him whatsoever.

The servant behind him was elderly, too, but he wore a soft smile that seemed to say he was glad to be there.

Not the count, who nodded to her with great formality. "Miss Servais, I presume?"

Sketching a curtsy, she said, "Good evening, sir." She refused to show him more deference than that. The family had ignored her and Grand-maman for decades, after all.

"You're right, my lord," the count's servant murmured to him. "She could easily be the princess's sister."

Which princess? she wanted to ask, but before she could, Grand-maman rose to eye the count uncertainly.

"Who is this ancient fellow, Monique?" she asked with the bluntness she'd developed of late.

Ignoring the way the man flinched, Monique said, "This is the Count de Beaumonde. Your eldest sister's husband."

"It cannot be." Grand-maman peered at him as she came near. "He is much too *old*."

The count bristled and scowled at Monique. "Did you not tell her I was coming to visit this evening?"

"I did," Monique said in a low voice. "But she doesn't remember. In her mind, you are still as young as when she last saw you."

As he took her meaning, his features softened profoundly. "Ah." He stepped into the room to approach Grand-maman. "Princess Solange, it is a great pleasure to meet with you again. You're looking very well."

Her grandmother preened. "Oh, Count, you always were such a flatterer."

The rare moment of remembrance made Monique feel momentarily grateful to the man. Until she reminded herself that he and the rest of the family had exiled Grand-maman from Chanay for eloping with a common actor without her father's permission.

Monique tamped down her anger. Grand-maman felt no resentment and never had. She'd always said she'd made her choice while fully knowing and accepting the consequences. That she would do it again, given the chance.

A thickness formed in Monique's throat. Her grandparents had been very much in love. Still, Grand-maman's choice had cost her time and again. Monique had learned from her example never to be so foolish as to choose romantic love over one's family.

The servant followed his master into the

room. "Do you remember *me*, Princess?" the man said hopefully to Solange. "You used to call me Chanceux, because of my luck at cards. We had some merry times when you were a girl."

Grand-maman's blank look showed that her rare moment of clarity was gone. "I—I . . . yes . . . of course. Chanceux." Abruptly she turned to Monique. "I'm very tired. It is late for visiting, no?"

"It is, Grand-maman." The lump in Monique's throat thickened even more. The old Solange would have exulted to have the royal family and retinue call on her after all these years. The new Solange barely knew who they were. "Would you like to retire now?"

"Yes." Grand-maman flashed the two men a vague smile. "Forgive me, sirs, but I am not so young anymore, you know."

What looked like regret crossed the count's features. "Of course. You must rest. Sleep well, my beautiful lady."

Solange brightened. "Thank you. I shall."

Then she went out into the hall. Monique was torn between going after her and remaining with their guests, but Grand-maman was still capable of preparing herself for bed alone, so Monique preferred to leave her with her dignity.

As soon as the elderly woman had vanished, the count said in grave tones, "How long has she been this way?"

Monique sighed. "About five years now. It's

why we stopped touring with Grandpapa's old
acting troupe. But it's worsened dramatically in
the past year."

He shook his head. "How sad to see such a
wonderful woman brought low."

She stiffened. How dared he? "Your concern comes a little late, sir. Where were you
when her father cut her off from her family just
because she chose to marry for love? Or when
my mother was born, and the doctor said Grand-
maman dared not have more children? Where
were you when my father abandoned my mother,
with me in her belly, shortly after being forced
to marry her? Or when Grandpapa and Mother
died of consumption, leaving Grand-maman to
raise me alone?"

She faced him down. "My grandmother *is* a
wonderful woman. She deserved better from the
Rocheforts."

The count looked momentarily taken aback
by her bitter words. They surprised her, too.
She'd never felt the loss of her royal relations to
any great degree. But Grand-maman had. Not
enough to leave the man she loved, but still . . .

"Why have you come here?" she demanded.
"What do you want from us?"

He pulled into himself as she'd seen her
grandmother do when faced with abject impudence. Usually from Monique. "I have come to
ask a favor of you."

"You have the gall to—"

"I would make it well worth your while. And your grandmother's."

That gave Monique pause. More money would make things so much easier. She could hire staff to look after Grand-maman around the clock. Then she could work more, which would enable her to save more to make Grand-maman's final days comfortable.

It had been just the two of them since Monique turned eleven. Without Grand-maman to raise her, who knew what would have become of her? Monique owed her everything. So if she had it within her means to give it to her . . .

Monique swallowed her pride. "What sort of favor?"

He exchanged a glance with his servant. "Do you mind if we sit down?"

"Of course not." She gestured to the sofa and to the wine in front of it. "Forgive me. I am not used to hosting royalty."

As her great-uncle took his seat, the servant said, "Except for your grandmother, of course. She is still a princess."

"Is she? You wouldn't know it to judge from how her family has treated her." When the count began to frown again, she added hastily, "And she doesn't consider herself one." Monique sat down in the other chair and began to pour the wine. "That life is behind her."

Not entirely, though. Memory played tricks on Solange these days. Sometimes it was as if the past decades had never happened and she was a girl again, frolicking in the gardens of Chanay.

"It doesn't have to be behind her." The count took the glass from her.

Monique narrowed her gaze on him. "What do you mean?"

"If you will do this one favor for us, we can take her home to the palace, care for her there, and make sure she is comfortable for the rest of her life." When Monique tensed, he added hastily, "You would of course come with her. You would be welcomed back into the family. You are, after all, granddaughter to a princess and second cousin to the reigning Princess de Chanay."

Monique could hardly catch her breath. Her main worry would vanish. Grand-maman would be taken care of. And Monique would at last have family when Grand-maman was gone.

A family who had not given her a thought until now.

She glanced away. "I suppose I would have to give up the stage." Her home, the only place she'd ever felt entirely at ease.

His gaze hardened. "Of course. No member of the royal family can be an actress."

It would be as if her past life vanished, swept away by the hand of Chanay royalty as if it had never occurred. It was a great price to pay. She loved acting; it was all she knew.

Then again, Grand-maman's condition worsened by the day.

"Forgive me, my dear," the count added, "but you must see that living as a royal in Chanay is vastly preferable to being on the stage, for both you and your grandmother. I'll admit that you are an excellent actress, one of the reasons we have come to ask this favor, but—"

"Yes, what exactly is it that you want of me that would wipe away the years when you wanted nothing to do with us?"

With a sigh, he sipped some wine, then set the glass down. "We want you to play your finest role yet. That of my great-niece Aurore, the reigning Princess de Chanay."

⌒⌒⌒

Two days later, the count ushered her into a lavish hotel suite in Calais. So the two of them could come here unencumbered, he had left his servant, Chanceux, in Dieppe to stay with Grand-maman. It was the first time Monique had been away from the woman who had mostly raised her, and that made her nervous.

But not nearly as nervous as the prospect of meeting her cousin Aurore.

She shouldn't have worried. The count had not lied about Aurore's situation. The princess lay insensible in her enormous bed, with three other ladies keeping watch over her.

But even with the young woman's cheeks flushed with fever and her eyes closed, Monique felt as if she were looking at her twin. Aurore had the same pale skin, the same full lips, the same ignominious bump on the end of her nose. Her cedar-brown hair was the same wildly disordered mass as Monique's. It too could probably only be tamed by scraping it up into a heavy chignon that threatened to escape its confines with her every motion.

They did have different chins—Monique had the cursed prominent one, while the princess's was small and delicate. The princess's cheeks were also marginally fuller and her neck a bit thicker, although illness might soon slim all of that, depending on how long she remained ill.

"Aurore has been this way for days now," the count said. "We dare not move her. But she was expected in London yesterday for the conference, and we can't put the delegates off much longer. We must either present her or take her out of the running for ruler of Belgium."

Monique nodded. He'd explained everything earlier, but she still found it a bit of a muddle. Politics. This was about political machinations involving the new independence of Belgium.

Apparently, the province of Belgium had broken off from the Netherlands and demanded to be its own country. Championed by the other major powers, who liked the idea of a buffer state between the powerful French and the equally powerful Dutch, Belgium had been granted its wish over the protests of the Dutch.

All that remained was to set out the terms of the agreement and to select a ruler for the new country.

That was the sticking point. Princess Aurore was the one most favored for the position. Firstly, Chanay lay in the middle of Belgium, and its royal line went back for centuries. Secondly, any other candidate would shift the balance of power.

The French wanted one of their dukes, and the Dutch wanted one of their princes. The English had proposed Prince Leopold of Hanover for his connections to the English royal family and his neutrality, but that had not gone over well with the French. So, the Princess of Chanay was everyone's first choice.

That was why the count wanted Monique to play Princess Aurore. Her Highness would remain in Calais in secret, being tended by her retinue and her mother at a secluded location, while Monique made an appearance in London to soothe all the delegates' concerns and show that Princess Aurore was worthy of the crown of Belgium.

"Will you step in for her?" he asked now. "As you can see, she is in no condition to do what she must."

Stalling for time, Monique said, "What is wrong with her?"

A pretty woman of about thirty rose from beside the bed, her face wrought with worry. "We aren't sure. She fell ill shortly after we arrived here and were preparing to make the crossing to England. We fear she has cholera, though no one else in the hotel seems to be suffering. The surgeon has bled her twice, to no good effect."

The count grew angry. "You bled her despite my instructions? Bleeding is foolish, especially given her symptoms."

An older woman stood to stare him down. "Do not blame Lady Ursula. *I* gave the order. I will not risk my daughter's life simply because you have these wild ideas about doctors."

Privately, Monique agreed with the count. Cholera was serious enough as it was, but if the use of an outdated "cure" like bleeding weakened the princess even more, it could prove fatal. No wonder her cousin looked so pale.

The count's lips thinned. He turned to Monique, his eyes hollow in his face. "You can see we need you. It will probably be some time before the princess has recovered enough to make public appearances."

If ever, Monique thought but didn't dare say it. The rest of them already seemed anxious about Princess Aurore's condition. "I'll admit that she and I do look somewhat alike, but surely people who have met her before—"

"*No one* has met her before, outside of the court of Chanay. Certainly no one attending the London Conference. The princess has never traveled much—she preferred to remain at home. And the only image of her is a court painting that few have seen. Besides, you even look well enough like her to match that."

"Yes, but looks aren't the only thing," Monique said. "The princess has had years of training and education in the royal family. I only know what Grand-maman has taught me and what I gleaned from my years in the theater."

The princess's mother snorted at that and excused herself. Clearly *she* did not approve of the count's plan.

After casting the woman a foul glance as she hurried out, the count turned back to Monique. "You won't have to appear in public often, and when you do, one of us will be always at your side to make sure you behave appropriately. It will take us a few days to journey across the English Channel in the private yacht, during which Lady Ursula, Aurore's lady-in-waiting, will be able to instruct you in—"

"Me!" Lady Ursula cried, clearly distressed. "But I had hoped to stay here with the princess."

The count's blue eyes sleeted over. "You're needed elsewhere. Aurore's mother and the servants will remain with her. Thankfully, the English are providing us with a fully staffed residence in London, so we won't require our own servants during our stay. But you, my dear, must go with us."

Lady Ursula's lips trembled, though she merely bowed her head and said, "As you wish, my lord."

Sparing her a dismissive nod, the count smiled

warmly at Monique. "Lady Ursula and I shall instruct you regarding the most important rules for proper behavior, but the delegates probably won't care if you make a mistake. They'll assume it results from your living isolated in Chanay all these years."

"But what if they *do* care? What if I stumble so badly that I ruin her chance at the throne? Or even worse, accidentally expose your scheme?"

"First of all, Aurore has no chance at the throne unless this succeeds. And if something goes wrong, we will simply proclaim you to be ill, whisk you back to the Continent, and take her home from Calais."

"Her." She curled her fingernails into her palm. "But not me. Or Grand-maman."

His smile no longer held any warmth. "Forgive me, my dear, but this contract of ours depends on your succeeding. If you don't, things will go back to how they were." When the pure ruthlessness of that made her suck in a breath, he softened his features. "And in any case, you *will* be successful. You're an excellent actress—surely you are accustomed to adapting to roles. Have you not played royalty before?"

"Well, yes, but all I had to do was act out someone else's script. What if I blunder? Use the wrong word for something?"

"I cannot see that happening. You speak English very well. To be truthful, you speak it better than the princess herself, which is a boon to us."

"Grandpapa was half-English," Monique reminded him. "He made sure I was fluent in it. Though I know I have an accent."

"The delegates will expect that."

"But it's not my facility with the language that I'm talking about. There are so many rules of deportment and—"

"We will teach you all that. And I swear that in most instances, one or the other of us will be around to steer you right or cover your errors."

That wasn't exactly encouraging.

Something else occurred to her. "Aren't you the least worried that someone who's seen me on the stage in Dieppe might recognize me?"

He waved that concern off with a flick of his bejeweled hand. "You wear wigs, costumes, and stage cosmetics—no one could discern the real you beneath all that. If my spies hadn't already told me of your resemblance to Aurore, I would never have recognized you from your work on the stage."

She blinked. "Spies?"

His mirthless laugh chilled her. "Come now, girl, did you really think the royal court forgot your branch of the family entirely? We did not, I assure you. One never knows when the heirs to the throne might perish, leaving some distant relation to inherit. As the oldest member of the family, I thought it important to keep track. That's why I could meet with you so quickly after the princess fell ill. I've always known exactly where your family was."

Because of his spies. She shivered. All this time, he'd had people watching them!

Though it seemed rather silly of him, to be honest. She was probably far down the line of succession, given that Grand-maman had been one of four children, all of whom must have had children themselves.

That actually relieved her. She had no desire to be a Princess of Chanay, forced to marry whomever the family deemed appropriate. She didn't trust love, but she didn't trust royal families either. There had to be some balance between marrying for love and marrying whomever was thrust upon you by political convenience.

"Even if someone *could* recognize you from Dieppe," the count went on, "it wouldn't be anyone you'd encounter at the few public affairs we'll be attending. Only those of the highest rank or political consequence will be there, and they aren't the sort to attend a provincial theater."

Though she bristled at his condescending tone, he had a point. Most of the foreigners at the theater were merchants and sailors, with the occasional courier thrown in. The highest-ranking gentleman she'd ever met in Dieppe had been . . .

Lord Fulkham.

Then again, he'd been only a baron. She knew enough about English peerages to know that a baron was nothing to a duke or a marquess or even an earl.

She struggled to remember what more Duval had said about the fellow's connections—and those of his friend—but that had been three years ago, and she'd been too irritated to pay attention. Still, a mere baron couldn't be anyone of consequence. And as the count had pointed out, her costume, wig, and makeup would have disguised her. Besides, their encounter had been brief.

Yet you remember him.

Yes. But that was different. He'd annoyed her. While *she* had probably barely raised any notice in his arrogant brain.

"So you will play Princess Aurore for us, then?" Calculation glinted in his eyes. "It's the role of a lifetime, you realize. If you succeed, it will be a tour de force."

True. She could never tell anyone, but still *she* would know. What actress worth her salt could resist attempting such a daring thing?

She did have one more concern. "What about when it's done and you replace me with the princess, assuming she recovers? Surely the people I meet in London will notice the difference between us once she becomes queen of Belgium."

"Once she becomes queen, she will be too busy ruling to meet with anyone you might have met through the conference. And I can manage that—only allow access to her for those people I know she didn't encounter. After a few years, it won't matter—they'll assume that any small differences they notice are due to age. And to her being married and having children, one hopes."

Poor Princess Aurore. They were already plotting out her future while she lay near death's door. But that couldn't concern Monique. She had her own family and future to think of.

"It will only be a couple of weeks at most," he went on, obviously sensing her weaken, "and Chanceux is more than happy to look after your grandmother in the meantime. Once it's done, you and Princess Solange can both travel back to Chanay with us to begin your new life."

Her new life. Bound to the royal family. Expected to behave appropriately, marry appropriately, live appropriately.

Her new life free of worry about Grandmaman.

That was the important part. Once Grandmaman passed on, Monique could choose to leave, to go back to her old life and do as she pleased. But for now . . .

"I'll do it," she said.

Two

There were few things Gregory enjoyed more than royal banquets. Not because of the pomp and circumstance or even the quality of the food and drink, but because they allowed him to root out secrets about those in the highest perches of power. He could learn a great deal from what a man said about his underlings, whether he ate or drank to excess, and how he treated the servants—or his wife.

Gregory also often gleaned interesting information from the gossip that ran rampant at these events. Some of it was inconsequential or patently absurd, but some of it could change the course of history. The fun came in figuring out which was which.

And tonight St. James's Palace was abuzz with discussions about the London Conference to determine the future of Belgium. The event was his bailiwick—his chance to change his own future.

Because of the recent English elections, the Duke of Wellington would soon be stepping down as prime minister, and Earl Grey would be taking his place. Even Gregory's superior—the foreign secretary—would be ousted.

Fortunately, although in most cases the undersecretary of the foreign office would be expected to leave, too, Grey had already asked Gregory to remain in his position. Gregory had made himself too valuable to both parties for either to want to replace him. Indeed, there was talk that if the London Conference went well under Gregory's management, he might even gain the position of foreign secretary under the new government. No more would he dwell in darkness as a spymaster.

He'd proved himself capable of moving behind the scenes. Now he wanted to be on the stage, to have a say in the ruling of his country. Fate had put the conference in *his* hands, and he meant to make the best of it.

"Look who it is," a voice came from behind him. "I should have known you'd be here, too."

He turned to see Jeremy Keane behind him, accompanied by his wife, Lady Yvette. In the past year, Gregory and the American had become friends, especially since the latter had proved an excellent source of information about his countrymen's habits. Given Gregory's present position, he figured it never hurt to be familiar with how an American's mind worked.

"What are *you* doing here, old chap?" Gregory

asked Jeremy jovially, pleased to find a fellow member from St. George's Club in attendance.

"I had to be in town for Guy Fawkes Day," Jeremy said. "I'm centering a whole series of paintings around it."

Lady Yvette shook her head. "Everyone else in England is avoiding London because of the bonfires and mayhem, but of course my husband must run toward it with great glee."

Jeremy grinned at her. "And you love that about me, admit it. My penchant for finding trouble is what drew you to me."

"And your dashing good looks," she said with an indulgent smile.

The couple exchanged a knowing glance that made Gregory grit his teeth. Nothing was more irritating than the sight of two people hopelessly in love. His parents had been in love once. It hadn't lasted long, and he doubted that the explosive finale had been worth the little bit of joy they'd gained in the beginning.

"I meant, what are you doing at a royal function?" Gregory asked testily. "You're not even British."

Jeremy widened his eyes in mock surprise. "Do you not realize just how famous I am, sir? I'll have you know that the king himself bought one of my paintings."

"That explains why you were invited, but it doesn't explain why you came. You always profess to find these affairs dull."

"Oh, but his wife *adores* them," Lady Yvette said brightly as she came up to kiss Gregory on the cheek. "So he puts up with them for my sake."

Jeremy chuckled. "I put up with them because of the reward I know I'll get for it later."

Lady Yvette blushed. They'd already been married a year, yet they acted like newlyweds. It was enough to make a bachelor want to slit his wrists.

And when Warren, the Marquess of Knightford, walked up with his wife, Delia, in tow, Gregory prepared himself for more of the same. But Delia was more interested in sharing gossip than in flirting with her new husband.

"You'll never guess who we just saw in Ambassadors' Court," Delia said, her eyes bright with excitement. "The Princess de Chanay. And she's much more beautiful in person than in that awful copy of her portrait they printed in the *Lady's Monthly Museum*. I don't know who they get to paint these things, but my sister-in-law could do far better."

Warren smirked at her. "In your opinion, Brilliana could do anything far better. Admit it. You're biased."

Brilliana was Niall's fiancée. Now that he'd been pardoned and had returned to London, he'd wasted no time in getting himself engaged . . . to Delia's widowed sister-in-law, of all people. So those two couples were quite cozily interconnected, since Niall was Warren's cousin.

Sometimes Gregory felt left out. Which was absurd. Spymasters couldn't afford the luxury of bosom friends. Too many secrets to keep. Indeed, he kept nearly all of *their* secrets, too, and not always by choice.

"Ahem," Jeremy said loftily. "While I don't deny that Brilliana does excellent work, *I* am, after all, the famous—"

"Artist," Delia and Yvette said in unison. Then they both laughed.

"We *know*, you old bastard," Warren said. "You remind us often enough."

"Well," Jeremy said, eyes gleaming, "at least I do something useful with my time. All *you* do is go to parties with Delia."

"Since when is art useful?" Warren drawled.

"Good God," Gregory snapped, "would you two shut up? I want to hear about this princess, and I honestly don't give a damn about who would paint her portrait best." He turned to Delia. "Were you able to speak with the woman? I haven't met her yet."

"That surprises me," Warren said. "I thought you had taken over for the foreign secretary since he's laid up with the gout. Isn't she part of the Chanay delegation to the conference?"

"She is, but—"

"Honestly, Warren," Jeremy interrupted, "doesn't your wife keep you busy enough not to have to dabble in politics?"

Delia rolled her eyes. "He reads three newspapers a day from front to back. You might say politics is his hobby."

"I thought brothels were his hobby," Yvette said cheerily. "Isn't he the one who gave that awful naughty watch to Niall?"

"Which I got from *your* brother," Warren pointed out genially.

"And which Brilliana hates," Delia put in. "But not for the naughty activity it portrays, oh no. She disapproves of the quality of the art."

Yvette laughed. "Of course she does. She has good taste. Which apparently our husbands do not."

"Except in women," Jeremy said with a wink.

"Hear, hear!" Warren said, and raised his glass of champagne.

God, this lot was cloying. And decidedly uninformative. "So, Delia, the Princess de Chanay . . ."

"Oh, I didn't get to speak to her. That greatuncle of hers hovers about her every minute. And I gather he only allows people of political importance to come near."

"People like *you*," Warren said. "Aren't you one of the people involved in making sure the delegates don't kill each other while trying to decide the fate of Belgium?" He gestured at Gregory with his glass and spilled some of his champagne on Delia in the process.

"Warren!" she cried. "This gown is brand-new!"

"Sorry, love," he said, not looking remotely repentant, though he did give her his handkerchief. "I'm a bit foxed."

"Obviously." She dabbed at her bodice with the square of linen.

He took the handkerchief from her to do some dabbing of her gown himself. "You missed a spot." He grinned as he dabbed all along her bodice. "And another. And this one. You missed a lot of spots."

"You are incorrigible, especially when you're foxed," she said, but her lips were twitching as if she fought a smile.

He whispered something in her ear, and she laughed.

Gregory couldn't stand it anymore. "Forgive me, but I see someone I must speak to," he lied, and headed in the direction of the doors to the gardens.

Clearly he needed more bachelor friends. Thank God Hart had recently taken up permanent residence in town. The chap had bought out his commission so he could work for Gregory infiltrating the foreign community in London. Gregory's sister-in-law, John's widow, used to do some of that work for him, but now that she was in love . . .

Bah. So many damned people in love.

And Hart wasn't here tonight, so Gregory was on his own with the happy couples. Ah, well, at least the delegates weren't all married. The Princess of Chanay wasn't, nor was her great-uncle, a widower. He would officially meet the princess tomorrow, but he knew the Count de Beaumonde from previous diplomatic situations, so he could probably finagle an introduction to the woman tonight. It wouldn't hurt to observe her in a less formal setting.

It didn't take long for him to spot the count coming in from Ambassadors' Court with a tall young woman on his arm, who was dressed in a gown of pink silk with cap sleeves that left her arms bare.

The princess? Probably. And quite a pretty one, too—with voluptuous breasts and a surprisingly slender waist, given her slightly broad shoulders. Despite her height, she walked with grace and didn't slouch, obviously not the least bothered by the fact that she towered over the shorter men in the room.

Something about the confidence in her walk nagged at his memory. Had they met before?

No, it couldn't be. From what he remembered of his reports, she hadn't been out in society terribly long, and she was famously reclusive to boot. Yet as they neared him, he realized she didn't seem as young as he'd initially thought. Mid-twenties, perhaps? If she'd had her debut recently, he would expect her to be younger. But perhaps the people of Chanay didn't toss their daughters out into the world as early as the English did.

Still, she looked the part of a debutante otherwise. Her elaborate coiffure—with curls the color of his favorite toffee piled atop her head and punctuated by a glittering tiara—was exactly something a maid on the marriage mart would wear. Oddly enough, the style reminded him of powdered wigs, though he couldn't imagine why. Those had gone out of fashion decades ago.

When she came nearer and he saw her face full on, his sense that something was familiar about her deepened. Could he be thinking of the portrait Delia had mentioned? No. Delia had been right—the woman's looks far exceeded that paltry image. Creamy skin, lush lips, a strong chin . . .

Her gaze narrowed on him with what he would swear was recognition, and he gave a start. Then she smoothed her features into politeness. It didn't fool him. He *did* know her, damn it. And she knew him, too. But from where?

The count spotted him then. "Ah, just the man I was hoping to see. Lord Fulkham, how are you? You're looking very well."

Bowing slightly, Gregory pasted a broad smile to his lips. "So are you, sir. I hope your accommodations are comfortable?"

"Quite so, I assure you. How long has it been since we last met—five years? Ten?"

"Ten! I'm not as old as all that. I believe we last saw each other in Paris at the Treaty of London, what, three years ago?" That was the trip when Gregory had stopped in at Dieppe to meet with Hart and gone to the theater to see—

His gaze shot to the woman. *Her.* Good God,

she was Mademoiselle Monique Servais. He would swear it. Despite her bland smile and entirely different attire, he would know her anywhere. The jutting chin, the thick lashes . . . those glorious emerald eyes.

She certainly wasn't the princess, so why did Beaumonde have her with him? Was she the old man's mistress?

The count caught him staring, and said, "Forgive me, I should have introduced you sooner. Aurore, this is the Baron Fulkham, undersecretary to the foreign office, whose opinion is supremely important in deciding your fate. Lord Fulkham, this is my great-niece, Princess Aurore of Chanay."

The words rang in his ears, so discordant and utterly wrong that he burst out with, "The devil you say!" When that made the count start, Gregory caught himself and added lamely, "You don't look nearly old enough, sir, to have a great-niece."

Beaumonde broke into a smile. "Be careful with this one, Aurore," he joked. "He has a silver tongue."

"So they tell me," he muttered, his mind racing.

He must have been mistaken about the woman's identity. Surely the count wasn't mad enough to pass off a known actress as a princess. Experienced in politics, the man was highly regarded for his fine character. He'd realize that if he was caught proposing an impostor for queen of Belgium, it would be the end of his position of power in his country. Chanay would be made a laughingstock.

So perhaps it was mere coincidence that this woman looked and acted like the actress. After all, Mademoiselle Servais had been in costume. And three years was a long time. He might not be remembering clearly.

Then he noted how she was gripping the count's arm, how she wouldn't meet his gaze, how false her smile seemed.

No, she *was* Monique Servais—he would stake his life on it. Though it made no sense.

"I'll admit, Your Serene Highness," he went on, "that I recognized you even without the introduction." He waited until she paled, then added, "From your portrait in the *Lady's Monthly Museum*."

"Someone did a portrait of me?" she said, sounding incredulous. "I don't recall sitting for one."

"I believe they simply copied an older painting of you. Though it didn't do you justice."

She shot her great-uncle a veiled glance. "An older painting of me. How interesting."

"It hardly deserved the title of 'painting,'" Beaumonde said, avoiding her gaze. "Terrible likeness. I agree with you there, Fulkham."

"Thank you, Uncle, but you're biased." The woman fluttered her fan before her face exactly as she had three years before, cementing Gregory's suspicions. "And I daresay I can hardly trust the opinion of a diplomat like Lord Fulkham either, since such men excel at giving compliments."

"Not always." Gregory fixed her with a hard look. "Sometimes we manage to step awry. Especially when confronted with a woman who stoops to conquer."

If she caught the reference to their discussion of Goldsmith's play in Dieppe, she gave no indication. "I assure you, sir," she said in the melodic tones he remembered only too well, "I have not come to London to conquer anyone."

"Except those of us attending the conference," Gregory said smoothly. "And you've made a good start, too." He glanced about the room. "Judging from the way everyone is looking at you, your beauty alone has the delegates smitten."

"You see?" Beaumonde said jovially to the woman. "He's quite the flatterer."

"In my line of work, it's called diplomacy," Gregory drawled. "And speaking of diplomacy, perhaps Her Serene Highness would wish to take a turn about the palace garden with me so I can make a more informal assessment of her ability to reign as queen of Belgium."

"An excellent idea!" the count cried. "She would be happy to accompany you. Wouldn't you, my dear?"

The faux princess's eyes frosted over. "I would, indeed," she said, then glanced at the doors, "but I believe they're about to announce that dinner is served."

"Not for a while yet," Gregory said. "Trust me, I asked." He always liked to know the schedule of an evening, the shape of the party . . . how to plan his maneuvers.

And one way or the other, he meant to get to the bottom of this mystery. Because an impostor playing the Princess de Chanay wasn't acceptable. There was too much at stake—for Belgium *and* for him—with this conference.

"Well, then," she said with a furtive glance at the count. "I would be delighted, monsieur."

Somehow he doubted that.

Monique fought panic as Lord Fulkham expertly maneuvered them through the crowded rooms of St. James's Palace toward the garden. Curse the count for throwing her to the wolves! And after he'd said he and Lady Ursula would always be at her side, too!

She should have known not to trust him. Ever since they left Calais she'd had the sense that he was hiding something. But she hadn't expected him to sabotage her masquerade after he'd gone to such trouble to set it up. Could he not see that Lord Fulkham was baiting him? Baiting *her*?

Probably not. To be fair, he didn't know of her former association with Lord Fulkham. He must never find out, either. Because she had to secure help for Grand-maman in her final days, and this pretense was the only way to do so.

But why, oh why, did Lord Fulkham have to be the man at the center of these proceedings? And why must he have recognized her? All his veiled remarks and his intense scrutiny—he remembered her. She was sure of it.

And why hadn't the count warned her that there was a portrait of Aurore in the *Lady's Monthly Museum?* She must finagle a chance to see it. She dearly hoped it was indeed of poor quality, and not a likeness that highlighted the few ways in which she and Aurore did *not* resemble each other.

When they reached the garden, her heart sank to see it so deserted. Apparently she hadn't been the only one to think dinner might soon be served. Even the band they'd heard playing out here earlier had packed up and moved inside, closer to the banqueting room.

You can handle this, she told herself. *You're an acclaimed actress, for God's sake. This is what you do—play roles. You've even played a princess before. So get to it, and show this pompous gentleman what you're made of.*

She went on the offensive. "Please forgive me if this is rude, Lord Fulkham, but I'm confused by what my uncle said concerning your part in these negotiations. I was unaware that undersecretaries were of such profound importance in English politics. I thought they were little better than clerks."

If she'd thought to insult him, his laugh

showed that she'd failed. "Some of them are. It just so happens that England has two kinds. I'm the political kind. Especially with the foreign secretary laid up in bed." He cast her a searching glance. "You have a better knowledge of English affairs than I expected."

She had her half-English grandfather to thank for that. He'd always kept up with politics in his mother's country. "And you, monsieur, have a better facility for 'diplomacy' than I expected. I think my uncle is right. You *do* have a silver tongue."

"I hope not. It would make it awfully hard to eat," he quipped.

A laugh sputtered out of her. Curse him. She didn't remember him having a humorous side. "You are very droll, monsieur."

"And you are very . . . different," he said.

She tensed. "From what?"

"From what I expected. I'd heard that the Princess of Chanay was a rather haughty young lady."

She had no idea if Aurore was haughty. Though it would stand to reason. Weren't all princesses haughty?

Not the way Monique played them. And it didn't matter how Aurore really was. According to the count, no one outside Chanay had ever met the princess, so Lord Fulkham couldn't be sure what she was like. He was merely trying to catch the woman he *had* met in an error.

Which meant she must be as different from Monique Servais as possible, to throw him off guard, make him doubt his eyes. Monique Servais had given him the sharper side of her tongue, so Princess Aurore must be engaging, flirtatious.

"A man like you should know better than to listen to rumor," she told him.

"Actually, rumor is my life's blood. There's generally a bit of truth in every piece of gossip. It's my job to find out which bits are true and which bits are trumped-up lies." He led her down a path. "For example, I heard that you were partial to theatrical entertainments. Is that the case?"

Curse the fellow, he'd heard no such thing. He was just baiting her again.

She fought the urge to stiffen, keeping her grip on his arm deliberately loose. "I enjoy the occasional play, yes. Doesn't everyone?"

"It depends. I like plays, but only tragedies." He shot her a veiled look. "Comedies set my teeth on edge."

She remembered only too well his ridiculous opinion of comedies. "I prefer operas," she said lightly. "Doesn't matter to me what the story is about as long as there's singing. Do you enjoy the opera, monsieur?"

That seemed to catch him off guard, for he frowned. "Not at all, I'm afraid. In real life people don't speak to each other in arias."

"In real life people do not dress so lavishly to

do their marketing, either, but one can still enjoy seeing such attire in that setting on the stage."

"Yes, those powdered wigs are quite entertaining," he drawled. "Especially when the actors and actresses are running in and out of the boudoir."

She could feel his eyes on her. Clearly he was referencing *Le mariage de Figaro* directly. Silly man. As if *that* would make her lose control and spill her secrets. "Oh, I do like that kind of opera myself. *Otello* is *so* dramatic. And that scene in Desdemona's boudoir makes me weep every time."

He halted to eye her closely. "You've seen Rossini's *Otello?*"

"Of course. In Paris. It was quite moving."

A triumphant look crossed his face. "I thought you rarely left Chanay."

Too late she remembered what the count had told her about Aurore's secluded life. She scrambled to cover her error. "That's true—I rarely do. But Maman took me to Paris to see *Otello* once when I was a girl. It's her favorite opera."

"You said that it 'makes me weep every time.' That implies you've seen it more than once."

Her heart thundered in her chest. "I meant 'every time I think of the scene.' I misspoke. English is not my native tongue, you know." She tipped up her chin. "And why do you dissect my words so, monsieur? Is it necessary for the prospective queen of Belgium to speak your language perfectly?"

"That's not why I 'dissect' your words, as you are well aware."

Merde, obviously he'd figured her out. She would have to tread carefully or else he would swallow her up, and with her, all her hopes for her and Grand-maman's future. "I have no idea what you are talking about."

"Come now, mademoiselle." He leaned close enough to show the hardening planes of his face. "It's time that you relinquish this pretense. You and I both know that you are Monique Servais and *not* the Princess of Chanay at all."

Three

Gregory had expected guilt. Shock that he'd found her out. Horror that he'd actually confronted her over it.

He had *not* expected the damned woman to laugh at him, long and loud, before saying, "Who on earth is Mona Servet?"

"*Monique* Ser— Damn it, you know whom I mean. You. *You're* Monique Servais."

Eyes twinkling, she cocked her head at him. "Oh? Tell me more. Why do you think I am not myself and instead am . . . am . . ." She waved her hand airily. "Some Frenchwoman."

"What makes you think she's French?" he countered.

That made her falter, but so briefly he could almost think he'd imagined it. Except that he hadn't.

"Servais is a French name," she said stoutly.

"Actually, there are Servaises in Belgium, Sweden, Luxembourg, and Canada, as well as Dieppe, France."

She didn't even blink at the mention of Dieppe. "Are there? I had no idea. Nor do I care. This Monique Servais is nothing to me." She arched an eyebrow. "And you still have not told me why you think I am she."

He crossed his arms over his chest, annoyed. This wasn't going as expected. "So you intend to brazen it out, do you?"

"Brazen *what* out? That I am some other woman pretending to be Princess Aurore? The idea is absurd."

"I agree. But true, nonetheless."

She shook her head. "You, monsieur, are quite mad."

When she turned on her heel as if to head back inside, he caught her by the arm. "No more mad than you and the count if you think you can perpetrate a deception of such proportions without consequence."

A cool smile crossed her lips as she faced him once more. Oh so delicately, she removed his hand from her arm. "Why would my country attempt such a thing at this critical moment in the negotiations? You must realize that such a tactic would be ludicrous."

"It would be, indeed. Which is why I must know the reason for it."

"You tell me. I have no idea." As if to erase the feel of him, she rubbed her arm where he'd been gripping it. "But you must have *some* theory."

Sadly, he didn't. He could think of no reason for the subterfuge. Yet.

"Well?" she prodded, obviously sensing the weak point in his argument.

He threw out the first thing that came to him. "Perhaps the princess is dead. And Chanay doesn't want to lose its chance at having Belgium in its pocket."

"The princess isn't dead." Just as he was about to pounce on that slip, she added, "She's standing right before you." Then she fluttered her fan again in what he'd come to realize was a telltale indication of her nervousness. "And if she *were* dead, then how could anyone reasonably expect her to be made queen of Belgium? Unless you believe that the Rocheforts mean to put an impostor on the throne. Not only would they be risking the royal line, but such a conspiracy would require my subjects—excuse me, the *princess's* subjects, according to you—to accept another woman in her place."

Another woman. Gregory kept waiting for her to forget herself and say, "an actress," which he had deliberately not mentioned as the impostor's profession, but so far Mademoiselle Servais had been better at maintaining her role than he would have expected.

So Gregory fell back on his usual tactics—fix her with a stare, keep his silence, and wait for her to crumble. Unfortunately, she seemed to be familiar with the strategy, because she did the same thing to him. And as the silence between them lengthened, it gave him time to look her over, to remind himself of her sensuous curves, to be drawn in by her beauty.

Damn her.

Meanwhile, she'd shown no sign of being the least affected by him in that way. Though she *was* an actress, which meant that showing no sign of her true feelings was her forte.

Apparently growing emboldened by his silence, she snapped, "Have you no answer to that?"

It was his move now. He'd best make it a good one. "For all I know, the Rocheforts *do* intend to put an impostor on the throne—someone they can manipulate, someone they can control. The real princess is not such a person. And there *is* a resemblance between the two of you, after all, which might even be good enough to fool the citizens of Chanay."

As he'd hoped, that seemed to startle her. The only reason this subterfuge was working was that no one outside Chanay had ever met the real princess. Including him. But Mademoiselle Servais needn't know that.

"Are you saying that you and I have met before?" Her voice was strained. "Because I do not remember that. And I think I would remember a man of your sort visiting Chanay."

He gritted his teeth to hear her persist in the

deception *still*. "Of course we've met before, as you well know. Not in Chanay but in Dieppe, where you lived as Mademoiselle Servais."

That didn't seem to faze her. "So you have *not* met me, then. And all your talk about the 'real' princess not being able to be manipulated is just . . . what? Speculation? Because you have some notion that I am this woman in Dieppe?"

"It's not a notion, damn it!"

He caught himself. The chit was annoyingly adept at making him lose control of his temper. And if he'd learned anything from his youth with Father, it was that controlling one's emotions was essential. Not only in his position, but in every aspect of life.

Forcing a measure of calm into his voice, he asked, "Why would I invent such a thing?"

"Because you once encountered a woman who looks like me, and have mixed us up." A brittle smile crossed her lips. "You saw that poor likeness of me in the *Lady's Monthly Museum* and think that I look different. But men do not realize how easy it is for a woman to change her appearance merely with a touch of rouge to brighten the cheeks, a bit of kohl to darken the eyebrows. We can make them doubt their very eyes just with our crème pots. And we often do."

True. Most men were unaware of such female secrets. But he was not just any man. Secrets were his game.

"How interesting that you should mention cosmetics," he said, "when I would imagine a princess of your standing is forbidden to wear them. But Mademoiselle Servais wore them all the time. She was an opera singer."

Would she correct him? He watched her expression, but she gave nothing away.

Instead, she broke into a smile. "An opera singer? How droll! Comic or dramatic opera?"

"That is hardly relevant."

She made a face. "No, I suppose not. But it is no wonder you are confused. An opera singer wears wigs and face paint and patches. How could you even tell what she looked like?"

He tried another untruth. "I saw her without all of that."

Only the sudden sharpening of her smile betrayed her reaction. "Did you?"

"Yes. Though even if I hadn't, I never forget a face, cosmetic changes or no. And I noticed Mademoiselle Servais's prominent chin in particular. The real princess has a very small chin, nothing like the opera singer's."

She laughed. "*That* is the source of your evidence? My *chin*? You do realize, sir, that no woman wishes to have, as you call it, 'a prominent chin.' So of course I asked the artist to reshape my chin for the painting. Even a princess wants to appear beautiful in her portraits."

"You know damned well that you're beautiful, prominent chin and all," he snapped. "You're certainly more beautiful than Princess Aurore."

"I'm not sure how that's possible, given that I *am* the princess." Her eyes shone merrily in the lamps of the garden. "But I shall take the compliment regardless."

God, she was as sly as a courtesan, and twice as tempting. "If you didn't, I'd be shocked, since you didn't seem to mind such compliments when I paid them before." He tried to provoke her with another lie, crowding her in and lowering his voice to a murmur. "You didn't mind *anything* we did before."

She blinked. *That* had shaken her. "Oh? Are you saying that this Mademoiselle Servais was your . . . paramour?"

"Can you claim otherwise?"

As if she knew what he was about, she met his gaze coolly. "Of course not. I am not she. What do I care if you have ten paramours?"

He considered his choices. He could give up the fight for now, and see what he could find out. Which might be difficult, given that even the very respectable Beaumonde was obviously part of the plot.

Or he could act to throw her off her game entirely. Because if he kissed her, the actress wouldn't dare call out for help from the guests—she wouldn't risk his voicing his suspicions before an audience. But she might lose her temper and give him what for. She hadn't liked him, after all.

Of course, if she *were* the princess, kissing her could ruin him. But she wasn't—he'd never been so sure of anything in his life. And *not* exposing her subterfuge could ruin him, too, if it came out later. He'd look the fool for not seeing through her disguise. His enemies would make mince-meat of his political aspirations.

He glanced around. The garden was empty, everyone having drifted inside. And nothing else had provoked her into making a mistake. Unfortunately, until he could get her to admit her masquerade, he couldn't get her to tell him why there'd been a need for it.

"Now, sir," she began, "if you are quite done, I should like to return to—"

"Not yet," he said firmly. Once she rejoined her companions, he wouldn't have another chance at unraveling this deception. At least not tonight.

He snagged her about the waist, taking her by surprise, and pulled her into a nearby gazebo obviously kept dark for a reason. Then he murmured, "We should take up where we left off in Dieppe."

"I told you, I'm not from—"

He kissed her, covering her mouth with his in a most insolent manner and praying she was *not* the princess. Though even if she was, she would probably try to extricate herself from the situation diplomatically, without insulting the man who could make her a queen.

She froze, then jerked back to glare at him. "What are you about, sir?"

He stared her down. "You know what I'm about. Reminding you of what we once meant to each other."

Her eyes glittered at him, and he held his breath, *sure* that she was about to call him a liar and tell him that Monique Servais would never have let him touch one hair on her head.

Instead, she smoothed her features into coyness. "We can hardly have meant *anything* to each other since we haven't met until tonight." She lifted a hand to cup his jaw, the impudent caress shocking him into rigidity—in more places than one. "Though I don't see why we can't mean something to each other now. I'm happy to pretend to be this Mademoiselle Servais for you in private . . . if you will champion me as queen of Belgium in the end."

"Are you actually attempting to *seduce* me, Monique?" he said, unable to mask his incredulity.

"Why not, if you pine for Monique so much that you would look for her in every stranger's face?"

"I don't pine for her, damn it!" He gritted his teeth. She was making *him* lose control. Forcing some calm into his voice, he added, "And if you think seducing me will buy my silence—"

"On what subject?" she asked in the silky tones he remembered only too well, the ones that had thrummed through his senses that night even when she'd been provoking him. *Especially* when she'd been provoking him.

She trailed a finger down his jaw in a sensuous stroke that stirred danger in his blood. God help him. He should have known she would be an expert at temptation.

"I don't need your silence," she murmured. "I *am* the Princess Aurore, after all."

"The Princess Aurore would not be touching me like this," he choked out.

"Clearly, you know nothing about me. But since you persist in this nonsense, I might as well receive a reward from it, *non?*" She wrapped her hand about his cravat and fixed her gaze on his mouth. "Seduction would be going too far, I think, but perhaps a little . . . mutual enjoyment would not be amiss."

Then she pulled his head down to her for another kiss. Bold. Hot. Yet somehow innocent. The way the real princess's might be.

That's when he realized his error. He'd assumed that *he* could remain unaffected through this little dance, that he would be immune to an actress's tricks. But the very smell of her—lilies and apples—seeped beneath his defenses. Her mouth was as delicious as he'd imagined, and her waist as tiny as he'd remembered it looking backstage.

If he had wanted her three years ago, despite her caked-on cosmetics and her outrageous gown and wig, he wanted her even more now that she was free of such things.

So this time when he kissed her, it was not on behalf of his country or his career. This time it was for *him* and him alone.

Four

As he clutched her to him, Monique wondered if she'd lost her mind, attempting this. But he'd kept pushing and badgering her, trying to make her slip up.

So she must make *him* falter, make him question his dangerous suspicions. Monique Servais had treated him with contempt, so Princess Aurore must kiss him into oblivion.

She couldn't just slap him and dart off; he might expose her to everyone. Or he might simply voice his suspicions to the count, who would see that as her not holding up her end of the bargain. She was supposed to convince people she was Aurore, and that was what she would do.

Looping her arms about Lord Fulkham's neck, she flattened her body against him. And then everything got more interesting.

"Damn you," he murmured against her lips. Then he took her mouth again with a shocking impudence, licking along her closed lips and inviting her to open for him.

So she did. And instantly regretted it. Because the moment he thrust his tongue into her mouth, she felt hot and aroused and so dizzy she had to cling to him for balance.

She'd been kissed in this manner a few times before, but never like this. His boldness made her body tremble and her mind swim as if through a fog. His tongue delved and searched, turning her into a quivering mass of wanting, and desire flashed over her like lightning through the sky, searing everything in its path.

The dark gazebo became their own private grotto as he kissed her more and more urgently, sending her up on her toes to enjoy his kisses to the fullest.

"God, woman, you have the most luscious mouth I've ever tasted," he murmured in English.

She didn't know that word, *luscious*, but she could guess what it meant. And the fact that she'd broken through his cool calm made her want to crow. "Do you taste many mouths?" she whispered.

"Enough to know that this is madness," he growled against her lips before trailing kisses down her jaw to her neck.

"But pleasurable madness, *non?*"

He tongued her throat, sending exquisite shivers along her spine. "*Oui.* A very pleasurable madness."

"Pleasurable enough to gain me a crown?" she asked, just to see what he would say. Or do.

He nipped her earlobe, and the tiny burst of pleasure-pain nearly made her swoon. She hated him for doing such things to her, for making her *feel* such things. But she wanted him, too. Madness, indeed.

"That will show, curse you," she murmured as she buried her hands in his hair to shift him away from her ear.

"No, it won't." He nuzzled her ear. "Though I wish it would. Actually, I wish I dared mark you somewhere more intimate, in a place no one would see but me."

The words brought her to her senses and reminded her that her purpose had been to catch him off guard. Which apparently she'd done. So now she must extricate herself from this . . . increasingly dangerous situation.

She drew back to cast him a chiding look. "Now you are being ridiculous. I am not that sort of woman."

His hooded gaze trailed down to her modestly cut gown. "The princess might not be. But *you* most certainly are. Actresses are known for their lovers."

A burst of anger swelled in her chest and she tamped it down with difficulty. He was probably waiting for her to lose her temper. "Well, I regret that as the princess, I cannot be your lover. I must be chaste when I marry."

That arrested him. "Marry? Is that what this masquerade is about? Snagging a husband for Princess Aurore?"

She planted her hands on her hips. "Why do you persist in this insanity? Surely you realize I cannot be both an impostor *and* snag Aurore a husband. The moment the real princess entered the man's bedchamber, he would know he'd been deceived."

"Unless it was an arranged marriage where the parties never meet. That happens often between countries seeking a political alliance."

She shook her head. "If the parties never meet, then there's no need for an impostor to masquerade. Your suppositions don't even make sense."

"Princess?" a voice sounded from outside the gazebo. "Are you out here?"

Lady Ursula! Oh, thank God.

Monique started to step out of the gazebo, but he caught her by the arm and whispered, "We'll continue this discussion later, Monique."

"Aurore," she hissed under her breath. "*Princess Aurore* to you. And if you ever call me Monique again, I will tell my uncle about your kissing me, and he will have your head."

"Then I will expose you for who you are."

She grabbed his hand where it lay on her arm. "You would not *dare* to make such a spurious accusation without proof. Especially when there's no proof to be had, because I *am* the princess."

"We'll see about that." He tucked her hand in the crook of his elbow. "One way or the other, I'm getting to the bottom of this."

"Your Highness?" Lady Ursula cried.

With his lips thinning into a line, Lord Fulkham led Monique out of the gazebo. "We're over here," he said, as poised as any politician.

"Are you all right, Princess?" the lady-in-waiting asked Monique, the lamplight falling full on her worried expression.

Hardly. Her heart thundered in her chest, and the flex of his muscle beneath her hand as he waited for her answer perversely catapulted an undeniable thrill through her. Juggling her two personas with a man who knew the true one was more difficult than she would have imagined. Especially when both personas were horribly attracted to the fellow.

She forced a smile for the woman's benefit. "I'm perfectly fine. Merely discussing politics with his lordship. Though I don't believe you two have met. Lady Ursula, this is—"

"I know who he is." Her eyes assessed him coolly. "The Baron Fulkham, correct? One of the Englishmen helping to decide who will become queen of Her Highness's country?"

"Indeed," he clipped out. "I take it you are *not* from Her Highness's country?"

"I am Lady Ursula Weber of Hanover, the princess's lady-in-waiting."

The woman was breaking all the rules of protocol by introducing herself. She must truly be agitated at finding them sequestered in a gazebo.

Casting him a dismissive glance, she turned to Monique. "Forgive me, Your Highness, but I was sent out here to fetch you for dinner. You're to be taken in by the Duc de Pontalba."

"Thank you." Relieved, Monique released Lord Fulkham's arm. "I enjoyed our discussion, sir." It wasn't entirely a lie.

"The enjoyment was all mine."

Before she could turn away, he captured her hand, angling himself so that her body blocked Lady Ursula's view. Swiftly, he lifted her hand to his lips, but he didn't kiss it. Instead, he turned it over and nosed her bracelet up enough so he could suck the tender skin of her inner wrist. Hard. Enough to leave a mark.

Why, the annoying devil had given her a love bite!

As she snatched her hand from him, he winked at her. Ooh, how she wanted to rage at him for it! But she couldn't, with Lady Ursula watching.

"I look forward to seeing more of you, Your Serene Highness," he said in a far-too-intimate tone.

Not if *she* had anything to say about it. All she could manage was a tight nod before turning on her heel and joining Ursula.

Her wrist burned where he'd sucked her skin. Though she knew her bracelet would cover the bruise—and her sleeves and gloves would do the same tomorrow—the thought of his having marked her deliberately, "somewhere more intimate, in a place where no one would see but me," had her pulse beating wildly in that very spot. It was all she could do not to rub it.

"Forgive me for not having noticed your absence sooner," Lady Ursula whispered to Monique. "I had no idea that his lordship had cornered you out here or I would have raced to your side."

"It's fine," Monique murmured. "He was a perfect gentleman."

The woman searched her face. "That's good. His reputation is stellar when it comes to women, but you never know with these Englishmen. They seem to think all ladies from the Continent are free with their favors."

"I can handle any fellows of *that* sort, I assure you. We saw plenty of them in the theater."

"Oh yes. I keep forgetting you were an actress. You just . . . look so much like Aurore and behave so much like a princess that I think of you more as one of the family. And truly, you are, you know."

Monique cast her a grateful smile. "Thank you. That's reassuring. My grandmother never gave up hope that the family might one day take her back. She made me learn all the rules and protocols, everything. I thought it was silly, but it made her happy. And now I'm glad of it."

Lady Ursula squeezed her hand. "Well, we appreciate what you are doing for the princess. Never think otherwise. I know the count can be overbearing, but he means well. And if Aurore could speak, I know she would tell you—"

Her voice grew so choked, she had to leave off to clear her throat. Then she pasted a smile to her lips. "Oh, look, there's the duke just inside the doors. He's a handsome fellow, don't you think?"

"Yes." But not half as handsome as a certain insolent lord.

No, she was not going to think of that man. With any luck, she'd avoid being alone with him in future, and this would all be over in a week or two.

She could only hope.

Gregory watched the two women disappear into the building but dared not follow right away. He was too aroused by his encounter with the "princess," whom he was almost certain was Monique. Whose luscious mouth had left him hard as stone.

Well, at least he'd left *her* with something, too. He hadn't really intended to "mark" her . . . until it occurred to him that such a mark could be useful. If her people tried to switch her off for the real princess in the next few days, he would know.

Right. That had been his only reason. It hadn't had anything to do with the intoxicating idea of her secretly having a reminder of him. An intimate reminder of their very intimate embrace.

He hardened again. Bloody hell!

The mark *hadn't* been about that. It had been about being sure of who was who, in case the two women really did look that similar. Such a strong resemblance would explain why the Rochefort family had picked Mademoiselle Servais for this subterfuge—that and the lack of decent images of the real princess.

Still, he couldn't fathom how the Rocheforts would have known of some obscure actress in Dieppe, no matter how accomplished she was. And even if they'd heard of her somehow, they couldn't have been aware that Mademoiselle Servais would resemble Princess Aurore to such a marked degree.

Unless it was the resemblance that had set everything in motion. Someone who had seen the portrait as well as the actress could have remarked upon the resemblance to Beaumonde.

But that didn't explain the reason for the masquerade in the first place. And Monique had told him nothing that would explain it, either, curse her. She hadn't slipped up and revealed her true self once. It was enough to make him question his own eyes.

Perhaps he just *wanted* her to be the actress, so he'd feel free to pursue her as a mistress. Even a man with his political connections and wealth couldn't marry a royal. The Princess of Chanay was under the same restriction as the English royals—she must marry another royal.

But he could take an *actress* as his mistress, if she agreed to it. Judging from their explosive kiss, she might. Actresses, after all, were experienced in such matters.

You need a wife, not a mistress. And she won't exactly fall into your arms after you unmask her.

True. Even so, the possibility of taking Monique Servais to bed made him . . .

Hard. Again. Damn her. It had been years since a woman had aroused him so profoundly. Three years, to be precise. Generally he was too careful to allow himself such an indulgence, but she got under his skin. He wished he knew why.

A pity there was no one with whom he could confer about her real identity, to at least confirm his suspicions. Unfortunately, he was the only one who had met her outside this arena.

Wait a minute—Hart had met her, too. It might not hurt to have the man's opinion to bolster his own. And if Hart agreed she was the actress, he could nose around the staff at the house where the Chanay contingent were staying to see if he could learn more.

The chap had turned into quite the useful investigator in the past three years. He'd be discreet and thorough.

Gregory would talk to Hart tonight at St.

George's. Hart had recently become a member, which had surprised some of the others, given the fellow's reputation with women. St. George's was supposed to be a place for pooling information to uncover rogues dangerous to members' female relations—in Gregory's case, it had been his sister-in-law—not a place for protecting such fellows. But Hart was an exception, given his connections to both Edwin and Warren.

Privately, though, Gregory suspected that Hart's reputation might not be as scandalous as the gossips claimed. For all the man's flirtations and talk of women, Gregory had never actually seen him in a brothel unless Hart was on a mission.

Thoughts of suspicions and missions banished Gregory's arousal, so he headed inside. To his surprise, he found Lady Ursula awaiting him.

She curtsied. "My lord, it appears that you are taking me in to dinner."

Ah, of course. He wasn't of sufficient rank for the princess, but he certainly was for one of her ladies.

"I would be honored," he told her, offering his arm. This could be a good opportunity. Perhaps *she* wouldn't be as tight-lipped about the masquerade as the impostor herself.

When he caught sight of Monique disappearing through the doors with the Duc de Pontalba, he tensed. The French duke was too good-looking by half, with his carefully coiffed blond hair and his surprisingly fit physique. Not to mention that the broad-shouldered fellow was possessed of a smooth tongue—the sort of chap one did not want to see nosing around one's sister.

Or one's mistress.

He grimaced. *She's not your mistress, you fool, and not likely to be, either—especially if you don't keep your head in the game. Pay attention.*

Lady Ursula leaned close. "They say that the duke is looking for a wife. It would be an eligible match, you know, a way of pacifying him when the French prince he's championing loses his bid for ruler of Belgium."

She was correct. As a high-ranking French noble, the Duc de Pontalba was one of the delegates in charge of choosing the ruler. But the Dutch would protest any French candidate. They wanted a buffer between their country and France, not a puppet ruler who would always side with their enemy.

"What makes you think his fellow will lose his bid?" Gregory asked the young lady. He judged her to be older than Monique by a few years, but she still had a fresh countenance and a wealth of flaxen hair. Any other man would find her quite beautiful.

He did not. She was slender, with the body of a gazelle, not his sort at all. She didn't smell of lilies and apples, or have a prominent chin and sparkling emerald-green eyes. Nor did she have full breasts that would make a grown man weep.

Lady Ursula blinked up at him. "I assumed that Princess Aurore is considered first choice. Is that not true?"

"Nothing is certain yet, so the duke's prince has as good a chance as anyone." That was laying it on a bit thick, but he wanted to gauge her reaction. Would she champion the impostor? Or try to undermine her?

She sniffed. "A Frenchman cannot rule Belgium. The people would revolt. They don't like the French."

"True."

They entered the dining room, and he looked for Monique. She was near King William, of course, with the duke on her other side and already watching her like a man waiting to pluck the best rose on the bush.

The hell he would.

"She is not for you," Lady Ursula said in an undertone.

Had he been *that* transparent? Devil take it. "Of course not. I wouldn't presume. I'm merely trying to determine how a possible alliance between them could alter the negotiations."

Liar.

Her face cleared. "Oh, of course. I never think of such things. I'm not very political." She ventured a smile. "I am more concerned that Aurore not be taken advantage of."

"Surely her years of preparation as a princess would make her able to head that off on her own." He watched Lady Ursula's face, but she betrayed nothing.

"Perhaps." She grew pensive. "Still, young women can be blind where an attractive man is concerned, especially those who have not been out in the world much."

Clearly the lady was part of the subterfuge, trying to smooth Monique's way in her role as the princess. Yet Lady Ursula didn't seem the sort to support such a masquerade. What the devil was going on?

He would have probed her for more information, but they were being seated now. And the next time he had a chance to speak to her, she was engrossed in a conversation with the man seated to her left.

Gregory leaned forward to see who it was. Ah, James Danworth, private secretary to the prime minister. No doubt he'd been invited because the prime minister was in the north at present. And now the fellow was either picking Lady Ursula's brain about the princess in order to report back to his employer, or he'd noticed the woman's attractions and was trying to court her himself.

Danworth *was* an ambitious sort. But somehow Gregory couldn't see him marrying an obscure German lady to further his ambitions. He'd be better off marrying an English heiress.

Gregory couldn't make out what they were saying over the din of the banqueting room, but fortunately, Danworth was *also* a member of St.

George's. So questioning him about the princess some other time should be easy enough.

Whatever the two were discussing was so engrossing that Lady Ursula never turned Gregory's way again, leaving him to spend the entire meal attempting conversation with the elderly countess on his right, who was famous for her reticence. By the time the main course arrived, he'd given up on trying to engage her and had turned to observing the princess's behavior.

Odd how she never made a slip, never used the wrong fork, never seemed ill at ease in such a setting. Some of it he could attribute to her ability as an actress. But the rest? Someone would have had to train her for months for this. He itched to know why they would go to so much trouble.

There *was* one point in the evening when the syllabub was served and she regarded it with a slight frown, her fingers toying with a dessert spoon as she looked over at Lady Ursula. How intriguing.

Lady Ursula picked up her syllabub and sipped from the glass. With a hint of relief on her face, Monique did the same. It was the only time he caught her trying to get direction from someone else on how to behave.

Though she still didn't succeed in drinking it without getting a charming line of the thick cream along her top lip. When she licked it off, she caught him staring at her, and a soft pink spread over her cheeks. It fired his blood, sent him right back to that moment in the garden when she'd kissed him with all the impudence of a courtesan. He held her gaze in a duel of wills that only ended when Pontalba leaned over to whisper something to her that made her stiffen.

Gregory had to fight the urge to leap over the table and throttle the man. Which was ludicrous. She was an impostor!

Yet something about her roused every protective instinct in his soul.

That shook him. God, it was going to be a very long night.

Five

St. George's was too crowded for Gregory's taste this evening. It probably didn't help that he was in a foul mood, having endured hours of watching Monique captivate everyone with whom she came in contact. Apparently, he was the only person in England who rubbed her wrong.

But he was also the only person in England who knew what it felt like to kiss her. That did soothe his damaged pride a bit.

He found Hart in the card room, finishing up a game of vingt-un with Niall, Warren, and Jeremy.

"I see I'm not the only one who abandoned the palace festivities early in the evening," Gregory said as he took a seat.

Despite his attempts to get near Monique after dinner, he'd been blocked by one person after another. Her dance card had been full of dignitaries, and she'd danced until the count had whisked her away.

After that, Gregory had seen no point in staying, especially since Danworth had left already. What a pity. Gregory was still trying to figure out what the man's interest in the princess might be. He intended to find out tonight, assuming that Danworth showed up here, which was a good bet.

Warren rose from the table. "We're not staying. My brother has the devil's own luck tonight."

"You play him at your peril, Fulkham," Niall added as he shoved his money toward Hart.

"Bunch of cowards," Hart complained. "They always run when the going gets tough."

"It has nothing to do with that," Jeremy said with a sly wink. "And everything to do with the fact that our wives are waiting for us. Eh, lads?"

Warren grinned. "Mine certainly is."

"I doubt that," Hart retorted. "They probably don't even realize you're gone. When I left your house, Warren, they were already in the midst of a hen party fit to make a bachelor's ears bleed. No doubt they're still at it. Why do you think I fled in search of more entertaining company?"

Niall snorted. "Scared of a bunch of women. Who's the coward now?"

Hart cast him a black look. "I can't even flirt with them. You lot are liable to shoot me if I do."

The three men laughed.

"Flirt all you like," Warren said lightly. "Delia can take care of herself—she knows just how to skewer you with her sharp tongue, and she rather enjoys doing so. Not to mention that I enjoy watching it. And I promise none of the rest would look twice at you, except to tease you."

"Or marry him off," Jeremy said. "That's the real reason he avoids them. They've got a list of prospective wives for him that would make his ballocks curl up and die."

Hart rolled his eyes heavenward. "You see what I'm up against, Fulkham? Watch out—the hens have got a list for you, too. I've heard them discussing it."

"So have I," Gregory said dryly. "Fortunately, I've been fending off matchmakers for years now, so I've got the knack of it. You merely tell the lady doing the matchmaking that no one could ever live up to her charms, and while she's preening over the compliment, you beat a hasty retreat."

Warren, Niall, and Jeremy laughed. Hart did not. He was still nursing a grudge at the others for quitting the game so early in the evening.

"And on that note, gentlemen," Warren said, "we're off to fetch our matchmaking wives home. Hart, don't beat Fulkham too badly. Leave him with his dignity at least."

Then the gentlemen were gone. Now it was just Gregory and Hart. Perfect.

Gregory took a seat opposite Hart. "Deal me in."

"Excellent," Hart said, brightening as he shuffled. "Another victim."

"I wouldn't count on that. Vingt-un is my game."

"We'll see." Hart handed the cards over to Gregory. "Stake of five pounds per hand?"

"I take it you need money," Gregory said. When Hart looked grim and cut the cards, Gregory added, "I have a better way for you to make it than vingt-un."

Hart lifted his head. "I'm listening."

"I need you to do something for me. It's important, which means—"

"Excellent compensation," Hart drawled. "I'm in."

"Don't you want to know what it is first?"

"No. I still owe Warren a bit of blunt for helping me pay off my debt to Brilliana for— It doesn't matter. Suffice it to say, I don't want that hanging over my head, even if he *is* my brother and unlikely to call in the bet."

"It's a matter of honor."

Hart nodded as he turned one card up.

"Very well." Gregory turned his up, too, then shrugged when he lost the chance to deal. "Do you remember that actress we met in Dieppe? Monique Servais?"

Hart gathered up the cards. "I should say so. How could I forget the only woman to have put the great Lord Fulkham in his place?"

"As I recall, she rebuffed you, too, old chap."

"She did not," Hart said. "I rebuffed *her* by running after you instead."

"If you say so." Gregory paused to watch Hart deal. "To be honest, most of that night is a blur."

It took a minute for those words to register

with Hart, but when they did, he turned instantly contrite. "Oh, God, I forgot. That's when you found out about—"

"John. Yes."

Some weeks after that horrible night, Gregory had learned the full extent of what had happened to his brother. John had ignored the advice of his superior. Instead of waiting a week until the officer they'd been watching was away on maneuvers, he'd searched the officer's tent for a certain treasonous letter while the man was supposedly in the mess.

Except that their suspect *hadn't* been in the mess. John had been caught. Or so his superior surmised, after the fool's body turned up in a ditch with his throat slashed.

It had been little consolation to Gregory that the officer had eventually been charged with murder, and later with treason once his tent was successfully searched and the letter found. John was still dead. Gregory had still failed him.

He thrust that thought to the back of his mind.

"So what's this about Mademoiselle Servais?" Hart asked.

"I think she's in town."

Hart eyed him askance. "What do you mean, you *think*?"

"I believe she's masquerading as the Princess de Chanay."

With a low whistle, Hart dealt himself a card

that brought him to fifteen. "That would be quite a feat, wouldn't you say?"

"Perhaps. Perhaps not." Gregory made a motion to indicate he meant to stand at nineteen. "It seems that the two women resemble each other."

Hart dealt himself another card and passed twenty-one. Shoving a five-pound note across the table, he listened as Gregory gathered up the cards and began to relate everything he'd noticed at the royal dinner, every suspicion he'd had about Princess Aurore. Of course, he refrained from speaking of their kisses. No need to mention *those*.

When Hart began to pepper him with questions, their card game was forgotten. And the man's skeptical remarks made him doubt his own theories.

Until Gregory remembered her reaction to him. "See here, Hart, if you don't think I'm right about this, check her out for yourself. I understand that she'll be touring Westminster Abbey tomorrow. See if you can get close enough to observe her, and then tell me your own impressions. I gather that you saw her in theater productions more times than I. You ought to be able to judge if it's her."

Hart settled back to fold his hands over his belly. "And if I think it is? What then?"

"See what you can learn from the servants at the town house we rented for them. We provided their staff, who will undoubtedly be more inclined to side with a countryman than with the strangers from Chanay. Anything you find out is better than what I know now, which is virtually nothing. All I have is my conviction that Mademoiselle Servais is impersonating Princess Aurore. I just can't figure out why. If you can do so, I will pay you well."

"All right. I'll see what I can learn." Hart shuffled the cards, then handed them to Gregory to deal. "Another game?"

"It depends. Have you seen Danworth here this evening?"

"I believe so. He was in the reading room having a spirited discussion about politics with some gentleman. But that was a while ago."

"I need to speak to him, so I'll have to leave you at present. But if you want to hang about until later . . ."

"Sorry, old chap, I'd rather saunter down to that new tavern in Covent Garden. The taproom maids are supposed to be particularly free with their favors, if you'd like to join me once you're done."

"Afraid not." He'd spent enough time in such places in his youth to know that they held more danger than pleasure, especially for a man with ambition. If he wanted a woman at the ready, he'd take a discreet mistress, as he'd done in the past.

But even those days were behind him. His political career required that he have a wife, so in future he'd be limiting his encounters with the fairer sex to eligible females. He drew the line at a marriage where he had to sneak around behind his wife's back. He wouldn't give his enemies any opportunity to turn his prospective wife against him, which meant no infidelities.

Not that he was looking for love or anything mad like that. But he wanted a comfortable, amiable match. A pity that he hadn't yet found a single eligible woman who struck his fancy.

Monique's mocking gaze came into his mind, and he scowled. She might strike his fancy, but she was *not* eligible. He could no more marry an actress than he could a laundrywoman. Which was a damned shame.

God, what was he thinking? He'd never want to marry a woman so devious anyway, even if she *did* have a luscious mouth.

"Enjoy yourself," he told Hart. "I'm sure you can find someone else here who'd join you at the tavern to dandle a taproom maid on his knee."

"Warren used to go with me, but now—"

"Delia would have his ballocks if he did."

"She's got his ballocks already," Hart grumbled. "Probably keeps them in a jar on her dressing table."

Gregory laughed. "Watch it, man. You're starting to sound peevish. Are you perhaps a little jealous of your brother's wedded bliss?"

"Jealous! Never." A flush rose over his cheeks. "I mean, Delia is pretty and all, but I have no intention of getting myself tangled in any one woman's apron strings. I prefer a more varied diet."

"Then you'd best steer clear of her for a while. The most determined matchmakers are always sisters-in-law." Although thankfully, now that his own was absorbed in planning her own marriage, he'd gained a reprieve. "I'll be waiting to hear from you about Mademoiselle Servais."

After walking through the club, Gregory found Danworth sitting alone in the reading room. Apparently the man's companion had left. "Danworth! Just the fellow I was looking for."

Danworth eyed him warily. "If this is about that bill you were hoping the prime minister would champion—"

"No, no, nothing like that." Gregory took a seat. "I'm just curious about your impressions of the Chanay party."

"Ah. I see." Danworth furrowed his brow, obviously gathering his thoughts before he spoke.

He was cautious that way. The third son of a squire, Danworth was one of those men who'd managed to insinuate himself into the highest echelons of society by being circumspect. He knew how to say the right things, dress the right way, and court the right connections, but without being a toady.

Aware of how much work that required, Gregory admired the man for doing it so effortlessly. He'd always suspected that Danworth's intelligence ran deeper than anyone realized.

How else could the fellow have gained the prime minister's loyalty for so long?

Gregory drummed his fingers on his knee. "I saw that you had quite a long and involved conversation with Lady Ursula. Had you met her before?"

"No. But she was most gracious in answering my questions about Chanay and the princess."

"What kind of questions? Is the prime minister taking a personal interest in the Belgium affair? Because the last time I spoke with him, he seemed to be willing to leave things up to the foreign secretary. Which, in this case, means leaving it up to *me* to negotiate."

Danworth blinked, then appeared to be considering the question. How odd. Gregory hadn't thought it a question that required lengthy reflection.

"It's not so much that he has an interest in Belgium, as it is that he wanted me to clarify a rumor concerning the princess and . . . er . . . Prince Leopold. Since Lady Ursula, like the princess, is from Hanover, I thought she could confirm or disprove the rumor."

Prince Leopold? Early on, he'd been England's top choice for ruler of Belgium. He'd been married to Princess Charlotte, heir apparent to the British throne, until she'd died in childbirth. The Belgians had liked him for the position. And since he wasn't French or Dutch, neither of those parties ought to have complained.

But the French had, of course. They were still eager to have one of their own princes put in place if they could get the other countries to agree. Barring that, they wanted the Princess of Chanay, since she spoke French and came from a French line.

"What's the rumor?" Gregory demanded. This could be important in the scheme of things.

Danworth scrubbed a hand over his face. "If I tell you, you can't tell anyone else. Since Prince Leopold is out of town, I haven't been able to confirm it with him. So it may be nothing."

"What's the rumor?" Gregory repeated, growing annoyed. If anyone should know this, it was him. He was in charge of this damned business, after all.

"There's talk—still just talk, mind you—that Prince Leopold has made an offer of marriage to Princess Aurore. If it's true—"

"It affects everything," Gregory said. "Yes, it certainly does." A union between Prince Leopold and Princess Aurore would all but ensure that one of the two would be chosen as ruler of Belgium. "When did this rumor surface? Before the process to confirm Belgium's independence began? Or after?"

"I . . . I'm not sure. I just know when *I* heard it. And that was recently."

Recently. So perhaps it had begun after Monique's masquerade, which meant the two things might be connected. Then again, as Monique had said, even the great Count de Beaumonde could hardly switch out one bride for another without comment.

"Was this offer made by the prince in person?" Gregory asked. "I was told that Princess Aurore rarely met with people outside of Chanay circles."

That seemed to give Danworth pause. "The *rumor* is that it was all done by correspondence, but I cannot imagine the prince's not at least attempting to see the woman. Still, as I said, I'm merely trying to clarify the rumor. It may be arrant nonsense."

"What did Lady Ursula say?"

Danworth snorted. "She wouldn't confirm *or* deny it, no matter how much I pressed her. She just kept changing the subject."

"Which means there must be something to the rumor, or she would have denied it outright."

"Or she's hoping for such a union even if it hasn't been brokered. Honestly, I wouldn't take it too seriously. You know how easily this sort of gossip spreads."

Gregory did, indeed. That was why he proceeded with caution when it came to women. Because any tales swirling around town about a man offering for the wrong woman could have disastrous consequences.

You didn't proceed cautiously with Monique. You kissed her most unwisely.

He grimaced. Clearly she was the exception to his rule. And it was starting to grate on him that every time he saw her, he let her be the exception. That simply wouldn't do. He'd worked too hard and long for his position—and the one he hoped to have someday—to allow his fascination with an impostor to overtake his good sense. If anyone found out who she was and that he'd known all along . . .

Damn it, that mustn't happen. So he'd better get to the bottom of this masquerade before someone like Danworth discovered it by accident and reported on it to the prime minister. Because then there would be hell to pay. And any possibility of his becoming foreign secretary would be over.

But attacking her with the truth hadn't worked. She'd merely laughed and flirted her way around his every remark. Even his kisses. So he needed another tack. Put her at her ease, make her think he'd given up while he waited for the evidence he hoped Hart might turn up.

Then, and only then, would he pounce.

Six

The evening after the royal dinner, Monique was standing with Lady Ursula in an English lord's ballroom when she felt the hairs stand on the back of her neck. She didn't even have to turn and look to see why. She *knew*.

It was Lord Fulkham. He had come . . . for *her*. To catch *her*. To bait *her*.

Last night, he'd watched her the entire time she'd been dancing, and tonight he had clearly decided to repeat the experience. Or to try to get her alone again. Which she didn't dare allow.

Only one person could help prevent that—Lady Ursula. The lady-in-waiting had been looking out for her, keeping her away from the man she most wanted to avoid.

She pulled Lady Ursula aside. "He's here."

"Who?" The woman scanned the ballroom. "Do you mean the duke?"

"No, of course not!" Monique cast a furtive glance over to where Lord Fulkham stood talking to a delegate from the Dutch contingent. "That cursed undersecretary. You have to keep him away from me as you did last night."

Lady Ursula's expression grew troubled. "I shouldn't have done that. The count was most displeased at me for it."

"But I'm glad you did." She squeezed Lady Ursula's hand. "You made sure that the men kept me dancing so he could never come near. I was so grateful."

The lady-in-waiting eyed her suspiciously. "You told me that Lord Fulkham did nothing wrong when you were alone with him."

Oh, dear. Playing a set role as an actress was far easier than juggling who she was with who she was supposed to be. And it was all *his* fault. She could escape fully into the role if not for him lobbing questions at her every moment.

Unfortunately, if she warned the count of Lord Fulkham's suspicions, he might send her back to the Continent, ending their bargain. She couldn't take that chance.

"Lord Fulkham didn't do anything he shouldn't have," she lied. "I just don't like him. He makes me nervous."

"As well he should, since he has a very important part in making the decision for or against you." Lady Ursula leaned close. "That's why you must spend time with him, reassure him of your worth. Can't you just put your feelings aside for a bit? Aurore needs you."

And so did Grand-maman. "He's very clever. I'm afraid he'll find me out." *Has already found me out.*

"Nonsense." Lady Ursula patted her arm. "You have been amazing. I confess I was skeptical when the count proposed this solution, but you are a quick study and good at improvising when you're uncertain." She smiled faintly. "I only wish I could see you on the stage. I know you must be magnificent."

The compliment caught Monique off guard. "Thank you. It isn't exactly a royal occupation." *To put it mildly.*

"Will you miss it?" the lady-in-waiting surprised her by asking. She seemed genuinely interested, too. "I mean, when you and your grandmother move to Chanay for good."

"*If* we move for good. I must bring this to a successful conclusion first."

"And I have faith that you will," Lady Ursula said kindly. "Still, when you move to Chanay, there will be no more applause every night, no more adventures on the stage . . . and off the stage." She cast Monique a wistful look. "No more freedom to do as you please."

If any other woman had said such things, Monique would have assumed she was making insinuations about supposed promiscuity. All actresses were believed to be promiscuous. But something in Lady Ursula's manner said that she didn't mean it that way.

"I haven't had much of that freedom anyway," she said softly, "not with Grand-maman ill."

Her life had revolved around her grandmother's care for so long that she'd forgotten what it was like to go for a walk alone or meet a gentleman at a café. Lord Fulkham would probably be shocked to hear that she was as chaste as her cousin Aurore probably was.

Her grandmother had been very rigid about gentleman callers. Monique's father had seduced Monique's mother, and Grandpapa had made the fellow marry. But shortly before Monique's birth, he had run off, proving his low character. So Grand-maman had been stricter with Monique, not wanting her granddaughter to be seduced.

Grand-maman had always said she'd been lucky that her own actor husband had proved a gentleman, but there were too many men out there who would take advantage of a pretty young thing.

By the time Monique had grown old enough to rebel at such restrictions, her grandmother had needed restrictions of her own. Then it had seemed impossible to add a beau into their lives.

Which was why once Grand-maman passed on, Monique would not stay in Chanay. She craved her freedom. She loved her grandmother and would miss her terribly, but she wanted to be young and alive again. So while she could live without the excitement of the theater, she could never live within the confines of royalty.

Not be able to say what she thought and go where she wished? Be forced to marry someone handpicked for political reasons? No, thank you. That was not for her.

Apparently it was not for Lady Ursula either, judging from her remarks. "Do you miss not being 'free to do as you please'?" Monique asked, partly to take her mind off Grand-maman's uncertain future, and partly because she was simply curious. "Do you wish you were not a lady-in-waiting to royalty?"

"Oh no, not one bit! I love being helpful to Aurore."

When her face clouded over, Monique asked, "Have you heard how my cousin is doing? Is there any word of her condition?"

Were those tears glistening in Lady Ursula's eyes as she shook her head? Poor woman.

Then she seemed to gather her composure. "The count says it's too soon to have received any message from Calais, and I daresay he's right. It's just that I was never as close to my family as you seem to be to your grandmother, so Aurore is all the family I—" She stiffened, then pasted a tight smile to her lips as she glanced beyond Monique. "Why, good evening, Lord Fulkham. How lovely to see you again."

Monique fought the urge to bolt. Smoothing her features into nonchalance, she turned to face him. "Yes, how nice to see you, monsieur."

It was a lie. It had to be a lie, even though he was dressed to impress. His perfectly tailored suit of black superfine heightened the crystalline blue of his eyes and the casually disordered waves of his dark hair, making her want to reach up and smooth the strands into place. Worse yet, his delicious brown silk waistcoat of some checked design made her think of chocolate wafers, which was apt, because she wanted to eat him up.

Mon Dieu.

His gaze seemed to take her in and like what it saw, too, judging from the sharp interest flaring in it. "You look luscious this evening, Your Serene Highness. That gown suits you."

"Luscious?" Lady Ursula said in her heavily accented English. "I do not know this word."

Monique did. She'd looked it up after he'd said it last night. How dare he use such a blatantly sensual word around Lady Ursula! "I think it means beautiful."

A wry smile twisted up Lord Fulkham's lips. "Exactly. So beautiful that I was hoping Her Highness might be willing to grace me with a waltz. Since she is not otherwise engaged at the moment."

"I'm sure she would be honored," Lady Ursula said before Monique could drum up some excuse. "Wouldn't you, Your Highness?"

"Of course," Monique said. "I am curious to see if his lordship is as good at dancing as he is at diplomacy."

He clearly didn't miss the sarcasm in her voice but apparently chose to ignore it. "I can show a good leg as well as the next man." He held out his hand. "Shall we?"

With a smooth nod, she let him lead her onto the floor, only to find that he hadn't lied. He danced very well for a pompous Englishman whom she still wanted to throttle.

She waited for him to resume his attack on her masquerade. If he did, he would find himself at a disadvantage; tonight she was prepared. He would not get the better of her.

"You do look luscious, you know," he drawled. "Every inch a princess."

"That's because I *am* a princess," she said sweetly.

"Of course. It was rude of me to imply otherwise last night. Forgive me."

That made her falter. "Very well. If I must." No, that sounded churlish. "You are forgiven." Yes, that sounded more regal.

The twinkle in his eyes said that she wasn't fooling him one bit.

They glided about the room, his hand resting on her waist as lightly as a caress while his other hand clasped hers in a gesture of possessiveness that reminded her of the mark he'd left on her wrist. The one he now had the audacity to rub with his thumb through her white kid glove.

"Tell me about Chanay," he said in a husky voice that made her belly quiver.

And sparked her temper. "Why? So you can pick at everything I say to use as evidence that I am this other woman friend of yours?"

"Hardly. As you pointed out last night, I've never been to your country. You could tell me that the sheep run Chanay, for all I would know." He smiled most charmingly, which instantly put her on her guard. "I merely thought you might be homesick and wish to talk about the place."

"I see."

He had to be still trying to trip her up. Did he think she would be so stupid as to not have learned anything about the country she was supposed to be representing?

Fortunately, Grand-maman had told her endless stories about Chanay. "What do you wish to know?"

"*Do* the sheep run the place?"

A laugh escaped her in spite of her caution. "Only when the shepherds have gone home for the day."

He smiled at her with genuine humor, and her heart flipped over in her chest. How foolish was that? She clearly needed a less susceptible heart.

Leaning close, he murmured, "We English have a saying, 'When the cat's away, the mice will play.' What happens when the shepherds are away?"

She edged away from that too-close mouth of his. "The sheep are eaten up, monsieur. Everyone knows that. Sheep are too trusting. They require good shepherds to keep them safe from . . . wolves."

He laughed. "If you're trying to say I'm a wolf

preying on the sheep, you are far off the mark. There isn't a sheep alive as quick-witted or as resourceful as you. Even when your shepherds abandon you."

She swallowed. "What do you mean?"

He glanced beyond her to where the others from Chanay were watching them dance with approving smiles. "Lady Ursula as much as thrust you directly into my hands. And the count has been more than eager to do the same."

"They are not my shepherds," she said fiercely. "I am perfectly capable of being my own shepherd."

"Exactly. That *is* a princess's purview, is it not?"

Now she was confused. Had he actually decided to believe she was the princess, or was he merely toying with her? Given his position, probably the latter. Either way, she had best be careful; he could not be trusted.

She tipped up her chin. "It is a queen's purview as well."

Glancing away, he twirled her about the floor as effortlessly as a man born to it, which, of course, he was. "So you think you would make a good queen, do you?"

"A better one than you," she quipped, delighted when that startled him into another laugh. "And yes, I think I would. I know what people want from their rulers."

His amusement faded to cynicism. "Ah. And what is that, pray tell?"

"Fairness. Honesty. Loyalty. And compassion."

He released a low whistle. "That is quite a list of qualities. What about a firm hand? What about justice?"

"There can be no justice where there's no fairness. And a firm hand should always be tempered with compassion."

That seemed to shake him. He gazed earnestly into her eyes. "It appears you think like a queen after all."

"Does that surprise you?"

"Nothing surprises me about you."

The look he then shot her sparked a need in her blood that burned through her veins the way his love bite had burned through her skin. He had this way of stripping her down to the essentials. No one had ever laid her bare like that.

The music ended, startling them both. He accompanied her to where the count now stood beside Lady Ursula. But before he left her, he said, "I would like to take you on a drive about London, show you some of the sights. Perhaps we could visit Hyde Park?"

"That would be wonderful," the count answered for her.

She bit her lip to keep from protesting. She was so very tired of having people answer for her.

To her surprise, Lord Fulkham ignored the count. "Your Highness? Would you like a tour of the city? Hyde Park is spectacular in autumn, with the leaves changing color. I think you would enjoy it."

Feeling the weight of Count de Beaumonde's gaze upon her, she flashed Lord Fulkham a thin smile. "That would be lovely, sir."

"Tomorrow, then?"

The count frowned. "Have you forgotten, Fulkham? Tomorrow is when the delegates are presented at Parliament."

The quick flash of annoyance on Lord Fulkham's face showed that he *had* forgotten. "Of course. Wouldn't want to miss that. But it's in the morning. The late afternoon is actually the fashionable hour during the Season, and it's the best time to go all year."

"Regrettably, we have another engagement in the afternoon," the count said, to Monique's vast relief. "But I'm sure we could manage it on the following afternoon"

"Excellent. I shall come at four p.m. I look forward to it." Lord Fulkham smiled at Monique with such intensity that a flame ignited low within her and licked fire along all the forgotten and desolate parts of her heart.

"As do I," she said.

And to her complete mortification, she realized that she meant it.

The next morning, only one person interested Gregory as he scrutinized each foreign delegate being introduced to Parliament. He told himself it was because she was an impostor, but the truth was, Monique Servais interested him no matter what role she played. He enjoyed sparring with her. He enjoyed watching surprise gild her features whenever he said something that caught her off guard.

He enjoyed watching *her*. Her malleable features displayed the subtlest of emotions. The characteristic served an actress—and an impostor—well. It made him wonder about the real Monique. He wanted to uncover her, to expose her . . . to explore her.

How reckless was that? She could destroy his entire career. Yet he was fascinated. Because she seemed not to know how dangerous she was, how dangerous was the game she played. That in itself intrigued him.

He glanced up into the gallery and noticed Hart standing there. Hart nodded, a signal that he had information to impart. Gregory looked about, noticed that the other MPs were half-asleep, and decided that he might as well speak with Hart now. *She* had not been presented yet, after all.

Rising from his chair, he made his way to the gallery and Hart. But as soon as he took a seat beside the fellow, Monique was presented.

Gregory couldn't take his eyes off her. She wore a demure, elegant gown of fawn silk that shimmered whenever a shaft of sunlight caught it as she moved. Her hair, too, was sedately dressed, no doubt to amplify her regal appearance. But it was her smooth aplomb and measured speech that made her every inch a princess.

Which she wasn't. She couldn't be. He refused to believe himself to be so far off the mark.

"You may be right," Hart said.

"About what?"

"Her being Monique Servais. I can't be sure, but I'm leaning toward your point of view."

Perhaps he *wasn't* going mad after all. "What did you learn?"

"Apparently, the count made a trip to Dieppe a few days before the Chanay contingent departed from Calais."

"Does anyone know why?"

"If they do, they're not saying. But it certainly *could* be because he was going there to engage Mademoiselle Servais in his scheme."

"It could." He listened as she made an impassioned speech about the importance of choosing the proper ruler for Belgium. She was articulate and clever. If she *was* the real princess, he would champion her no matter what the cost. "Did you learn anything about *why* he might have wished to engage her?"

"No. That's the trouble. I tried to find out, but when it came to information of that nature, the servants clammed up."

"Or they didn't know anything. The English servants would have been told that she was the princess. They have no reason to believe otherwise. Did you speak to the French ones?"

"There really weren't any, so no. Have you any theories?"

"None right now. I need to know more." Gregory paused to watch as she seduced a roomful of men into believing whatever she said. It was astonishing what a pretty, young female could do to further her cause. He refused to let such manipulation affect him.

Right. Because you're not attracted to her in the least.

He scowled. He could handle Monique Servais. If that was really who she was. "Do you have time to take a trip?" he asked Hart.

"To Dieppe?"

"Exactly. I'd go myself except that I have to be here for the conference, especially with the foreign secretary indisposed."

"I can go. The steam packets cross from Newhaven to Dieppe in nine hours these days. I could probably be back with a report for you by Friday. What do you want me to find out?"

"Whatever you can about Mademoiselle Servais. See if the count visited her personally, and if so, when. And do some research into her background. I can't figure out why they would choose her, beyond her facility as an actress. The more you learn, the more I'll know how to act."

"Very well. I'll discover what I can."

"Excellent."

They sat in shared silence a moment. Then

Hart cleared his throat. "If she *is* Mademoiselle Servais, she plays the role of princess to perfection."

"She does, indeed."

"Are you sure she isn't—"

"Aren't you?" Gregory snapped.

Hart cocked his head to listen. "I just can't be certain. She does have the same dulcet voice. Not to mention that sensual glide of a walk, like a swan on the water . . . or one of the finer French courtesans in the salons of Paris, who knows all the secrets of flirting and uses them to her advantage. It's something in the way her hips swing ever so slightly, making a man want to reach out and grab—"

"Yes," Gregory said irritably, "I know what you want to grab." Randy bastard. "No princess walks like that. Besides, Princess Aurore has never been in Dieppe acting on the stage."

"So why the masquerade?"

"I don't know. That's what I'm trying to figure out."

He could feel Hart's gaze on him as the other man assessed the tension in his face.

"You like her," Hart said accusingly.

Gregory forced a smile. "I think she's talented at pretending to be someone else."

"If that's what she's doing. And it's more than that. You *want* her."

He certainly did. But he would never admit that to Hart, of all people. Gregory drew himself up. "Unlike you, I do not fall for the blandishments of actresses."

Hart uttered a mirthless laugh. "If you say so." He rose. "I'll let you know what I find out."

"Be quick about it, do you hear? The delegates plan to make a decision soon."

"I'll do my best."

Barely aware of Hart slipping from the gallery, Gregory kept his gaze trained on Monique Servais. She did have the practiced grace of a princess. But Hart was right—something lay underneath it, a sensual quality that roused his blood. It called to him as no other woman ever had, made him want to unwind the barely restrained masses of her hair and luxuriate in it.

The effect she had on him made no sense. He was a practical man, well aware of the restrictions of his position. And she tempted him to toss them all to the wind just for another taste of that warm mouth.

He dropped his gaze to her wrist and the glove that covered the mark he'd made. An intense satisfaction coursed through him. At least *there* she was his.

Yet not his, either. She wasn't the sort of woman to be owned. Which fascinated him. Most women wanted to adopt the high status of a husband so they could be sure of their place in society. She clearly did not. Or else she was sure enough of her own place to be content.

That gave him pause. Could he have been

right the first time? Could she be the count's mistress, who just happened to look enough like the princess to be her twin? It seemed an odd coincidence. But it would explain why the count had asked her to take Princess Aurore's place.

Gregory also had to wonder about Princess Aurore. What would make the woman give up her duties to an impostor? Was she merely extremely shy? That would be in keeping with the reclusiveness she was famous for.

Perhaps this whole thing had come about because her people were afraid Aurore couldn't present herself well enough to secure the position of queen. So they called in a woman who could, knowing that once Aurore was chosen, she could surround herself with sycophants who could keep people at bay.

Though that made sense, it didn't seem likely. It was too much of a risk. Which left another more disturbing reason—that there was a sinister purpose behind it. Or worse yet, that she really *was* Princess Aurore and he was utterly wrong about the masquerade.

Damn it, he was tired of thinking about it. Until he had real information, he couldn't puzzle it out. So he would just have to hope that Hart learned the reason for it in Dieppe. Because otherwise, Gregory would seriously have to improve his game at eliciting secrets from whoever that devilishly fetching creature was.

Seven

Monique trod the carpet in the drawing room of the strange English town house so enthusiastically that she feared she might damage the flimsy soles of her delicate shoes. She'd wanted to wear sturdy half boots, but those wouldn't do for a fine princess, oh no. The slippers must be kid, the stockings silk, and the gown of the finest green gros de Naples with a line of fussy pink bows and gigot sleeves.

Apparently her cousin had a fondness for pink, which was evidenced by her hat—an enormous creation in blossom silk with birds and fake apples that hurt Monique's head. She hated all of it. It made her wonder at her cousin's taste. Not to mention the common sense of the person who'd packed Aurore's attire for autumn in England. Monique had been freezing ever since her arrival!

Still, the ladies here seemed no better off,

wearing flimsy satins and silks in the evening. They did have lush velvet cloaks, as did Aurore, but Monique was used to dressing more warmly in Dieppe, to the heavy brocade gowns and the hot lamps of the stage. She envied the English ladies in the streets wearing sensible wool. She preferred *warm* clothes. Grand-maman had always laughingly told her that she'd inherited the thin blood of some ancient Italian ancestor, and Monique had never believed it more than now.

She swallowed hard. She missed her grandmother. That servant of Count de Beaumonde's had better be treating Solange well, or Monique would roast him on a spit!

"Are you ready?" said a crisp male voice from the doorway.

She started. The count was hovering about as usual. "As ready as I'll ever be."

Her great-uncle entered. "You needn't be nervous. You already have Lord Fulkham wrapped about your finger. The man is entranced."

The trace of bitterness in the man's voice gave her pause. Granted, Aurore wasn't known for her male conquests, but she'd seemed pretty enough. Surely she would make a good match eventually.

"He's not entranced," she said. "He is . . . careful. He asks probing questions and demands answers."

The count poured himself some coffee from the pot always kept at the ready for his use, even now, in late afternoon. The man drank more coffee than anyone Monique had ever met, always flavored with a finger of brandy. It did make her wonder if the brandy was the real reason for the coffee, though he never seemed intoxicated.

"Are you having trouble giving Fulkham answers?" the count asked. "Shall we go over the information I gave you before?"

"No need. He's not interested in the exports of Chanay or in how the ministers advise me. He wants to know my opinions on governing."

And why I am masquerading as Princess Aurore. Though she could hardly tell the count that.

She could handle Lord Fulkham. She must.

Nervously she adjusted the gold bracelet she wore to cover his love bite. It gave her a secret thrill to know it was there. Curse the man for that.

"You must play nice with him," the count said. "Encourage him."

She stiffened. "What do you mean?"

"Being an actress with many admirers, you must realize how men are. Flatter him and soothe his fears. I'm sure you know how."

Stifling a burst of temper, she said, "Of course." Though she did *not* know how. She'd learned from her grandmother never to encourage men who wished to conquer her. Otherwise, they only became more strident, more demanding . . . more dangerous.

Or so Grand-maman said. But the undersecretary was dangerous for an entirely different reason. Because she was far too susceptible to him, though God only knew why.

"I will do my best," she said. "But he is predisposed toward choosing a man to rule Belgium." She wasn't sure of that, but it made sense. Men always favored other men.

The count frowned. "He won't continue to be so if you make him enamored of you. Men think with their . . . you know. And he is no exception."

This time she had more trouble hiding her anger. Why did everyone assume that actresses were whores? Elizabeth Farren had been famously chaste until she married the Earl of Derby. And Monique knew plenty of women in the theater who did not take lovers, who did not want to be a man's toy.

Well, a *few* women, anyway. And she was one of them, having learned that even marriage could prove treacherous to one's future. She would find a man who would accept her profession, who understood her need to be free, who would allow her a voice in her future. Who would not tear her family from her.

It certainly couldn't be Lord Fulkham, since he seemed determined to expose her, which would end her hopes of taking care of Grandmaman in Chanay.

One of their English footmen came to the door. "Lord Fulkham is here for Princess Aurore."

"Send him in," the count said.

When Lord Fulkham entered she tried not to

be impressed, but it was difficult. The man certainly knew how to dress. Most of the Englishmen
in the streets looked frumpy and ill-kempt. While
the members of Parliament carried themselves
better, their overhanging bellies and red noses tes-
tified to their overindulgence in food and drink.
And the lack of hair was common enough for her
to think the English a race of bald men.

Not Lord Fulkham. Looking ever so smart in
his royal-blue coat, ivory waistcoat with brown
stripes, and buff trousers, he emanated power in a
way that other English lords did not. Their attire
was fussy and extravagant. His was understated,
hiding his important rank the same way his
body's lean, clean lines hid his surprising strength.

It made her nervous. She always liked to know
what kind of man she was dealing with, and he
shielded his true character at every turn.

"Good afternoon, Your Serene Highness," he
said in a voice like warm chocolate. A pity his
eyes were like the frozen ices from Gunter's in
Berkeley Square.

She raised an eyebrow. "I'm looking forward to
our jaunt through your little park."

That warmed his gaze, and he chuckled. "The
king would be amused to hear you refer to his
park as 'little.' "

"The princess hasn't had much chance to see
the city, I'm afraid," the count cut in. "Too many
appointments and parties."

The ice returned to Lord Fulkham's eyes as he

trained them on the count. "We do like to keep our guests busy. It prevents them from wandering too far afield."

"Wandering?" A frown crossed her great-uncle's brow. "Who has been wandering?"

"I understand you were recently in Dieppe, sir," Lord Fulkham said.

Though the count showed no surprise, her heart jumped into a frenzied rhythm. Lord Fulkham had apparently done some probing into the Chanay contingent. Either that or he was trying to provoke her great-uncle into revealing her role in the scheme. Then he would expose their former association and ruin everything.

Merde.

"I was indeed in Dieppe, not that it's any of your concern," the count said, as matter-of-factly as if Lord Fulkham had just mentioned a ride into the English countryside. "I have relations there, so I thought I would take advantage of being in Calais, close enough to take a steam packet there in one day, to pay them a visit. You do realize my family is from very near there, do you not?" His voice hardened. "Your spies must have told you. I was raised in Rouen. I met my late wife, great-aunt to Princess Aurore, in Paris."

Monique fought to hide her surprise. She had not known that, though she had known the count wasn't native to Chanay.

"What spies, sir?" Lord Fulkham said smoothly. "You are guests here. We don't spy on our guests."

The count flashed him a tight smile. "Of course not. And I do not spy on my English friends, either."

The words seemed to give Lord Fulkham pause, as they were obviously meant to do. "I should hope not. That would be most unwise."

She fought the urge to shiver at the veiled threat. Was this the world of diplomacy? If so, she wanted none of it. Thank God it would be Aurore enduring these games and not she.

Time to end it. "Lord Fulkham, I thought you had come to take me for a drive, not trade words with my great-uncle." She held out her hand. "Shall we go? I am most eager to see this Hyde Park you spoke of."

He forced a smile. "Certainly, Your Highness. I would be honored."

"The princess's maid will, of course, be attending her," the count said.

That gave Monique pause. "I expected Lady Ursula to join me."

The count's hard smile answered that. "She is feeling unwell, so Flora will go."

Sacrebleu. The sympathies of her English maid would not be with her, but with the very handsome Lord Fulkham. "Of course."

Oddly enough, Lord Fulkham looked as if he disapproved. "Such a shame that Lady Ursula is ill. Do give her my sympathies."

Count de Beaumonde nodded, and Lord Fulkham left with her. Before they even reached the foyer downstairs where her maid stood waiting with her cloak, the undersecretary said in a low voice, "You see how he throws you to the wolves? Why do you let him?"

"I don't know what you mean," she retorted. "Are you a wolf, sir?"

He stiffened. "I could be. That is the point."

"But you and my uncle know each other well, do you not? So he's aware that you can be entrusted with a princess."

"Hmm," was all he would say.

But his remark made her wonder. Was he truly concerned about her? Or simply trying to drive a wedge between her and the count?

If so, he was succeeding. It unnerved her how easily her champion Lady Ursula was whisked away and a foreigner put in her place.

They set out beneath a steady drizzle. At least his curricle had a hood that protected them, although poor Flora was left to sit on the back with nothing but a bonnet and a cloak to shield her from the weather.

"It appears I picked a bad day for a drive." Lord Fulkham handled his horses exceedingly well, maneuvering them onto the street with ease. The beasts were probably as afraid to cross him as everyone else seemed to be. "I hope it isn't too uncomfortable for you."

"It is fine, although England seems very rainy. Is it always so?"

"Yes. That's what makes it so very green."

"My country is green, but it does not have constant rain."

He turned pensive. "True. France manages to have the best of both worlds."

"As does Chanay." When his lips curved cynically, she added, out of spite, "We have wonderful summers, full of sunshine and golden blooms. Can you say the same for England?"

"I can say the same for *my* part of England. My estate, Canterbury Court, is in Kent. We suffer some of the rain, but we have more sunny days than the north and even than London. That's why we're called the garden of England."

"It sounds beautiful," she said, and meant it. "Why do you spend so much time in town if you have such loveliness at your estate?"

His shoulders tensed. "I have duties."

"But must your duties to England be your first concern? If you have sufficient property to live comfortably in the country, why do you and your fellow statesmen toil in the city for much of the year?"

He flashed her a rueful smile. "You sound like my mother. She wishes I would stay in the country all the time."

"I can understand why. In my opinion, large cities are too restless. So many people, so much noise, so much dirt. I prefer the green." And the wonderful, turbulent sea. Though if she mentioned that, he would pounce on it as evidence of her true identity, since Chanay was landlocked. "The country provides a solitude that is soothing."

"And tedious. Not to mention silent."

"Wouldn't you prefer silence to this . . . this . . ." She waved her hand to indicate the major thoroughfare they'd pulled onto. "*Cacophonie?*"

"Not when silence hides lies." An edge entered his voice. "In the country, with its privacy, it is too easy for brutality . . ." He caught himself. "For the brutality of nature to run unchecked."

His shadowed features made her think he was no longer speaking of trees and fields, but of mankind. *Human* nature. She wondered if she could get him to say more. She would like to understand him better.

"We're here," he said, ending her chance as they drove through a massive stone arch into an enormous expanse of green that stretched as far as the eye could see.

No wonder he had laughed at her calling it "little."

He steered the curricle onto a wide, muddy track. "This particular section of Hyde Park is called Rotten Row. The name became bastardized from *route de Roi*, since it's used by royalty." He shot her a bland smile. "We English always murder the French language whenever we get the chance."

"True," she said lightly.

"Rotten Row is where the rich and powerful of London go to see and be seen. Normally it's quite crowded. But this isn't the Season, and the weather isn't particularly fine, so there aren't as many here as usual."

"Oh," was all she could answer. It seemed to her to have plenty of people, even in the drizzle. Colorful carriages jockeyed for space on the muddy track, mounted riders held to the edges, and a few brave souls strolled in the grass, umbrellas held high. Apparently they wanted to "see and be seen" no matter what the weather.

But these weren't the sort she cared about. In her experience, the rich and powerful always trampled upon the poor and the nobodies. Only too well, she remembered how the *haut ton* of Dieppe had treated her when she'd begun as an actress. Their praise had come with a slice of contempt.

As she'd become more successful her circumstances had changed, which had only made her more cynical. The people who'd treated her badly before now fawned over her, though she was the same person as always. So how could she take their opinions seriously?

He had not changed how he saw her. *He'd* never fawned. And still didn't. It was oddly reassuring.

She gazed beyond the people in their fancy coaches to the birches and Dutch elms with their changing colors, a riot of golds and reds and oranges. "You're right; the trees *are* beautiful in autumn. Even in the rain. *Especially* in the rain, which gilds them with drops of silver. So very lovely."

He fixed his gaze on her. "That's all you can say? No mention of the luxurious carriages? The costly gowns? The jewels?"

Belatedly, she realized that what she'd said wasn't very princess-like. "How can I see the costly gowns and jewels? Everyone is inside their equipages, hiding from the rain."

A smirk crossed his lips. "And the luxurious carriages?"

She waved her hand. "I do not care about carriages."

"I see." He turned off the dirt track he'd called Rotten Row and onto a less crowded path. "Even mine?"

His tone was flirtatious, so she matched it. "I like *yours*, of course, monsieur. It is the perfect combination of comfortable and useful."

He stiffened. "I take it that the count told you to flatter me to ensure my cooperation in making you queen."

Even though it was true, she bristled. "Do you not trust me to have my own opinions?"

He searched her face. "Do you? Have your own opinions, I mean?"

"Of course."

"Then tell me what you would think of being queen of Belgium."

That caught her off guard. She forced a smile. "I would . . . like it very much."

"Would you? Why?"

"Because I am from Belgium. So I have a strong opinion of the proper position of the nation."

"Ah. And what is that?"

She blinked. "I beg your pardon?"

"The position of Belgium. What is it?"

She took a moment to give the matter some thought before drawing her faux regality about her like a cloak. "Right now, the position of Belgium could be better. It is finally free, yes, but like a newborn babe, it is forced to bow to the wishes of adults with competing goals." Much like *her*, come to think of it. "Belgium has never governed itself or defended itself against intruders, and now must find its way through the morass of protocols and conflicting expectations. Thus, it is important for Belgium to take command of its future aggressively before anyone—"

An explosion occurred somewhere nearby, startling the horses and momentarily confusing her.

"Get down!" Lord Fulkham ordered, and when she stared stupidly at him, not quite aware of what was going on, he shoved her off the seat and into the well between it and the dashboard. Then he cracked the whip and sprang the horses into a run.

Again came a noise like an explosion, but this time she registered what it was. A gunshot. Someone was firing at them!

Terror froze her in place. Flora was screaming as the curricle raced along, and Lord Fulkham was cursing under his breath. The whole while, Monique clung to the seat behind her with clammy hands and kept her head down, her pulse galloping as fast as the horses.

Why on earth would anyone shoot at them? Was this a common occurrence in the parks of London? What if they hit Lord Fulkham? What would she do then?

Her stomach churned, and her throat closed up. She couldn't breathe. Oh, God, she didn't want to die! Not now, not here, so far away from her home!

Within moments they were back on Rotten Row, where men in uniform were already riding toward them, drawn by the shots, which thankfully had stopped now that they were surrounded by crowds.

Lord Fulkham reined the horses in and glanced down at her, his mouth drawn with concern. "Are you all right?"

He lifted her back into the seat. She bobbed her head.

"Flora?" he called back to the maid, shocking Monique. Gentlemen of rank never cared about servants.

At least the maid had stopped that awful screaming. "I—I'm f-fine, sir," she stammered just as the first uniformed soldier reached them.

Lord Fulkham turned to the soldier. "Captain,

there was a man shooting from among the silver birches back by the Serpentine," he said, sounding eerily calm. "Find him! I must get the princess away."

"Yes, my lord," the captain said, and rode off.

Her heart still in her throat, Monique clutched her bonnet with one hand and the side of the carriage with the other as Lord Fulkham tooled the curricle out of the park. His lips were set in a hard line, and his eyes blazed.

She had never seen him like this. "D-do you think the danger is over now?"

"I can't be sure, and I'm not taking any chances."

The curricle careened through the streets until he pulled it up in front of the Mayfair town house. Before the grooms could even rush out to put down the step, Lord Fulkham was out of the carriage and around to her side, reaching up to clasp her by the waist.

He lifted her down as easily as he'd lifted her onto the seat. One would think she was light as a croissant. She was not. Indeed, sometimes she enjoyed her croissants a bit too much. Yet he gave no sign of being overtaxed.

With a hoarse cry, Flora jumped down and ran up the steps into the house most uncharacteristically, clearly rattled by the shooting. Lord Fulkham kept Monique in his grasp, trapped between the curricle and his rigid form.

"Are you certain you're all right?" he asked.

She fought for calm. "Of course. Don't I look all right?"

He scanned her, from the top of her ridiculous hat to her collarette to her—

"Oh, God," he said hoarsely. For the first time that afternoon, she heard a tremor in his voice.

"What?"

He grabbed the gigot part of her left sleeve and thrust his finger through two holes in it. "A bullet came through here." His voice grew ragged. "A few inches to the right, and he would have hit your heart."

Her heart, which had not been hit, nonetheless dropped into her stomach. "You . . . you think he was aiming for me."

The count came out of the front door and hurried down the steps. "What happened? Flora is hysterical and babbling about gunshots."

Veiling his gaze, Lord Fulkham released her. "We should discuss this inside."

Her great-uncle glanced from him to Monique. "But the princess appears unharmed."

"Only by sheer luck and her assailant's bad aim." His lordship grabbed her sleeve again to display the holes. "Someone shot at her."

The blood drained from her great-uncle's face. "Surely not!"

Lord Fulkham took her arm to compel her forward. "We should go inside now, sir. I won't chance her being in the villain's sights again."

With a shaky nod, the count led the way.

Lord Fulkham didn't release her until they were in the drawing room. As she removed her hat with shaky hands and set it on the marble-topped console table, he strode up to her great-uncle. "The princess was fired upon. We cannot let this stand."

The count drew himself up as only an old royal could. "Of course not. *If* she truly was being fired upon. How can we be sure it's not merely the result of your country's lax rules about violence among the lower classes? Perhaps there were people in the park using their guns recklessly—or worse, criminals seeking to intimidate you so they could rob you. Or rob someone else. The shooting might have nothing to do with the princess at all. Your countrymen may merely be behaving wildly. Guy Fawkes Day is in two days, is it not?"

His words gave her pause until she reminded herself that she'd seen none of the "lower classes" in the park. Perhaps Count de Beaumonde was simply unaware of what sort of person frequented Hyde Park. And what was Guy Fawkes Day?

Although she was ready to give the elderly man the benefit of the doubt, Lord Fulkham clearly was not, for his face flushed with anger. "This is *not* my countrymen being 'wild,' damn you, and the mayhem of Guy Fawkes Day doesn't begin until the fifth. Something else is clearly going on."

The count crossed his arms over his chest. "Like what?"

His lordship shot her great-uncle an incredulous look. "That ought to be obvious to you. *Someone* is intent upon assassinating the princess. And you and I must figure out who—before Her Highness ends up dead."

Eight

Gregory stared the count down, fury scorching him like a wildfire. Because as the oddness of the count's reaction sank in, he began to realize what this was actually about.

The bastard had intended Monique to take the place of the real princess so that if someone attempted to kill Princess Aurore, Monique would die instead. Why else have a masquerade?

But did *Monique* see that? Probably not, or why would she have gone along with it? She couldn't possibly have realized it in the beginning—although she might be starting to recognize the truth now.

And the fact that she was being used as a pawn infuriated him the most. When he thought of those holes in her sleeve, his stomach roiled.

But apparently not the count's, given how his hard gaze skewered Gregory. "Why on earth would someone wish to assassinate my great-niece?"

"I can think of any number of reasons," Gregory snapped, "the main one being that she is the top candidate for ruler of Belgium."

"Still?" she asked, then paled as she clearly realized what she'd inadvertently implied: that his knowledge of her masquerade might have put her out of the running. Swiftly she tried to recoup. "I wasn't sure how my presentation went yesterday, and you were *most* aggressive in your questioning of me today."

Now was his chance. He could unmask her in front of the count, who clearly wasn't going to acknowledge the masquerade or reveal whether he knew that Gregory knew of it. Gregory could just lay everything out in the open—voice his suspicions and put an end to the danger for her.

And risk ruining himself in the process. Because if by some slim chance he was wrong about her identity, the count would have him removed from the conference. The man had powerful friends, especially if Prince Leopold was sniffing around Princess Aurore.

Even if Gregory was right about her, he still couldn't prove it. And the count wasn't going to admit it based on Gregory's three-years-old memories of an actress in a theater, dressed in costume and makeup and the rest.

So confronting him might merely result in the count's denying him further access to the "princess." Gregory dared not chance that, for her own sake as well as his. Especially now that she was in danger.

Better to play it safe. "I questioned you aggressively," he told her, "because that is my job. But everyone knows you are first choice. Which is precisely the problem. Anyone could resent that—the French, the Dutch, even some Englishmen who want Prince Leopold in that position."

The count, damn his hide, was already shaking his head. "You are utterly wrong. This incident has nothing to do with the London Conference or the choice of a ruler for Belgium. Your country merely has no control over its citizens. It was a random attack by criminals. My great-niece should probably not be taken out into a public park again, not because of some attempt on her life, but because your countrymen are mad!"

"It's more than that, and you know it." Gregory glanced over to where Monique stood shivering, clearly still unnerved by what had happened. "Are you willing to risk her life to prove me wrong?"

The count blinked. "Well, no, but I don't think—"

"I have a suggestion for how to protect her that will satisfy your concerns as well as mine."

Beaumonde eyed him warily. "Oh?"

"You mentioned Guy Fawkes Day. You are right about its becoming quite a wild event—lots of people starting bonfires, creating mayhem, and making nuisances of themselves in the name of the holiday. So most events involving the conference will be suspended for the next five days, and many of the English members of the conference are retiring to the country in an effort to avoid the celebrations. You and the princess should do so as well."

"Leave London?" the count said, clearly outraged. "That hardly seems wise when events of the conference are still going on."

"Nothing but social events. And it hardly seems wise to *me* to risk your great-niece's life so she can dance at some ball where anyone could fire upon her!" When the Frenchman blanched, Gregory fought to govern his temper. "My estate, Canterbury Court, is in nearby Kent. You and your retinue are welcome to visit while the conference is in recess. I can think of no better way to protect Her Highness than to remove her from the reach of the 'lower classes' you denigrate."

Beaumonde drew himself up stiffly. "I can take care of my great-niece."

"Of course you can," Gregory said. "But under these circumstances—"

"Under these circumstances," the count said, "it is better that Aurore stay here than in some isolated part of the countryside."

Patience, man. Do not let him rattle you. "At my estate, I can control who comes in or out," Gregory said evenly. "She won't be surrounded by hundreds of people—any one of whom could pick her off with a rifle and escape undetected in the crowds. It will be much easier to make sure she remains safe."

"His lordship is right." Monique surprised him by chiming in. "What if this villain truly was trying to shoot me?"

"He wasn't," the count said firmly. "I can't believe it."

"You can't take the chance," Gregory countered. "Because if she *was* the target—"

"I tell you, there was no target!" The count began to pace the drawing room. "This is a . . . what do you English call it? . . . 'tempest in a teapot.'"

"Hardly that," Gregory said, frustrated by the man's refusal to see the truth. He turned to Monique. "What do you think?"

She looked nervously from him to Beaumonde. "I—I'm not sure."

Damn it, the man clearly had some hold over her that made her reluctant to gainsay him. But the thought that she could lose her life because of the count's stubborn refusal to admit the truth—or because he had some plot afoot that might actually *involve* her being assassinated—chilled Gregory's blood.

He ignored the count to say to her, "Your Serene Highness, I should like to speak to you alone, if I may."

When she looked startled, the count narrowed his gaze on Gregory. "Why?"

"Before she makes a decision that could lead to her death," Gregory said bluntly, "I should like to be sure she knows what she's getting into."

Beaumonde scowled. "I hardly see why that is

necessary. She trusts me to make such decisions for her."

"Perhaps she shouldn't," Gregory said without measuring his words.

The count drew himself up in clear outrage, but before he could retort, she laid a hand on his arm. "Of course I trust you, Uncle." She cast him a look of wide-eyed worry that would bend any man to her will, even the rigid count. "But you were not there when it happened. It was terrifying. So I should like to discuss the matter with his lordship alone to determine for myself if *he* is overreacting."

The count fixed her with a quelling look. "Why not do it in my presence?"

She matched his gaze with a determined one of her own. "Are you forbidding it?"

That brought the man up short. He had to realize that "forbidding it" would put her even further on her guard. "Of course not, but—"

"I *am* still the ruler of Chanay, am I not?" she said in the unforgiving tones of royalty.

The count's eyes glittered, but he offered her a jerky nod.

She cast him a thin smile. "So I have the right to make these decisions for myself, to speak to whomever I must in order to ascertain what should be done. A few moments alone with his lordship is all I require. You may wait outside while we discuss it."

If the situation hadn't been so dire, Gregory

might have laughed at how Beaumonde bridled at that, clearly disturbed that his creation was turning into the very thing she was pretending to be.

Apparently noticing how intently Gregory was watching the exchange, the count smoothed his features into calm. "If that is what you wish, Your Highness."

"It is."

Bowing his head to her, Beaumonde left the room.

Thank God. Perhaps Gregory could finally talk some sense into her.

~~~

Now that Monique had Gregory to herself, she wasn't sure what to say. He was watching her expectantly. But how to talk to him without admitting to the masquerade? Because if there was still a chance that she could pull this off, she must ignore his attempts to elicit a confession.

Even at the risk to her own life?

She shuddered. For all she knew, Gregory had engineered this afternoon's shooting just to frighten her into telling the truth. She had best tread very carefully—with the count *and* with him.

Pasting on a tight smile, she faced him. "Are you absolutely sure that someone wants to kill me?"

Frustration knit his brow. "Aren't *you*? Do you really think anyone wants to do away with me or Flora? We have no holes in *our* sleeves, after all."

"But how could anyone have known we would be at the park?" she pointed out.

"Oh, for God's sake, servants talk—sometimes idly, sometimes with malice, and sometimes for pay. I daresay it would have been easy enough to learn your schedule."

She raised an eyebrow. "All our staff here was hired by *your* government. Are you saying that your foreign office hired servants who couldn't be trusted?"

"I'm saying that *no one* can be trusted when it comes to politics."

"Even you?" she asked.

Her candor seemed to take him aback. Then a dark cloud shadowed his brow. "You don't think *I* had anything to do with this."

"Why not?" she persisted, ignoring his scowl. "You were the one who convinced me to go for a drive, the one who then turned your curricle off into a more secluded path."

The deadly calm that came over his features was far more frightening than any anger. "And why exactly would I plot to have you killed?"

When he put it so bluntly, it seemed . . . rather unlikely. And accusing the undersecretary of the foreign office of attempted murder was probably not the wisest tactic. But, to paraphrase the English saying, in for a sou, in for a franc. "Because you wanted me to be frightened enough by the shooting to admit to this . . . masquerade you keep accusing me of."

His jaw flexing, he bore down on her. "So you think I hired people to fire on you in a public place where anyone might get in the way. You think I risked the chance that my lackey might miss and instead hit me or the servant my office hired, and all to *scare* you into admitting what I know to be true? I daresay that if I did such a fool thing, it would make me the most reckless man in politics, and undeserving of my very career."

She swallowed. He had a point.

"Look," he went on, "I realize I rubbed you the wrong way the first time we met in Dieppe—"

"We did not mee—"

"But no matter what you think of me," he continued, heedless of her protest, "I do have a conscience. I'm not the sort of man to risk a woman's life—any woman's life—for a political reason. I would certainly never risk yours."

The fierce tone of those last words took her by surprise. "Then who would?" she asked, her heart in her throat.

"I don't know. And until I figure out who might have reason to assassinate—"

"Stop using that word!" The very thought of this being about assassination stripped the breath from her throat. "As my uncle said, no one is trying to assassinate me."

"And you believe him?" Cynicism edged his voice. "Hasn't it occurred to you that there's a *reason* you were asked to masquerade for Princess Aurore? Perhaps your precious count didn't want to risk *her* being the one killed. Perhaps he knew she was in danger."

The words sank into her flesh like shark's teeth. He was wrong—the masquerade had come about because Aurore had been sick with—

Wait. What if Aurore hadn't been sick, but *poisoned*? It could look the same, could it not? What if the villain had assumed that he'd botched the murder when Monique showed up in Aurore's place, so he'd come here to finish the job, thinking she was Aurore?

If so, Lord Fulkham *could* be right about her great-uncle. The count had realized he must protect the real princess, and had put Monique in her place to draw the killer away.

Lord help her.

"What?" Lord Fulkham pressed her. "Tell me."

The urgency in his voice snapped her out of her musings and reminded her that for all his apparent concern, Lord Fulkham was not her friend. Perhaps he hadn't orchestrated the attack, but he could still be trying to use it to trick her into confessing all now that he'd learned whatever his spies in Dieppe had told him. Because clearly he'd found out something from them.

Apparently not enough to feel comfortable confronting her great-uncle with his suspicions, though. Which meant she still had a chance at brazening this out.

She stripped off her gloves with all the nonchalance she could muster. "If I were an impostor, your claims might make sense, but since I was *not* asked to masquerade for anyone, your supposition that someone is trying to assassinate me is absurd."

"It's not absurd, damn it!" Without warning, he caught her by the arms as if he wanted to shake her. "You were nearly killed, for God's sake!"

The genuine distress in his voice shook her. "But I wasn't."

He merely clenched his hand in her sleeve, the very one whose holes had so disturbed him earlier. "You were lucky, that's all. You might not be so lucky next time." His jaw tautened. "At least consider the *possibility* that you were the target, and let me try to get to the bottom of what happened today. Come to Canterbury Court while I arrange for my people to do some digging into who might want the princess—*you*—dead."

Her breath was coming as quickly as his now. "I don't understand why you care so much. You think I'm some impostor—"

"All the more reason to care what happens to you. No one should have to die for another without first agreeing to the sacrifice. And you have not. I daresay you had no idea what this was really about when you began it."

The truth of that remark hit home, sticking in her brain like a bit of childhood doggerel. "I—I don't know what you mean."

"Yes, you do. In your heart you know those

bullets were meant for *you* . . . or rather, for Princess Aurore."

She scowled at him. "I *am* Princess Aurore."

"Fine." Gripping her shoulders, he growled, "Maintain your role. Play the princess if you must. But at least let me keep you safe while you're doing it. Come with me to Canterbury Court, where I can look after you."

The fervency of his words stirred an unruly need deep in her belly. And the way he was staring at her . . .

She couldn't look away, but she was equally afraid to fall into those deep blue eyes. "I—I don't know if my uncle will allow it."

"If you're the princess," he said hoarsely, "then you damned well have the right to *demand* that he allow it, don't you?"

She gave a shuddering breath.

"Monique—"

That sparked her temper. "*Aurore*," she said firmly. "I told you never to call me Monique again."

Something unholy and dangerous flickered in his eyes. Then he said in a guttural rasp that made the words sound more like a prayer than an appellation, "Your Serene Highness." He moved his hands to clasp her head. "*Please*, I beg you, let me protect you. I cannot bear the idea of your being hurt if I can prevent it."

She caught her breath. It was a supplication, not an order. And the raw emotion in his features sent a shiver of anticipation along her nerves. Because she could tell he meant every word.

As if realizing he'd exposed too much of his true feelings, he stiffened and added, in a dryer tone, "After all, it would be disastrous to my career to have a princess die on my watch."

But she was having none of that nonsense. He'd gone too far, and she knew this wasn't about his career. She could see it in the stark fear for her that glimmered in his eyes.

He started to draw his hands from her head, but she caught them, covering them with her own. Then she stretched up to brush a kiss to his cheek. "All the same," she said softly, "thank you for caring. And for quite possibly saving my life."

A harsh breath hissed out of him before he drew her head back to him so he could lower his mouth to hers. As his lips hovered a scant inch away, he murmured, "You're welcome . . . Princess." Then he kissed her.

And the world exploded into a million colors. Unlike their last kiss, this one was fierce and all-encompassing. His mouth took hers over, possessing and commanding it until her legs began to wobble and her heart to race so much that she had to grip his neck to keep from collapsing.

God, the man could kiss. His tongue drove hard and deep as his fingers buried themselves in her hair, threatening to dislodge her hairpins.

That should have alarmed her, made her see sense. Instead it drove her to tangle her tongue with his, to see if she could arouse him the way he was arousing her. Apparently she could, for he moaned low in his throat and dropped his hands to her waist to pull her against the thickness in his trousers.

She might be chaste, but she knew what *that* signified. She'd spoken of it in the sly words of a play, heard actresses jokingly comment on its power in their lovers, even felt its presence in the few men who'd dared to grab her and try to bend her to their will.

But never had the feel of it sent an unchecked thrill through her. Never had it sparked a heat that threatened to set fire to her blood. Never had it made her want to lift her skirts just to get closer to the promise of it.

That was dangerous. Which was why, no matter how much pleasure it gave her, she must put a stop to things before they went too far.

Nine

Gregory growled a protest when Monique pressed her hands against his chest to put some distance between them, though he knew that what they were doing was wholly unwise, especially with her great-uncle on the other side of the door.

"Lord Fulkham—" she began.

"Gregory." Holding her gaze, he lifted her hand and peeled back her sleeve to expose the love bite he'd left on her wrist. "Call me Gregory, at least when we're alone." Then he licked the place he'd marked her, watching her cheeks flush and her eyes turn sultry.

"*Gregory*," she breathed.

It was one more intimacy between them. He tried to tell himself these were necessary steps to get her to lower her guard and admit the truth, but that was just a lie meant to preserve his sanity. Because deep down, he knew this was no strategy or scheme.

He wanted her to be his, simple as that. And the sound of her melodic voice crooning his Christian name was turning him as hard as the marble-topped table behind them.

Seizing her mouth once more, he plundered it with ruthless intent. She wanted him. He would make her want him enough to be honest with him, no matter the cost.

As she returned his kisses with ungoverned passion, he backed her toward the table, then swept her hat off it so he could lift her onto the marble. She didn't make so much as a mew of protest, which emboldened him to do what he'd been wanting to do all afternoon—unfasten the hooks down the front of her bodice so he could slip his hand inside to fondle one breast.

She tore her lips from his to stare at him wide-eyed. "Gregory, you shouldn't," she chided in the dulcet tones that had captivated him from the moment he'd met her.

But she didn't push his hand away, and when he pulled her corset cup down enough to thumb her nipple through her shift, she gave a throaty gasp that sent his blood into a frenzy.

"Why shouldn't I?" he ground out. "You like it."

An uncertain smile crossed her lips. "Perhaps a little." When he kneaded her breast and a moan of pure pleasure escaped her, she rasped, "All right, perhaps more than a little."

He bent his head to kiss her again, but she turned her head. "My uncle—"

"I don't give a damn about your uncle," he said as he turned to kiss her heated cheek, her elegant neck, her perfect ears, "since he clearly doesn't give a damn about *you*." His fury that the man might be using her as a pawn made his words come out harsher than he'd intended.

She threaded her fingers through his hair as if to pull him away, yet she didn't stop him from exploring the delicious fullness of her breast with his fingers and palm. "But *you* care, I suppose."

The hint of sarcasm in her tone inflamed him. "Enough to want to make sure nobody harms you." His voice roughened in spite of himself. He tongued her bared throat. "Do you have any idea what it did to me to realize some arse was firing upon you? Yet your 'uncle' won't even acknowledge that it happened."

"He's not as bad as all that."

"Really? Because it looks as if he only cares about whether you become queen, and naught else."

She swallowed convulsively, and he felt the motion against his lips.

It only made him angrier at the count. "I hate men who use women, who hurt them. Men like your uncle." And his bastard of a father. "You deserve better."

A desperate laugh escaped her as she met his gaze once more. "How do you know what I deserve?"

He paused in his fondling to regard her with a serious look. "I'm not blind. Yesterday I watched you cleverly and articulately convince a roomful of men that you could rule Belgium. Today I watched you bravely keep your head as Flora screamed on the back of the carriage."

"But on the inside I was terrified," she admitted.

"Good. You have enough sense to recognize the danger. Or I hope you do, anyway. After I saw those holes in your sleeve . . ." The memory of it made his throat tighten. "Do you realize how close you came to death?"

"But you were there to protect me." Her features soft, she reached up to stroke his cheek with a tenderness that uncurled something wild and reckless within him.

"I didn't do a very good job of it," he said hoarsely, "considering how close the first shot came."

"Yet here I am. Safe. With you."

"Yes. And I mean to keep you safe with me until this is over." This time when he took her mouth, she let him, rising to the kiss like a swan taking flight. And when he resumed fondling her breast, she pressed it against his hand.

So, once more he slid down into the insanity that was Monique.

Monique knew she was courting danger, but his words about her bravery and cleverness had seduced her. Perhaps that was what he'd intended, but she didn't want to believe it. Because what he was doing made her feel alive, young, free. Every inch of her responded to the excitement of it.

He kissed a path down her neck. "I want to taste you." He rubbed her nipple again. "Here. Now."

"Oh yes," she breathed. "*Please*."

Desire had her in its grip, and she wanted to explore it. Especially with the only man who'd ever heated her blood.

Now his mouth was inside her gown, closing over her nipple, licking it through her flimsy chemise, then sucking it hard and making her gasp from sheer pleasure.

No man had ever gone so far with her. Now she had to wonder why she'd resisted such intimacies for so long. What he was doing to her was *magnificent*.

"Even here you smell like lilies," he murmured against her breast. "Do you sleep in a garden?"

She laughed lightly. "I bathe every day with scented soap. I'm told that's rather . . . fastidious for someone from—" She halted just before she said "France." "From Chanay."

He glanced up at her with a smirk that said he'd caught her near slip, but he didn't comment on it. Instead he returned to courting her body with his mouth and teeth and tongue. As she grabbed his head to hold him close, he paused long enough to rasp, "Shall I mark you here, too? I could, you know."

"Don't you dare!" she choked out, though the idea of his leaving a love bite where no one could ever see but her shot a perverse thrill through her. "You are . . . very wicked for a politician . . . my lord."

"You bring it out in me." Eyes alight, he started dragging up her skirts. "I don't generally try to seduce princesses within hearing of their uncles."

A sudden knock at the door made both of them freeze.

"Speaking of uncles—" Gregory ground out.

"Oh, God," she hissed as she slid off the table, "do you think he heard what we were saying?"

Gregory looked amused. "Not through *that* door." He chucked her under the chin with a sigh. "But all the same, we'd best stop this before he storms in."

As she swiftly set her gown to rights, Gregory strode for the door. He glanced back at her and waited while she smoothed her hair into place and tucked a final few tendrils in.

But even after she nodded to show she was ready, he didn't open the door. "We *are* agreed about your coming to Canterbury Court, aren't we?" he asked softly.

She stiffened, but nodded again. What choice did she have?

Relief flooded his features. "Good." Then he swung the door open.

Her great-uncle marched in. He had Lady Ursula with him, who looked decidedly pale.

Monique had to wonder if her new friend really *had* been ill earlier, as the count had claimed, or, more likely, had been told the situation. Either way, Lady Ursula appeared as if she might faint.

Meanwhile, the count's gaze scoured the room, then zeroed in on the table. "Why is your hat on the floor, niece?"

Curse it all. She'd forgotten about her hat.

As she fumbled for a plausible answer, Gregory said blandly, "I knocked it off. I'm afraid I became a bit . . . impassioned in arguing my case."

Dear God, the man liked to live dangerously. How could he even *think* to use that word with her great-uncle?

But the count didn't seem to care. He circled the room slowly, as if looking for evidence of perfidy. Apparently finding none, he came toward her. "I hope you have convinced him that we cannot go to the country."

"Perhaps we should consider—" Lady Ursula began.

"Quiet, girl!" the count said. "I will handle this."

Monique bristled, both at his treatment of the lady-in-waiting and his apparent assumption that she would simply fall in with his plans.

She would not. She must hold her ground, though she would undoubtedly have the devil to pay for it later. Gregory was right—her safety could not be ensured in London with so many people around. And she did not wish to die for Aurore.

Not to mention that Gregory had planted

seeds of doubt in her mind regarding her great-uncle, which were sprouting with the count's continued resistance to Gregory's plan.

"Actually," Monique said stoutly, "I agree with his lordship. The country might be safer. And there really is no reason I must stay here for the next few days, is there?"

"Of course there is," he said coldly. "The Duc de Pontalba is remaining in town, and he is one of the delegates you should sway to your side before the vote takes place, after everyone returns." He cast Gregory a sly glance. "Unless his lordship is prepared to invite *him* to the country as well."

"That would give the princess an unfair advantage that none of the other possible candidates have," Gregory said. "They might protest."

"*You* are a delegate, too," the count pointed out. "So if she went, she would have an unfair advantage with *you*. How is that any different?"

"I am not merely a delegate to the convention. I am in charge of her safety. Which is precisely why I shouldn't like to have the duke there. We don't know for certain if he had anything to do with the shooting."

The count scoffed. "A *duc*? He would not risk such a scandal. The very idea is ludicrous."

From her time in the theater, Monique wasn't so sure. Dukes always thought they had the right to do anything in their power, scandal be damned.

Still, she'd spoken long enough with Pontalba

to think he wasn't the sort to engineer an assassination. He wasn't so much a schemer as a man sure of his own position. And he'd seemed less interested in the results of the convention than in getting under her skirts.

That, too, was fairly typical behavior for a duke, in her experience.

A sudden commotion sounded in the hall, of boots tramping and loud voices. One rang out above the rest. "I must speak with Lord Fulkham. *Now.*"

Apparently that was enough to send a servant in to announce the man. "My lord, there's a captain of the guard here to see you."

"Good," Gregory said. "Send him in."

It was the same captain who'd helped them at the park. As he entered, he nodded courteously to her. "Your Serene Highness. I hope you are well."

Monique flashed him a smile. "I am, thank you."

"She'll be better," Gregory said, "if you can assure her that the villain is in your custody."

The captain's face clouded. "I'm afraid not, my lord. We scoured the woods, but were too late to apprehend the villain. There were enough people on horseback in the park to make it difficult to determine who might have been involved."

"Damn," Gregory muttered, threading one hand through his hair.

"We did find a witness who said he thought he saw a young man wearing a green frock coat and brown riding breeches, with a brown Tilbury hat, on horseback, shooting from behind a silver birch. But after two shots, the man galloped toward the Stanhope Gate and got through it before the witness even registered what was happening."

"Did you dispatch men into Mayfair?" Gregory asked.

"Yes, and St. George's Fields, too, but no one matching the man's description was discovered. My soldiers are still searching."

Gregory shook his head. "He'll be long gone by now. Have your men see what they can learn in the stews and elsewhere. This was probably a hired assassin. We must find out where he was hired, and that may lead us to who he is, and thus who hired him."

"Yes, sir," the man said deferentially, clearly used to taking such orders from Gregory.

"You should also increase the patrols around the park and especially around the residences of those involved in the conference, in case the princess isn't the only person being targeted."

"Very good, my lord." The captain bowed and took his leave.

As soon as he'd gone, Gregory rounded on the count. "You see, sir? We have a witness who claims the gunshots were a deliberate act and not random recklessness. *Now* will you listen to reason and remove the princess and her retinue from London?"

"Will you invite the duke to your estate as well?" her great-uncle countered.

When Gregory bristled, Lady Ursula said, "You

could also invite Prince Leopold. That would make it more fair. Then there would be two delegates— you and the duke—and two candidates for ruler— Her Highness and the prince. No one could complain about that. After all, it's not as if the entire convention could go."

Monique gaped at Lady Ursula. What on earth had possessed the woman to suggest that another candidate be included? And why Prince Leopold, of all people? Why not one of the other candidates presently in London? Everyone knew that Prince Leopold was out in the countryside and only intended to return next week, when the convention reconvened to announce the decision on who was to rule Belgium.

"See here," the count said to Lady Ursula, "I know that the prince is your distant cousin, my dear, and that he and your family were friendly even before you were born, but that is no reason to suggest including him."

The prince's connection to Lady Ursula came as news to Monique. She couldn't help noticing that Gregory wore the same inscrutable expression as when he was trying to hide his opinions, though she could guess what they were.

So she stepped in. "I don't think it's terribly polite of us, Uncle, to be suggesting extra guests to his lordship, when he's been good enough to invite us to his home in the first place. Why, we have no idea how large his estate is, or if he could manage a party of such size."

"Canterbury Court is more than sufficient for such a party," Gregory said, with a hint of amusement that surprised her. "Indeed, my mother will be overjoyed at the idea of having so many important guests at the estate. She almost never gets the chance to entertain."

"So you do not mind including Prince Leopold?" Lady Ursula asked.

"Not at all. Including him would satisfy any of my objections about including Pontalba."

That gave Monique pause. She could see from the glint of calculation in his eyes that he knew something about Prince Leopold that he wasn't letting on.

Apparently so did the count, for he scowled. "How do we know that the *prince* wasn't part of the assassination attempt?"

Gregory leapt upon that statement with great glee. "So now you're acknowledging it was an attempt to murder the princess?"

Her great-uncle rubbed his chin nervously. "I'm merely saying that he's even more likely a suspect than the duke, since he's in the running for the position."

"But very low on the list. We English prefer him, but none of the French or Dutch or Austrians do." Gregory cast her a considering look. "And given that rumor says he's interested in marrying the princess, I doubt he would risk her life."

Marrying Aurore? Monique's stomach knotted painfully. If that was true, the prince must know Aurore personally. Judging from the gloating glance Gregory shot her, he'd realized that, too. So he was including Prince Leopold in this party solely in hopes that the man would expose Monique as an impostor.

Oh, Lord. Lady Ursula had led them right into a trap.

Monique frowned. That made no sense. Why would Lady Ursula have made the suggestion if she'd known that Prince Leopold could expose their scheme?

"Actually," the count said, "Prince Leopold made an offer of marriage to Aurore through an emissary some months ago and was rejected. So he may not have taken kindly to that. Perhaps he sent someone to shoot at my great-niece so she would be frightened into accepting his offer."

Gregory laughed outright. "Who's being ludicrous *now*? The prince can have his pick of royals in Europe." He shot Monique a furtive, knowing look. "Of course, if he fell in love with her when he met her—"

"They've never met," Lady Ursula said swiftly.

"Ah," Gregory said, disappointment fleetingly crossing his face.

Relief swamped Monique. Hah! His plan to have the prince unmask her wouldn't work after all, thank God.

Though it was still curious that Lady Ursula wished to include the man. Bringing Monique into contact with Aurore's spurned suitor didn't seem wise.

"Well then, I see no issue with having the prince come." Gregory dusted off his hands. "So that's settled, as far as I'm concerned. Princess?"

Monique felt trapped between the count's disapproval and Gregory's insistence. But the captain's words confirming the deliberate nature of the shooting had frozen her blood. She had to get away, if only to have a place where she could breathe and figure out whom she could trust. "Yes, I would prefer that, too," she told Gregory.

The count assessed her and Gregory with a long look, then shrugged. "Very well. We will decamp to your estate. Tomorrow?"

Gregory nodded. "In the afternoon. I have a few matters to attend to before I can leave London, including sending an invitation to Prince Leopold in Brighton. Then we can set off for Canterbury Court, if that meets with everyone's approval. I'll speak to Pontalba myself tonight."

"Excellent," her great-uncle said.

Meanwhile, Lady Ursula appeared oddly cheery about the excursion to Kent. Monique would try to find out why once she had the lady-in-waiting alone.

Gregory turned to Monique with a veiled smile. "So, Your Serene Highness, you're finally going to get your wish."

"My wish?"

"You said you weren't fond of the city, and it

looks like you'll get to spend time in the country-side. I hope it does not disappoint."

She nodded. Before they left town, she'd have to ask her great-uncle about the real reason for Princess Aurore's illness.

As soon as Gregory took his leave and the count turned to her as if to chide her for forcing him to go to the country, she asked the question that had been burning in her brain.

"Was my cousin poisoned, Uncle?"

The count blinked, and Lady Ursula gasped. Clearly, neither of them had expected that question. "Of course not!" he said. "She has cholera."

He certainly looked as if he believed it. But she wasn't entirely convinced. "So you did not put me in Aurore's place to protect her from another assassination attempt."

"What?" His shock was palpable. "Why would I do such a thing? If I'd thought Aurore was at risk, I would have whisked her back to Chanay and given up on the idea of her being queen." He was red in the face now. "*Mon Dieu*, she's my great-niece! As are you, I might point out. I would not risk either of your lives. What would even make you think—"

"I was *shot* at, Uncle! What am I supposed to think?"

That unsettled him. "I am still not convinced that anyone was trying to hurt you specifically—"

"Yes, I know. Meanwhile, if you're wrong, I could be risking death over this scheme."

Looking concerned, Lady Ursula stepped forward. "My dear, surely you've heard that cholera has been raging through the Continent."

"In Russia, Germany, and Hungary. Not France," Monique said. She had indeed seen the reports in the papers of the death toll mounting.

"Calais is where nearly everyone in Europe goes to cross the English Channel, niece," her great-uncle snapped. "In our hotel alone, there were foreigners of every stamp. She could easily have caught the contagion from one of them."

He had a point.

"And as for someone shooting at you," he said, "your champion Lord Fulkham seems more than eager to prevent that from happening again."

"But you tried to keep him from doing so," she accused.

Conceding her point with a shrug, he said, "I was not happy to hear that you would be kept away from the other delegates. But once he included the duke, I thought better of his suggestion. Besides, Fulkham *is* the man most influential in making the selection. So it would probably do you good to have him more to yourself for a few days."

He drew himself up, making clear that he was done with the discussion. "Speaking of this upcoming house party, you must excuse me. If we are to travel tomorrow, I must see to the arrangements."

Narrowing his gaze on her, he added, "But if you ever again put me in the position you did today, forcing me to agree to your terms in front of someone like Fulkham, I *will* put an end to this scheme, as you call it. And you will be back in Dieppe in a flash, looking after your grandmother alone again. Is that understood?"

She swallowed the hot protests that rose in her throat. "Yes, Uncle."

"Good," he said, and stalked out the door.

Lady Ursula came up to lay a reassuring hand on her arm. "Pay him no mind. The count's bark is worse than his bite. He's fond of you, though he won't admit it."

"Or show it," Monique said bitterly.

The lady-in-waiting laughed. "You didn't hear him after your presentation to Parliament yesterday. 'She was spectacular, Ursula, a true stateswoman! I daresay Aurore could not have done better if she tried. I told you she would be perfect.' He's proud of you, though he's afraid to show it for fear that you will take advantage of his soft spot for you."

Monique snorted. She hadn't noticed any soft spot. But Lady Ursula was clearly a peacemaker in the household.

Which reminded her . . . "Did Prince Leopold truly offer for Aurore?"

Lady Ursula's face clouded over. "He did. And was refused."

"Why?"

The lady-in-waiting moved away to go stand by the fireplace and warm her hands, though it was hardly cold in the drawing room. "Aurore does not wish to marry anyone. And of course she must. So she and the count and her mother argue about it incessantly."

"Why doesn't she wish to marry?"

"Who knows?" Her voice sharpened. "She's young and impetuous and has some notion that a husband will curb her freedom."

"Which he will," Monique pointed out.

With a laugh, Lady Ursula faced her. "Indeed. That's why *I* have never married. That, and the fact that the one I love cannot marry me."

Monique's heart constricted. "Oh, I'm so sorry." She wanted to ask who he was, but she didn't want to make her ally uncomfortable.

"Don't be," Ursula said brightly. "One cannot always have whom one wants. It is simply the way of the world."

"True."

The thought depressed her. Because she was beginning to think that the only man *she* might want was Gregory. And there was no way on earth he would ever marry an actress and impostor, even if she *was* also related to a princess. His life was here, and her life was in Chanay with Grand-maman. Best to remember that before she fell for his sensual charms.

Ten

The following day, Gregory headed for Apsley House to meet with the Duke of Wellington, who was about to lose his position as prime minister. Which meant this discussion could be tricky. Wellington was hard to manage on a good day, but given the current political climate, he was downright cantankerous.

Still, he liked Gregory . . . most of the time. And it would be political suicide for Gregory not to inform the man of his plans to whisk so many important people out of town.

As he drove by the Hyde Park entrance, yesterday's events flooded his mind, and a chill settled in his bones. Monique could have been killed. The image of her lying in a pool of blood had haunted him ever since the shooting, making him anxious to leave town. Something was definitely amiss, and he meant to figure out the whole matter, but first, he must keep her safe.

The way he'd kept Mother safe all those years ago.

He scowled. And he'd do it again, if he had to, not just for Mother but for Monique. They were both in his charge now, whether the impudent Mademoiselle Servais liked it or not.

Though he did wish he knew why Princess Aurore—presumably the real one—had refused Prince Leopold's offer of marriage. Perhaps she really was as shy and reclusive as all that. Perhaps the idea of him as her husband had terrified her. Otherwise, it made no sense. It seemed an excellent match to him.

Could *that* be behind the masquerade? Had Beaumonde brought Monique into it in hopes of renewing the arrangement? Gregory didn't see how that could work. Surely the two women weren't *that* much alike.

Unless the real princess was dead.

A chill ran through him. There was always that possibility. If someone had succeeded in assassinating Princess Aurore, and the count hadn't been willing to give up on having the royal family of Chanay in power in Belgium . . .

Surely he wouldn't be so insane. And would Monique agree to a lifetime of playing someone else? It seemed unlikely.

And what was the business with Lady Ursula

being a relation of the prince? How did that fit in? These were questions he hoped to answer once he had all the parties trapped at his estate in the country.

But first he must deal with Wellington. As Gregory was shown into the man's study, the prime minister rose to greet him with a handshake. "I heard there was some trouble across the way yesterday," Wellington said without preamble. "You have it under control?"

"I do. Indeed, that's why I'm here."

"I figured as much." Gesturing to the chair in front of his desk, Wellington took his own seat behind it. "The captain of the guard says the Princess of Chanay was fired upon while you were taking her for a drive?"

"Yes, sir." Gregory briefly went over the previous day's fiasco and explained the measures he'd taken. Now came the difficult part. "I have proposed to the princess and her great-uncle that they and their retinue decamp to my country estate while the conference is in recess for the holiday."

Wellington steepled his fingers. "Is that really necessary?"

"If we want to make sure no more attempts are made on her life, yes." When the duke frowned, Gregory added, "I've invited Pontalba to join us, as well as Prince Leopold, to make it more of a house party. That should also squelch any accusations that I'm trying to keep the Chanay contingent away from the delegates."

"Ah. Turn it into a social event—very wise. But then, you are nothing if not wise."

Gregory chalked up the trace of bitterness in Wellington's tone to resentment that Gregory would be continuing on with the government when *he* would not. "I do my best," he said blandly.

"And I know your mother can easily manage such a party. A very clever woman, Lady Fulkham."

"Indeed she is," Gregory said, with more emotion.

His mother was the cleverest woman he knew . . . except perhaps for Monique. Still, Mother was going to have his head for giving her so little notice. He'd sent the message off last night. He could only imagine the chaos going on at Canterbury Court right now as servants scurried to ready all the guest chambers.

Fortunately, there were plenty of them—and he'd instructed his mother to spare no expense in hiring more servants to help. Although this would still be a major feat, Mother understood the trials of playing hostess to politicians. Her father had been chancellor of the exchequer before the family had fallen on hard times. Which was how she'd ended up married to Gregory's arse of a father.

"You don't mind, do you?" Wellington said.

"Hmm?" Gregory said.

He'd missed the prime minister's last remark, damn it. He was going to have to do something about his bloody woolgathering of late. It wasn't like him.

"Danworth," Wellington said, eyeing him oddly. "Including him won't be a problem, will it?"

"Not at all." Great. Another person to add to the growing party. "Though I'm not sure why it's necessary."

"Not necessary perhaps, but a good idea under the circumstances. Since I can't go myself, I need someone there to represent me. And who better than my secretary?"

Wellington liked to keep his hand in things, even when he was on the verge of being booted out of office.

"Of course. We will be glad to include him."

"Good, good. I shall let him know."

With that, Gregory took his leave, musing upon how the addition of Danworth might change the dynamics of the group.

Danworth could be trusted to protect the princess in a pinch. And he had a reputation for being an excellent shot, which Gregory doubted was the case for either the duke or the prince.

Besides, ladies loved the witty and engaging Danworth. He could be counted on to keep Mother and Lady Ursula entertained.

And Monique?

Gregory stiffened. He'd rather take on *that* task himself.

God, what was wrong with him? Yes, she felt like heaven in his arms. Yes, she amused him. But that didn't mean he should be thinking about her incessantly, worrying about her incessantly . . . wanting her incessantly.

His blood roared in his ears. All right, so he wanted to bed her. Who wouldn't? But he must not let that cloud his judgment.

Especially not until he determined precisely what the count was up to with this masquerade.

~ᕫ᠊ᕬ

Monique wasn't sure what she'd expected of Canterbury Court, but it certainly wasn't *this*. Though she'd realized Gregory was a man of great political importance, she hadn't expected him to also be a man of substantial riches.

They drove through impressive gardens, which he explained covered twenty acres, before reaching the Palladian-style house. It looked stylish and refined—like the gentleman himself—and obviously spacious enough to hold the entire party with ease.

Indeed, when the count asked how many rooms it contained, Gregory said, "Thirty or so. Depends on whether you include dressing rooms, pantries, things of that nature."

The way he tossed that off as if it were nothing astonished her. Then again, perhaps it *was* nothing to the count and Lady Ursula. Though they did look quite impressed as Gregory's comfortable traveling carriage drew up in front and a large retinue of servants stood on the steps to welcome them.

Perversely, the show of wealth and consequence put Monique even more on edge with him. She might be connected to a royal family, but she was just the poor relation, the one they would never even have approached if not for her startling resemblance to their precious princess. So if this masquerade *did* end successfully, and if, by some chance, Gregory pursued a relationship with her despite her subterfuge, it could never be a legitimate one.

He might consider making her his mistress, but no more. A man with his ambitions couldn't marry a French actress, considered by most in English society to be beneath contempt. Best to keep that in mind at every turn, before she let his kisses and caresses turn her head and make her consider the impossible.

But how she wished Grand-maman had prepared her for what to do when the smile he shot her as he personally helped her from the carriage gave her such foolish, raging urges. How was she to handle the heat that built in her belly as he placed her hand firmly in the crook of his arm, and oh so swiftly touched the wrist with his love bite?

It was fading now—she didn't even need to hide it anymore—but she was still aware of the place of it, like an invisible itch that needed soothing.

"Does this meet with your approval, Your Serene Highness?" he murmured without a hint of sarcasm, probably because her great-uncle was close on their heels.

"You know perfectly well that it's lovely. Your gardens alone were worth the trip."

His heated gaze dropped to her lips. "Then I shall be sure to give you a tour of them later."

Oh, she knew what *that* meant, and the very thought of being alone with him sent her heart into a ridiculous frenzy.

"Yes," Lady Ursula interrupted brightly, "I'm sure we would all enjoy a tour of the gardens."

Monique sighed with resignation . . . and maybe some relief.

Her great-uncle said, "Not I. I am quite tired after our journey. But you young people should go, by all means."

"Gregory!" A woman whom Monique had at first taken for a housekeeper because of her apron came running down the steps.

When Gregory released Monique's arm to kiss the woman's cheek, Monique realized belatedly that it must be Lady Fulkham, which he confirmed by saying, "Here we are, Mother, just as I warned. Do with us as you will."

The woman with salt-and-pepper hair and blue eyes a shade lighter than Gregory's drew back to wag a finger at him. "*Not* as you warned. You said you would be much later."

He flashed her an affectionate smile. "Is that why you're still wearing your apron?"

Looking down at the offending garment, she

blanched, then hurried to remove it. "Lord, what you must think of me, greeting royalty dressed like *this*."

"We think you are very gracious to take us all in at such short notice," Monique said swiftly.

Lady Fulkham smiled at her and curtsied. "You must be the princess, though I wouldn't have guessed it from that portrait in the *Lady's Monthly Museum*. You are far prettier. Welcome to Canterbury Court, Your Serene Highness."

"Thank you," Monique said. "We're pleased to be here." How many people had seen that stupid portrait? It wasn't even a good likeness of Aurore, according to Lady Ursula.

Her great-uncle stepped up next to her. "My niece is right—we are quite delighted to be here, Lady Fulkham."

Gregory introduced him and Lady Ursula, then frowned when the count took his mother's hand and lifted it to his lips to kiss.

"May I say," her great-uncle murmured, "that I had no idea his lordship's mother was so beautiful, or we would have been here at dawn."

The woman withdrew her hand with a polite laugh. "And I had no idea that gentlemen from Chanay were so prone to flattery."

"As it happens, I am not from Chanay originally. I'm from France, where we have a deep appreciation for fine ladies."

He winked at her, and Monique nearly fell over. Her great-uncle could *wink*? She'd assumed that that particular muscle was permanently atrophied.

Apparently Lady Fulkham regarded his wink with skepticism as well, for she raised an eyebrow ever so slightly, reminding Monique of Gregory when he was being sarcastic. But the lady merely said noncommittally, "I hope that you will enjoy your stay."

Lady Ursula stepped forward. "I know we will. And I must share my companions' thanks for your kind hospitality. I'm sure we are causing you some difficulty, descending on you with little warning."

"Not at all. I love guests, I assure you." With a twinkle in her eyes, the lady added, "Besides, how else was I to coax my terribly busy son home for a visit? He can bring the entire royal family with him, as long as it means I get to see him."

"Good God, Mother," he bit out, his cheeks flushing.

A delighted laugh spilled out of Monique. She'd never seen Gregory nonplused, and she couldn't resist teasing him. "Why, Lord Fulkham, do not tell me you are a bad son. I would never have guessed."

"Oh, he's a wonderful son," Lady Fulkham said quickly. "But you know mothers. Our children can never come home often enough."

"I'm afraid I wouldn't know," Monique said. "I don't have children."

"Yet," the count said. When everyone stared at him, he added, "You don't have children *yet*."

That remark surprised her . . . until she

remembered that he was speaking of her as the princess, not as herself.

Perhaps that was why Gregory's frown deepened into a surly scowl. "Yes, well, now that we've dispensed with the introductions, I suggest we go inside. I confess myself eager for a glass of wine and a chance to warm my hands by the fire. It's damned cold today."

"Gregory!" his mother said with a furtive glance at Monique. "Such language in front of the princess!"

"Don't worry, Lady Fulkham," Monique said dryly. "I've heard far worse from my great-uncle when he thought I wasn't listening."

The woman regarded the count thoughtfully. "You don't say." Then she glanced past them down the drive. "Where are the others? I did hear from Prince Leopold, accepting your invitation and saying he would be able to come tomorrow, but aren't there supposed to be more guests?"

"They'll be here in time for dinner," Gregory said. "The duke travels with a larger retinue than the princess, I'm afraid, and Danworth is stopping to visit a friend before continuing on here."

His mother's face brightened. "Mr. Danworth is coming? You neglected to mention that."

Gregory had told Monique and the count that the prime minister's private secretary was coming, but she hadn't understood why. It clearly had something to do with politics.

"How fun!" his mother went on. "Danworth

is much better at remembering the popular bon mots than you are."

"Forgive me, Mother, but I have a few more important things to keep track of than the latest witticisms," he said irritably.

Lady Fulkham patted her son's hand as if he were a little boy. "Of *course* you do. And all of us in England are very grateful for your sacrifice."

Monique practically bit off her lip, trying to keep from smiling. She could never have imagined the self-assured, arrogant Gregory being alternately chided and soothed by his mother. It made him seem more . . . human, somehow.

He shot Lady Fulkham an exasperated look, which softened into a contrite smile. "Sorry about that, Mother. I don't mean to be so cranky."

Lady Fulkham beamed at him. After that she was all business, showing them inside, offering them refreshments, and directing servants. A very efficient woman, Gregory's mother. One would think she'd been expecting them for weeks; she had everything under control.

At least now Monique knew where Gregory got his powers of restraint. She could have used some of those right now to keep from gawking at his lovely home. It was even grander than the London town house.

The central staircase was of Italian marble, for pity's sake! The wallpaper was patterned silk, the curtains were brocade, and she would have sworn that the painting in the foyer was a genuine Van

Dyck. Not that she would have known what it was if the count hadn't remarked upon it—but judging from Lady Ursula's reaction, the artist was important enough to impress the royal family.

Which begged the question—why was Gregory bothering with politics in London if he had expensive paintings lying about his home? Why not simply enjoy the life of a landed gentleman? It made no sense.

By the time she was led into her bedchamber, she wasn't surprised to find it full of the finest Sheridan furniture, with silver fittings, embroidered bed hangings, and an ancient tapestry on one wall, which had probably been woven by some famous person as well. That was clearly why Lady Fulkham had called this the Tapestry Room.

Flora was already unpacking her trunks. "Oh, Your Highness, isn't it wonderful? I know you are used to lovely houses like these, but this is the grandest one I've ever seen! And her ladyship seems *so* very kind that I'm sure . . ." Flora prattled on in her usual way.

Lady Ursula had cautioned Monique that she was supposed to use a harsh word or two to put Flora in her place, as was the way of princesses, but she could never bear to do it. Too many times, she had been the recipient of lowering comments made by fine ladies at the theater who were jealous of the interest their husbands showed her. It had taken years for her to grow a skin thick enough to deflect such remarks.

While Flora might need to grow that sort of skin eventually, Monique wouldn't be the one to toughen her up or destroy her view of the world as a place of wonders. Let the girl enjoy her brush with "greatness."

Flora cast her a sly look. "So *are* you going walking in the garden with his lordship?" She held up a walking dress of cerulean-blue watered silk. "Because this would be perfect. Brings out the green in your eyes. His lordship will be falling all over himself at the sight of you in this."

Monique tensed. Had Flora noticed the charged atmosphere between her and Gregory whenever they were in the same room? If the girl had, then *everyone* might notice. Oh God, she must take more care to hide her feelings.

"Why would I want that?" she asked, a little too sharply.

Flora blinked. "Because he can make you queen of Belgium. That's what you're hoping for, isn't it?"

Stop being a fool, Monique. The girl isn't talking about your mad infatuation with Gregory. "Oh. Of course."

But only because of what *not* becoming queen of Belgium would lose her.

She *must* stop thinking of Gregory as a man she desired, or she might find herself and Grandmaman dumped unceremoniously back in Dieppe, and this whole insane scheme would be for naught.

Eleven

The duke arrived before Gregory got the chance to show Monique and Lady Ursula around the gardens, which annoyed him even more than Mother's treating him like an ungrateful son.

His mother *knew* why being at Canterbury Court was difficult for him. Yet she couldn't accept it. Sometimes it frustrated him.

And now something else was frustrating him—the way Pontalba and Monique were flirting. He wanted her to himself, damn it. But only so he could delve more into why she was masquerading.

Not because he wanted to taste her mouth again or hear her laugh or see the wonder rise in her eyes when she viewed his gardens. No, indeed. Nothing so base as jealousy fueled his irritation.

God, he was such a liar.

It irritated him that Pontalba had offered

Monique his arm for the stroll, leaving Lady Ursula to Gregory. He had to wonder if it was by design.

Had Monique planned it that way? If so, was she just currying the duke's favor in hopes he would throw his vote toward her as queen? Or was there more to it? Was she hoping to hedge her bets in case she ended up a poor actress back in Dieppe? A woman could make much of being the mistress of a man like Pontalba.

The very idea made Gregory's gut twist. That would happen over his dead body. If she was seeking a protector, *he* would be first in line.

So he had to grit his teeth when she batted her lush lashes at Pontalba. "Do you have gardens as beautiful as these at *your* estate, Your Grace?"

"With apologies to his lordship, I believe mine at Valcour are even more lovely." The duke placed his hand over hers intimately. "You would much enjoy viewing them, I'm sure."

Gregory had to fight the urge to knock the man's hand from her arm. Instead, he said, in his most bored tone, "It's a pity the princess will never get the chance. Given that she'll probably become queen of Belgium, she'll be much too busy ruling the infant country to visit one of France's many provincial dukes."

It was the first time Gregory had given any indication of his bias toward a candidate for ruler, but he'd done it deliberately to witness the duke's reaction and figure out his true intentions.

Did Pontalba merely mean to court the woman for his country's sake, or was he playing a deeper game involving his own candidate?

Besides, Gregory was proud of his gardens, even though he was rarely here to enjoy them. His mother had worked hard to improve and expand them, and Gregory resented Pontalba's disdain. Especially in front of Monique.

Unfortunately, Pontalba didn't rise to the bait. "*Pardonnez-moi*, my lord, I did not mean to offend. And of course, you do not have the space on your estate for the extensive gardens I have at Valcour. But you do much with what you have."

Gregory fought to keep an even keel. If not for the smug look in Pontalba's eyes, he wouldn't have managed it, but he was *not* going to let the duke know he'd drawn blood. That didn't mean, however, that he would allow the arse to win the pissing match, which was all this was.

"Thank you, sir," Gregory drawled. "Given my busy schedule, I prefer the amount of land I have. I can't be here as often as I wish, since the cabinet and the prime minister depend upon me too heavily. Of course, you don't have those constraints. I heard you were sent to the London Conference because the fellow who was supposed to come had other obligations."

When Pontalba's smugness vanished, Gregory congratulated himself on giving as good as he got.

But before the arse could retort, Lady Ursula surprised Gregory by jumping in. "I would hardly call an estate of two hundred acres 'small,' Your Grace."

Pontalba visibly started. "No," he said grudgingly. "I suppose not."

"Oh," Monique put in, "you were not here when Lady Fulkham told us of its size earlier." Then, with a furtive glance at Gregory, she added, "But I'm sure yours is equally large, Your Grace."

So she meant to placate everyone, did she? Gregory was still stewing over that when she said, "Lord Fulkham, I understand that you have a knot garden on the property. Do you think we could see that? I do so love knot gardens."

Gregory doubted that the actress had ever seen a knot garden in her life, but no point in challenging her. "Of course. This way, Princess."

Deliberately, he took them the long way around to the acres at the back of his home, so he could show them the terraced gardens, the stone bridge over the pond, and the view out over his extensive woodlands. By the time they'd reached the knot garden, the duke had grown silent about his precious Valcour.

As well he should. Since the revolution, few of the ducal titles in France had substantial property attached to them. Pontalba might be a duke, but Valcour was probably derelict and uninspiring.

Though that didn't stop the man from leaning over to whisper in Monique's ear from time to time, making her laugh or flirt or blush. It was the blushes that roused Gregory's temper. *He* should be the only one making her blush.

Damn it, he must stop this obsession with her. He still needed answers, and he was squandering his opportunity to ask Lady Ursula the important questions.

Forcing himself to ignore Monique's flirtations, he said, "So you are related to Prince Leopold, are you?"

The smile Lady Ursula had worn for most of their stroll faltered. "We are distant cousins, yes. When he was sixteen and I was seven, I used to trail after him everywhere. His family and mine were very close. We even came to see him a few times in England after he married Princess Charlotte."

He narrowed his gaze on her as a thought occurred to him. "You would have been, what, fifteen then?"

"Yes."

"So, not that much younger than the princess."

"Pardon me, sir, but there is a vast difference between a fifteen-year-old and a twenty-year-old. One is essentially still a child, the other a woman."

A fifteen-year-old was not a child, as she well knew. What if Lady Ursula had wanted Prince Leopold for herself? That would explain why she might try to eliminate Princess Aurore.

Though the lady-in-waiting didn't strike him as the murdering sort. And it didn't explain why she would attempt to kill *Monique*. Unless she was worried that Monique might charm the prince, too. If Lady Ursula had spoken to Danworth and heard of the prince's interest in renewing the courtship, that might have been enough to do it.

Still, if the count were to be believed, the prince's initial offer had been refused some time ago. So why would Lady Ursula try to kill Aurore if the woman was no longer a rival? It made no sense.

But something was still afoot with Lady Ursula. She'd been too eager to have the prince come here. Gregory just hadn't figured out why yet.

He pressed her further. "Those differences in age between men and women aren't so bothersome in later years, are they? For example, a man of forty, like Prince Leopold, must not seem that old to a woman of thirty-one." *Like you.*

She merely turned his implication back on him. "And a woman in her twenties, like Princess Aurore, must not seem that young to a man of thirty-five, like yourself."

He stifled an oath. "Do you honestly think I have designs on the princess?"

"Don't you?" She nodded to where Pontalba had just straightened the princess's shawl. "Every time he whispers to her, you go rigid as a pike."

"Only because of her political importance," he lied. "That sly weasel is up to no good with her. Either he's trying to ruin her chances to become queen so he can put his own candidate in . . . or he's hoping to dazzle her with a courtship so he can rule with her himself. I don't trust him."

Lady Ursula regarded the couple thoughtfully. "I don't particularly like him, but I'm not sure he's as villainous as you think." She cast Gregory an enigmatic glance. "Still, if you want, I can get him away from her."

He lifted an eyebrow. "And what do you require in exchange?"

"Nothing. Just your promise that you won't . . . press her into anything untoward."

"Like a mésalliance with me, you mean?"

"Like a compromising situation."

He stiffened. "I could certainly promise you that." But he was playing with words. He *could* promise her that, but he didn't intend to.

All the same, he would say almost anything to get Monique away from that arse Pontalba. Because he honestly didn't trust the smarmy fellow.

As soon as they reached the knot garden, he moved away from Lady Ursula to approach Monique. "What do you think, Your Highness? Is it what you expected?"

She surveyed the garden with an odd concentration. "It's . . . different."

"From ones you've seen before? Probably. Some use box hedges to form the strands of the knot, but my mother uses rosemary. I think she hopes that the old saying 'Where rosemary flourishes the lady rules' will prove to be true if she plants enough of it."

"Well, rosemary's hardy stems make it a good choice. And the addition of purple lavender is delightful. I only wish I could see it when it's blooming." Monique sniffed the air. "Even so, it smells heavenly, as do the wild marjoram and sage. What a fine selection of plants. Your mother has a good eye for what belongs in a knot garden. Not to mention a good nose. "

Gregory cocked his head. She'd managed to startle him. Again. "You *do* know your knot gardens."

"My grandmother always dragged me to see them." A wistful note entered her voice. "She loves—" Monique caught herself. "*Used to* love them."

He knew that Princess Aurore's grandmother was dead. But not Monique's, perhaps? He suddenly remembered the discussions at the theater three years ago about her aging grandmother. Damn, he wished he could reach Hart to have him pursue that line of questioning.

Although there really was no need. Hart would be sharp enough to cover it. He'd become quite adept at spying.

Apparently noticing Monique's slip, Lady Ursula said, "You miss your grandmother terribly, don't you, Your Highness?" She glanced at Gregory. "The princess still speaks of her as if she is with us, though she's been gone ten years."

Her "Highness" said nothing, merely gave him a sad smile. It twisted something inside his chest.

He *must* talk to her alone. He offered her his arm. "Since you like knot gardens, Princess, I have something special to show you if you will come with me."

She eyed him warily and didn't take his arm.

Lady Ursula said, "Why don't you two go on? I'm rather tired after our long trip today." She turned to Pontalba. "Your Grace, would you accompany me back to the house? I'm afraid I might get lost."

His lips thinning, the duke glanced from her to Gregory, but the Frenchman could hardly refuse. "Of course, madam. I'd be happy to."

As soon as they'd gone, Monique stared him down. "What are you up to, Gregory?"

"How would you like to see a knot garden in process?"

Her eyes widened. "What do you mean?"

"Mother has laid out a scheme for a new one by our garden pavilion. She just hasn't planted it yet."

"Oh, that sounds wonderful!" Tucking her hand in the arm he offered again, she let him lead her on.

Now what? Asking her point-blank about her masquerade hadn't worked heretofore, but Lady Ursula's remarks had given him more ammunition for tricking her. Yet some small part of him was loath to do it. She looked so very pleased with the idea of seeing Mother's newest garden project.

And she looked so fetching in that blue walking dress that made her eyes appear almost azure beneath the shade of the trees. He just wanted to stroll with her and pretend that they were not at odds, that she wasn't an impostor whom it was his duty to expose.

As if she, too, was reluctant to discuss the elephant between them, she said, "I don't understand why you never come here. It is so very . . ." She uttered a sigh. "*Lovely*. If I had these gardens—"

"Have you no gardens in Chanay?"

She shot him a veiled look. "We're not talking about me. For once, can't you just answer a simple question without turning it back on me?"

"I don't like to talk about myself," he said honestly.

They skirted a patch of calla lilies as she said, "If you told me more, I might be willing to tell *you* more."

That started an uneasy roiling in his gut. "Spilling one's secrets is dangerous for a man like me, Princess."

"I'm not asking for your secrets. Just something to help me understand you. What has caused an ambition so powerful that it makes you spend all your time in the city, when you could live a life of ease here amid all this glorious green?"

"For a woman who spends her time in theaters

far from the countryside," he snapped, "you have an astonishing affinity for green."

Blanching, she halted in her tracks. "I'm sorry. I thought you would take my request seriously. It appears I was wrong."

The hurt in her voice surprised him. And when she turned on her heel as if to go, he said in a low voice, "Princess, please."

That made her pause.

A frustrated breath rushed from his lips. "Fine," he bit out. God, he would surely regret this in the end, but he couldn't have her running from him. Not anymore. "What do you wish to know?"

Twelve

Monique was certain that delving into the mystery that was Gregory Vyse was a mistake. He wiggled more under her skin with every view she got of his real life, the one he led beyond his ambition.

But she couldn't stop prying. Perhaps it was the actress in her, wanting to figure out what made him behave as he did. All she knew was that he fascinated her, which men rarely did.

"I already told you what I want to know," she said baldly. "Why do you spend all your time in London when you could be here?"

Muttering a curse, he headed down a graveled walk. She followed his aimless ambling.

After a while, he spoke. "Let's just say that this place holds bad memories for me."

"Of what?"

"Not what—who. My late father." He remained silent a long time. "My parents didn't exactly get along. My father was a mean drunk, and my mother generally got the brunt of his temper. So there were lots of arguments."

"Oh." She wanted to ask if those arguments had grown physical, but she'd said she wasn't asking for secrets, and he might consider that one. Still, she would love to know. "How . . . er . . . bad were the arguments?"

"Bad." His jaw seemed carved out of granite. "So bad that they used to wake my little brother, even though he slept in the nursery a floor away."

That startled her. "You have a brother?"

He winced. Clearly, he hadn't meant to reveal that. "*Had* a brother. He's dead now. I learned of his passing the night I met you, after the play."

She tensed. Curse him—he couldn't even tell her one important thing about himself without trying to provoke her into revealing the truth about the masquerade.

Then she realized he hadn't even registered what he'd said, because he went on without so much as looking at her. "He died doing something for me." His voice turned bitter. "In the service of what you call 'my ambition.'"

The pain in his words cut through her. She laid her hand on his arm as they walked. "I'm sure that's not what you intended."

Pulling free of her, he raked his fingers through his hair. "Of course not. Yet the result is the same—John is dead and it's my fault." He scanned the woods they were passing. "And every inch of this place is haunted by him. Him *and* my father. One good ghost, one bad ghost—though it hardly matters. They're still ghosts." His tone grew acid. "They rather spoil my enjoyment of all the 'green.' "

"I'm sorry," she whispered. "I did not mean to call forth your ghosts. And now that I see what a sacrifice you were making by offering your home to us and being forced to come here, I'm sorry for that, too."

"Don't be." He dragged in a long breath, then faced her with a half smile. "Believe it or not, your being here makes it less . . . ghostly." Before she could even take pleasure in that, his smile faded and he said in a hard voice, "And now it's *your* turn to answer a question."

Oh, Lord. Knowing what the question would be, she went on the defensive. "First, you promised me another knot garden. I have yet to see it."

That smirk of his returned. He could tell she was stalling, but he merely swept his hand forward. "It's right there."

She gazed beyond him to a large clearing with an octagonal-shaped brick pavilion at the end. Walking past him, she surveyed the ground, then gaped at the design marked in powdered chalk. "And here I thought you were making it up just to get me alone."

"Unlike a certain female I know, I don't generally make up things when the truth will suffice."

Ignoring the barb, she strode around the design, careful not to step on the chalk marks that not only laid out the pattern but described in words what plants went where. "Kudos to your mother. Does she intend to have a true knot garden with the effect of overlapping hedges to make the strands? I can't tell from the design." She stopped in the middle of an enigmatic circle. "Might she be planning a fountain here?"

"How the devil should I know?"

"*Sacrebleu*, you really do not spend much time at your estate, do you?" She eyed him askance.

"Not since my father died, no. And even when he was alive, I spent most of my time right there." He gestured to the pavilion. "I used to sneak books up there from Father's library and read the day away." His voice hardened. "Or the night, if they were fighting."

Her heart constricted at the thought of the lonely little boy reading to avoid the painful realities of his parents' marriage. "Is that why your mother is putting the knot garden here? To coax you back home by improving your favorite spot?"

He snorted. "If it is, then it won't work."

"Don't be too sure. Your mother's work is amazing, and I daresay it will look spectacular from up in those windows. This is a very ambitious effort for a knot garden."

"Where do you think I get my ambition from?" he quipped.

With a laugh, she shook her head. "Lady Fulkham is quite a force, isn't she?"

"Since she runs this place in my stead, she has to be." He came over to stand beside her. "I've offered time and again to hire a manager, but she won't hear of it. She likes to keep her hand in."

Monique kept her gaze fixed on the design. "Apparently she's not as bothered by ghosts as you."

"No," he said softly. "Though she ought to be." Just as Monique was about to ask why, he added, "So how long ago did Prince Leopold offer for you?"

The abrupt change of subject caught her off guard. Especially since it wasn't the question she'd expected. And she didn't know how to answer.

She chose to be careful. "I'm not sure. I was only informed of it a few months ago. It might have been before that, however."

"You're lying," he said bluntly. "I saw the surprise in your face when Lady Ursula suggested including him in this party. And when the count mentioned the offer of marriage, you were stunned. I'd already heard rumors of it, but apparently *no one* had informed you of the prince's interest in Aurore until that very moment."

"Gregory—" she began, turning away.

He stepped in front of her to clasp her shoulders. "I should warn you that even as we speak, one of my men is in Dieppe, trying to determine exactly what deal you made with the devil that led you here. Actually, you know my man, Lord Hartley. He was with me at the theater the night we saw your play. More recently, he witnessed your presentation in Parliament and agreed with me that you quite possibly *are* Monique Servais."

The gloves had come off. He was clearly done waiting for her to confess.

Leaving those words to knock about in her brain and make her frantic, he released her before continuing. "So rest assured—your masquerade will be exposed eventually. I won't stand by and let an impostor take the throne of Belgium. I was willing to let the idiotic scheme ride at the beginning, to give me time to figure out what was going on, but not after I heard about Prince Leopold's designs on Princess Aurore. Surely you cannot think I would let you *marry* the man in her stead."

"I have no intention of marrying the man!" she protested. "And he's already been refused, so his designs don't matter."

"They matter far more than you think, you little fool. Don't you see? A union between Prince Leopold and Princess Aurore would ensure that the two together are made rulers of Belgium. It would solve so many diplomatic issues that all sides would eagerly approve it."

His expression grew fierce. "Your dear 'uncle' or manager or whatever you choose to call him would like that very much indeed. So you may find yourself pressured into such a marriage, especially if the princess is dead and Beaumonde hopes to put you in her place."

"Dead!" Had he heard something the count wasn't telling her? Had the princess not survived her cholera or poisoning or whatever it was? If Gregory had spies everywhere, as apparently he did—

She seized his coat lapels. "What have you heard? What has happened?"

He met her gaze coldly. "To *whom*?"

"Damn you! You will make me say it, won't you?"

"I will. Or I will drag you in front of the count and make *him* say it, if I must."

"No, you can't, *please*. I'll do anything . . . just don't let him know you know the truth."

"You didn't tell him about our previous—"

"Certainly not. And you mustn't, either." She shifted away, frantic to think how to convince him. "Surely there's a way we can . . . All I need is . . ."

An idea occurred to her, and she whirled on him. "You said you want me. Well, you can have me." Though his expression grew stormy, she persisted. She'd been on the verge of having to take a protector in Dieppe—how was this any different?

Besides, she was attracted to Gregory, which was more than she could say for any of her admirers at home. "Just let the masquerade play out. I swear to you that there is nothing wicked about it. And if it turns out that it does involve marriage to Prince Leopold or anything like that, I will confess the truth myself, even if you and I have already—"

"Shared a bed?" he roared. "What kind of monster do you take me for? I would never accept such a bargain. You may not believe this, but I *am* a gentleman. Not to mention, I am perfectly capable of wooing a woman into my bed without forcing her there." Eyes glittering like the hardest of diamonds, he stepped up close. "If ever I make love to you, it will be a mutual decision, not some form of blackmail."

"It . . . it's not blackmail. It's quid pro quo."

His harsh laugh cut through her. "What the devil do you know about 'quid pro quo'? You're an actress."

She tipped up her chin. "One of my admirers is a lawyer."

"One of your admirers *at the theater*," he prodded.

A frustrated breath rushed out of her. "Yes, yes! Of course I am Monique Servais." She swallowed. "Though I can't believe you recognized me after three years, despite all the makeup and clothes and wig—"

"Sorry, my sweet," he said. "You could cover yourself in mud, and I would still recognize *you*."

The heat flaring in his gaze gave her hope. "Then why won't you just—"

"I told you." He lifted a hand to brush something from her cheek, and only then did she realize she was crying. His voice roughened. "I don't believe in hurting women. Forcing you to my bed would be tantamount to rape, and thus vastly unsatisfying for both of us, trust me."

Rape. The hard word jangled in her ears. "Not if I chose to be there."

"An act done in desperation is not a choice. And while I might back you into a corner to get the truth out of you, when it comes to warming my bed, I only want what's freely given."

He trailed his hand down her cheek, gathering tears as he went. "So you have only one recourse. Tell me the truth. Tell me why this is so important that you would offer your body to secure it. Then perhaps together we can figure out a solution that won't require scandalizing the world and ruining your future."

The slender offer of other alternatives, coupled with the kindness in his words, so took her by surprise that her defenses crumbled. She caught his hand and turned it to kiss the palm. Then, as she wondered where to begin, she pulled away to go roam the path laid out by his mother's chalked design.

"Does it have anything to do with your grandmother?" he asked.

That startled her. "How did you—"

"I overheard you speaking of her three years ago. And then just now, you were talking about—"

"Yes," she said bitterly. "Apparently, I am not quite as good an actress as I thought I was."

"You're magnificent," he said fiercely, surprising her yet again.

"Even though I'm a *comic* actress?" she retorted.

He looked chagrined. "I should not have said what I did that night. To be honest, I was perturbed to find myself so attracted to a provincial French actress." He ventured a smile. "Especially one who had managed to impress me with her talent, yet professed herself annoyed at the prospect of meeting me. But trust me, I knew from the moment I saw you on the stage that you were extraordinary."

She snorted. "If I were so extraordinary, I would have been better in my role as Princess Aurore, and you wouldn't have guessed my identity the first time you saw me."

"It wasn't a lack of acting ability that handicapped you, my sweet. Because you were not actually on the stage. I suspect that when you're being yourself you're probably honest. And lying about oneself is vastly different from playing a role in the theater."

Therein lay the rub, to paraphrase Shakespeare. On the stage, she was aware that everyone *knew* she was playing a role. She had permission, as it were, to lie egregiously. To inhabit the character, to be wholly someone else.

But in life . . .

She didn't particularly like lying about being a princess to people who didn't realize they were watching a play.

"Your grandmother," he prodded. "She's the reason you're doing this. Why, exactly?"

Monique sighed. He was not going to let this go. "My grandmother is . . . ill. She's not in her right mind anymore, hasn't been for some time. Because of our connection to the Chanay royal family—"

"Wait," he interrupted, "you truly have a connection to them?"

"Yes." She flashed him a sheepish smile. "As it happens, I'm Princess Aurore's cousin."

He gaped at her. "Really?"

She took a perverse pleasure in shocking him. "I'm her second cousin."

"*That's* why you resemble her. You're related!"

She smiled faintly. "In truth, we look astonishingly alike. Probably because my grandmother is one of her great-aunts."

"So how did you end up in—"

"Dieppe? Grand-maman fell in love with an actor in her youth. As the youngest of four children, she thought she ought to be able to marry whom she wanted. Her family disagreed. So she married him in secret." Anger crept into her voice. "And for her misbehavior, the royal family cast her out. She and Grandpapa joined his troupe and traveled the Continent, as did my mother before—" No, she would not tell him that embarrassing detail. "Anyway, we became a family of actors, which we've been all these years."

Gregory cast her an incredulous look. "So the count really *is* your great-uncle."

"Yes. He was married to one of Grand-maman's sisters. That's why he chose me. He promised that if I pretended to be Princess Aurore until she gained the throne of Belgium, he'd make sure that Grand-maman spent her final days in the home of her youth. Chanay. The place she loves and misses. The place she was banished from when she married Grandpapa."

"Good God."

And for once, she quite agreed.

Thirteen

Gregory's head reeled. Monique was Beaumonde's great-niece. A member of the Chanay royal family. In a way, she was as legitimate a descendant as Princess Aurore. Just probably not directly in line for the throne, or the Rocheforts wouldn't have ignored her branch of the family for so long.

A thought occurred to him. She was decidedly *not* the count's mistress, which meant . . .

Well, he didn't know what it meant, except that it pleased him inordinately. He hadn't liked the idea of her with that ancient relic, Beaumonde.

But that should *not* be what he was focusing on. Her revelation raised a number of questions. "How did the count know about you and your resemblance to the princess?"

She shrugged. "Apparently he's kept an eye on our family all these years. I had no idea. Though

I knew I was from the royal line of Chanay, Grand-maman seemed sure that they had no use for us. They'd never made any overtures until he approached me in Dieppe a short while ago."

"And you agreed to his mad scheme be-cause—"

"It's just me and Grand-maman, and I can't take care of her on my own anymore," she said bluntly. "I can't afford to hire anyone to watch her day and night, now that she's started to wan-der. Even good actresses don't make that much money. So my only choice is to quit working and descend into poverty with her, or"—she wrapped her arms about her waist—"take a protector, which I have no desire to do."

The thought of her being forced into that position twisted something in his chest, even as he realized with self-loathing that *he* had wanted to be her protector. But he wouldn't have wanted it at the cost to her freedom of choice. It would have been mutual.

Right, his conscience clamored. *Mutual.*

She went on in a hollow tone. "Plus, the more Grand-maman sinks into . . . senility, the more she longs for her home. So when my great-uncle offered to allow us both to return to Chanay and live there free of worry if I would just pretend to be my second cousin, it seemed the perfect solution." She shot him a dark look. "I had no idea I would run into *you* again, my lord. Or that you would remember me."

"I would imagine not. Our encounter was brief." He arched an eyebrow. "Although I should point out that you remembered me as well."

She tipped up her chin. "Hard *not* to remember a man of such arrogance."

He ought to take offense, but she looked so adorably put out that he had to bite back a smile. "Is that all you remembered of me? My arrogance?"

Coloring, she glanced away.

"So I did not imagine the attraction between us that night," he murmured.

"As I said," she retorted. "A man of arrogance. In any case, your remembering me has ruined everything, especially considering the position you're in."

That jerked him back to the reality of the situation. "Yes, let's talk about that. Princess Aurore is in line for the Belgian throne." He bore down on her. "Is she dead?"

She blinked. "I thought you said that—"

"I don't know what has happened to her. But something clearly has, or you wouldn't be here in her stead."

A heavy sigh escaped her. "The last time I saw her, she was very much alive. But ill."

That gave him pause. "In what way?"

Her expression was conflicted. "I—I'm not sure. They told me she had cholera. That's why they needed me. They didn't want to risk her losing her chance at being queen simply because she was sick." Her voice grew choked. "But after you said it was *me* someone was trying to kill . . ."

His blood ran cold. "You wondered if she'd been poisoned."

Wide-eyed, she nodded. "My uncle says that is ludicrous. I just don't know whether to believe him. This world of politics and shady doings is not my purview." She began to roam the knot garden design again. "I'm an actress, not a diplomat. I wouldn't even know how to tell if she *was* poisoned." Her voice lowered. "Though she did seem very ill. When I saw her, she was insensible and apparently had been so for a few days."

That didn't sound good. "Where is she now?"

"In Calais. She fell ill as they were preparing to make the crossing to England."

Interesting. "So it was only then that the count came to you?"

"Yes. He took a steam packet to Dieppe to meet with me and Grand-maman."

That confirmed what Hart had learned. And it meant that it was possible the count hadn't initially intended to put Monique forward as a substitute. That he might have been trying to fix a bad situation in the only way he knew how.

On the other hand, if Beaumonde had been aware of Monique's resemblance to Aurore all along, he might very well have chosen to assassinate his great-niece and put Monique in her stead rather than risk Aurore's bumbling through the conference.

"What about preparing you for the role?" Gregory asked. "How could he have known you would understand enough about what was required of a princess to step into Aurore's shoes?"

"I asked the same thing!" she cried. "I mean, Grand-maman has tried through the years to teach me the proper behavior just in case they ever . . ." Her voice hardened. "But of course that didn't happen until they found themselves in difficulty. And he said we had enough time on the crossing to prepare me. He did seem . . . rather out of sorts about the whole matter."

"I can well imagine," Gregory said dryly.

The count struck him as a man who wouldn't set up such a havey-cavey plan unless he was forced into it. If Beaumonde had intended all along for Monique to take Aurore's place, he would have eliminated Aurore in enough time to prepare Monique to replace her. This smacked of the actions of a desperate man, not a scheming one.

Besides, if the count had wanted to replace Aurore, why would he then have hired someone to shoot at Monique? If she was supposed to be the future of Chanay and Belgium, it made no sense. So Gregory could probably rule out Beaumonde as the one trying to kill Monique.

Unless, of course, the count had somehow learned about her former association with Gregory.

A chill swept him. "Are you certain your great-uncle doesn't know that we met before?"

"How could he? *I* never told him."

"And you never told Lady Ursula. Or your maid or—"

"Are you mad?" She faced him down. "I want Grand-maman taken care of, and he's made quite clear that if this masquerade isn't successful, his promise to bring her home is for naught. So I haven't told a soul. I was hoping to brazen it out until the whole thing was over."

Her expression turned pleading as she drew nearer him. "Which is why you *must* keep silent. If you reveal to my uncle that I've failed to convince you I'm Aurore, then I will be packed off to Dieppe without so much as a farewell. He will only honor his promise if Aurore becomes queen. Otherwise . . ."

The desperation in her eyes sliced through him. Damn her. Damn the count. He couldn't let this nonsense stand. And yet . . . "What is supposed to happen to Aurore if you *do* succeed in being chosen as ruler of Belgium?"

She sighed. "Aurore will take my place. By then, he hopes, she'll be well, and she can go to Belgium and assume her throne. Then Grand-maman and I will go to Chanay as ourselves. Relations to the crown. But after Grand-maman dies, I intend to return to Dieppe and my position at the theater."

How did she still manage to surprise him? "You would choose being an actress over living as a relation to royalty?"

"A *poor* relation, forced to submit to their will in everything? Absolutely. I love my work at the theater. And I crave . . ." She trailed off with a sigh. "You wouldn't understand."

He stepped nearer. "Try me. What do you crave, Princess?"

Her eyebrow lifted. "You realize I'm not truly a princess."

"To me, you are." He caught her hand and brought it to his lips, kissing each finger and reveling in the way she blushed. For a woman who'd probably gone through quite a few lovers, she had a surprising air of innocence about her. "Tell me, my sweet, what you crave."

She searched his face, as if to determine his sincerity. Then she flashed him a sad smile. "Freedom. To be myself. To live my life and practice my craft. To not always be worrying about how I shall care for Grand-maman, or what will happen if—"

A loud cry broke the stillness of the clearing. "Princess? Fulkham? Where are you? I've returned!"

A vile oath escaped Gregory. "Pontalba, damn him." Gregory had more questions, needed to know more before he could make a decision about how to handle this matter. "Come with me."

Before she could protest, he tugged her across the path and into the pavilion.

At least she went willingly. She too must realize that they weren't done. "Gregory?"

He held a finger to her lips. "Keep quiet, and he'll go away."

She nodded, though her eyes showed she wasn't as certain.

They could hear the fellow approaching, far too near for Gregory's comfort. Pulling her deeper into the pavilion, he dragged her up the stairs that led to the second floor, with floor-to-ceiling windows that indeed overlooked Mother's proposed new garden.

He released Monique and rounded the chaise longue near the window to stand where he could observe the duke. With the afternoon sun shining full on this side, the man shouldn't be able to see them. Which was a good thing, since Monique came up behind him so she could look out the window, too.

As Pontalba surveyed the clearing, he scowled and muttered to himself, "Damn it, I could have sworn I heard them out here somewhere."

Monique tensed, and Gregory shot her a reassuring glance.

"What the hell is this, anyway?" the duke said in French. "A bunch of chalk lines on the ground? These English are mad, I swear."

The leap of fire in Monique's eyes amused Gregory. He could see she was itching to march out and give the man a piece of her mind about Mother's designs. It made him want to kiss her.

So he did.

And to his shock, she responded beyond his

wildest dreams. She opened her mouth, let him deepen the kiss, then tangled her tongue with his, as if she'd never wanted anything more.

He was no fool—he took advantage, kissing her with all the urgency in his loins. He wanted her. Even now that he knew who she was, and what she and her great-uncle had planned, he still wanted her. In truth, it was hard not to want a woman who would risk everything for her grandmother.

But even before he'd known that about her, he'd desired her. Because when it came to her, all his vaunted control and logic went right out the window.

Right now, his entire *life* didn't make sense. She was the last person he should desire—an actress who could do nothing to further his career. Who could actually harm it irreparably.

Yet he didn't care. All he knew was he wanted to keep kissing her, holding her, touching her . . .

"Is he gone?" she whispered against his mouth.

The words drew him briefly from the sensual cloud she wrapped around him every time their lips met. He looked out. "I think so. I don't see him."

"Good," she whispered, then tugged his head back down to hers.

The kiss rapidly spiraled beyond his control. Her mouth, so soft and wet, made him want to plunder and ravage her like some conqueror of old. He manacled her waist with his arm and smoothed his other hand down over her skirts to cup her sweet bottom, pleased to find how shapely she was beneath her petticoats.

God, how he wanted to taste her, caress her . . . take her.

She tore her mouth free to murmur, "You see how it could be between us? All you need do is promise not to say anything to the count."

That sparked his anger, making him clasp her head in his hands. "I told you I will not let you barter your body for my silence."

Her eyes narrowing, she slid her hand down over his rapidly hardening cock and rubbed it, silkily at first, then more roughly. "Are you sure? Because it seems to me that your *body* is more than willing to barter for mine."

He hissed a breath through his teeth. "You don't play fair, my sweet."

"Says the man who marked my wrist with his love bite." She stretched up to press a kiss to his neck just above his cravat. "Shall I mark *you*, my lord? So that every time you look in the mirror, you remember how you had a chance at me and threw it away for your ambition?"

"Not for my bloody ambition, for damned sure." A groan escaped him as she licked the spot, tantalizing him with her tongue. "I risk my ambition more with every hour I let this masquerade go on. Even if I did agree to your terms and keep silent, I can't prevent someone else's unmasking you. And if it comes out that I knew the truth and didn't speak, I'll be ruined."

She drew back to stare at him. "How would it come out, when the only ones who know of it are you and I?"

"And Hart and Lady Ursula and the count. Not to mention the princess and whoever else is looking after her in Calais." He thumbed her lips, so sweetly swollen from the ferocity of their kisses. "I've been in politics long enough to realize that secrets known by a number of people don't stay secret for long."

That brought a frown to her brow. "Even when those people have a vested interest in staying silent? Except for Lord Hartley, who I assume is under *your* control, the others have to keep the secret or lose everything."

"And what about the assassin? Do you think *he* will keep quiet? He knows you're not Aurore. First, he tried to poison Aurore. Then, when the count's response was to put a substitute in her place, the assassin shot at the substitute. Whoever is bent on not letting Aurore take the throne will resort to revealing the truth about your masquerade, if that's what it takes for him to get what he wants."

She pondered that a moment, then brightened. "Not necessarily. If Aurore was poisoned—and we're still not sure she was—he could have managed that without ever actually seeing her. Besides, the count put her into seclusion in Calais once I stepped in, so this villain could have just assumed the poison didn't work and still be trying to kill the woman he thinks is Princess Aurore."

"I suppose that's possible." He hardened his tone. "But that only means *you're* in more danger than we thought. And that the count knew it from the beginning."

"He didn't."

Gregory eyed her closely. "What makes you so sure?"

"I asked him about it. He truly believes that Aurore has cholera and that the shooter was not trying to shoot at *me*."

"Then he's a fool." The very idea that she was putting her trust in the count, who clearly wasn't concerned for her welfare, made him want to shake her.

"Perhaps so, but he's my only hope of making sure Grand-maman is cared for."

"What about me?" he bit out without thinking.

She gaped at him. "You? *You* want to expose me."

That stung, even though she was right. "I seek only the truth."

"Which would destroy me. And Grand-maman."

He cupped her chin in his hand. "I don't wish to destroy either of you."

"Then don't say anything to my uncle." When he stiffened, she added in a pleading tone, "Think of it this way. You can't catch the assassin if you end my masquerade. And you want to catch him, don't you? Assuming there is one? Because if he's trying to kill his competitor for the crown, you don't want him winning, do you?"

That made sense. Either that, or his cock was guiding his brain. Which rarely happened. Except, apparently, around *her*. "Let's say I allow this travesty to continue until we . . . find the culprit. That would mean you'd be acting as bait for this monster."

"Not here. You said I'd be safe at your estate." She lifted a guileless, trusting gaze that fairly slayed him. "And if I'm not, you'll protect me. I know you will."

Fighting the absurd satisfaction that her faith in him brought him, he growled, "Then how am I to catch the bastard, if you stay here safe?"

"You said you had spies. I assume that your men will be looking into what happened at the park. My being here for five days will give them time to find him."

"And if they don't? You expect me to further risk your life by bringing you back to London?"

She stared off through the window as if seeking answers in his mother's design. "I don't know. Perhaps the soldiers will have scared him off. He might not try again." She gave a shuddering breath. "All I know is that there's no future for me in Dieppe if this does not succeed. My great-uncle will make sure of that. He doesn't want Aurore to lose her chance."

"That's something else you haven't considered. What if she dies in the end?"

Monique shrugged. "Then I will 'die' and the masquerade will be over." She met his gaze. "I have no desire to rule Belgium. I'm only making sure that Aurore can do so."

"I suspect your uncle would have something to say about that."

She frowned. "What do you mean?"

"He wants the throne for Chanay. If Aurore dies, I daresay he'll want you to take her place."

"Well, I wouldn't!" she said hotly. "And he can't make me."

"He's making you do *this*."

She thrust out her chin. "Yes, but this is to help Aurore. And Grand-maman. The other would be wrong."

Gregory shook his head. She was so refreshingly naïve in some ways.

"Besides," she said, "what do I know about ruling a country? No, he wouldn't ask that."

"Are you sure? Perhaps that was his plan all along—to put you in Aurore's place."

The shock on her face made it clear that hadn't occurred to her. "I would never agree to that!"

"Even to take care of your grandmother?"

A troubled frown knit her brow. "Not even for that."

He shouldn't believe her, but he did. She seemed caught between a rock and a hard place. As was he. Because the minute he revealed her identity, it could come out that he'd known all along. She might even admit it herself to save her own skin.

Then everyone would question why he hadn't acted from the beginning. And all his protests that he hadn't been sure of who she was would fall on deaf ears.

Damn. He should have exposed her the moment he'd suspected the truth. But he hadn't, so now he was in a quandary. "How about this?" he said. "The decision won't be made until we return. So for now, I'll let you go on with your masquerade while I try to find out if anyone truly is trying to murder your cousin, and why. By then we should know if Princess Aurore has survived, and we can move on from there."

He was stalling, giving himself time to think his way out of this mess.

But judging from the way her face brightened, he had just given her the keys to the kingdom. "Oh, Gregory!" she cried, and threw her arms about his neck. She kissed both his cheeks. "Thank you, thank you, *thank you.*"

"Hmph," he grumbled. "I know I'm going to regret this."

"You won't, I swear," she told him. Then she kissed his mouth. Sweetly. Tenderly.

His pulse broke into a stampede. "What are you doing?" he growled as he jerked back from her.

She stared up at him with eyes as luminous as the setting sun shining through the window behind her. "Making sure you don't regret this."

"Monique—"

She cut him off with a kiss that set his body afire. No woman had done that to him in a very long time. He was always too conscious of his position and what it would cost him to have a dalliance with someone he couldn't trust.

But she made him want things . . . *need* things . . .

Clasping her close, he kissed her with all the fervent longing in his blood. And she gave as good as she got, twining her tongue with his, pressing her breasts against him, and making him ache down deep where he never ached. Not for anyone.

What did it matter if she did it out of gratitude, really?

But the rational part of him knew it mattered. It protested this lapse in his conscience. Yet the part of him that desired her stifled all protests, reminding him that she was no young virgin, that she could be his for the taking. That she was soft and giving in his arms, her mouth a wonder and her body eager for him. He wanted her so badly, he could hardly think.

So he abandoned thought and, without looking back, plunged in where angels feared to swim.

Fourteen

Gregory's eager response heartened Monique. She truly did want to show him her gratitude, so he wouldn't regret this. So he would think twice before confronting her great-uncle.

It wasn't because she wanted to banish his ghosts. Or because this secluded spot made her yearn to explore the attraction between them. Or because every time he kissed and caressed her, it unwound a little more the coiled rope of past longings and urges and needs that she'd spent years ignoring. Years suppressing.

With him, she wanted to suppress nothing.

Taking her by surprise, he swept some books off the chaise longue behind them, sat down, and then dragged her onto his lap. Men had tried to pull her onto their laps before, and she'd fought them.

She didn't fight Gregory. She looped her arms about his neck again, eager to let him do as he would with her.

"From the moment I saw you on the stage," he whispered against her cheek, "I wanted to touch you. Explore you." He trailed kisses down her jaw. "To have you in my arms like this." He covered one breast and kneaded it through her gown and undergarments. "To have you at my mercy."

The idea of *being* at his mercy shot a thrill through her. Cursing herself for wearing so many clothes, she arched her neck to give him better access to her naked throat.

"Then you are a better actor than I," she murmured as he licked the pulse beating wildly there. "I could not tell that you wanted me so."

"Couldn't you? I suppose not. I was too caught up in my—"

"Self-importance?" she quipped.

He drew back with a scowl. "Is that what you thought? Because it's not true. I was merely irritated that Hart was there, that you seemed to fancy him over me." He nuzzled her throat. "You didn't, did you?"

That hint of uncertainty surprised her. "He was nothing compared to you," she admitted. When a self-satisfied smile crossed his face, she added, "Although I *was* irritated that you disapproved of my art."

"I could tell. The truth is, I was merely annoyed with myself for falling under your spell like all your other admirers. For desiring you as badly as the rest of them." His voice hardened, and he began to unbutton her front-opening bodice. "The way I desire you now, to distraction."

The admission warmed her down deep. "You can have me, if you wish."

He paused to stare at her with the unreadable expression of the diplomat. "This is not . . . just gratitude, is it?" Vulnerability crept into his features. "Because if so, I couldn't bear that."

She vacillated between protecting herself and confessing the truth. The truth won out. "No." She tongued his throat, the light scruff of beard there reminding her that he was a real man, not like the sycophants who surrounded her in the theater. "It isn't merely gratitude."

Apparently that was all he needed to hear, for with a groan, he got her gown open somehow and fell upon her breasts, sucking and teasing and driving her out of her mind.

Meanwhile, his hands roamed down to drag up her skirts and burrow through her petticoats until he discovered the opening in her drawers. "My sweet princess . . ." he murmured as he delved inside her curls with his clever fingers. "My darling girl—"

"Not a girl," she corrected him, "and not a princess."

"But *mine*," he said. "At least for now."

Those last words were a taunt she had to return. "Yes, Gregory. As you are mine . . . for now."

If he realized it was a taunt, he didn't show it. Instead, he took her mouth again as he drove two fingers inside her, tantalizing her, arousing her. At the same time, he thumbed the part of her that throbbed and ached for him, and her blood rushed through her veins . . . and lower.

It was so intense she nipped his lip.

He drew back with a chuckle. "The actress has claws."

"Teeth," she muttered, and shifted atop his growing arousal. "Though I can show you my claws if you wish."

"Go ahead." He resumed his caresses with relentless intent. "I don't mind being scratched if it means having you."

She couldn't imagine any other man saying that to her. It turned her to mush, made her desire him even more. With him, she didn't have to be the princess or the sophisticated Mademoiselle Servais. He seemed to actually like the woman who hid her softness beneath her prickly remarks. With him, she could be herself.

"Gregory . . ." she whispered on a breath, which was all it took to have him plundering her with his hand below while his mouth plundered her breasts above.

Oh. *Mon. Dieu!* She began to see why Grandmaman and Maman had thrown away everything for a man. Clearly Monique had their reckless blood running rampant through her veins, because the way he was caressing her made her want to tear her clothes off and let him do as he wished with her body.

"My sweet Monique," he said as he fondled her. "You're so . . . wet for me."

She squirmed against his hardened *verge*. "And you're so . . . firm for me."

"You have no idea," he growled. "I've been 'firm' for you since the day I met you. I've thought of you often since then."

Drawing back to stare at him, she said, "Truly?"

His eyes had the heavy-lidded gaze of a man aroused, and he thrust up against her bottom as if to confirm it. "Do you doubt me?"

Her throat went dry. "No."

"Good." He shifted her off his lap and onto the chaise longue so she was reclining on it while he hovered over her. "Because I can think of nothing but tasting you and taking you. Here. Now."

She was so blinded by her need that she could only nod.

To her shock, instead of opening his trousers, he slid down the chaise longue so he could place his mouth on her *minou*. Then he began to tongue her. *There*, where no man had ever kissed her.

What a revelation. She knew of this intimacy—actresses spoke of such things from time to time—but she'd had no idea it would feel so . . .

Incredible. Delectable. To have a man arouse her while ignoring his own arousal . . . so *magnifique!* "*Gregory*," she begged, hearing the plea in her voice with a tiny bit of shame. But not enough to stop her from saying, "Please . . . *please* . . ."

"Whatever you wish, my sweet," he said, his very tone a smug smile.

He could smirk all he liked as long as he kept licking and teasing and caressing her *minou* as if feasting on her. It overwhelmed her . . . the heat of his lips, the delicious pleasure of having his tongue inside her . . . the very knowledge that he could seduce her body with just his mouth. How unfair!

But fairness ceased to matter as she felt a sort of buzz beginning in her loins. As he continued his ministrations, it rose to weaken her thighs, swamping her with such glorious sensations . . . "*Sacrebleu* . . ." she breathed and buried her fingers in his silky hair to clutch him more tightly to her. "*Oui* . . . Take me . . . like that, yes . . . oh, *oui* . . ."

The buzz grew to a pounding in her ears, then a roar of sensation between her legs, then an outright explosion that rocked her from her head to that soft, silky place he was ravaging with such intent.

"*Mon Dieu!*" she screamed as the explosion shattered her into shards of herself. She lay there trembling in ecstasy, marveling at the beauty of it, while he wiped his mouth on her drawers. Then, as her joy began to wane, she whispered, "Oh, my dearest *Gregory*. That was . . . was . . ."

"Indescribable?" he teased.

"Amazing."

"Good." His eyes shone jewel-bright as he moved up over her. "Because you, my princess, deserve 'amazing.'" He rubbed against her, the fine wool of his trousers abrading her bare flesh ever so slightly. "I want to be inside you. Will you let me?"

Even as she reached down to unfasten his trousers, she cast him a provoking smile. "You were just now inside me."

With his hands gripping either side of the chaise longue, he hovered over her. "You know what I mean, Mademoiselle Tourmenteur," he growled, and bent his head to nip at her earlobe. "Tease me at your peril."

Smiling coyly, she reached in his trousers to cup his rampant erection through his drawers. "Are you sure it will be *my* peril, monsieur?"

His eyes slid shut. "Oh, God, yes. Touch me there." When she began to rub him, he rasped, "You may torment me as much as you wish as long as you keep . . . doing . . . precisely that."

It was as if his words unleashed the coquette in her. It made no sense, but she reveled in his hunger, delighted in his thirst for her. Perhaps because in that moment, he was just a man and she a woman, and all the subterfuge and machinations between them vanished.

While she stroked him through his drawers, he began kissing her again, his mouth as ravenous as a bird of prey's. The firm thrust of his *verge* against her hand inflamed her, though it also made her curious to know if it really could give such enjoyment as her fellow actresses claimed. It seemed so . . . massive—

"Fulkham!" came a shout from below. "Where are you, old chap?"

They both froze.

Gregory muttered a string of curses. "*Danworth* is out here now? Why the hell is everyone in the whole damned party looking for us? Can't they leave us alone for one bloody moment?"

Amused by his burst of temper, she gazed up into his scowling face. "Perhaps he too will go away if we keep quiet . . . and *you* stop cursing."

"Not Danworth." He pushed up from the chaise longue and began to straighten his disordered clothes. "Not if he has any inkling that we're out here. He'll send a search party for us, blast him. Especially given the reason we came to my estate in the first place."

"He *knows* of that?" she asked in alarm, jumping up to put her own clothing to rights.

"The prime minister told him. That's the reason he's here: because Wellington wants to make sure the 'princess' is kept safe."

She glanced out the window to see Mr. Danworth coming down the path toward the knot garden, searching the area with what appeared to be concern. He would be upon them in moments if he entered the pavilion.

Gregory came up beside her to tuck a tendril back into her coiffeur. "You stay up here and finish straightening your hair and clothing while I speak to him alone."

"Yes, you would not want your friend to think

that you might actually desire the princess, eh?" The bitter words left her before she could stop them. "Especially since you intend to expose me in the end. A dalliance with an actress, an impostor, couldn't possibly help your career."

He swore under his breath. "Monique—"

"Forgive me," she said instantly, and meant it. She faced him, the remorse in his gaze making her wince. "I should not chide you for doing what any man would do when a woman throws herself at him."

His jaw tightened. "It's not as simple as that, damn it."

"Isn't it?" A wave of sadness swamped her. "We could never have a legitimate connection even if you wished it—even if *I* wished it. Half of good society has met me and thinks they know who I am. To marry you, I would have to be exposed for a fraud. And that would ruin you. Not to mention that it would leave Grand-maman with no one to take care of her."

The sound of Mr. Danworth entering the pavilion downstairs struck terror in her that only deepened when the man cried, "Princess? Fulkham?"

Gregory wasn't the only one who could lose everything if they were found in a compromising position that might cause a scandal.

She had to fix this, since he wouldn't. Touching a hand to her hair to make sure it was presentable enough to pass, she swept past Gregory to the stairs. "We're up here, Mr. Danworth! You must come see."

Gregory tensed. "What the devil are you up to?" was all he had time to growl before Mr. Danworth was hurrying up the stairs.

She met the man at the staircase. "Lady Fulkham has set out a new knot garden. It is truly a magnificent design. You probably couldn't tell it from outside, but you can see it wonderfully from up here."

Mr. Danworth glanced beyond her to Gregory and raised an eyebrow.

Taking his cue from her, Gregory rolled his eyes heavenward. "The princess is a bit obsessed with knot gardens. I suppose they're a favorite in Chanay. She wouldn't rest until she got a look at Mother's new design from a better vantage point."

"Oh *yes*," she gushed, "and it's wonderful." Clasping Mr. Danworth by the arm, she tugged him over to the windows. "Look there. Do you see how the edges curl around what is marked to be a lilac bush? Lord Fulkham tells me that his mother plans to have overlapping hedges and embroidery effects and everything. I only wish I could see it once it's completed."

"I'm sure Mother would be happy to host you here again," Gregory said dryly from behind her.

She ignored him to focus all her attention on Mr. Danworth, who was peering out the window incredulously, as if incapable of believing anyone cared that much about a garden.

"And look over there." She pointed to the far corner. "That circle will be a birdbath. Imagine how lovely this garden will be once the robins and the sparrows come to preen in the sun. Not to mention the butterflies."

"Butterflies?" Mr. Danworth asked, rather stupidly.

"Of *course* there will be butterflies. The painted ladies will come north in the spring and lay their eggs, which cocoon. Once their young emerge—"

"Right," he said. "More butterflies." Looking over at Gregory, he said, "She really *does* enjoy gardens, doesn't she?"

Gregory only shrugged, though his eyes glittered at her as if to say, *We are not done with our discussion.*

Determinedly she lifted her face to Mr. Danworth and flashed him a flirtatious smile. "Why are you here? Did you come to call us in to dinner? Or were you hoping for a private word?"

The man looked suddenly uneasy. "Er . . . I merely thought . . . that is . . ."

"A private word with your friend," she added. "Lord Fulkham."

Relief spread over Mr. Danworth's features. "Yes. Of course. With Fulkham. Or rather . . ."

"Pay her no mind, Danworth," Gregory drawled. "Her Highness likes to toy with us Englishmen." He smiled thinly. "She thinks we are all too serious by far."

"But not *you*, Mr. Danworth," she said, and tugged him toward the door. "Lady Fulkham says you know all the choicest bon mots. Is that true?"

Casting a nervous glance back at Gregory, he said, "I know one or two." And with that, he proceeded to regale her with some as she let him lead her out of the pavilion, with Gregory following.

Along the way she flirted and teased, waxing philosophical about plants and insects and anything else she could think of. By the time they reached the house, she was fairly certain she had distracted him from dwelling on the impropriety of her and Gregory being alone together in the pavilion.

Now, if only she could distract herself from wishing she and Gregory had been alone a bit longer. Which was absurd. She had dodged a figurative bullet this time. Next time she might not be so lucky. And the last thing she needed was to give her virtue to a man who would end up destroying her.

It didn't help that once they entered the house she found the count waiting for her, obviously annoyed about something.

He took her aside as soon as he could get her alone. "Now, see here, girl, Danworth is of no importance. Don't waste your smiles on *him*."

She bristled. "Did you not see that I was also with Lord Fulkham?"

"Yes. But I gather that you avoided the duke in

order to spend time with Fulkham. That isn't a good strategy either. Pontalba was quite put out. Meanwhile, Fulkham is clearly already in your clutches. Do not slight one fellow for the other. You must charm them both if we are to succeed. And unlike Fulkham, who fancies *you*, the duke is already predisposed toward *his* candidate."

She tightened her hands into fists at her sides. Oh, the things she wanted to tell him—that she was done with the masquerade, that Lord Fulkham *knew* she was Monique Servais . . . that if the duke breathed his garlic breath on her one more time, she would shove her scented handkerchief down his throat.

Instead, she flashed the count a brittle smile. "I shall do my best to please you, Uncle."

That seemed to bring him up short. "Well . . . then . . . see that you do." He paused. "You do realize I say these things only for your own good. This is too important for all of us."

How well she knew.

Fifteen

That night at dinner, Gregory had trouble concentrating on his guest's chatter. After his encounter with Monique, he'd gone into nearby Canterbury to speak with the constable, figuring it wouldn't hurt to find out if anyone suspicious had been lurking about.

Thank God he had, for the constable had informed him that a stranger from London had been in town a few days before. But it hadn't had anything to do with the princess, because the fellow had been asking about *Gregory*. About his father's death. About why no one had found it suspicious that the previous Lord Fulkham had broken his neck falling down a staircase.

The constable, of course, had told the man the truth—no one had found it suspicious because the baron had been well known for his drunkenness. Indeed, it had not been the first time the man had taken a tumble while drunk.

Still, though Gregory knew no one could ever find out the truth, it unnerved him to have someone asking about it. Unfortunately, the constable only had a name for the mysterious London investigator: Tom Smith, obviously an alias. The constable knew nothing more that could tell Gregory what this was about.

Bloody hell.

Well, there was naught he could do about it at present. He had to focus on getting through the next few days with Monique. On making sure she stayed alive . . . and that he didn't do something unwise.

Like bed the woman.

God, even now he wanted to do so. Tonight she was at her most effervescent—flirting with Pontalba and Danworth, charming Mother, and teasing Lady Ursula and even the count in a way that seemed to startle the old Frenchman.

But she persistently ignored Gregory. Not that he could blame her. First, he'd nearly ravished her. Then they'd had a close call with Danworth. If she hadn't acted swiftly to allay the fellow's suspicions, Danworth would now be wondering why they'd been up there alone, seemingly hiding from the world.

But she'd made everything seem perfectly natural, despite her lips swollen with Gregory's kisses and her coiffeur tilted off-center. He couldn't help admiring her aplomb. For a woman who'd spent her life as a commoner, she could play the princess to the hilt.

Indeed, she was presently enchanting every person at the table, including him, with her self-deprecating remarks about her encounters with the English.

"So when I asked His Majesty about the ancient queen, he was quite insulted," she told the other guests. "Thank heaven Lady Ursula explained to him that I meant the 'previous' queen and not his wife. Only then did I realize that 'ancient' in English may look like *ancien* in French, but it is decidedly *not* the same in meaning." She covered her cheeks fetchingly. "How very *embarrassant!*"

Mother laughed. "I can only imagine. Especially since Queen Adelaide is nearly thirty years younger than the king."

"But my explanation must have satisfied him," Lady Ursula put in, "since he then went on to ask the princess to waltz with him."

"Did he really?" his mother said. "I confess I'm surprised. I thought he never waltzed with anyone but the queen." Her tone turned dry. "Or Mrs. Jordan, back when she was alive."

"*Mother,*" Gregory chided. "Must you gossip about His Majesty?"

"Who was Mrs. Jordan?" Monique asked.

His mother ignored him, intent on sharing a juicy tidbit with the few at the table who'd likely never heard it. "She served as the king's mistress for twenty years before she died and before he married. He lived with her in his own house. Why, they had ten children together! You may actually have met some of them. All the FitzClarences are his by-blows by that actress."

As Monique's smile turned brittle, Gregory stifled a groan. A quick glance at the count showed the man blandly nodding as Lady Ursula colored and turned a sudden, inordinate attention to her fish.

God, when those two had chosen an actress to impersonate Aurore, they should have told her about the king's former mistress, given that the FitzClarences were in and out of the palace and royal functions with regularity.

"His Majesty has always been unorthodox," Gregory explained. "He never expected to be called upon to rule, so since he couldn't marry Mrs. Jordan—"

"Why couldn't he marry her if he wished?" Lady Ursula asked. "He's a prince." Inexplicably she cast a furtive glance at the count. "He ought to be able to do as he pleases."

"That's a lovely idea," Gregory said, not even trying to hide his sarcasm. "Unfortunately, no matter how enticing the concept, English law forbids it."

Monique stared at him, her expression so vulnerable it cut him to the heart. "Because he was a prince? Or because she was an actress?"

"Both, I'm afraid. Royals cannot marry anyone unsanctioned by the king, and William's father, George III, would never have sanctioned such a marriage."

"But *lords* can marry actresses, can't they?" Lady Ursula put in. "I have heard of it. Wasn't Lord Derby's late wife a former actress?"

Gregory tore his gaze from Monique. "His second wife, yes. Which was why they weren't much accepted in society. It's considered beyond the pale."

"I don't know," his mother mused aloud. "The Duke of Bolton married an actress, and the Earl of Peterborough married an opera singer, which is practically the same."

"Both were second wives," Gregory pointed out.

"What about Louisa Brunton? She was the Earl of Craven's *first* wife."

Damn it, why must his mother press this? "Certainly it's been done, but when you can count the number of such marriages on one hand, it clearly isn't common. Most lords are too conscious of their position to risk such a union."

"Which is precisely why British lords are so very dull, sir," Monique said with forced lightness. "They follow rules rather than their passions." When he shot her a black look, she added, "Present company excepted, of course."

"No, no, you're right," his mother had the audacity to say, "at least about my son, anyway.

While I would not call Gregory dull, he can sometimes be overly a slave to rules. Although he wasn't always like that."

Mischief leapt into Monique's eyes. "Do tell," she crooned.

"Well . . ." his mother began.

"Mother," he said in a warning tone, "our guests have no desire to hear about my youthful peccadilloes."

"On the contrary," Danworth said, a certain glee in his face, "I would thoroughly enjoy such tales."

The thought of Danworth spreading Mother's stories at St. George's made Gregory scowl at him. Besides, he was still annoyed with the man for preventing him and Monique from continuing their delightful, though unwise, encounter.

"I, too, would find it entertaining," the count said, with a bit of a smirk. "Wouldn't you, Pontalba?"

"Most assuredly," the damned Frenchman drawled.

"You see, Gregory?" his mother said. "They all think you too rigid and serious, and I mean to show them that you *can* break the rules sometimes. That even you have a reckless side."

Oh, God.

"Anyway," she went on, "even as a small boy my son was quite a pistol. Seven months after his brother was born, he got jealous of the baby getting so much of my attention, so he hid poor

John under his bed. When I came to the nursery, Gregory met me at the door and announced very loftily that the fairies had flown off with John, and there was naught we could do about it."

Everyone chuckled.

"Then, even as Gregory was spinning his sad tale, John crawled out giggling from beneath the bed. Apparently, he found the whole thing a fine game. Seeing that his plan had gone awry, Gregory burst out with, 'Ooh, look, they must have flown him back! They're quick, those fairies.' "

As the room erupted in laughter, Gregory grumbled, "For God's sake, I was four years old."

"Almost five," she corrected him. "And as willful a lad as I ever saw, even when your father—"

She caught herself before she could say "disciplined you." Which had been Father's euphemism for knocking him about.

Gregory took a long swig of his wine, wishing it were something stronger. He rarely drank spirits, but tonight he might have to make an exception.

"Then there was Gregory's first year at Eton, when he was ten," Mother went on. "He attended at a younger age than some gentlemen's sons, because his father felt it would be good for him. As did I."

Actually, Mother had talked Father into sending him away, trying to protect her son from the man's worst abuses. And Gregory had always been grateful to her for that. No punishment for minor offenses at Eton had ever been as terrifying—or painful—as Father in a drunken rage.

"Slowly I began hearing reports of him," Mother went on. "A polite letter from the head-master, a not-so-polite letter from another boy's mother . . . even a note from a local rector. And they all said the same thing. Apparently, my son had become quite the prankster."

"*You?*" Monique said to him, half-incredulous. "A prankster?"

Gregory shrugged. "School was too easy. I had to entertain myself somehow."

Mother rolled her eyes heavenward. "He sent a fake note to one of the older boys, suppos-edly from a maid the lad fancied, stating that she would love to kiss him in the arbor. So this poor fellow did what he thought she'd asked and got himself slapped for it."

Lady Ursula giggled behind her fan.

"Served him right if you ask me," Gregory muttered as he broke off some bread. "The chap was always talking vulgarly about that poor girl." It had reminded him of how cruelly his father had spoken of Mother when he was in his cups.

Monique shot him a penetrating glance, which he ignored.

"Another time," his mother continued relent-lessly, "he put icicles in a fellow's boots right before the lad went to don them."

For the first time since she'd begun laying out his youthful indiscretions, Gregory smiled. "*That* one was funny, actually. You should have heard the whoop he gave." When he caught sight of the rest of them regarding him with surprise, he sobered. "But to be fair, he did it to me a week later."

"Not so amusing then, eh?" the count said.

"I don't know," Gregory said defensively, and downed some wine. "Certainly woke me up."

"But the worst," Mother put in, "was the one that nearly got him expelled when he was twelve."

"Good God, don't tell them that," he growled, but he was shouted down by the clamor of the others wanting to hear it.

Mother paused for effect, waiting for everyone to quiet. "It was late October. The school called me and my husband down to Eton to tell us that our son had attempted to murder the riding master."

When the others gasped, Gregory muttered, "Oh, for God's sake, I did *not* attempt to murder anyone." And if he had, the person would have been dead—though he shouldn't admit that, given what had happened a couple of months later.

"It took us a while to piece the story together," Mother went on, "but apparently, Gregory had substituted bicarbonate of soda for the usual contents of a salt cellar."

"I only wanted to ruin the man's meal, not frighten him out of his wits," Gregory put in.

"Unfortunately," Mother said, "the part of the meal that the fellow chose to salt was his favorite dish—a salad generously dressed with vinegar."

When the others looked at her blankly, Gregory sighed. "It seems that when bicarbonate of soda and vinegar are put together, it makes a . . . rather impressive foaming effect. Which I did not know at the time."

"Apparently no one did," Mother said, a certain glee in her voice. "Including the subject of the prank, who thought it was an attempt to poison him, no matter how much my son protested."

Gregory snorted. "Father recognized the truth at once. He'd had a friend who was a chemist, so he called the riding master a fool for panicking over it."

"Yes, his father thought it rather a fine joke," Mother said dryly. "Eton wasn't inclined to agree, but he threw some money at them, and the problem went away."

"*Mon Dieu,*" Monique breathed, her eyes wide. "I confess I am astonished. You were quite the wild child, Lord Fulkham."

"Until then, yes," Mother said. "But that sobered him into being more circumspect from then on." She shot him a furtive glance. "Turned him into the rigid fellow you see before you."

Gregory could barely suppress a hot retort. That stupid prank hadn't been what changed him. The change had happened a couple of months later, once he'd discovered what he was truly capable of.

That had been what had taught him that emotions were volatile and must be contained whenever possible. That passion could lead to recklessness and murder.

"Well," he said blandly, "a lad has to grow up sometime. Now, if we're done dissecting my misspent youth, perhaps we should discuss our plans for tomorrow."

Pontalba settled back in his chair. "I thought it was Guy Fawkes Day. Shall we not go into your local village to observe the celebrations? I've heard it's rough and raucous, a delightful melee."

Gregory frowned at him. "It is indeed, even in Canterbury. And a melee isn't so delightful if it means risking the well-being of a princess, her lady-in-waiting, her great-uncle, a duke, and the prime minister's secretary."

"Don't forget your mother," the count added from his seat beside her. The fellow actually patted Mother's arm reassuringly. "She should not have to endure the behavior of hooligans."

"Why, thank you, sir," Mother told the count with a flirtatious smile that struck Gregory speechless. "It is very kind of you to worry about me. Though I'm not sure it's necessary."

Gregory shook off the horrifying image of his mother being swept off her feet by the courtly count. Why, the Frenchman was at least ten years her senior! "All I was saying is, in such circumstances, I cannot guarantee anyone's safety. Which is why the only celebrations taking place will be on the estate."

"But we *will* wait for the prince to arrive, won't we?" Lady Ursula asked.

Her continued interest in Prince Leopold's impending visit still perplexed Gregory. After dinner, he would have to take her aside and question her more thoroughly about her relationship to the man. And this time, he wouldn't let her change the subject, as she had earlier.

"We'll have no choice but to wait," Gregory replied. "Guy Fawkes Day activities generally involve fire—burning the Guy in effigy, bonfires, the occasional fireworks. All of that is far more interesting when done and seen at night."

"Fireworks!" Monique crowed. "I should love that!"

He cursed his quick tongue. "Sorry to disappoint you, but no fireworks here, I'm afraid." It would be too easy for someone to shoot at her unnoticed with all the noise and smoke around. "We never have them," he lied. "But we might be able to see the ones from Canterbury in the distance."

Mother narrowed her gaze on him. She knew he was lying about the fireworks, but at least she was keeping quiet about it. Later he would tell her the real reason for his caution, if only to make sure she fell in line with all his plans. Though he hated to alarm her unduly.

"In any case," he went on, "everyone will have the morning and afternoon to enjoy other pleasures on the estate. We've got fishing and—" He caught himself before he could say "shooting." That wasn't wise, either, under the circumstances. "Swimming. Also, the drives around the estate provide some lovely views. Or if you prefer to ride, I have a number of suitable mounts."

Pontalba brightened. "That sounds most amiable. I do enjoy a stirring gallop." He looked over at Monique. "What do you say, Princess? Shall we go for a ride in the morning?"

She flashed the duke a gorgeous smile. "I would be delighted, Your Grace. Her ladyship told me there's a man-made waterfall on the grounds, and I should very much like to see it."

Gregory was stewing over the idea that she actually meant to go off with the duke alone when his mother said, "And perhaps the count and Mr. Danworth would accompany me and Lady Ursula into Canterbury for some shopping."

"Good God, Mother, I *just* said—"

"You also just said that nothing actually happens until late afternoon. Which is true. There will be a few ragged boys dragging their effigies around asking for a coin 'for the Guy,' but it's not wild, the way it is in London. And since the two most important members of your party— the duke and the princess—are going riding, why shouldn't we have a taste of town? We'll come back before dinner." She batted her eyelashes at the count. "That is, if the count is willing to accompany us."

"I would be most honored," Beaumonde said, and took her hand to kiss it.

Gregory bristled. What the devil was going on between his mother and the count? If the damned fellow thought that buttering up Mother would influence Gregory's vote for Princess Aurore, he had another think coming.

"Actually," Lady Ursula said from across the table, "I would much rather just stay in your lovely house, Lady Fulkham, if you don't mind. You have quite an extensive library, and I'd like nothing more than to explore it."

"Of course, if you wish."

Hmm. Was Lady Ursula's true reason for staying behind to make sure she got to see Prince Leopold alone? This got more curious by the moment.

"That leaves me," Gregory said. "I suppose I'll be going riding with Pontalba and the princess."

"Don't be silly," Monique said, a hint of frost in her tone. "I'm sure you have many matters to take care of at the estate after your long absence from it."

"Not so many that I can't enjoy a rousing ride." He lifted an eyebrow at Pontalba. "You don't mind if I join you and Her Highness, do you, old chap?"

Pontalba blinked, obviously aware that he'd

landed in the middle of something beyond his ken. "Certainly not. Fine by me."

Damned arse had *better* say that. Because Pontalba had to know that it was more important not to offend the undersecretary of the foreign office than to cozy up to the princess, no matter what the duke's romantic interests.

"Then it's settled," Gregory said smoothly, ignoring Monique's daggered glance. He was bloody well *not* letting her go off alone with anyone, no matter what the reason. He had to keep her safe.

This isn't about keeping her safe, and you know it, his damned conscience said. *This is about jealousy, pure and simple.*

Perhaps. But he was not allowing her out of his sight if there was even a remote chance that something could happen to her. And that was that.

As she pled a headache and slipped out of the drawing room after dinner, Monique was seething. Between Gregory and her great-uncle, she felt like one of those mythical angels dancing on the head of a pin. One minute she had to pacify the count. The next minute she had to hold Gregory and his suspicions at bay. What in creation did they *want* from her?

She snorted. She knew what Gregory wanted

from her—a convenient mistress, no doubt. Once he exposed her, he knew she'd have nowhere to go but to him.

But then, why hadn't he exposed her right away?

Because of his cursed ambition, that was all. He needed this conference to be successful.

I risk my ambition more with every hour I let this masquerade go on.

She knew that was true. He could have exposed her that first night, yet he hadn't. And even after she'd offered him her body . . .

I told you I will not let you barter your body for my silence.

A sigh escaped her as she climbed the stairs toward her bedchamber. He was such an enigma. He desired her, but his conscience resisted. She'd never met a man who would do that. And just when she thought she knew exactly who he was, he did or said something that reduced all her convictions about his character to rubble.

His mother's tales rose in her mind. A prankster? The self-controlled Gregory? How could that be?

Then again, he had also enjoyed showing her a knot garden he'd known she would appreciate. Had roused her body *and* her mind, making her wish for what had never troubled her sleep before.

What was she to make of him?

Men! They were a plague upon women.

She reached the second floor, and as if to punctuate her very thoughts, Gregory stepped out of a room into the hallway. Had he been waiting for her? Why wasn't he still in the dining room with the other gentlemen?

"In here," he snapped, and pulled her into the room.

When he released her and moved away, she took the time to look around. It was clearly a study, done up in beautiful polished mahogany and brass accents. The study of a rich man, confident in his importance. In his wealth and power.

And yet . . . "Your curtains are lavender," she said inanely.

He froze, then followed her gaze. "They're purple," he protested. "I like purple. Reminds me of royalty."

She snorted. It was a very *light* purple— lavender or lilac. Hardly the color of royalty. It reminded her yet again that he had sides to him she couldn't fathom, like a faceted gem with shimmering depths.

At her silence, he sharpened his tone. "It's an appropriate color for entertaining *you*, don't you think, Your Serene Highness?"

"There's no need to mock me," she said, choking down her hurt at the pointed barb. "I didn't choose this. Trust me, if I'd had a choice of roles, I wouldn't have chosen that of an ingénue like Aurore."

"No." His eyes blazed at her. "The role of an

artless, simple girl doesn't suit you. You play the seductress much better. As Pontalba can attest."

His bitter tone startled her. She strode right up to him. "Are you jealous?"

"Of that self-important scoundrel?" Contempt laced his words. "Hardly."

"Then why did you insist on going with us tomorrow morning?"

He stared her down. "Have you forgotten that you're in danger? Do you even know *how* to ride? It doesn't seem like a skill an actress would acquire."

"On the contrary. My grandmother could ride quite well, so she learned how to perform a few horse tricks with Grandpapa's troupe. When I was a girl she incorporated me into her act, so yes, I *do* know how to ride, your lofty lordship."

"Still, you shouldn't risk your life to—"

"We've already established that the duke is an unlikely assassin. And you keep insisting that I'm safe on your estate."

A sullen scowl knit his brow. "That doesn't mean I trust the arse."

She thrust her face up into his. "Admit it: Your insinuating yourself into the situation has nothing to do with concern for my safety. It's about your not wanting me for yourself, but not wanting anyone else to have me, either."

"What?" He caught her about the waist, his eyes alight. "You have no idea what I want." His gaze scoured her a long moment, finally coming to rest on her mouth, and he lowered his voice to a ragged murmur. "No bloody idea at all."

When he looked as if he might kiss her, she fought the swirling need that pooled in her belly at just being in his arms and wrenched free of him. "Oh, I think I do. You want to have your cake and eat it, too. You want me in your bed, but not in your life or your heart."

"Do you think *Pontalba* wants you in his life and his heart?"

The clear jealousy in his tone made her want to provoke him. "Perhaps."

That didn't seem to sit well with him. "Do you desire him?"

No, she thought. *Fool that I am, I desire* you, *you thickheaded dolt.* But she wouldn't give him the satisfaction of knowing that.

Strolling along the length of his desk, she ran a finger casually over the burnished wood the way she'd run her hand over *his* burnished wood this afternoon.

She waited until she heard his sharp intake of breath before she went on. "You know, I'm not entirely sure *how* I feel about the duke. I'm barely acquainted with him. That's why I intend to ride with him tomorrow. So I can come to know him better." Thinking of the count's remarks earlier, she turned to face Gregory and added in a hard voice, "That's also why I don't want *you* there."

His jaw flexed. "That's a pity. Because I mean to join you whether you want me there or not."

A part of her thrilled to that. But he kept using her real identity to pressure her, and it was time to call his bluff.

She strode toward the door. "I'm tired of this. If you want to expose me, do so. Otherwise, stop bullying me. Or I will reveal the truth myself and take you down with me."

It was a bluff, too; all the power was on his side. But she felt better for saying it.

And, gathering her faux royal dignity about her, she walked out.

Sixteen

Gregory sat at his desk for a long time after Monique left, long after he heard the others come up to their bedchambers. He was supposed to be sifting through a stack of documents requiring his signature, which his mother had conveniently marked so he could skim them quickly.

But his mind kept wandering back to Monique's threats.

If you want to expose me, do so. Otherwise, stop bullying me. Or I will reveal the truth myself and take you down with me.

She had him hemmed in. He could either go along until the masquerade was done, or expose her and risk exposing himself. Granted, he could merely dismiss her as a lying foreign actress, but there would still be a scandal. It would almost certainly ruin his chances at becoming foreign secretary.

Worst of all? He didn't really think she'd do it. He'd backed her into a corner, and she'd lashed out as a wounded animal might.

He snorted. Right. A wounded animal. She had him so tied up in useless emotions like jealousy and anger and desire that he couldn't even see her clearly. Damn her.

Realizing he wouldn't get any more work done tonight, he left his study and went out into the hall. He found his mother standing at the top of the stairs, gazing down them as if into a portal of the past.

The look of sadness on her face made his blood run cold. "Are you all right?"

That pulled her out of her trance. "You're still up?"

"No, I'm walking in my sleep."

She swatted his arm. "Don't be sarcastic. You always do that—make jokes when you're upset."

"I'm not upset," he said through gritted teeth. Not about anything involving her, anyway.

Her expression grew troubled. "Forgive me for telling our guests about your antics at school. I hope it doesn't hurt your career."

That was what she thought had upset him? "I doubt some gossip about my childhood pranks will affect my future, Mother. Don't worry about it."

Glancing down the stairs, she whispered, "I sometimes miss him, even after all these years. Is that wrong?"

He tensed. "Wrong? No. Hard to believe? Yes."

"He wasn't always a monster, you know. In the beginning, when he was mostly sober, we had some good times."

"That must have happened before I was old enough to remember, because I never saw him sober." An anger as old as sin sharpened his tone. "I only ever saw him in a drunken rage—at you, at the servants, at me and John. I only ever saw that fist of his, seconds before it landed on your jaw . . . or stomach or—" He fought for calm, fought to put his emotions back in the box where he kept them. "Why are we talking about this, for God's sake?"

She reached up to touch his cheek. "Because I want you to know I don't blame you."

The words snagged on his memories, making him choke down a flood of remorse. Then he realized where they were and glanced about to see who might be close enough to overhear. "Mother, we can't talk about this here."

"You're right. I'm sorry." She flashed him a wan smile. "I'm not used to having so many people about. But you understand what I'm saying, right?"

That she "sometimes" missed the arse who'd sired Gregory and John and had hit them whenever they'd made a wrong step? That she actually *missed* the arse who'd beaten her whenever he was in his cups, which was most of the time?

Oh, and then there was the fact that she didn't blame her son for defending her that night and shoving his father so that he lost his footing and tumbled down the stairs to his death.

Gregory could scarcely comprehend her train of thought. But then, he'd lost only an abuser when he'd killed his father. She'd lost a husband. Guilt coursed through his veins like a shot of bad whiskey.

"Yes," he said tersely. "I understand."

They stood there a moment in a companionable silence, both of them lost in the past as his father's ghost hovered between them.

Then he shook off the chill that gave him. Her mention of Father had reminded him of what he'd learned yesterday. "As long as you insist upon discussing this, I have something I should warn you about." Leading her into the study, he closed the door. "Someone has been asking in town about Father's death."

She blanched. "Who?"

"I don't know. But you need to be very cautious about what you say to people. Has anyone asked *you* about it?"

"Not lately, no." She thrust out her chin. "And even if they did, it's not as if I'm going to tell them that my son killed his father, accidentally or otherwise."

He sighed. There were times when *he* wondered what his motives had been that night. Had he merely been defending Mother with that shove? Or had he acted with the full intention of killing his father?

He could never be sure, and the thought often plagued his nights. "Just be careful, all right?" he told her.

"You be careful, too."

That took him by surprise. "When have I ever *not* been careful?"

"Not about *that*," she said with a wave of her hand. Her gaze turned sly. "Careful about the princess."

Crossing his arms over his chest, he said, "What do you mean?"

"You *know* what I mean. You fancy her."

Oh, God, now even his *mother* could tell how he felt about Monique? "Don't be absurd. She's from a royal line extending back for generations. She would never be able to marry a mere English baron, no matter what his political position."

"Which is why I said to be careful. Because I think she fancies you, too. And if the two of you are involved—"

"That will never happen," he clipped out. Remembering what Monique herself had said, he added, "Nothing can ever come of a . . . er . . . friendship between me and Princess Aurore."

Again he considered telling his mother about the attempt on Monique's life, but something held him back. There was no need to go that far; Mother wasn't in any kind of danger. Besides, he wasn't sure he could trust himself to discuss the situation impartially, and whatever he let slip would only fuel her suspicions concerning him and Monique.

Clearly unconvinced, she cast him a searching glance.

He knew better than to fall prey to *that*. "Good night, Mother," he said firmly.

She hesitated before stretching up to kiss his cheek. "Good night, son." Then she left.

A short while later, Gregory went off to bed himself. But he rose the next morning in a foul mood, having tossed and turned most of the night.

He'd had no luck the evening before in cornering Lady Ursula to find out why she was so fixed on the arrival of Prince Leopold, so he'd hoped to encounter her this morning. But she was still abed, and Monique and Pontalba had headed outside a while ago to choose their mounts for their ride.

Bloody hell. He had best join them before the impudent female decided to go off alone with the duke. Gregory meant to protect her from Pontalba, no matter what.

Are you jealous?

Damned right he was. He *hated* that. It made him behave like an ungoverned fool, which he'd fought most of his life to avoid. Yet the thought of her and Pontalba together . . .

Christ, he wouldn't think about it. It didn't matter.

And where the devil was Hart? He should have been back from Dieppe by now. Not that Gregory didn't believe Monique's tale about why she was doing this. When she'd spoken of her grandmother, her emotions had been palpable. Still, he wanted to confirm her tale.

Because when it came to Monique, his cock was definitely leading him . . . right down the garden path to hell.

Scowling, he descended the steps of the manor house to find the groom holding his horse while she and Pontalba waited for him on mounts that were clearly growing restless.

Today she was resplendent in a riding habit of brownish-purple crushed velvet, with a jaunty top hat of pink silk that had a strip of lavender gauze streaming from it.

Whoever had picked out her clothes certainly did like pink. But after last night's discussion, he had to wonder if she'd chosen the purple gown just for him.

God, he really was becoming besotted. "Ready for a ride, I see," he said, hoping he sounded nonchalant.

"It's a lovely day for it," Pontalba said. "Don't you agree, Princess?"

"*Certainement*," she said absently, searching Gregory's face with an acute gaze that made him uncomfortable. "Monsieur, you do not look at all well this morning. Are you sure you wish to ride?"

Ride? God, yes. Unfortunately, his mare wasn't what he wanted to ride. "I'm fine, Your Highness. Merely distracted by affairs of state involving this damned conference."

She took his meaning at once and colored fetchingly, rousing heat in all the wrong places. "Yes, I'm sure that such matters often distract you."

Climbing into the saddle, he muttered, "You have no idea."

"Still," she said, "you must be used to it by now."

Blackmail? Impostors? His career teetering on the knife's edge of destruction? Hardly. "Certain things, one never gets used to." He prodded his horse into a walk. "Shall we?"

"Lead on, sir," the duke said. "I am most eager to see your waterfall."

The sun shone full on the lawn as they headed at a walk for the wilder part of the estate that lay past the woods. He did love his woods in autumn—the cool shadows, the flashes of evergreen and orange and red, the crisp crackle of dead leaves underfoot. A pity they could not ride through them rather than next to them, but since there was no path for it, that would be difficult.

"How far do your woods extend?" Monique asked.

"All the way to the main road. They provide the firewood for the estate. We've got alder, ash, and oak. Some birch. They're also stocked with pheasant and partridge for hunting."

"We should have gone hunting today!" the duke exclaimed. "I do enjoy such sport."

"It's not the season for it," Gregory lied. He wasn't about to give his guests firearms and hope that no one took the opportunity to shoot Monique "accidentally."

"Well, your woods are very green," she said blandly, obviously referring to their conversation yesterday, and Gregory shot her a sharp glance.

The duke said, "Not really, my dear. Just the evergreens and the oaks. They're more orange and brown than anything."

It took all Gregory's effort not to laugh outright.

With a roll of her eyes for Gregory's benefit, Monique pointed to a spot at the end of the woods. "And what is that in the distance?"

"An Ionic temple Mother had built for effect," Gregory said. "To be honest, I've never understood the appeal of follies that do nothing but look pretty and enhance the grounds. A pavilion that one can use is fine. An elegant little chapel, for those who are very religious? Fine. But anything else seems pointless and a bit absurd."

"Yet you don't mind gardens," Monique said, a hint of laughter in her voice. "Even though they too only look pretty and enhance the grounds."

He smiled at her. "Perhaps I like the green as much as certain people I know." When her cheeks pinkened, he added, "Besides, gardens are useful. You can take your exercise in them, grow flowers to cut for the house, and provide herbs for Cook. But what do you do with an Ionic temple?"

Pontalba was watching them in confusion. "If you dislike such ornamental creations, why did you approve the building of this one?"

He shrugged. "Mother needs her little projects to entertain her out here in the country. She isn't much for town, so I don't mind indulging her."

Feeling Monique's gaze on him, he glanced over to find her regarding him with an enigmatic expression. "You're a good son."

"I try to be." He couldn't prevent the edge sharpening his words. "Though, according to my mother, I don't always succeed. If she had her way, I'd be here whenever Parliament isn't in session."

The glint of pity in Monique's eyes, showing that she clearly remembered yesterday's conversation, made him grit his teeth and look away. What in God's name had prompted him to tell her about Father and John?

It was the way she listened, no doubt. She didn't comment or judge. And that seemed to pull things out of him that he kept secret from everyone else.

The conversation petered out then, and for a while the three of them rode in silence.

Then Monique said to Gregory, "If you don't

mind, monsieur, I should like a more vigorous ride. Race you to the temple?"

Gregory was about to say it wasn't a good idea when Pontalba said, "Yes, indeed!" and urged his horse into a canter.

Then he and Monique were off, bolting down the edge of the woods, laughing as they vied for first place.

Bloody hell. The woman would be the death of him yet.

Gregory spurred his own horse into a gallop, determined to stay close to her. He had nearly caught up to them when he heard a noise and saw Monique's pink hat go flying off. Only when her gelding broke into a panicked run did he realize the noise had been a gunshot.

With a sick roiling in his stomach, he goaded his mare into a run, too, determined to reach her before her damned horse threw her. At least she didn't appear to have been hit by the shot. She was crouching low in the saddle and keeping her seat remarkably well. Still . . .

He choked down panic. He had to keep his head about him and pray that he could catch up to her. His mare *was* the quickest, but her gelding was frightened, and fear lent wings to a horse.

As Gregory went thundering past the duke, another shot sounded from close by. He had to get to her!

Pontalba cried, "I'll go find the bastard!" and peeled off, headed for the woods. Gregory had no time to wonder about that, no time even to look back for telltale signs of smoke. He was coming up on Monique now. As he got even with her, he reached over and jerked her onto his mount.

Just in time, too, for a third shot rang out and her gelding went down. The bastard had shot the horse, damn him! Monique gave a little cry, and for a moment he feared she'd been hit. Then she maneuvered herself better onto the saddle between his arms, and he realized she hadn't been.

But that didn't quell his terror. She was still in danger, and if he couldn't get her away . . .

He dug his heels into his mare's sides, desperate for more speed. Monique was shaking, her breath coming in quick, desperate gasps. Like his. He leaned over her, hoping to shield her with his body. Then, with his heart knocking in his chest, he steered his mare toward the temple. At least they could find shelter there.

And he'd heard no more shots. Belatedly, it occurred to him that he shouldn't have let the duke go into the woods alone—Gregory was responsible for Pontalba's safety, too, after all— but right now he could only focus on getting Monique out of danger.

Moments later, they reached the temple. They both slid to the ground. Grabbing her by the hand, he yanked her behind a pillar. The building had no entrance—it really was just for show— but the columns were large enough to block the view of anyone in the woods, and he was certain that was where the shots had come from.

He pinned her against the pillar, wishing he could surround her completely with his body. He barely resisted the urge to run his hands over every inch of her to make sure she was all right. "You're not hurt, are you?"

"*Non*," she whispered, and laid her head against his shoulder.

"Thank God," he said fervently, and pressed a kiss into her hair. "When I saw your hat fall . . ."

He couldn't bear to think what he would have done if that shot had hit home.

They stood there frozen a long while, hardly daring to breathe. But as the moments ticked by and no more shots came, they both began to breathe more easily. He glanced around the edge of the pillar but saw nothing except her horse lying in the field, obviously dead. Damn that villain. Gregory would hunt him down just for that alone.

"Do you think it's safe now?" she whispered.

"Probably. No doubt the duke frightened the shooter off." He drew his head back behind the pillar. "But I'm not taking any chances. We should remain here a while longer."

She nodded. More time passed before she ventured, "Why are they doing this? *Who* is doing this?"

"I wish I knew." His voice hardened. "I'll tell you one thing, though—it wasn't local ruffians

shooting recklessly. They were bloody well aiming for *you*."

"I know." Fear darkened her eyes as she gazed
up at him. "You must have some theories about
who would want Aurore dead."

He thought about telling her of Lady Ursula
and her suspicious—possibly romantic—interest
in Prince Leopold. Then it dawned on him that
the lady-in-waiting had supposedly been in bed
when they'd left. She could have been waiting
for them to leave the house before following
them.

Then there was Pontalba's eagerness to go
after the shooter. What if he'd hired someone to
do the deed and, when the shots hadn't hit their
mark, decided that he'd better silence his accom-
plice?

"I have a few ideas," he said, "but I would
rather investigate them before I speak of them to
anyone." He kissed her brow, his frenzied pulse
having slowed only a little. "First, however, I must
see you safe inside the house."

The sound of hooves approaching made both
of them tense up, and instinctively, he tightened
his grip on her.

"The damned fellow is gone," Pontalba said
from beyond the pillars.

Gregory stuck his head out to stare at the
duke, who looked the worse for wear after
tramping through the woods. "Are you sure?"

Grim-faced, Pontalba nodded. "I followed the

last plume of smoke just in time to see a chap running through the woods for the road. By the time I reached the road myself, no one was there. He must have had a horse waiting, because I saw a spot where the grass was trampled and eaten."

"Did you get a good look at him?" Gregory moved from behind the column, and Monique followed him.

Pontalba shook his head no. "He was wearing a green jacket and a brown hat. That's all I noticed."

Just like the man who'd shot at her in the park. A chill swept down Gregory's spine. The assassin had *followed* her to Kent? That didn't bode well for keeping her safe.

"So it could have been anyone," Gregory said.

"Anyone who could access the estate from the main road, yes." When Monique clutched Gregory's arm, Pontalba added, "Is something going on here that I don't know about?"

Feeling Monique freeze beside him, Gregory shrugged. "Someone shot at me in London." No point in alarming more people than was necessary. Or handing the duke fodder for his argument that his candidate would be the best choice. "I thought it was a random occurrence, but apparently not. I do have enemies, you know."

Pontalba cursed under his breath. "Well, keep your enemies well away from *me*. They could have hit me or my horse as easily as they hit the princess's."

"Indeed," Gregory said. "Which is why I shall have men posted along the road. With any luck, the show of force will be enough to scare the fellow off." He stared down at Monique. "All the same . . . forgive me, Princess, but I fear this will mean no bonfires on the estate tonight. I simply don't have enough servants to protect every part of my land that adjoins the road."

"Certainly not," she murmured. "You must keep your guests safe."

He must keep *her* safe. "Precisely. Which is why we should all return to the house now."

"Absolutely," Pontalba said. "I must change out of these clothes, anyway." Pasting on his usual courtly expression, he turned to Monique. "If you prefer to use my mount, Your Highness, I don't mind walking."

"She'll be riding with me." Gregory wasn't sure Pontalba was involved in the attempts on her life, but he wasn't taking any chances. "No need to wait for us. With two riders on one horse, it will take us a while to return."

Pontalba bowed, then jumped back into his saddle and rode off. Clearly, he wasn't as eager to act the part of gentleman with a gunman possibly still roaming the woods.

"Do you think it's safe to return?" Monique asked him.

"Probably. Though we should take a different route."

She nodded.

He headed over to where his mare grazed contentedly near the temple. His pulse had slowed to a normal pace, but every time he thought of how close she'd come to death . . .

"Gregory?" she said behind him.

He turned to look at her. "Yes?"

Her eyes shone bright with emotion. "Thank you for saving my life. Again."

Despite everything, his heart flipped over in his chest. "You're welcome."

He could only pray it was the last attempt. Because next time she might not be so lucky.

Even after they had returned to the house, Monique couldn't stop shaking. It had become abundantly clear to her that no matter what her uncle said, someone was trying to kill Aurore. Had probably *been* trying since before Monique's involvement.

After leading her to a settee in the drawing room, Gregory pressed a glass of sherry on her, and she gladly sat and sipped it as he questioned the servants. From them, they learned that no one had returned from Canterbury yet. That the duke was upstairs in his bedchamber and had called for a bath. That the prince hadn't yet arrived.

And, more disturbing, that Lady Ursula had left to go for a walk right after they'd headed out for their ride.

When that made Gregory curse, Monique felt her heart sink. She gulped down the rest of her sherry. It couldn't be. How could the lady-in-waiting be involved? Lady Ursula was her *friend*, for pity's sake!

Gregory barked some orders to the footmen, sending one of them for the constable. As they left to do his bidding, he came to sit next to her on the settee, looking solemn. "That day when we went for a drive, I thought it was the count's decision to have Lady Ursula not accompany you. I assumed he wanted to throw us together for his own purposes. But now I'm not so sure." Taking her hand, he searched her face. "You seemed surprised that day to hear she was ill. Had you had any indication of that before our carriage ride?"

"No," she said, her heart sinking further.

"She didn't look particularly ill after we returned."

"True. But I just can't believe . . . I can't imagine that she would—"

"I know, it's hard to accept." He squeezed her hand. "But we must consider the possibility, given that she was absent for both shootings, yet near enough that she could have been the one pulling the trigger."

"But . . . but does she even know how to fire a gun?" Monique said. "Besides, everyone who saw the shooter said it was a man!"

"A woman can dress as a man and fool people. Not to mention that she might have hired an assassin. This morning she could easily have gone off to tell her henchman what time we left. Whoever shot at you already knew that we'd be riding to the waterfall this morning. And there's only one path to get there, so it would have been easy for the man to lie in wait."

"Yes, but *why*? Why would she do it?"

"I have an idea. But first, has she said *anything* to you about her feelings concerning the union of Prince Leopold and Aurore?"

She thought back to her brief conversation with Lady Ursula that day. "All I remember is her saying that Aurore didn't want to marry. That's why she turned down Prince Leopold's offer."

"Did she say why?"

Monique was trying to recall the details of the conversation when Lady Ursula herself burst into the drawing room.

"The servants told me someone fired a gun at you again!" she said, hurrying over to Monique. "Are you all right?"

It was hard not to notice the leaves clinging to her skirts, or her disheveled appearance. Monique wanted to cry. Could Gregory be right about her?

Gregory rose to put himself between Lady Ursula and Monique. "Where have you been?"

She gaped at him. "I was walking through your gardens. Why?"

Aware that his staff could be listening, he walked over to shut the door, then leaned against it to glare at her. "Because you've been absent both times the princess has been fired upon. You seem inordinately interested in a possible union between Princess Aurore and Prince Leopold. And you are the *only* one who keeps asking about when he will arrive. Tell me—is that mere coincidence?"

Lady Ursula blinked. "What are you insinuating?"

"That you're jealous of Princess Aurore's hold over the prince because you want him for yourself."

Such a motive hadn't occurred to Monique.

Apparently, it hadn't occurred to Lady Ursula either. "What?! I can assure you I have no designs on my cousin. We're like sister and brother!"

Pushing away from the door, Gregory advanced upon her. "Then you should explain why you were so intent upon having him here at my estate."

His words reminded Monique of something the lady-in-waiting had said a few days ago. "You told me that the one you loved couldn't marry you." Monique rose to stand beside Gregory. "Was that Leopold?"

Lady Ursula stared at the two of them united, and her face crumpled. "No, it wasn't Leopold."

Monique glared at her. "I don't believe you."

"It wasn't him!" Lady Ursula wrung her hands. "I can't tell you who it was."

"You'd better," Gregory snapped. "Because I won't stand by and let you hurt Monique."

"Monique?" Lady Ursula looked shocked. "You know who she is?"

Keeping the secret hardly seemed to matter anymore, now that Monique's life was in danger. "He knows." She drew in a ragged breath. "He's always known. As it happens, he met me three years ago in Dieppe when he saw me play Suzanne in *The Marriage of Figaro*. So the first day he 'met' me as Princess Aurore, he recognized me."

Lady Ursula blanched, then dropped into the nearest chair. "*Mein Gott.*"

It was the only time Monique had heard her speak in her native tongue. "That's why I've been trying to avoid him all this time. That's why I wanted you to keep him at bay."

"And I failed you," Lady Ursula whispered.

"In more ways than one, if you're behind these shootings," Gregory bit out.

"What? I'm not! How can you even think so?"

"Because you keep asking about Prince Leopold." Monique wrapped her arms about her waist. "You're the one who insisted on including the prince in this house party. No matter what you say, I can only assume it's because *he's* the one you love and can never have."

"No, no, no . . ." Lady Ursula was chanting, burying her head in her hands.

"If not him, then whom did you mean?" Monique pressed her.

The lady-in-waiting slumped in her seat. "You won't understand."

"You must tell us," Gregory demanded. "Otherwise, I shall assume that you and Leopold—"

"Aurore!" Her voice fell to a ragged whisper. "The one I can't have is Aurore."

"What the devil?" Gregory said.

"She's the one I can't marry, the one I love with every breath of my soul." Lady Ursula looked at them with bleak pain in her face. "I was always only talking about Aurore."

And to Monique's shock, the young woman burst into tears.

Seventeen

Gregory could only stare at the poor woman disbelievingly. "But if you weren't bent on gaining Prince Leopold for yourself, then why were you so obsessed with his interest in Aurore?" Even as the words left his mouth, the truth dawned on him. "Ah—you saw him as your rival for the princess's affections."

Lady Ursula nodded through her sobs, her face wracked in a private agony he could well imagine, given his own obsession with Monique.

Meanwhile, Monique just gaped at him. "I don't understand. I know that she loves Aurore, but—"

"It's not a sisterly kind of love, *ma chérie*," Gregory explained. It still amazed him how naïve and unworldly Monique could be sometimes. "She's *in* love with Aurore."

In his line of work, it wasn't unheard of. Granted, it was slightly more common for men to be enamored of other men, but he'd certainly encountered women who loved women in a romantic way.

Though many of his peers found such a love distasteful, he wasn't one of them. Too many years skirting the edges of society as he performed the tasks of his dark, secretive business had taught him that there were all kinds of love in the world. And given his own past crimes, he could hardly throw stones at someone for the "crime" of loving a person of the same sex.

Lady Ursula fought to compose herself. "I—I love Aurore as . . . as another woman might love a m-man." She met Gregory's gaze. "I've loved her for years."

The look on Monique's face told him she comprehended now. "That's why you begged not to be forced to leave her. Why you resisted coming here."

The lady-in-waiting bobbed her head. "She was ill. I wanted to stay with her and take care of her." Her voice hardened. "But of course the count wouldn't allow it. He and Aurore's mother have never approved of our . . . friendship."

"You mean, they *know*?" Gregory put in.

"Not everything," Lady Ursula admitted. "They think we're merely too close, that I'm the one who influenced her to refuse Leopold." She brushed tears from her cheeks. "And I suppose that's true. But I didn't convince her of anything she didn't already feel. She didn't want him." A softness entered her voice. "She wants *me*."

"So she shares your feelings?" Gregory asked.

Lady Ursula nodded. "We . . . we have been in love for years." She sighed. "Not that anything can come of it. We could never rule Chanay together the way she would like. Still, she remains adamant that she will have no *man* for a husband. That she loves only me." She cast Monique a helpless glance. "I'm sorry—I should have told you, but I thought . . . I was afraid—"

"That I wouldn't understand." Monique flashed her a wan smile. "I confess that I really don't. But that doesn't mean you're wrong. What I still don't comprehend is why were you pushing to have the prince come here if not to gain him for yourself?"

Lady Ursula shrugged. "I needed to find out why he was considering renewing his suit to Aurore. She'd refused him because unlike some men she might marry, Leopold would never countenance a wife who—"

"Was in love with someone else," Gregory finished.

"Exactly. I know him well enough to be sure of that." She scowled. "So I honestly thought he and Aurore had parted ways for good. Then Mr. Danworth told me that Leopold was interested in approaching Aurore again."

"Wait a minute," Gregory broke in. "I thought Danworth was asking you to *confirm* Leopold's interest."

She blinked. "Why would he ask *me?* I mean,

Leopold and I are related and were friends long ago, but I have only seen him a few times since he took up residence in England. I assumed that Danworth knew something I didn't, since Danworth knows him better, is friendly with him."

It was Gregory's turn to be shocked. "What do you mean, 'friendly'?"

Lady Ursula shrugged. "They've known each other for years. I believe they became boon companions after Leopold married Princess Charlotte."

His mind reeling, Gregory roamed the room and tried to make sense of her claims. There was a close connection between Danworth and Leopold? Hard to believe. Then again, Gregory had still been at university at the time—it wasn't as if he could have known.

So what was Danworth's game now? Why would he lie and say he wanted to confirm the "rumors" about Leopold renewing his interest in Aurore if all he'd had to do was ask Leopold?

Unless Danworth thought that stirring such rumors would make Leopold a more attractive candidate. Which begged the question—how far would Danworth go to help his friend?

Would he stoop to murder? It seemed unlikely. What could he gain from it except Leopold's gratitude? That was rather far to go for such a thing.

Still, the merest possibility of it made Gregory uneasy.

Lady Ursula was watching him with avid interest. "What about the count? Does he know about your . . . past association with Monique?"

Damn. Now he had to explain all *that*.

"Of course not," Monique said. "If he did, I'd already be headed back to Dieppe. And you mustn't tell him, either. It wasn't my fault that his lordship met me before I came here. I've done everything my uncle asked, and my grand-mother deserves her reward."

"Absolutely," Lady Ursula said in a placating tone. "If you keep my secret about Aurore from him, I will keep yours."

That reminded Gregory of something. "Are you sure that Beaumonde is unaware of the full extent of your feelings for the princess? Is it possible he's hoping to put Monique in Aurore's place because Aurore refuses to marry?"

Lady Ursula gaped at him. "Then why have someone shoot at Monique?"

"Good point." Gregory scrubbed a hand over his face. Today's attempt had rattled him so much, he wasn't thinking straight. "It's unlikely there are two assassins—one for Aurore and one for Monique."

Lady Ursula smoothed her skirts. "And you're assuming that Aurore's illness was caused by poison. It might just be cholera."

Gregory stared her down. "You don't believe that, and neither do I. It's too much of a coincidence that someone would make two attempts on Monique's life no more than two weeks after Princess Aurore falls deathly ill."

"True." Worry furrowed Lady Ursula's forehead. "But I don't see how anyone could have poisoned her. We were always with her."

Monique went to sit beside the woman. "It would be easy enough to slip something into even a princess's food, especially in a hotel. And how would you know?"

As usual, Monique went right to the heart of the matter. Gregory stared at the lady-in-waiting. "Is there anything that Princess Aurore preferred to drink or eat that no one else generally partook of?"

Lady Ursula shook her head, then paused. "Actually, she did always like hot chocolate before bed." She lifted her gaze to him. "But I was the one to fetch it."

"And who gave it to you?"

"Someone in the hotel's kitchen."

"The same person every night?" he prodded.

"We were only there one night before Aurore fell ill." Lady Ursula frowned. "But come to think of it, the kitchen maid who gave it to me wasn't there the next evening when I went to fetch wine for Aurore in hopes that it would settle her stomach. Indeed, I never saw the maid again."

Gregory nodded grimly. "There you go. Find that maid, and we find who poisoned Aurore. Or was paid to poison her."

Lady Ursula had gone deathly pale. "That means *I* was the one to hurt Aurore!" She burst into tears. "I—I put the p-poison in her hands m-myself!"

Monique laid her arm around the woman's shoulders. "You couldn't have known what was in the chocolate. It wasn't your fault."

Pacing the room, Gregory thought through everything they knew so far. "I somehow doubt that even the maid knew fully what she was doing. She was probably paid by someone. And the assassin hung around until he got word that Aurore was ill. Then he likely saw no point in remaining there to watch her die."

"If that's true," Monique said, "he must have been shocked to see me show up at the conference."

"Indeed," Gregory said. "Which would explain why he then set out to kill you. He thinks you're Aurore. He thinks she survived somehow, and he's trying to finish what he started."

"Even if he knows I'm *not* Aurore," Monique said, "he might want me gone to make sure no one from Chanay takes the Belgian throne."

"No," Gregory said firmly. "If he knew about the masquerade, he could just expose you and be done with it. So he has to be operating under the assumption that you're Aurore. It's her he's trying to eliminate."

He faced the two women with a scowl. "Which is why, Monique, you have to withdraw from the conference and return to Dieppe. Make up some excuse for why you no longer want to be ruler of Belgium. It's too dangerous for you to keep playing Aurore."

"You *know* I can't do that!" she cried as she jumped up.

He gestured in Lady Ursula's direction. "You don't owe her and the count *anything*. For all we know, Beaumonde was perfectly aware that Aurore had been poisoned, which is why he put you in her place."

"That's not true!" Lady Ursula rose to face him. "I didn't know, and I'm almost certain he didn't, either. Cholera is running rampant across the Continent, so we assumed that she contracted it along with everyone else."

"Yet no one else in your party has fallen ill," he ground out.

Lady Ursula glanced away. "That doesn't mean that she was poisoned. Count de Beaumonde hopes every day for her recovery from the disease. I have heard him say so."

"And he never lies." Gregory snorted his disbelief. "Do you think he really wants to watch his great-niece rule Chanay—or Belgium—without an heir? He's too much of a politician not to know about Aurore's intention never to marry. And he would not allow that."

"You're wrong!" Lady Ursula insisted. "He's Aurore's uncle first. He wouldn't wish to see her hurt."

"To be honest, I don't care what happens to Aurore," he said hoarsely. "I only care about

Monique." The vehemence in his words seemed to catch both women off guard.

Not surprising, since it damned well shocked *him*. But he pressed on, forcing coldness into his tone to hide the terror swirling in his blood. "And if she continues in this masquerade, she risks her very life. I won't allow it. It would put a permanent stain on these proceedings." He dragged in a heavy breath. "So if she doesn't abandon her masquerade and return to Dieppe, then you both force me to expose her."

Monique only stared at him with a look of pure betrayal, but Lady Ursula cried, "You can't! If you do, it will ruin the count and me *and* Aurore, not to mention Monique. We'll be mocked by all of Europe. And Chanay will never recover from the embarrassment."

"Embarrassment!" he cried. "Do you not understand? Monique could *die*, for God's sake. She nearly died today. And I refuse to stand by and watch her murdered!"

A rap came at the door, startling all of them.

"What is it?" he barked.

There was a moment's silence, before a timid voice said, "Captain Lord Hartley is here to see you, my lord."

Gregory fought to steady his pounding heart. "It's about bloody time," he growled as he strode for the door and swung it open, making the footman jump. "Put him in my study, and tell him I shall be there directly."

He doubted that Hart had anything substantial to add to his information, but at least the man could confirm how much of what Monique had told him was the truth.

Not that Gregory didn't believe her. He clearly had gone far beyond insanity, because he believed every word out of her mouth.

Though he still wasn't entirely sure he could trust the rest of the group from Chanay. Turning on the women, who stood together as if preparing to fight him, he ordered, "Stay here. We're not done with this discussion. Do you understand me?"

Eyes widening, they nodded.

And with his temper thoroughly roused, he marched out.

❧

As soon as Gregory was gone, Monique sank onto the settee. "What shall we do? He'll ruin everything."

Lady Ursula sat down and took her hand. "I don't think so. It's clear he cares about you too much to do that."

Monique wished she could believe the woman. But Gregory's threats had struck a chill to her soul. "He wants me in his bed, that's all. Once he gains that, he'll pack me off to Dieppe without a thought, the way he has packed his mother off here to run his estate without him." A thickness clogged Monique's throat. "His lordship . . . doesn't like to let people too close."

"Really?" Lady Ursula squeezed her hand. "He kept your secret all this time when he didn't have to."

"Only because he wasn't sure it was me."

She snorted. "Perhaps. But he could have confronted the three of us privately, and he didn't."

I risk my ambition more with every hour I let this masquerade go on. Even if I did agree to your terms and keep silent, I can't prevent someone else's unmasking you. And if it comes out that I knew the truth and didn't speak, I'll be ruined.

Monique shook off the tantalizing thought that he'd kept silent out of concern for her. "He behaved cautiously, as he always does, probably to avoid the risk of being wrong. His future in politics is at stake, apparently."

"Still, I saw real terror on his face when he spoke of not letting you be murdered. I think he cares more than you know. Perhaps even more than *he* will admit."

Monique stared down at their joined hands. "Even if he does, it makes no difference. Gregory—" She caught herself. "Lord Fulkham could never marry me. I am one of those actresses beyond the pale whom he spoke of at dinner last night."

"I don't know; I think you're wrong. But if you're not . . ." Lady Ursula sighed. "We must find a way to convince him not to expose you."

"I can't imagine how. I already offered to share his bed in exchange for his silence."

"My dear!" Lady Ursula cried, clearly shocked. "I should hope there's no need to do *that*. Unless you really *want* to join with him, of course."

She avoided Lady Ursula's penetrating gaze. "I—I wouldn't mind so much, actually." Oh, who was she fooling? She would eagerly share his bed, if only to experience the thrill of having been his, even for a short while. "But he refused my offer. He said that bedding me as some sort of . . . payment for his acquiescence in the masquerade would be akin to rape."

"Did he? Interesting." Lady Ursula looked pensive. "It appears that our ruthless Lord Fulkham is actually a gentleman when it comes to women. I suppose I should believe it, given what they say about him."

"What do they say?"

"That he has no mistress, which is odd for a bachelor. But apparently his position in the foreign office takes precedence over anything else." She leaned close. "And Mr. Danworth says he's been looking for a wife to cement his future."

"Of course he has." A quick flash of pain hit her heart. If anyone knew about Gregory's ambition, it was she.

"But that's mostly idle gossip. You know how rumors start in society."

Monique knew how they started in the theater, and she doubted that society was much different. But she also knew that a man like Gregory had to have a wife . . . one who was respectable.

Then something else Lady Ursula had said struck her. She stared at the lady-in-waiting. "Why do you call him 'ruthless'?"

Lady Ursula shrugged. "The count says he has a reputation for doing whatever it takes to achieve his political goals." She leaned close to whisper, "I've also heard it said that he is unofficially a spymaster."

Monique gaped at her. "Really?"

"Supposedly he has any number of fellows who do his bidding, seeking out secrets and such."

Her stomach sank. Gregory had practically said as much the last time he'd confronted her about her identity. And Lord Hartley was one of his spies. Still, he could scarcely have learned anything new about her in Dieppe. She'd already told Gregory everything.

She swallowed. That didn't mean Lord Hartley couldn't have uncovered some nasty gossip. There were plenty of untruths about her circulating in Dieppe—about her supposed lovers, about her supposed weakness for drink . . . all the vile things people said concerning actresses. What if Lord Hartley had encountered that sort of information and Gregory believed it?

A servant entered the room and bowed low. "His lordship would like to speak to you in his study, Princess."

With her heart in her throat, Monique rose. "Of course."

Lady Ursula stood as well. "I am not letting you face him alone."

"Thank you." The more she knew of Lady Ursula, the more she liked her. And she could use the moral support.

They followed the footman to Gregory's study, but before they could be ushered inside, the door opened and a man came out. She instantly recognized the burly fellow with dark brown hair and a flirtatious smile.

"Mademoiselle Servais," he said, bowing. "How good to see you again."

She nodded stiffly. "Captain Lord Hartley. I hope your trip went well?"

Shuttering his features, he glanced from her to Lady Ursula. "Well enough."

Monique swallowed. No telling what horrible things he'd dug up in Dieppe.

Gregory appeared in the doorway. "Come in," he said, his expression tense.

That made her even more nervous.

As soon as she and Lady Ursula entered, he closed the door and turned to her, his eyes as icy as the frozen reaches of the far north. "When the hell were you going to tell me that you're third in line for the throne of Chanay?"

Eighteen

Gregory watched Monique to see her reaction, unsure what to expect. He was taken by surprise when she gaped at him.

"What are you talking about? I'm not . . . I can't be . . ."

He pressed his advantage. "According to the fellow left in charge of your grandmother, *she* is second in line for the throne. Which makes you third."

At least the part about the grandmother had proved to be true. Hart had found out from friends of Monique's that Princess Solange had grown increasingly ill over the past year. That Monique had been desperate to find help for her.

But the other part . . .

He went on in a harder tone. "First in line is your grandmother's older sister, who is doddering on the edge of the grave, as is, apparently, your grandmother. Once they both pass on, *you* are the successor. After Princess Aurore, of course."

There was no mistaking Monique's shock. "That's impossible."

Lady Ursula gave a heavy sigh. "She didn't know. Trust me, she had no idea."

Gregory crossed his arms over his chest. "And why the devil should I trust *you* when you've been keeping secrets all along?"

"Because I have nothing to gain by telling you this," the young woman said stoutly. "The count told me we were not to tell her how far up she was in the succession. He was"—she cast an apologetic glance at Monique—"afraid she might take advantage of the knowledge."

"I can well imagine." Gregory focused his attention on Lady Ursula. "If Monique had known she was essentially next in line—assuming that Princess Aurore didn't survive the poisoning—she might not have been so eager to follow the rules that you and the count set for her."

"Me!" Lady Ursula exclaimed. "I just do as I'm told."

"Except when it comes to Princess Aurore."

The woman's face fell. "Yes. I would do anything for Aurore."

Now he felt as if he were beating up a puppy. God, both women were driving him mad.

Monique still hadn't seemed to grasp the truth of the situation. "I—I don't understand." She glanced from him to Lady Ursula. "How can I be third in line? Grand-maman had three siblings. Surely they all had children."

Lady Ursula shook her head. "Actually, no. The count and his princess wife were unable to produce a child. Aurore's grandfather had one son, the previous Prince of Chanay, who only sired Aurore. And your grandmother's other sister has been a spinster all her life. So with your parents dead and your having no siblings, *you* are the only descendant of the new generation, aside from Aurore."

"You're sure," Monique said.

"Of course I'm sure!" Lady Ursula drew in a calming breath. "If Aurore dies, your grandmother will be heir apparent until her seventy-two-year-old sister dies. And given that your grandmother is ailing . . ."

"When *she* dies, Monique will become Princess de Chanay," Gregory finished.

Clearly, no one had explained it all to Monique. There was no mistaking her reaction at hearing that she was essentially next in line for the throne of Chanay. Not even the best actress in the world could fake the astonishment on her face.

"*That's* why the count has been keeping track of my family's whereabouts all this time," Monique breathed. "*Mon Dieu.*"

She looked as if she might faint. Hurrying to her side, Gregory offered her a chair, which she took, clearly in a state of shock.

"If you would leave us, Lady Ursula," he said, "I need to speak to Monique alone."

The lady-in-waiting crossed her arms over her chest. "I'm not going anywhere without her."

"It's a bit late to be trying to protect her, don't you think?" he ground out. "Until now, you've abandoned her every time you thought it would suit the count's purposes."

The young woman bristled. "Now see here—"

"Besides," he cut in, "I just received a message that the prince is scarcely an hour away, give or take thirty minutes. And you did want to speak to him alone before everyone else returns from town, didn't you?"

"It's fine, Lady Ursula," Monique added. "I think I can be trusted to spend a few moments alone with his lordship."

Lady Ursula looked conflicted. But in the end, she nodded and left the room. Clearly, if the choice was between seeing to her true love's welfare or Monique's, she would choose Princess Aurore every time.

Gregory shut the door to the study, his heart pounding as he saw the lost expression on her face. It tugged at his sympathies. "What am I to do with you, my sweet?"

She glanced up at him warily. "I don't know, my lord." Rising to walk over to the window, she stared out. "I don't know anything anymore."

He understood; the news had certainly caught him off guard. Mother's remarks last night stuck in his head. Who could have known that her warning about not taking up with a princess might have proved sound?

Because she truly *was* a prospective princess,

which meant she could never be his. Unless Aurore lived, in which case he might have a chance . . .

He cursed under his breath. The last thing he needed was a woman who would turn his life upside down. He had too much to accomplish. She would be wrong for him in every way.

Yet he didn't care. He wanted her in his bed. And, God help him, in his *life*. Which was impossible.

"Monique—" he began.

"This changes nothing," she said, whirling to face him. "Perhaps if Aurore dies, it affects things, but if she lives . . ."

Clearly she had thought through all the same paths that he had.

"You're still in danger as long as you pretend to be her," he said.

"I suppose." A sudden softness spread over her face as Monique approached him. "But I have complete faith that you will find the culprit before anything happens to me. You must. Because even if I leave England, the killer will still be at large and might try to murder my cousin again in Chanay."

"Doubtful. Once she is no longer a contender for the throne . . ."

"We can't be *sure* that's why this killer is after Aurore. It might have nothing to do with the conference at all. If what Lord Hartley learned is true, it . . . it might have to do with the succession."

"The only one to benefit from Aurore's death is *you*," he said dryly, "so if it has to do with the succession, then you've been trying to shoot yourself."

She glared at him. "Who is below me? Did Lord Hartley say?"

"There's no one. You are last in the line. Another Prince or Princess of Chanay would have to be chosen, and since that would be a complicated process, no one person could be sure of becoming ruler. So no one has anything to gain yet by shooting both Aurore and you."

"All the same, if I return home before the conference ends, the scoundrel might follow me, assuming I'm Aurore, and unravel the whole deception. Then what? There's a chance we could all be exposed." Her eyes searched his face. "That you could be ruined."

It took all his will to resist the urge to pull her into his arms. "If that should happen, then let the bastard find out you're an actress." Despite his attempt to sound uninvolved, he couldn't stop his fear for her from creeping into his voice. "At least you'd be safe."

"But I'd be back in the same situation as before," she pointed out. "With the count refusing to take me and Grand-maman back into the family."

"Considering your place in the succession, he wouldn't pursue that."

"You don't know that. If Aurore survives—and

she's young and strong, so she might—she could still live a long and healthy life. Despite what Lady Ursula says, Aurore might yet choose to marry and have children. And with each one, my grandmother and I drop further in the succession. Until we know how Aurore is—"

"I've already ordered Hart to Calais to learn that," he ground out. "He leaves at dawn tomorrow morning."

She stared him down. "Then we should wait to act until he returns."

God, the woman would be the death of him yet. "The delegates will vote in four days." Desperate to convince her, he grabbed her by the shoulders. "Whoever is trying to murder you will make damned sure he or she kills you before then."

Frustration lit her features. "For pity's sake, Gregory, do you *want* to see me the mistress of some elderly theater patron? Or whoever proves the highest bidder? Because that's how I will end up if Aurore lives and I have not met the terms of my bargain with the count. He will discard me and Grand-maman like so much trash."

"I don't believe that," he said hoarsely.

"Then you don't know him as well as I do. I must see this out. Please *let* me." Her voice dropped to a whisper. "I know you want me out of your hair as quickly as you can manage, but—"

"You're wrong, damn it." He smoothed his hands down her arms to her waist, unable to stop himself from touching her. "I don't *want* you to leave. But I also don't want you to die."

She cupped his jaw with a touch so tender, it made him groan. "Yet you'd sentence me to a living death with a succession of protectors in Dieppe."

God, what a choice she laid before him. Because she might be right about the count. He simply didn't know. Obviously, the man hadn't paid her branch of the family any attention until now. And he possibly wouldn't pay it any more if Aurore lived, but lost her bid to become queen of Belgium.

Still . . .

"You could be *my* mistress," he said before he reconsidered. "Return to Dieppe and wait for me until this is over and we find out about Aurore. Hart would accompany you and keep you safe before going on to Calais. Then, if Aurore lives and the count cuts you off, I could bring you and your grandmother back to England." His blood ran hot at the very thought of having her as his own. "I could set you both up somewhere—"

"So I could hide away for the rest of my life, to prevent anyone from recognizing me as the woman who'd played Princess Aurore? Because that's what I would have to do to keep from ruining your career." Her breathing grew ragged. "I said I wanted freedom, and you offer me a gilded cage."

The accusation cut him bone-deep as he recognized the fairness of it. Or rather, the unfairness of what he was offering her. "What about if you stay in Dieppe, and I pay for your grandmother's care while you continue in the theater? That's what you want, isn't it?"

She eyed him skeptically. "And you would do that out of the kindness of your heart? For a woman you would never see again?" She caressed his cheek. "Or are you simply proposing to make me your mistress in France?"

Would never see again? The very thought of it made his chest seize up.

His *chest*, not his heart. This was not obsession. Not need. Certainly not love. It was plain, old-fashioned desire.

God, even he wasn't fool enough to believe that.

He caught her hand and pressed a kiss against the palm, then against the spot where he'd once left his mark. When desire leapt in her eyes, he said hoarsely, "And if I were? If I wanted to make you my mistress there?"

"It wouldn't work, and you know it. We'd never see each other. And what would happen when you wish to marry?" When he opened his mouth to protest that, she pressed her finger to his lips. "Don't lie to me or yourself. We both know you must marry eventually and you can't marry *me*. Nor do I want to find myself with a string of by-blows—"

"There are ways to prevent that."

She snorted. "Foolproof ways? Because I've

seen actresses find themselves with child despite using French letters. Besides, I want children eventually. But not ones who will never see their father. I grew up without a father. I don't want that for my own children."

"Instead you want to go to Chanay and marry some . . . cursed fellow your great-uncle picks for you? Or return to Dieppe after your grandmother dies in hopes of marrying some French noble like the duke?"

A sad smile crossed her lips. "Would that bother you so much?"

"Yes," he admitted. "Because part of what you said last night is true. I want no other man to have you."

The moment he spoke the words, he knew they were true. He couldn't bear the idea of her with another man, in marriage or otherwise. He wanted her for his own. And as she'd pointed out numerous times, that would never work.

"You only want me because you haven't had your thirst quenched, my lord." She slipped her hand inside his coat. "But we can easily remedy that."

She was trying to distract him from his insistence that she go back to Dieppe before the vote. Before someone made a successful attempt on her life, which would destroy him.

Yet his cock rose at the thought of having her, even so. The bloody woman was shattering all his control. "Monique—"

"Shh," she whispered as she rose to kiss him. "I want you, too, my lord. Here. Now, while everyone is still in Canterbury and the duke is at his toilette. While I can still have you. Give me this, at least."

He let himself indulge in a long, hot kiss, in the delicious sweetness of her mouth and the tempting softness of her body in his arms. Then he drew back to rasp, "What about your determination not to have any of my . . . by-blows?"

"You said there were ways to prevent it—"

"No foolproof ways," he reminded her.

She untied his cravat and drew it off inch by tantalizing inch. "I will risk it just this once, if only to gain the memory of being with you. That will have to last me a lifetime."

"And afterward, you will agree to return to the Continent with Hart?"

Her answer was to pull his head down to her for another inflaming kiss. It wasn't an answer, but he didn't care anymore. Her remark about his not seeing her again was stuck in his head, and the thought of never having the chance to be with her blotted out the fact that he was a gentleman, that he should not do this, that they could be caught together . . .

Nothing mattered but taking her to bed.

Nineteen

Monique watched Gregory stride to the door and lock it, shedding his coat and waistcoat as he returned to her. She knew this was madness— why this man? Why now, when her life was in upheaval?

But she also knew she wouldn't regret it. For once she would take her pleasure where she could, and to hell with those who would keep her from it.

She watched with avid interest as he took off his shirt, revealing a chest that seemed sculpted of marble, all carved lines and beautiful symmetry. Even the smattering of raven curls over it turned her knees to jelly.

When he caught her staring at him, he gave a low chuckle. "Like what you see, Princess?"

"Perhaps," she said coyly. "Though I want to see more."

Heat flamed in his face like lightning on the

sea, drying the very breath in her throat. "As would I." Gesturing to her riding habit, which fastened in the front, he ordered, "Unbutton it."

His tone of command sent excitement roaring through her, as did the idea of having him watch her remove her clothes. Though she fumbled a little in her haste, she had her riding habit off in a matter of moments, followed by her chemisette.

His gaze seared her as he surveyed her in her corset, chemise, stockings, and riding boots. "God save me," he rasped.

That break in his usual control—and the noticeable thickness in his trousers—freed her to tease him. "Not even God can save you from me, monsieur." With a coquettish smile, she lifted one foot and set it on the chair so she could unlace her half-boot and slide it off. Then she deliberately hitched up her chemise to expose her lacy drawers and garters.

She was rewarded by his harsh intake of breath. Just as she removed her garter and started to take off her stocking, he said hoarsely, "Let me," and walked over to peel it slowly down her leg.

At the same time, he slid his other hand between her thighs and inside the slit in her drawers to find the place where she was already wet and eager for him.

It was her turn to strive for breath as he fondled her so deftly that it made her gasp and moan for more. With a smile that was half smirk, half pleasure, he pulled her foot off the chair, then hooked his hand behind her knee to lift the other leg so she could set *that* foot on the chair.

This time he was the one to remove her boot, garter, and stocking with a series of bold, hot caresses that ignited her senses. By the time her stockings were pooled on the floor at her feet, she thought she might melt into a puddle on top of them.

"Turn around," he commanded her.

"Yes, sir," she said impudently. "Whatever his lordship demands."

His low laugh resonated deep inside her belly. "*Whatever* I demand? I'll have to see that to believe it."

She put her back to him. "Do you always order your paramours about like this?"

"I don't have a string of paramours, as you seem to think," he said, a trace of irritation in his voice. "They're . . . inconvenient."

Yet he had asked her to be his mistress. She told herself that it meant nothing. All the same, it felt like it meant something.

"Wives can be inconvenient, too," she said, trying not to tremble like a silly schoolgirl as he loosened the laces of her corset, the brush of his hands over her chemise-clad back making her yearn for more than this one encounter.

"So I'm told." He pulled her corset off over her head, then pressed a kiss to her bare shoulder. "I would give much to see you with your hair down, Princess."

"You can't," she said with true regret, then added tartly, "unless you're prepared to put it back up again."

"Don't tempt me to try it." He ran his tongue along the nape of her neck. "Though I confess that having all of this exposed is enjoyable, too. It makes me want to mark you again."

"Don't you dare!" She swiveled to face him, only to find him laughing. "It's probably a good thing we can't marry," she said petulantly. "You would be a most trying husband, I'm sure."

"Probably," he said, obviously not the least insulted. With eyes darkening, he reached for the hem of her chemise. "But there are advantages to marriage, too." His guttural tone gave her pause. "Like being able to have the wife of one's dreams in one's bed."

Her breath caught in her throat. "Would I be . . . the wife of your dreams?"

His only answer was to kiss her, hard and deep and so fiercely that her heart felt as if it might fly out of her chest. She told herself to not even hope for it. What good would it do to dream, when nothing could come of it? He would not give up his ambition for her.

But that didn't mean she couldn't enjoy their one time together. And she intended to do so, to revel in it and fix it in her memory for all her days.

He drew back to drag her chemise over her head, then gaze on her naked as if it were his right. And it was. She'd given it to him.

His eyes smoldered a hot blue as they scoured her naked body. "You may never be queen of Belgium, *ma chérie*, but you are a queen nonetheless."

"In appearance, you mean," she said, faintly disappointed.

"In everything. Diplomacy. Intelligence." He lifted an eyebrow. "Talent in the theater." As that made her smile, he filled his hands with her breasts, thumbing her nipples to fine points. "And in bounty of bosom. Most assuredly."

She laughed in spite of herself. "For a fellow who strategizes his every move, you are still such a *man*."

Eyes gleaming, he pulled his hands from her breasts so he could work loose his trouser buttons. "Shall I show you how much of a man I am?"

"Oh yes." She'd never actually seen a man naked, except on statues, and that could hardly be the same.

He shoved off his trousers, then swiftly divested himself of his drawers. And that's when she thought better of her plan to lose her virtue to him. Because that massive engine thrusting out from between his thighs like a cannon headed for war was far more daunting than she'd expected. It was as arrogant as he, with ballocks the size of plums.

"*Sacrebleu*," she couldn't help whispering.

That made him falter. "You *have* done this before, haven't you?"

She considered revealing the truth. But then

he would put a swift end to this. He was a gentleman, and he had some insane notion that she might end up a princess one day.

"What do *you* think?" she said, perversely not wanting to lie to him.

Thankfully, he came to the obvious conclusion and drew her into his arms. She ought to be insulted, but she was merely glad that he would do as she wanted and take her to his bed.

Or at least figuratively, since instead of leading her to his bedchamber, he hoisted her onto his desk and murmured, "Good. Because I can't wait any longer to have you, my sweet."

Then he was parting her legs and finding that soft, silky place that yearned for him and sliding up inside her as if heading home.

She choked down a gasp. My, my, but that was . . . not what she'd expected. Did every woman have to endure that large *verge* pressing up into her? More importantly, did every woman find it *pleasurable?*

Perhaps she was merely the exception. He seemed so thick, so intrusive.

"You're as tight as a virgin," he whispered, before taking her mouth in a leisurely kiss that roused her blood and made her less tense down below.

She tore her mouth free of his. "And how many virgins have you deflowered, monsieur?" she asked with forced nonchalance.

"None." He kneaded her breast so silkily she gasped, which brought a self-satisfied gleam to his eyes. "I don't believe in taking a woman's innocence outside of marriage."

Then he began moving inside her, and all thought of having lost her virtue to a man who didn't actually believe in *taking* a woman's virtue faded. Because this wasn't what she'd expected *at all*.

Yes, his hard *verge* inside her was still uncomfortable. But the more he drove inside her and the more his clever fingers caressed her breast and her *minou* at the point of their joining, the more she found herself moaning and shimmying against him, trying to gain more of the delicious sensations he provoked.

"Monique," he whispered in a ragged voice. "My dear, sweet princess. I could die happy inside you."

She could die happy with him inside her, too. Because a hunger unlike any she'd experienced was building within her. She wanted to eat him up, to absorb him into her, to have him be part of her as no man ever had. And the more he lunged into her, the more she ached to have him deeper, further, more thoroughly hers.

Her cravings grabbed her by the throat, making her arch up into him, strain against him in search of more pleasure as he thrust inside of her.

"Ah, yes." He spread kisses over her cheeks and throat and shoulder. "Show me what you want, my dearest. And I will give it to you, I swear."

"I want *you*," she murmured, hating herself for the admission. "*Please*, Gregory . . ."

With a growl, he increased his rhythm. His fingers thrummed against her where they were joined and the craving intensified until she was clutching him close and moaning and aching for something she couldn't fathom . . . until it rose inside her like a phoenix lofting toward heaven.

"Gregory . . ." she moaned against his mouth. "My God, *Gregory*!"

And she catapulted into the sky, her body shaking and her heart feeling as if it might shatter into a million stars.

Then he drove hard and cried out something as he spilled his seed inside her. She could have sworn he'd said, "My love," but that was impossible. He didn't seem to believe in love.

Unfortunately, she was beginning to. Because she realized, as she held him close and tried not to cry over the glory of it, that she felt something for him she'd never felt for any man.

Could it be love? She hoped not. Because love was dangerous and wretched and made one hurt the way Maman had been hurt by Papa. Love cut one off from one's family the way Grand-maman had lost hers.

She simply couldn't go through such pain.

Gregory couldn't seem to let go of Monique. He should have pulled out before spilling himself inside her. At the very least, he should have hunted up the French letters he kept somewhere in his bedchamber.

But he'd been afraid to ruin the moment, to lose his chance. And some part of him was sure that if he'd lost his chance, he would have regretted it all his days.

He drew back to stare at her. "That was . . . miraculous. I shall not forget it for years to come."

A tentative smile curved her lips. Her luscious, tempting lips. "Nor will I."

His softening cock slipped from her as he pulled out of her embrace, reminded that the duke and Lady Ursula were still in the house somewhere. As he bent to pick up his drawers, he noticed the blood staining not only her thighs but his cock. He stared at it, hardly able to believe his eyes. "Did I hurt you?"

She glanced away with a veiled expression. "No, of course not."

Suddenly he remembered what she'd said that first night in London—*I must be chaste when I marry.* He'd assumed it was part of her role, but what if . . .

Oh, God. The evidence was hard to ignore— the tightness of her quim, the way she'd embraced every pleasure as if it were entirely new . . . the blood smearing her thighs.

Half in a trance, he took out his handkerchief and wiped the blood from his cock before pulling on his drawers. Surely he hadn't . . . Surely she wasn't . . . "Were you chaste before I took you?"

Avoiding his gaze, she murmured, "Why does it matter?"

He caught her head between his hands. "Because it *does*." He stared her down. "Answer me. Were you a virgin?"

She shrugged. "I suppose you could put it that way."

He'd deflowered her. He'd taken the innocence of the future Princess de Chanay without a thought for the political consequences, all because he couldn't stand the idea of not having her.

Damn it all to hell. How could he have done that? "Why didn't you tell me beforehand?"

"Would you have bedded me if I had?"

"Of course not!"

A rueful smile crossed her lips. "That's why I didn't tell you."

He couldn't comprehend it. If she'd told him, he would never have dishonored her. But he'd assumed . . . "I don't understand. You're an actress."

Her temper flared as she slipped off the desk to move away from him. "That doesn't mean I'm a whore."

"I wasn't implying—"

"Of course you were," she said irritably. "Everyone assumes that actresses are whores." Her voice lowered to a murmur. "But it isn't necessarily true."

The enormity of what he'd done hit him. He'd taken the innocence of a *princess*, who might one day rule in Chanay, even if she didn't end up doing so in Belgium. It was unconscionable.

"We must marry," he said baldly.

That seemed to catch her by surprise. Ever practical, she picked up her petticoat, though her expression remained shuttered as she returned to where he stood by the desk. "Why must we? Nothing has changed from before."

"Everything has changed. I took your innocence."

"No," she said firmly. "I *gave* it to you of my own volition."

"In hopes of keeping me silent about the masquerade, or convincing me to let you stay, or—"

"*Merde*," she spat, his first clue that he'd stepped far awry with that remark. "I *desired* you. That is all." She used her petticoat to wipe the blood from her thighs and his desk with furious motions. "Though I don't know *why*, given that you are the most arrogant, infuriating . . ."

A string of French slurs followed, none of which he blamed her for. The words *I desired you* sounded in his head, as tempting as her nudity. "Monique, forgive me. I did not mean—"

"To insult me? To imply that I am some sort of seductress trying to trap you into marriage?" Still fully nude, she faced him and planted her hands on her hips. Her lush, very distracting hips. "And why on earth would I marry you when you clearly think me a blackmailer and manipulative *putain*?"

"I do not think of you as a whore," he snapped. "And *pardonne-moi*, *chérie*, but you did offer me your body for my silence only yesterday."

"Yes! Offered! From the beginning! I did not give it to you in hopes I could make you pay for it later, and then try to be so wicked as to demand that you—"

"Enough," he said, suitably shamed. "You're right. I should not have said that."

That seemed to mollify her a little. Sullenly, she dragged on her chemise, then pulled her loosened corset on over her head. "I do not understand why you would offer marriage when you think such awful things of me."

"And *I* don't understand why you would give me your virtue. Especially now that you have possibilities."

When she merely put her back to him and said, "Will you tighten my laces, my lord?" he muttered a curse under his breath and went to do so.

He regarded the back of her head and the stretch of skin he'd only half-jokingly spoken of marking. Even now, he wanted to suck her skin, taste her quim, be with her again and again.

His damned cock roused at the thought. "Please, *chérie*, tell me why you would behave so recklessly."

She was quiet another long moment as he tied off her corset. Then she sighed. "Perhaps I just wanted to make sure that my first time was special. I knew I could trust you to make it so." Turning in his arms, she faced him with a wistful smile. "And you did."

He fought the surge of satisfaction that those words roused in him. "All the same, you see now why we must marry."

"So you may throw your future away on a French *putain?*"

"Don't call yourself that," he said sharply. "Never again."

She stroked his cheek. "It is what the world will call me, *mon coeur,* once it learns that I have been an actress for years. That I have been lying to everyone about who I am."

He gritted his teeth. She was right about *that.* "We'll find a way around . . . exposing your past. Somehow."

Her mocking laugh echoed in his ears. "I would love to hear how you intend to do that. It's impossible."

"Nothing is impossible," he said in true annoyance. He crossed his arms over his chest. "Have you no faith in me?"

"It doesn't have anything to do with you." A weariness spread over her features. "I simply know how the world works, *mon coeur.*"

It was the second time she'd called him *my heart.* It should alarm him. Instead, it made him want to whisk her away somewhere safe and make her his yet again. "What if I don't care about my career?"

She snorted. "Then you are lying to yourself. We both know you care very much. And if I took what you love away from you, you would come to resent me." Her voice dropped to a whisper. "I could not bear that."

Those words revealed that she cared more than she let on, and the realization struck him down deep, in the place where he kept all his darkest secrets. He wondered if she, of all people, might understand what he'd done in his youth and why. That she might accept his past and not judge.

The idea tantalized him, made him want to explore it. He reached for her, but before he could drag her into his arms, a knock came at the door.

Bloody hell. He'd be very happy to have all of this over, so he could sort out his feelings for Monique and his insane wish to have her as his wife, though it would surely mean the end of his career.

"What is it?" he called to the intruder, only too aware that he was naked except for his drawers.

With a frown, Monique left his side to continue putting on her clothes.

"My lord, the constable is coming up the drive," came the voice of his most trusted footman.

Damn. "I'll be right there," he called out.

"Very good, sir," the footman said.

As soon as the servant's footsteps receded,

Monique murmured, "You have many responsibilities. You must attend to them."

And leave her be? With this matter unresolved? "I don't care about my responsibilities. I care that I just deflowered—"

"I do not wish to gain a husband who is forced into marrying me." Her gaze was direct and rather chilling as she gestured for the door. "Go speak to the constable and see if *he* might know who is trying to kill me. Go uncover all the many secrets you excel at revealing. I don't expect anything of you." She cast him a wan smile. "All I want is to finish out the masquerade so I can take care of Grand-maman."

The words carved a guilt on his heart that was nothing like the one put there by his murder of his father. Because she obviously didn't expect him to behave as a gentleman in this matter and accept his responsibilities. He'd never had a woman think so little of him, and it chafed at him.

"This discussion is not over," he said. "Don't think that it is, *ma chérie*."

"You should put some clothes on," she retorted, very much like a wife. She pulled on her chemisette and then her gown, and fastened the latter up hastily.

He shook his head. Despite all the political difficulties involved in this affair, she would actually make him a very good companion. Perhaps it was time to explore ways out of this mess that could result in his wedding her.

"I'll take care of the constable," he said. "You might wish to go to your bedchamber and make sure that you are . . . presentable before the prince arrives."

He wasn't sure why he'd said that until she glowered at him. And then he knew. He'd wanted to be certain she was his and no one else's. That given the choice, she would choose *him*.

And now he had his answer. Astonishing how gratifying he found it.

Oh yes, he had a new purpose. Somehow, he meant to make sure that she could be his wife . . . and that he could keep his career safe in the process.

Because any other choice was rapidly becoming unthinkable.

Leaving the room, he headed downstairs to meet with the constable in the drawing room. He gave the man the same story he'd given the duke—someone had shot at him in London and now in the country.

The constable took careful notes. "I'll look into it, m'lord, but there's so much mayhem going on, what with today being Guy Fawkes Day and all, that it could have been just 'bout anyone. You're sure it was the same fellow as what shot at you in town?"

"I'm sure. One of my guests, the Duc de Pontalba, saw the man from behind and the description matched. He tried to go after him, but the fellow escaped toward Canterbury."

"Then I should like to speak to this duke, if I may," the constable said.

"Of course. I'll have him fetched."

Gregory opened the door to the drawing room only to find that the prince had arrived, along with, oddly enough, Danworth. Perhaps Lady Ursula had been right about the two men being friends.

"Fulkham!" Prince Leopold called to him. "Thank you so much for the invitation, old fellow. Given that the conference is leaning toward Princess Aurore as a candidate, I confess I was rather surprised to be asked here."

"We decided to make it a more international group," Gregory said blandly. "Besides, with your relation Lady Ursula and your good friend Danworth attending, it only made sense to have you as well."

Gregory noticed that Danworth looked suddenly uncomfortable.

The prince smoothed his features into nonchalance. "Of course, my relation and my . . . er . . . friend."

"I suppose that's why Danworth went to meet you on the road?" Gregory queried.

"Not at all," Prince Leopold said. "I merely happened to spot Mr. Danworth as I was passing through your quaint village on my way here."

"And not the others?" Gregory pressed him.

The prince blinked. "The others?"

"I went into Canterbury with his lordship's

mother and the count this morning to shop," Mr. Danworth said hastily. "But we got separated."

Hmm. He would have to ask Mother exactly *when* Danworth had left them. "Well, I do hope my mother and the count return in time for dinner." He glanced at the clock. "It's getting late, and I would hope—"

"Lord Fulkham!" said a voice from the doorway of the drawing room. "May I speak to you a moment?"

The way Danworth blanched at the sight of the constable gave Gregory pause. "Of course."

He walked over to the constable, who whispered, "That fellow there is Tom Smith."

Gregory fought the urge to glance at Danworth. "The one in the blue coat?"

The constable nodded. "He's the one who asked about your father's death."

His heart thundered in his chest. "Thank you," Gregory said. "Please speak of this to no one. I will handle it. Do you understand?"

The constable nodded, albeit a bit reluctantly.

"The duke will be down soon to speak with you. So please take a seat."

Again, the constable understood his meaning. "Of course, my lord."

Gregory returned to his guests, his mind reeling. What reason could Danworth have had to ask about Father's death? Unless this was part of an investigation into Gregory's suitability to become secretary of the foreign office.

But why would such an investigation be mounted by the party leaving office? Could Danworth have found a way to move on to the opposition party, the same way Gregory had?

The arse seemed to have gathered his composure. "Who *is* that fellow, Fulkham?" Danworth asked in his loftiest tone.

Gregory forced a shrug. "The constable from Canterbury. We had an incident this afternoon, which I had to report." He waved his hand dismissively. "You know how these locals are during Guy Fawkes Day. Very reckless."

Danworth's face showed no reaction that might indicate he'd been part of the shooting. Then again, he worked for the prime minister and knew how to play the game.

No matter. Tonight Gregory would confront him with what he knew and demand an explanation, about both "Tom Smith" and the attempts on Monique's life.

And if Danworth was behind the latter?

Gregory would eviscerate him.

Twenty

Her heart torn in two, Monique stood in her bed-chamber making herself "presentable." She didn't know how to interpret Gregory's proposal of marriage. Had he meant what he'd said? Or was it merely part of his rules of honor that said he must offer for any virgin whose innocence he took? He certainly hadn't voiced any eagerness to marry her out of love.

She sighed. She would adore being Gregory's wife, being *loved* by Gregory. Because somewhere along the way she'd fallen in love with him, however unwisely. He might be a proud, hardheaded Englishman, but he was also kind. And protective. And so sweetly passionate that . . .

Tears welled in her eyes, and she brushed them away ruthlessly. Marriage was impossible, and they both knew it. So it didn't matter if she loved him or not. Their paths were set, and those paths went in opposite directions.

As soon as she'd changed out of her riding habit, she headed downstairs. As she reached the ground floor, she heard an unfamiliar male voice speaking rather pompously. So it was unlikely to be the constable.

Her blood stilled. Prince Leopold?

Pasting a smile on her lips, she sailed into the foyer, where stood not only a man royally bedecked, but also, inexplicably, Mr. Danworth, along with Gregory.

"Ah, here she is." Gregory cast Prince Leopold a thin smile. "I understand that you have not yet met the princess?"

Prince Leopold regarded her with a keen interest that gave her pause. "Sadly, no."

Gregory swiftly performed the introductions, although it seemed rather pointless, since each was well aware of the other's identity.

Smiling amiably, the prince stepped forward to take her hand. "It is a very great pleasure to meet you, Princess. I would have arranged a meeting sooner if I'd known how very lovely you are."

As he lifted her hand to his lips for a kiss, she had to admit he was quite attractive. From what her great-uncle had told her, he was at least forty, yet not a strand of gray streaked his hair, and he dressed quite well. He also had an air of command about him that reminded her vaguely of Gregory.

Still, his compliments gave her pause. Why would he be interested in her—in Aurore—after she'd supposedly rejected him? "It's good to finally meet you, too, Your Highness," she said blandly.

Lady Ursula rushed into the foyer, then halted. With widening eyes, she smiled at Prince Leopold. "Cousin! How wonderful to see you here at last!"

A change came over him that arrested Monique's attention. "Indeed," he said, rather dismissively, making poor Lady Ursula pale. Then he turned to Monique. "I'm fatigued from my journey, Princess, but I do hope to enjoy your company at dinner."

She nodded, aware that Gregory was scowling most unwisely. "I would be honored, sir."

The prince turned to Mr. Danworth. "Thank you for joining me in my carriage. I would never have found the place otherwise."

Mr. Danworth nodded. "I was happy to help, Your Highness."

How strange. The two men were cordial, to be sure, but they didn't seem to be the great friends Lady Ursula had described. Were they putting on a show? Or had Lady Ursula simply been lying about their friendship?

She could tell from Gregory's face that similar thoughts were passing through his head. But he merely ordered the servants to show the prince to his room.

As soon as Prince Leopold was gone and Lady Ursula and Mr. Danworth had headed up to their own rooms to dress for dinner, Gregory came to her side.

"Are you all right?" he asked.

She stiffened. "Why wouldn't I be?"

Gazing up the staircase to where his guests had disappeared, he said, "I don't know. But clearly *something* is going on with the prince and Danworth."

"Lady Ursula said they were friends, but they didn't seem friendly to me."

"Exactly. It worries me. The constable told me—" He caught himself.

"What did he tell you?"

His gaze grew shuttered. "Nothing. At least, nothing that I'm sure of the meaning of yet."

She understood; she wasn't sure what *anything* meant yet.

Before she could remark on his words, the entrance opened and his mother came in, laughing along with the count, who looked thoroughly enamored.

"Mother!" Gregory said sharply. "Where the devil have you been?"

"We were having a very pleasant time in town," Gregory's mother said, with a knowing glance at Monique's great-uncle.

The count smiled down at her. "We were, indeed. Your mother is a delightful woman, Fulkham."

When Gregory bristled, Monique had to suppress a laugh. Clearly, he didn't approve of any possible relationship between his mother and the count. But Monique thought it was sweet. Much as she resented the count's behavior toward her and Grand-maman, she also recognized that he needed a softening influence.

Like Lady Fulkham.

"Tell me," Gregory said in a firm tone, "was Danworth with you the entire day you were in Canterbury?"

The count and Lady Fulkham exchanged a glance. Then Lady Fulkham shrugged. "We lost track of him quite early. I'm not sure *where* he went."

Gregory's jaw tightened. "I see. Well then, that is that."

What an odd thing to say. But with no more information to go on, Monique didn't know what to make of it.

"Dinner is in less than an hour," he added. "Perhaps you two should go upstairs to change clothes."

"Oh!" his mother said. "Of course." She cast the count a flirtatious glance. "I do hope you will sit next to *me* at dinner."

The count took her hand in his and pressed a kiss to it. "I would be honored, my lady."

Gregory rolled his eyes. And as soon as the pair had disappeared up the stairs, separately, he said, "What is your great-uncle up to, Monique?"

"I have no idea. Perhaps he just likes your mother."

"I doubt that," Gregory ground out. "He has some reason for flirting with her, I'm sure."

The remark made her sad. "That's the trouble

with you, Gregory. Everyone you work with has an ulterior motive, usually political. But sometimes people just want to be with other people for no reason beyond simple liking." *Or loving.*

He stared at her. "I don't trust your uncle."

She shrugged. "I don't trust him either. But he appears to like your mother a great deal. And I think those feelings are genuine." She crossed her arms over her chest. "Not all of us are trying to use our gender to gain something, you know. Sometimes we just desire certain people because we desire them."

As he gaped at her, clearly skeptical about the idea of his mother desiring anyone, she left him to mount the stairs. If he couldn't even accept that his mother might wish to find a companion, then what was the chance he would accept that *she* did?

Once the constable had finished questioning the duke, Gregory had packed the man off, promising to learn more about why Danworth was looking into the death of his father.

Gregory considered speaking to the count about this latest attempt on Monique's life, but that would only make the man want to return to London right away, and Gregory wasn't sure that was wise. He still needed to do some more investigation.

Dinner that night was interminable. The shooting was discussed at length, but thankfully everyone accepted his story that *he'd* been the target. Except perhaps for the count, who looked thoughtful. But no one else gave away anything that could help him figure out who'd been behind the attempt on Monique's life.

Gregory also couldn't help noticing that Prince Leopold was enormously interested in Monique. And why wouldn't he be? She was a vivacious and clever beauty who knew how to engage any man's attention.

In truth, she would be wise to court the prince's affections. If Aurore died and Monique eventually took her place, then Leopold would be well served by having her as his wife. Was that Monique's aim?

Gregory watched her avidly, jealousy burning in his chest. But to be fair, she showed no true interest in the prince. It was Gregory she fixed upon. Gregory whom she deferred to.

Clearly, he was a fool, vacillating about what she wanted. *Whom* she wanted. It was clear that he was the only man who had her affections.

Very well, then he would make sure that the way was paved for the two of them. Even if it meant changing his hopes for the future.

With that in mind, he asked Danworth to join him in his study after the ladies retired to the drawing room. It was time to figure out where the prime minister's secretary stood in all this.

And why Danworth had questioned the constable about Gregory's father.

When Danworth entered his study, he seemed wary. Not surprising, given what Gregory had learned. Did the fellow realize that Gregory knew so much? Did he care?

"What is this about, Fulkham?" Danworth demanded, clearly on the defensive.

Gregory forced a smile. "You tell *me*. I understand that you've been asking in town about the circumstances surrounding my father's death."

Danworth fixed him with a dark glance. "I have, indeed."

Surprising that the man was admitting it.

The fellow crossed his arms over his chest. "The constable told me that your father died as a result of a tumble down the stairs while he was drunk."

"Yes," Gregory said tersely. "My father was often drunk. What has that got to do with anything?"

"Well, I asked the constable why no one ever suspected your mother of causing your father's death, and he said that they knew for certain that she'd had nothing to do with it. That if anyone had killed him, it was a male." Danworth smirked at him. "Because when your father was found, he was clutching a button in his hand. And not the sort of button found on a woman's attire. A boy's button."

Gregory's blood ran cold. The night of his father's murder, he'd lost a button off the school jacket he'd been wearing when he'd defended his mother. He'd looked for the button, but hadn't been able to find it anywhere. So he'd assumed it had been lost somewhere in the depths beneath the staircase.

No one had ever told him it had been found on the body. But then, he'd been too young for anyone to consider making him privy to the investigation. "A *boy's* button? How in God's name could anyone be sure of that?"

"Well, the constable wasn't, because he didn't recognize the design. He said it must have been from a servant who was trying to keep his lordship from falling. Fortunately, I knew better. I could see that it came from an Eton jacket."

Oh, God, the constable had actually shown the arse the button. "I don't see why that matters." Gregory hoped he sounded far more bored and nonchalant than he felt.

"It matters," Danworth said as he approached Gregory, "because since the constable still has the button, it could easily be called into evidence."

"To prove what?" Gregory said. "That my father was tossed down the stairs by some anonymous Etonian?"

His sarcastic tone didn't seem to faze Danworth. "I'm saying that *you* are the person who tossed your father down the stairs. I'm saying you killed your father."

Gregory fought the sick feeling swelling in his belly. "Ah, I see. And why would I do that?"

Danworth shrugged. "I have no clue. But I do

know one thing. If word got out about this, you'd be ruined."

That was certainly true. "Assuming that anyone would believe it." Gregory stared the man down. "And who would? Especially since I was away at Eton at the time."

"You were not. You had come home for the holiday already."

Gregory tensed. "What makes you think so?"

With a smirk, Danworth circled the study. "I found someone in Canterbury who remembered seeing you on your way home." He lifted an eyebrow. "A certain shopkeeper was adamant that you passed through town the very night your father died. He saw you looking out of a coach window. Imagine that."

"Imagine that, indeed," Gregory clipped out, his tone cold. "Some shopkeeper *thought* he saw me peering out of a coach window on a night more than twenty years ago? Assuming that I did anything wrong, which I did not, no court in the world would convict me on the basis of such flimsy evidence."

Danworth snorted. "I've no need to prove it in court. I merely need to prove it in the court of public opinion, and I damned well have enough evidence to do that. Any insinuation of your being involved in your father's death would ruin you in politics for decades to come. Especially if the papers got hold of it."

Gregory certainly couldn't refute that. "So

what do you want from me?" he snapped. "I assume that you want *something* or you wouldn't have gone to such trouble to drum up this ridiculous tale."

Danworth marched toward him. "I want only one thing from you. It would cost you very little. I want you to throw the weight of your influence behind Prince Leopold to be chosen ruler of Belgium. *Not* Princess Aurore."

That told Gregory two things. One, Danworth was still unaware of "Princess Aurore's" true identity. And two, the man might very well be behind the attacks on Aurore's and Monique's lives.

What a pity that he couldn't prove it. Danworth might have been missing for part of the day, but Gregory somehow couldn't see the man hiding in the woods in an attempt to assassinate Monique. Or lurking about in Hyde Park for the same purpose.

Still, Danworth was a damned good shot, so it was conceivable. And it didn't rule out the possibility that the man had hired someone to do the deed for him.

But before he accused Danworth of anything, he needed more information. "Why are you determined to put Leopold on the throne?"

Danworth crossed his arms over his chest. "As you know quite well, Wellington is about to lose his position as prime minister. As long as I remain tied to him, I will lose any chance of advancement." Bitterness crept into his tone. "I'll end up an aging private secretary to an ancient relic of a politician, whose only usefulness is in writing his memoirs. But if Leopold becomes king of the Belgians, he has promised me a post there worthy of my talents. No more toadying to the likes of Wellington, no more putting up with nonsense from lords like you."

"And all you have to do to gain your post is to blackmail *me*."

The bloody arse shrugged. "You may call it blackmail if you wish. I would call it quid pro quo. A favor for a favor. I keep silent about your family secrets and you put your influence behind Leopold."

"I see. And whose idea was it to ask for this 'favor'? Yours? Or the prince's?"

"Leopold knows naught of this. But I daresay he'd have no quarrel with it if he did."

Gregory wished he could be sure of the truth of either of those statements. "And what about attempted murder?" He bore down on Danworth. "Does he know about *that* little strategy of yours for eliminating his competitors?"

A slight twitching of the man's eyelid gave Danworth away, though he stood his ground. "I have no idea what you're talking about. I haven't attempted to murder anyone."

"Forgive me if I don't believe you. As you already know, we're here in the country precisely because someone shot at the princess in Hyde Park a few days ago."

"I thought you said *you* were the target?"

"You know damned well I was not."

Danworth stared coldly at him. "I was nowhere near Hyde Park then. Ask Wellington."

"Oh, don't worry, I intend to." And while he was at it, he would ask if Danworth had been dispatched to Calais around the time of the princess's poisoning. "But even if you had nothing to do with that attempt, I know you damned well had something to do with the second attempt on the princess's life this morning."

"I don't even have a gun with me. How could I possibly have shot at the princess?" Danworth snapped, though sweat broke out on his brow.

Gregory pressed his advantage. "According to my mother, you conveniently disappeared for most of the shopping trip. Which makes you the only one of my guests not accounted for during the attack."

"Your mother?" Danworth snorted. "She was so busy cozying up to Beaumonde that she wouldn't have noticed if I *had* been there."

"Do I detect a note of jealousy?" Gregory said, seizing on his opponent's weakness. "Were you hoping to feather your nest by gaining my mother's affections yourself?"

Though Danworth colored, he shook his head. "I have no need of a wife so much older than I, sir. I can have any woman I want."

"True. Which is why I question your flirtations with her. Or were you perhaps hoping that she might tell you something about my father's death that you couldn't learn by deceiving the constable?"

He saw he'd hit his mark when Danworth's jaw flexed. "No deception was required. The man was more than ready to reveal what he knew."

"Because you told him you were an investigator from London interested in implicating my mother. You knew that would make him provide an alternate view of the crime."

"I knew that would make him tell the truth." Danworth drew himself up. "In any case, it doesn't matter. You can't prove I did anything wrong—you're just lashing out because I've uncovered your nasty little secret." He strode up to Gregory with a menacing smile. "You've heard my terms. If you wish to continue in your present career, then you must advocate for Leopold when we return. Otherwise, I will reveal to the world the truth about how your father died. And what your part in it was."

Gregory desperately wanted to tell the arse to go to hell, but he couldn't. It wasn't just he who would suffer. It was Mother. And Monique, if she chose to marry him.

"Well then," Gregory said noncommittally, "I suppose I have a decision to make."

"You do, indeed. Just be sure to make the right one, my lord. Or I swear I will make you and yours regret it."

And with that, the arse walked out.

Twenty-One

As Mr. Danworth left the study, Monique slid behind a massive ornamental display case in the hall and prayed he wouldn't notice her. Fortunately, the man seemed too caught up in what had just occurred to pay his surroundings any mind. That wasn't surprising, given what he'd said to Gregory. Clearly, Mr. Danworth thought he held all the cards.

And perhaps he did. She had come up here after leaving the drawing room, hoping for a chance to continue this afternoon's discussion with Gregory in private. Instead, she'd heard Mr. Danworth threaten him most appallingly.

Waiting until the wretch disappeared up the stairs, probably headed for his bedchamber, she slipped into the study.

The moment the door closed, Gregory said, "What now? You wish to blackmail me into something else?" He turned, then started. "Oh.

It's you." He tensed and wouldn't meet her gaze. "What are you doing here?"

Her heart ached to see him looking so lost. "I came to talk to you, and I overheard—"

"What Danworth said?" He crossed his arms over his chest. "How much did you hear?"

"Most of it, I think."

That seemed to deflate him. "Wonderful. So I suppose I can add you to the list of people who despise me."

His acid words broke her heart. "Don't be absurd. I could never despise you. But I don't understand how he could threaten such a horrible thing. Clearly, he is cobbling together a bunch of nonsense—"

"I wish he were." Gregory went to pour himself some brandy from the decanter on his desk. "Sadly, he is not."

That shocked her. She'd been sure that Danworth was simply taking advantage of an accidental death to strike out at Gregory. "So what he claims, what he threatens to expose—"

"Is the truth. Yes." Twirling the glass he held in his hand, he stared down into the amber liquid. "You might as well know it. The world will hear it soon enough."

Her blood clamoring in her veins, she walked up to take the glass of brandy from him. "Not if I have anything to say about it," she said firmly. "I'll reveal the truth about my masquerade, and that will be an end to it. You will champion Prince

Leopold, who will become king of Belgium, thus ensuring that none of your secrets come out."

"And you will be forced into poverty with your grandmother?" A faint smile curved up his lips as he faced her. "I think not."

"I will not save Grand-maman at the risk to your future . . . and that of your mother. I refuse to see your family embroiled in scandal on my behalf. Grand-maman and I will manage somehow. You have far more to lose than we ever did."

His confident demeanor faltered a little at that. "You're amazing, do you know that?" he said in a voice wrought with emotion. "You just heard that I am a murderer, yet here you are, springing to defend me."

I am a murderer.

No—she couldn't believe it. With her heart pounding, she laid her hand on his arm. "I know the situation can't have been as cut-and-dried as Mr. Danworth implied."

Now he looked desperate. "Ah, but it was." He dragged in a shuddering breath.

She had to know it all. "Tell me about it, *mon coeur.* How did it happen? *When* did it happen?"

He gazed off across the room. "When I was twelve."

When he said nothing more, she prodded him. "What were the circumstances?"

For a moment, she thought he wouldn't answer. Then he drew himself up as if preparing for an onerous task. "I had just come home from

Eton for the holidays. My father was drunk and in a foul temper. He lashed out at my mother as always, and I defended her, as always."

His gaze grew distant. "Father and I were at the top of the stairs—the ones right outside that door there, actually—and I got so angry that I thrust myself between them, determined to keep him from hurting her. I'd done it often enough before. She'd done it for me, too."

Snatching the glass of brandy back from Monique, he took a long swallow. When he continued, the matter-of-fact tone with which he'd begun his recitation shifted to something more tortured. "Father pulled his fist back to punch me, and I shoved him. He fell, all the way down the staircase, head over heels. He—" His voice cracked a little before he gathered himself to continue. "He ended up in a crumpled heap at the bottom. His neck broke on the way down, and he . . . died instantly."

"So you didn't *mean* to kill him," she said softly.

He uttered a harsh laugh. "Didn't I? I've never been sure. Perhaps I did. Perhaps I took my chance to rid us of the plague that was my father." His voice hardened. "All I know is that when he died, I had not one moment of remorse. Do you hear me? Not. One. Moment." He downed the rest of the brandy, his eyes bleak. "If anything shows that I'm a killer at heart, it's that."

"Oh, Gregory, that's not true. You did feel remorse, or you wouldn't have spoken of the ghosts that torment you here."

"Only because I remember so much of what my father did to my mother. Only because every time I return, I realize how little . . . I regret killing him."

"You were twelve!" she cried. "You were acting as impulsively as any lad that age and trying to protect your mother. No one would blame you."

"You think not, do you?" He poured himself more brandy and stared into its depths as if finding the past in them. "As a result of his death, I inherited everything. I gained my title and my fortune by shoving my father down the stairs. Plenty of people will see only that."

Unfortunately, that was probably true. "Then you must do what Mr. Danworth says. Vote for Prince Leopold. Use your power to get him chosen as king."

Even if it meant that she had to return to Dieppe with Grand-maman and take a protector. She couldn't watch Gregory and his mother be destroyed in the press by . . . by a devil like Danworth.

"I am *not* going to let that arse win," he said fiercely. "I'm certainly not going to reward Leopold by giving him what he wants after he used such tactics to gain it, assuming that he knew what Danworth was up to." He set down his glass to fix her with a tortured gaze. "And I damned well will not overlook the fact that Danworth tried to murder you in order to gain his aims."

She swallowed. She'd heard that part, too, after all. "You don't know that for certain."

"I can't prove it, no." He caressed her cheek. "But I *know* it as surely as I know that Danworth is up to no good. And I won't let him get away with it."

"Then you and your mother will suffer. You'll lose your career and your future," she whispered. "I can't bear that."

He stared at her a long moment. "Why do you care? All I've done is give you grief, threaten to expose you . . . take your innocence. You ought to be handing me over to Danworth on a silver platter."

"I would never do that!" she cried, her heart in her throat. "I love you! So I can't stand by and watch while you are destroyed."

❧

I love you. The words rang in his ears. Clearly, he was losing his mind, because never had three words sounded so sweet.

And so very maddening. All he could think was how he wanted to take her to bed and make love to her until the sun came up. She'd just heard how he'd murdered his father, yet she was on his side. He didn't know whether to exult or to despair. If Danworth—and possibly Leopold—

had his way, she would be headed back to Dieppe in two days, with nothing to show for all her effort.

He couldn't endure that. "I don't care what Danworth says—Aurore will be chosen as queen of Belgium. And you and I will marry. Somehow. I shall not stand by and watch you suffer at the hands of Danworth or anyone else."

A despairing look crossed her face. "Yesterday you told me you couldn't allow the masquerade to continue, and now you'll put Aurore, whom you've never met, in the position of queen of Belgium? Why?"

"Because she's the best choice politically, assuming she lives."

"That's not the main reason. You just don't want Danworth to win. But Aurore may not even live. So choose Leopold, save your career, prevent a scandal, and stop being stubborn about it, for God's sake!"

"I *am* stubborn," he growled. "It's why I've progressed this far in my career. I don't give in to blackmail, and I especially won't give in to it if it means watching you suffer."

"Gregory—"

He dragged her into his arms. "You're mine, *chérie*. And I think it's time I convinced you of that."

If he couldn't convince her with words, then he would convince her this way. He took her mouth, reveling in how she melted against him.

There had to be a way for them to marry. He would *find* a way, damn it.

In the meantime, he would show her that they were meant to be together. He'd been at a disadvantage before, not knowing she was an innocent. But he knew now, so he could show her what things *could* be like between them . . . if he took her the way she deserved.

Pulling back from her, he drew her toward the door that led to his adjoining bedchamber. "Come with me, my sweet. This time we will do it right."

She didn't even pretend to be confused about what he meant. "Did we do it wrong last time?" she said with a tender teasing that lodged somewhere down deep. "Because it certainly seemed right to me."

"I could have taken more care with you, *ma chérie.*"

"I have no complaints."

He led her into his bedchamber and closed the door before saying, "I aim for better than that." Then he thrust her against the door and kissed her hard and long, until he felt her soften against him.

She had put her faith in him, though he wasn't sure why, given what she now knew about him. And he meant to prove himself worthy of it. He undressed her with great care, eager to see her body unveiled for him yet again.

And as before, he marveled at her perfection—

full breasts, a slim belly that would make a man weep, and hips the right size for a man who liked a bit of flesh on his woman.

She blushed. "Why do you stare at me so?"

"Because I take great pleasure in looking at you."

Seemingly self-conscious, she averted her gaze from him. "I'm not as pretty as some."

"You're a goddess," he said, and meant it.

"With too prominent a chin and unruly hair and—" When he laughed, she cast him a hurt look. "What?"

"Forgive me, dearest, but surely a woman who entrances every man in her orbit knows that she's gorgeous."

She pouted in a way so classically French that he got hard just seeing it. "I still don't like my chin."

"Well, I love it."

When the word *love* made her shoot him a questioning glance, he cursed himself, not wanting her to put too much stock in what *had* to be a mere slip of the tongue. Men like him did not fall in love. It was too . . . reckless.

He chucked her under her much-maligned chin. "It's pert and assertive, just like you. As for your hair, I've only seen it covered in wigs, trussed up under hats, and wrapped up into fat chignons. Never down and loose." He reached for her coiffeur, tugging it free of its pins. "So I mean to remedy that."

With a satisfaction that sent his cock rousing even more, he watched her honey-brown tresses cascade down over her shoulders to nearly her hips, which was saying something, given how tall she was.

"There," she said tartly. "Are you happy now? You have finally managed to unleash my hair."

Unleash was a good word. Because it was messy and thick and glorious. And all his. *His.*

He filled his hands with it, kissed its "unruly" mass, and then used hanks of it to caress her nipples until she sighed and melted. "Do you know what I see when I look at you?" he asked.

"A fake princess?"

"Not fake—but no, a princess is not what I see." He backed her toward the bed, stripping off his clothes as he went. "I see the woman who will be my wife. The woman I will have in my bed for the rest of my days. The woman who will bear my children."

The words sounded more like vows than he'd meant them to, and the alarm in her face gave him pause. "Oh, Gregory, we can't marry. It will ruin you!"

"We can. We *will*. And it won't." He tumbled her down onto his bed, relishing the sight of her lying there, exactly where he wanted her. "I shall make it happen, my sweet. You just have to trust me to manage it."

He had no plan yet, but he would find one somehow. He still had four days to do so.

Parting her legs with his knee, he moved between them and bent to kiss her mouth, but she caught his head in her hands to prevent it. "Are you marrying me solely because you took my innocence?"

He froze. The vulnerable look on her face told him what she wanted—the same words of love she'd given him. Words of love that would lay his heart bare to the knife, that would put the power to destroy him in her hands.

The man who ached to possess her wanted to say them, if only to please her. The cautious spymaster knew better.

The spymaster won out. "To paraphrase a certain fetching actress, 'I desire you. That is all.'"

There was no mistaking the flicker of disappointment in her face. And seeing it made him feel as if he'd just told the first real falsehood of his life, even though he'd lied many times as a spymaster.

But never to himself. Never about something this important. And never to someone he cared about.

Then she smoothed her features into a seductive expression and said, in a coquettish voice just a shade forced, "Well, then, sir. What are you waiting for?"

He seized the reprieve eagerly and set about arousing her in every fashion he knew. He tongued and sucked and fondled her breasts. He kissed every inch of her delectable belly, licked her navel and then her quim, brought her to the brink of satisfaction until she was moaning and begging and clearly needing him as much as he needed her.

Desperately, madly. *Now.*

Only then did he slide inside her, reveling in the smooth wetness of her . . . in the tight fit of her, like a hot glove . . . in the sweet, luscious smell and taste and essence of her surrounding him as he pounded into her in search of that unnamable thing he wanted and dared not reach for.

Her face grew flushed and her eyes glazed over. "Gregory . . . oh yes, *mon coeur* . . . yes . . . like that . . . *mon amour, mon amour, mon amour!*"

And as she reached her release, her delicious quim squeezing and kneading his cock, the words *my love, my love, my love* chimed in his brain, triggering his own explosive climax, which seemed to go on and on until he fell exhausted atop her.

And as he lay there, pillowed by her softness, with her arms wrapped about him and her legs entangled with his, he thought, *My love.*

But he was too much of a coward to say it.

Twenty-Two

Monique lay in Gregory's arms, her heart broken and bleeding. She was foolish to expect love from a man like him. Yet now that she knew how desperately she loved him, she wanted him to love her in return. And he just didn't. He desired her, but that was all.

It wasn't enough. After all these years, she finally understood why Grand-maman had gone against her family, why she'd fled with Grand-papa, why she'd never regretted her decision. Because love was a powerful feeling that made one do mad things.

Like give oneself to a man who apparently couldn't love. Or at least couldn't love *her*.

"Gregory?" she murmured.

"Hmm?"

"I must go. My maid will wonder what I'm doing."

He pulled her close. "It's early yet. Stay awhile."

He gazed into her face with heavy-lidded eyes. "You're a princess. You can stay out as late as you like."

"I'm not a princess, and no, I can't."

She tried to leave his arms, but he held her fast. "Please, my sweet," he said hoarsely. "Don't go just yet."

Her eyes burned with tears. "All right."

In truth, she didn't want to go. She wanted to stay in his arms forever, but that was unwise. And he knew it. He just didn't want to accept it.

She ought to argue with him about his plans. She ought to point out again the futility of going against Danworth. But she didn't have the heart for it, and she doubted anything she said would change his mind.

Besides, he looked so peaceful lying next to her, with his arms wrapped about her.

"What will you do?" she asked.

He clearly knew what she meant. "I don't know. But Danworth has no evidence."

"What does it matter, as long as he has insinuation on his side? As he said, all he need do is rouse suspicions concerning your father's death, and you'll be ruined. He won't need to prove it in a court of law."

"True." His brow furrowed as if something had occurred to him, and he shifted to lie back and stare at the ceiling. "Insinuation is a powerful thing."

"Yes! That's what I've been saying!"

Glancing over at her, he smiled. "Have you any idea how fetching you are when you're in a temper?" He slid his hand over her breast. "How desirable?"

She fought the need he roused in her blood. "*Mon Dieu*, you're insatiable," she said, removing his hand. "I must go."

With a sigh, he fell back against his pillow. "I suppose you must. And I have to speak to Hart tonight, anyway."

"About what?"

"You'll see," he said noncommittally. Then he folded his arms beneath his head as if settling in for the night.

She wanted to laugh. It had been a long day, so she understood why he might be tired, but he looked so adorable as he fought sleep that she also wanted to snuggle up against him and stay the whole night.

How horrible that she couldn't. She waited until she heard his breathing even out before she left the bed. For a moment she just stood there, staring at him, memorizing every inch of him.

She knew what she must do, no matter what he seemed to think about it. Perhaps the count would take pity on her and take Grand-maman in nonetheless. Or perhaps Lady Ursula could convince him to do so.

But to persuade them of that, she'd have to tell them Gregory's dirty little secret, and she just couldn't. Even the thought of him suffering abuse as a boy at the hands of his father made her throat close up and her heart constrict.

No, she mustn't tell a soul. It was too dangerous.

She gathered her clothes and dressed as best she could without help. With any luck, she could make it to her bedchamber without being seen. She'd just have to hope that Flora kept her mouth shut. But first . . .

Slipping into the study, she found some paper and a quill pen. Perhaps she was a coward to do it this way, but she couldn't argue with him anymore. He always overwhelmed her with his assertions that he would take care of matters that she knew he couldn't change. So this was the only way.

Sitting down at his desk, she began to write.

When Gregory awoke, he was disappointed to find that Monique had left. Though he wasn't surprised. She was far more conscious of her reputation than he seemed to be these days.

He thought over what had occurred to him earlier: a plan to gain everything he wanted while also thwarting Danworth. Monique had put the idea in his head by speaking of insinuation. It had dawned on him that insinuation could work for *him*, too. He would need to do research—speak to some people, have Hart speak to some people, lay out everything beforehand—but it just might work.

And if it didn't?

Fear seized his gut. If it didn't, he would lose everything. And Monique would, too, if she chose to stay with him. But at least her future—and that of her grandmother—would be secured. And he would have her. Forever. They'd be joined together in scandal, but that was better than letting Danworth succeed in his blackmail. Or get away with his attempts to murder her.

Gregory rose from the bed. It was worth any risk to make sure that didn't happen. And how strange that the idea of having her as his wife made him almost giddy with excitement. He hadn't felt giddy since he was a boy and he and John had gone fishing together on one of those rare occasions when Father had gone to London without them.

He pulled on his drawers and went into his study. That's when he noticed the sheet of paper on his desk. Odd. It was a letter from Monique. And as he read it over, he began to scowl.

Dearest Gregory,

I know that you think you're doing what is right, and I admire you for it. Truly, I do. But I refuse to be the cause of scandal for you and your mother, especially after all you've endured.

So tomorrow morning I shall leave with your friend Lord Hartley and return to

Dieppe. Let the count explain the reason for it, if he can.

As for you, you must do what your conscience dictates, but if you are as wise as I know you are, you will act to preserve your future and your family.

And forget about me. It would be one thing if you loved me, but as you said, it is only desire for you. I don't want to see you toss away everything for desire when you can find that with any pretty woman. You need a wife whom you can love as I love you. Clearly, I am not the one who fits that requirement.

Just know this. I shall never forget you.

With much affection,
Monique

He balled the letter up in his fist and tossed it into the fire. Damn her! Had she no faith in him? She'd fully intended to sneak away without his knowledge. How could she?

It would be one thing if you loved me . . .

Love, hah! Why did she think he despised the very idea of it? Because of things like *this*—people using the idea of love to get what they wanted.

He scrubbed one hand over his face. No, that wasn't fair. She wasn't trying to get anything from him. She was trying to save him. But didn't she see? That was precisely the problem with loving someone. It made you do mad things, reckless things . . . dangerous things.

Mother's love for Father had nearly destroyed her, and might very well destroy Gregory, too, if he didn't make his plan work. Every friend of his at St. George's who'd fallen in love had ended up in some sort of trouble for it. And he'd had a hand in helping two of them *out* of their trouble.

Still, they'd also ended up happy after facing that trouble with their wives, together.

Scowling, he went to put on his clothes. That didn't change the fact that she'd tried to sneak out without saying any of this to his face. Clearly she'd thought he wouldn't see the letter until morning, until after she'd left with Hart.

Hart! Damn. The man was supposed to leave at dawn. In a moment of panic, Gregory glanced at the clock, then let out a relieved breath. One a.m., thank God. He hadn't slept *that* late, at least.

Dressing hurriedly, he headed downstairs in search of Hart. He wasn't surprised to find the fellow in the drawing room playing cards. He *was* surprised to find him playing cards with Mother, of all people.

"What are you doing up so late?" Gregory asked his mother.

"Keeping Lord Hartley company," she said primly. "He said he's leaving before dawn to go on some fool's errand for you, and he saw no point in retiring to bed only to have to rise again in the wee hours of the morning."

"Actually, I need him to go on that fool's errand now," Gregory said.

"Good heavens!" she cried. "You and your friends are all quite mad. First, Danworth has to rush off to London, and then—"

A chill swept over him. "Danworth is gone?"

"Yes. He left right after he finished his meeting with you in your study."

"Bloody coward." No doubt the arse had feared that Gregory might murder him in his sleep.

But it was just as well the chap had fled to town; it would make things simpler. And quite possibly mean the end of the attempts on Monique's life. "Did Prince Leopold leave with him?"

Mother blinked. "No. Why would he?"

"No reason." And that might be one more sign that Leopold wasn't fully aware of what Danworth was up to. Or that he didn't want anyone to guess that they were friends, in case Danworth's machinations didn't work. "Hart—"

"I know." He stood. "You want me to go now. I'm packed and ready. I was just waiting for morning."

"I need you to wait for one more thing. You and I must speak with Lady Ursula before you go."

"Don't be ridiculous, son," Mother said. "She retired hours ago."

"We'll have to wake her, then. Actually, Mother, it's a good thing you're up. You can rouse her while I give Hart a few last-minute instructions."

"Can't it wait until morning?" she said.

So Monique could slip away with Hart? Not a chance in hell. "I'm afraid not. It's more important than you can possibly know." When his mother just stared at him, he added, "*Now*, Mother. Please go fetch Lady Ursula right *now*."

Mother rolled her eyes, but rose to do his bidding. As she walked away, he thought of something.

"Oh, and Mother? Whatever you do, don't wake up Mo— The princess. That's crucial. She needs her sleep."

His mother sniffed. "So do we all, thanks to you and your schemes." Then she stalked off up the stairs.

As soon as she was gone, Gregory sat down to tell Hart what was going on. Although it was necessary to reveal his darkest secret to his most trusted ally, it still chafed him that he must do so.

To Gregory's shock, Hart didn't condemn him for what he had done in his youth. He only asked questions to clarify the facts. Gregory was grateful for that. Perhaps Hart might see a crack in Danworth's scheme that Gregory had missed.

"Sounds like an accidental death to me," Hart mused. "No one would probably even prosecute you for it."

"They won't have to. In Danworth's hands, the tale will still ruin me."

As he explained what the bastard wanted, Hart's expression turned deadly. "That devil. I had no idea Danworth was so despicable."

Gregory nodded grimly. "I always knew he was ambitious, but I never guessed he would do *anything* for his ambition, even blackmail a man."

"Or commit murder?"

"That, too, quite possibly."

"So what do you mean to do about it?"

Gregory laid out the entirety of his plan for Hart. Then he asked, "What do you think? Will it work?"

"I'm not sure. If it does, it could solve everything. But it relies on a number of factors beyond your control."

"I realize that." For a moment, terror gripped him at the idea of all the ways this could go wrong, of the possibility that in four days he would be watching his life go up in flames.

He shook off the thought. "But I know you'll do your part as best you can."

"Absolutely." Hart reached over to grip his shoulder. "You gave me a chance years ago, and I've never forgotten it. I'll do everything in my power to give *you* a chance."

"Thanks."

Just then, Gregory's mother returned with Lady Ursula, who looked rather tired in her nightdress and wrapper.

Gregory rose. "Thank you, Mother. You can go to bed now."

"The devil I will!" She crossed her arms over her bosom. "I haven't had this much excitement in years, and you're not going to pack me off like some child while you plot and scheme."

He should have known he wouldn't be able to keep her in the dark forever. "Fine, you can stay." He pointed to the settee. "But only if you keep quiet until I'm done with Lady Ursula and Hart." Then he turned to the lady-in-waiting. "Madam, I need you to tell Hart exactly where the count has hidden Princess Aurore in Calais."

As Mother blinked at that, Lady Ursula's face lit up. "I'll travel with him and show him."

"No, you will not," he said firmly. "It's bad enough that *I* must leave to take care of certain matters in London. I can excuse myself as needing to handle an emergency regarding the conference. But if *you* leave, who have no excuse for doing so, it will spark too much speculation. It's imperative that no one else know of Hart's mission—not the count, not Prince Leopold, no one—and that means you must stay here. Do you understand?"

She bobbed her head. "It's not as if Prince Leopold and I are very friendly these days. I think he blames me for Aurore's refusal of his suit. He probably expected me to influence her to accept."

"Ah." That explained why Leopold had treated her so coldly.

Taking some paper and a pencil from a writing desk, he handed them to her. "Write it down. Draw a map if you have to."

It didn't take her long. And as soon as she was done, Hart headed off. Gregory sent Lady Ursula back up to bed, but there was no getting rid of his mother until she learned exactly what was going on.

He'd been dreading this, but she needed to know, given that her life might be upended, too. He sat on the settee next to her.

Before he could even begin, she asked, "Is this about Danworth?"

He tensed. "What makes you think that?"

"Because the day after you warned me of people asking about your father's death, Danworth struck up a conversation with me about it. He made some comment about how hard it must have been for you to see your father die so tragically. I told him in no uncertain terms that you were away at school."

Hmm. What if Danworth had been bluffing about that shopkeeper? What if he'd attempted to get the truth out of Mother and hadn't succeeded, so he'd just made something up?

"Thanks for telling me, Mother. Yes, it has to do with Danworth. And as I guess you've deduced, it also concerns a different princess from the one who is here—although Danworth doesn't seem to know that. Here's the thing . . ."

It took him a while to tell her everything. When he was done, she seemed surprisingly calm.

"Someone was bound to find out the truth someday. I suppose we're lucky we've managed to hide it for this long."

"My plan *will* work, Mother," he said. "All I'm asking is that you continue to keep quiet unless forced into testifying in court. But I honestly don't think it will come to that."

"I hope not." She patted his hand. "You're a good son."

They sat a moment in silence. Then she dragged in a heavy breath. "So you mean to marry this actress/princess, do you?"

That put him instantly on his guard. "I do."

"Does she love you?"

"She says she does," he said, his voice more unsteady than he would have liked.

His mother caught his tone, as always. "And do you love *her*?"

"You too?" he said irritably. "What does that matter? You loved Father. Look how that turned out."

"True. But love is always a risk. Indeed, I find it strange that you will take any number of risks in your career—fomenting schemes and hiring spies and whatnot—without a thought, but you won't take a chance on love."

He scowled. "That's different."

"How?"

Because love could rip out your soul and tromp on it, leaving you with nothing. "Because when I take risks in my career, what results is by *my* choice. If I take a risk with my heart, the results depend on someone else's choice."

"On her being a good person, you mean. Unlike your father."

Mother knew how to cut right to the point. "I know already that she's a good person." He'd seen it in myriad ways. That wasn't the issue.

"Then forgive me if I'm wrong," his mother went on softly, "but it seems to me that you have already put your heart at risk, or you wouldn't be fighting her over sacrificing herself for your benefit. You wouldn't be dreaming up a scheme that could ruin your future, just for the chance of being with her."

She rose to lay her hand on his shoulder. "I think your heart has already chosen, son. You just need to let it have its way. Otherwise, you'll spend the rest of your life wondering if, because you were too afraid to take the risk, you missed your one chance at finding the person who makes you whole."

With a squeeze of his shoulder, she left.

Long after she was gone, he sat pondering her words and considering how he'd lived his life. Perhaps Mother was right. He'd spent twenty years thinking that insulating himself from emotion would protect him from feeling too much. And it had worked. It had made him numb. To the world, to people . . . to the realities of his own childhood agonies.

It had also kept him from living a full life. Enjoying his own estate, having friends without thinking what purpose they served. Loving a woman who might love him back.

Thickness clogged his throat. He'd been ignoring the needs of his heart to avoid having the pain of a broken one, but he had lost the joy of a full one in the process. So perhaps it was time he considered the needs of his heart.

Because if he didn't, he might lose the only thing he'd ever truly wanted.

Twenty-Three

Wanting to be sure to catch Lord Hartley before he left, Monique had asked Flora to wake her an hour before dawn. She'd considered speaking to him the night before about letting her join him on his trip to London, where she could then catch a steam packet to Dieppe, but she'd worried that he might reveal her plans to Gregory. So she'd decided it was best to take him by surprise just as he was leaving.

She'd then packed a large reticule with a few essentials. None of Aurore's gowns and lavish nightwear would be going with her, since they weren't hers to take. Instead, she was wearing the clothes she'd gone to Calais in.

"Flora," she now said, "would you please go down and ask Lord Hartley if I might have a word with him before he departs?"

"Of course, Princess."

Monique had just finished dabbing perfume in

all the important spots when Flora came back in, sooner than she'd expected.

"I'm sorry, Your Highness," she said, looking a bit anxious, "but his lordship left for London some hours ago. I believe Lord Fulkham asked him to leave earlier than planned."

Monique stared at her, stunned. Gregory must have seen the letter earlier than she'd anticipated, and then packed Lord Hartley off to prevent her from leaving. Why, that . . . that devious *canaille*! How dare he! He knew perfectly well she couldn't just set off for Dieppe on her own.

Ooh, she would give him a piece of her mind!

She marched out her door and down to Gregory's bedchamber. She didn't even have to burst in, for his door was open and he was ordering some footmen to carry out his trunks.

She waited until they had disappeared downstairs before she marched in and slammed the door behind her.

He turned, his face lighting up. "Ah, there you are. I was just coming to—"

"Take your leave?" she snapped. "Which you would not allow *me* to do?"

A shadow crossed his features. "Hear me out, my sweet. I have a plan to save us."

"I have one, too." She stood there, shaking with anger. "But you won't let me implement it because everything has to be *your* way, in *your* time, even though it will mean . . ." She choked up, thinking of him burning his future down about his ears.

Afraid that she might burst into tears, she turned on her heel and headed back for the door. "Well, you follow your plan. But *I* am going to the count and demand that he return me to Dieppe. He can do as he wishes with me, but at least—"

"Wait, darling, *please*—"

"I will not!" she cried, and reached for the door handle. "There's no reason to!"

"I love you, Monique. Isn't that reason enough?"

For a moment, she thought she had imagined the words. She froze, her hand still on the handle. "What did you say?"

He came closer. "I love you. I'm *in* love with you. Or, in case you don't understand it in English, *je t'aime*."

Wary, she turned to face him. "You're just saying that to keep me from leaving."

"No. I do want to keep you from leaving. But that's not why I'm saying it." His eyes shone with sincerity. "I'm saying it because it's true."

Her pulse began to race. "How can that be?"

Uttering a self-deprecating laugh, he said, "I'm not sure. I'm still . . . getting used to the idea myself." He neared her with caution, as a rider might approach a spooked mount. "I always said that love was reckless, unwise. Because my career—my ambition, as you call it—had always been about assuring outcomes, measuring risks, managing the future. Being in control."

"The way you weren't in control with your father," she whispered.

He glanced away, naked vulnerability in his face. "Right."

It should have occurred to her before. The rigid rules, the iron restraint he kept over his emotions, were necessary to him because he'd had no say over his father's abuse, no way to change it. "Your ambition has always been about not being that little boy at the mercy of a cruel father with an unpredictable fist."

His gaze shot to her unerringly. "Right again. About not being that little boy who'd persisted in hoping for some crumb of affection, even when the man whom he wished would offer it was incapable of that."

A lump lodged in her throat. He was opening his heart to her, and she had never thought it would happen. Despite the frantic beating of her own heart, she kept very still, eager to hear him say it all, needing to know that he meant it.

"After Father . . ." He dragged in a ragged breath. "After I killed him, I swore never to let myself be that vulnerable again. Never to let my emotions guide my actions. I thought if I just worked at it, I could control how I felt, as I controlled everything else."

A faint smile crossed his lips. "But if I've learned anything in the past few days, it's that controlling one's heart is impossible. The heart takes its own course, no matter how hard one tries to guide it. And mine . . ." He reached for her, his eyes luminous with emotion. "Mine set a course for you from the moment I met you. I just . . . didn't want to admit it."

"Oh, Gregory," she whispered, lifting her hand to his cheek with the first stirrings of joy in her soul. "My heart set a course for you, too. No matter what path I take, my heart will always be yours."

He caught her hand in his, then turned it to kiss the palm. "Then put your faith in me, *mon amour.* I meant it when I said I had a plan that I think will work. I'm rather adept at scheming, as you've noticed. But you must trust me. Can you? Because without you, my plan will surely fail." His voice dropped into his usual ironic drawl. "And then you and I will have to escape to the Continent and leave my mother's lovely gardens behind just so we can be together."

"I wouldn't want that," she said through a voice thick with tears. Choking them down, she tried to match his tone. "You wouldn't like living on the Continent. Too many comedies and operas being performed, and not enough tragedies."

"I will live the rest of my days in an opera house if that's the only way to have you as my wife," he said fiercely, gripping her hand in both of his. "But I think we can do better. Will you let me do this for you? For us both? Will you take a chance on me?"

She hesitated only a moment before nodding. "But only if you tell me the plan. We do this together, or not at all."

A brilliant smile broke over his face. "I wouldn't have it any other way. Now, here's what we're going to do . . ."

~

Monique paced the London town house, scarcely able to contain herself. It had been three days since she and Gregory had professed their love and he'd left for London. Two of them she'd spent at Canterbury Court, pretending to be Princess Aurore, to be unaware of the treacheries swirling beneath the surface around them. She'd fended off the flirtations of both the Duc de Pontalba and Prince Leopold while praying that Gregory could make his mad plan work.

At least in the country, she'd been able to avoid the count, since he and Gregory's mother seemed to have struck up a friendship. They'd been very chummy, though Monique wondered if they would stay that way once the count found out she meant to marry Gregory and not some fellow of his choosing.

On the drive back yesterday evening, however, she'd been closeted with the count and Lady Ursula for hours, and the enormity of what was about to happen today in London had hit her.

Everything could go to hell in a short while. Not

knowing how Gregory's machinations had gone while he'd been in London was driving her mad, but he'd insisted they not see each other until the vote today. He couldn't risk Danworth's catching wind of their plans. Better that the wretch not know what had hit him until it happened.

The count entered the drawing room. "It's time to go, niece. Ursula awaits us in the carriage."

With a nod, she followed him out the door. But as soon as the carriage set off with the three of them, she couldn't seem to catch her breath. If this went wrong . . .

"Are you all right?" Lady Ursula asked.

"Just . . . nervous," she said.

The count reached forward to pat her knee. "Relax, niece. It's almost over now."

His faux kindness was too much to be borne, given all that had happened and the way she was strung tight as a wire over the stage. "Almost over for *you*, perhaps, Uncle." She couldn't hide the resentment in her voice. "But if the delegates vote for one of the other candidates, I will be returning to Dieppe forthwith, no better off than I was before."

At least that was what she *would* have been doing, if not for Gregory.

A flush rose in his cheeks. "Actually, I should have told you before, but . . . well, I still intend to bring you back to Chanay once this is done, no matter what the vote is. I always did."

She gaped at him. "What?!" Then she shot Lady Ursula an accusing glance. "Did you know this?"

"No, I swear!"

The count crossed his arms over his chest, looking sullen. "I had to make sure you saw the charade out to the end. That you put the full force of your ability into it."

Rage roared up inside her. "You mean you only threatened to abandon me and Grand-maman to *spur me on*? To make sure you got your money's worth out of me?"

He shrugged. "You could look at it that way."

Oh, that was . . . She couldn't believe . . . She was going to kill him! All of this had been avoidable! If she'd known that the count was predisposed to help her, no matter what, she could have told him about Gregory from the beginning, and they could have worked matters out to determine how best to proceed. If Gregory had known the reasons for her masquerade, he might better have countenanced it. He might not right now be preparing to lose everything, if necessary, to gain her.

That brought her up short. She couldn't regret that. Or the circumstances that had led to her finding love with Gregory. But that didn't mean she wasn't still furious with her great-uncle.

"What a truly awful thing to do," she snapped. "I don't *want* you to take care of Grand-maman. She would be better off in a garret somewhere than with the likes of you, damn you!"

"Now, niece—"

"No! I shall not listen. When this is over, I want nothing more to do with you. I shall marry Lord Fulkham, and Grand-maman will live with *us*."

Lady Ursula smiled, having obviously already figured out how things were going with Gregory.

But the count scoffed. "Marry Fulkham? He would never marry an actress. It would hurt his career."

"But I'm *not* just an actress, am I?" she said bitterly. "I'm third in line for the throne behind Grand-maman and some great-aunt of mine."

She had the great satisfaction of watching him blanch before his gaze shot to Lady Ursula. "You *told* her?"

"Not I. Lord Fulkham told her."

Confusion clouded his features. "But then he would have had to know—"

"My true identity," Monique finished. "Yes, he knew from the beginning, because he'd met me years ago. And I was too afraid to tell you because of your stupid threats. Instead, I lived in terror that he would expose me."

She glanced out to see them pulling up in front of the assembly hall where the conference had been held. "Oh, why am I even bothering to tell you? It doesn't matter anymore."

"But truly, niece," her uncle said. "He means to *marry* you?"

A footman opened the door to the carriage

and bowed to her. "Your Highness. They're waiting for you inside."

She paused to stare at her uncle. "Yes, *marry me*. But before then, he means to risk everything for me. So just stay out of our way, will you? Because if you ruin this for him and me—"

"No, no, I won't," he said hastily.

"Good. Because if you do, Uncle, I swear I shall never speak to you again."

Then, lifting her head and taking on the mantle of Princess Aurore for the last time, she descended from the carriage and went to meet her fate.

Twenty-Four

Gregory stood backstage at the assembly hall, his stomach in upheaval and his heart racing. Hart wasn't here, despite having sent a message earlier saying he would arrive there soon. Where the devil was he? Something must have happened. And if he didn't get here in time . . .

"My lord, they're ready to begin," a servant said.

Damn. He would have to stall the proceedings somehow.

But that shouldn't be difficult. The conference had been full of boring speeches on the importance of keeping Belgium neutral. Surely he could manage one of those.

With a steadying breath, he walked out onto the stage. And that's when he saw her. His love, sitting in the audience with her trusting gaze fixed on him.

Three days without her had only firmed his

determination not to fail her . . . or his mother or any of the other people dependent upon him. In those three days, he'd learned much, uncovered much, and even spoken to Wellington, who'd confirmed that Danworth had made a trip to Calais around the time of Aurore's poisoning. It had been clear that Wellington had never been involved in any of this, and Gregory had promised not to drag him into it.

So Gregory was better prepared than he had been before. But that didn't mean everything would go smoothly. And if Hart didn't come . . .

He refused to worry about that right now. This would work. He would *make* it work, damn it, with or without Hart.

He began by thanking the delegates and their candidates, stating how important this matter was, and in general stretching out the time. As he talked, he noticed Danworth looking smug and certain, as if he'd guessed that Gregory was stalling . . . except that Danworth probably thought Gregory was merely putting off the inevitable.

Then the doors in the back of the hall opened, and Gregory spotted Hart with a young woman.

Gregory stared in disbelief. It couldn't be.

"My lord!" Hart called out, ignoring all protocols. "Before you proceed, there is someone here who must speak."

Everyone turned toward the back of the room, and several gasped. Because standing there, dressed in a resplendent gown, was a woman who could have been Monique's twin, if not for her pale, sickly countenance. And her less-than-prominent chin.

His heart swelled with relief. "Princess Aurore!" he announced. "Please, do come to the stage!"

With a regal manner, she swept up the center aisle, and the room erupted into whispers and furtive glances at Monique, who sat serenely, as if she'd expected this great surprise. Even Danworth looked startled, along with most of the delegates.

As Princess Aurore came to join Gregory at the podium, he stood aside to give her the floor.

"Thank you, Lord Fulkham," she said with a kind smile for him. "And I must beg the pardon of the delegates. I would have been here sooner, but I have been very ill. A couple of weeks ago, someone attempted to poison me and very nearly succeeded in killing me."

After a collective gasp sounded in the audience, she went on. "In my hour of need my second cousin, the famous actress Monique Servais, was kind enough to step in for me." She gestured to Monique, who acknowledged her with a smile. "Fortunately, Lord Fulkham, recognizing the dangers of having the work of this conference thwarted by a villain, concocted a plan. My cousin would take my place here while I recovered. And in the meantime, his lordship would try to discover who the assassin was."

Gregory released a breath. Thank God the

princess had been willing to go along with their rewritten version of events. Though she would have been a fool not to, since it exonerated her people as well.

It also really started the delegates murmuring.

"From what I've been told," she went on, "my poor cousin Monique has since endured two attempts on *her* life—first in London and then at Lord Fulkham's estate, where he'd taken her to try to protect her from harm. Fortunately, his lordship was finally able to discover who the assassin was. Lord Fulkham? Will you tell us what you learned?" She moved aside.

Gregory couldn't help noticing the sudden tension in Danworth's face. "Thank you, Princess. In the past few days I have found out that only one man from the conference—other than the princess's retinue, of course—was in Calais during the time of the poisoning."

He narrowed his gaze on his enemy. "The prime minister's private secretary, Mr. Danworth."

As the room erupted into shocked cries and horrified whispers, Danworth jumped to his feet. "How *dare* you, sir? What possible reason could I have had to poison Princess Aurore?"

"You wanted to put your good friend Prince Leopold in the position of king of Belgium in exchange for being offered a position in his government."

Gregory shifted his stare to Leopold. There

was no mistaking the shock that crossed Leopold's face. "What?" the man cried and jumped to his feet. "I swear I had nothing to do with Mr. Danworth's actions!"

If Gregory hadn't already suspected as much, he might have dismissed the prince's assertions. But as it was, he nodded to the prince. "Would you like to speak, sir? To defend yourself?"

"I most certainly would!" Prince Leopold marched up onto the stage. "Mr. Danworth, my friend there, if you can call him that, promised to use his influence with the prime minister on my behalf. And yes, in exchange I promised him a position in my government in Belgium, should I be fortunate enough to become king."

When that started another murmuring among the crowd, he added, "But I would *never* have countenanced assassination! I thought he meant only to speak to the prime minister. And perhaps to make his case to Lord Fulkham, a member of his club, which is what he promised. I had no idea—"

"This is all nonsense!" Danworth cried. "I never attempted to assassinate anyone. And how are we even to know that this . . . Servais woman is actually the cousin of Princess Aurore?"

"Will *my* word in that regard suffice?" the count called out, to Gregory's surprise. The older statesman rose, clearly having caught the gist of where things were heading. "I brokered the exchange— with the help of his lordship, of course. My great-niece, Monique, is third in line for the throne behind two elderly relations. She would have become the princess in truth if Aurore had died." He crossed his arms over his chest. "If you don't believe me, I can show you the entire line of the Chanay royal family."

"Besides," Gregory cut in, "I have managed to hunt down the assassin Danworth hired to try to kill Mademoiselle Servais." That had taken some doing, but once he'd known of Danworth's involvement, Gregory had been able to track the man's friends and acquaintances and unearth the shooter in his hovel in Spitalfields.

As Danworth paled, Gregory exulted. "Under the threat of prosecution for attempted murder, the former servant of Mr. Danworth has been more than eager to cooperate with the authorities. He confessed to having been paid by Mr. Danworth to shoot at Mademoiselle Servais not once, but twice."

"This is absurd." Danworth narrowed his gaze on Gregory. "His lordship is merely trying to smear my name to avoid having his own past unveiled. I recently discovered that he was responsible for the death of his father!"

There were more gasps, more eyes turned toward Gregory.

Now came the tricky part. "I don't suppose you have any evidence to support that claim," Gregory drawled. "Because I was at Eton at the time of my father's death, as anyone can attest."

Just as he'd guessed, Danworth's assertion that a shopkeeper had seen Gregory had been a bluff. "I—I'm sure that someone at Eton could confirm—"

"So you have no evidence," Gregory said coldly. "Who's trying to smear a fellow's name *now?* Because, unlike you, I have ample evidence to validate my own case. I can prove your involvement in the attempt to murder Princess Aurore and her cousin."

Princess Aurore whispered something in his ear.

"Her Highness tells me that my friend, Lord Hartley, who went to fetch the princess for this meeting, discovered that you paid a maid to put poison in Princess Aurore's evening chocolate. Then there's the testimony of His Grace, Wellington, that you were sent to Calais. There's your former servant, who confessed to firing upon the princess's representative at your behest . . ."

Danworth glanced about in a panic. "And in your case, there's a button. A button that was clutched in Lord Fulkham's hand. I—I mean, the *previous* Lord Fulkham's hand. Ask the constable! He will tell you!"

"A button?" Gregory gave a caustic laugh. "That is your evidence? Fine, go ahead. Bring the constable down to London. Let's see what he has to say."

When Gregory had gone to speak to the constable, the man had professed that he didn't know of any button, and that even if he had, it was long gone. Gregory suspected that after years of patronage by the Fulkhams, the constable didn't want to bite the hand that fed him, and Gregory certainly wasn't going to make him do so.

Rage filled Danworth's face as it dawned on him that he was not going to win this fight. "You bloody bastard. You always have to succeed, no matter who you trample upon. You couldn't let one crumb fall from the table for a mere private secretary like me, who has served his country well until now. All you had to do was vote for Leopold, but because some whore of an actress whispered in your ear about attempted murder—"

"Some cousin to the princess, you mean," Gregory hissed, unable to keep his temper one minute more. "And I was *with* her when your man shot at her. Both times! If she had died—"

Realizing that everyone was gaping at him, he fought for control, then continued in a more measured tone. "If Mademoiselle Servais had died in the place of Princess Aurore while in England, it would have been a heinous blot on these proceedings and the country you claim to be serving. So yes, I take issue with your actions."

Danworth's gaze shot daggers. "Well, you will hear from me further! I have not yet—"

"All right, gentlemen!" Gregory cried to the police officers waiting in the back. "You may place Mr. Danworth under arrest now."

As the buzz in the assembly hall grew deafening, the officers marched forward with grim intent. Nothing like a bit of official theatrics to seal the fate of a blackmailing arse. Danworth could rouse questions about the death of Gregory's father all he liked, but the image of him being dragged away in shackles would take precedence in the minds of the delegates.

Or so Gregory hoped. This had always been a risk. He glanced over at Monique, who ventured a smile in return. A risk well worth taking.

He steadied his breath, then turned to the business he was good at. He brought the gavel down on the podium enough times to gain quiet in the room. "Now that we've taken care of that," he said, "perhaps we should go on with the vote."

Princess Aurore put a hand on his arm. "If you don't mind, my lord, before you vote, I have something else to say."

Gregory tensed. *This* he hadn't anticipated. "Of course, Your Serene Highness," he said, and stepped back.

"While I am enormously grateful to my cousin for putting herself in my place, nearly dying has given me a new perspective on life. So it is with great regret that I must withdraw as a candidate for ruler of Belgium." She slid a quick glance and a smile toward where Lady Ursula sat. "I prefer to continue my uneventful life in Chanay, with the people I know and love. And Belgium deserves a ruler who would put it first. That would not be me. Thank you."

As she left the stage, Gregory stood there stunned. The irony did not escape him. If the princess had said that in the beginning, he could have voted for Prince Leopold without going against his conscience.

Except that he would never have known for sure if Leopold had been part of the scheme. And Danworth would have gotten away with trying to kill Aurore and Monique.

That wouldn't have passed the demands of his conscience. How refreshing to know that he still had one.

Curious to see what the Chanay contingent thought of Princess Aurore's announcement, he glanced to where the count and Lady Ursula sat beside Monique. Lady Ursula was beaming; no surprise there. But the count wore a rather pensive look on his face, and that *was* a surprise.

What the devil was that about?

The room had gone very quiet, and it suddenly dawned on Gregory that they were waiting for him to guide the proceedings.

He stepped once again to the podium and cleared his throat. "Well, then, it appears we have one less candidate to vote for."

Pontalba rose. "*Two* less, don't you mean, Lord Fulkham? How do we know that Prince Leopold wasn't behind Danworth's actions all along?"

"Because in my investigation of this matter, I didn't find one shred of evidence supporting that.

Nor did Danworth ever say that he was acting at the prince's behest."

As Pontalba took his seat, it was clear his words had still had some impact on the assembly. There was nothing Gregory could do about that. But the fact was, with Princess Aurore out of the running, it was in England's best interests to put Leopold in place. And the Dutch would never vote for a Frenchman, nor would Austria, Prussia, or Russia.

So, with that in mind, he called for a vote.

Monique wasn't entirely surprised when Prince Leopold was chosen in the end. She'd had a chance to get to know him over the past few days when Gregory was gone, and it had become apparent to her that he would make a good ruler. Putting aside his flirtations, which she chalked up to his attempt at making a sound political alliance, she judged him reasonable, responsible, and eager to serve. No one could fault those qualities in a king.

Nor had she been entirely surprised when Princess Aurore withdrew as a candidate. Clearly, the princess had known that becoming ruler of Belgium would seriously damage any future between her and Lady Ursula. And it was obvious, at least to Monique, that the two women were thoroughly in love. Monique only hoped that their life together would be a happy one, despite their not being able to publicly acknowledge their affections.

Now that the vote had taken place, the conference attendees were dispersing to attend a lavish reception being held at St. James's Palace. Gregory came over to greet them.

It was all Monique could do not to run up and throw herself into his arms. But he and she had agreed that the best thing for his career and her future as his wife would be a sedate courtship conducted in full view of society. Gregory insisted that he wouldn't have any trouble selling that to the press after her heroic actions.

And judging from the delegates who kept stopping to say how appreciative they were that she had risked her life for the good of the conference, he might be right. She seemed to be the woman of the hour.

But she knew better than anyone how swiftly such adoration could turn to scorn. It was the only fly in her ointment. Danworth's words *some whore of an actress* still rankled.

Not that you could tell from the heat in Gregory's eyes as he met her gaze. He banked it swiftly, though, and turned to hold out his hand to the count. "Thank you for supporting me in this endeavor. I'm only sorry that things did not turn out as you had hoped."

With a snort, her uncle shook Gregory's hand and glanced over to where Princess Aurore and

Lady Ursula were conversing in low voices. "One can never predict what the young will do. I try to give them the benefit of my years of experience, and this is how they thank me."

Then he gave a Gallic shrug. "On the other hand, I am getting rather old to be guiding an obstinate princess. I'm not sure how I would have liked being a queen-maker in Brussels. Indeed, I may wish to do some traveling instead." A gleam lit his eyes. "I may even extend my visit to England, assuming that your lovely mother would be willing to show me some of the countryside."

Gregory's shock was comical. "My mother."

"Yes." The count looked almost mischievous. "Lady Fulkham. I do believe you know her?"

"Apparently not as well as I thought," Gregory mumbled.

Monique stifled a laugh. "I'm afraid my uncle and your mother have become even friendlier in the days you were in London."

Her uncle glanced about the room, which had now emptied out to leave only the five of them standing there. He stared Gregory down. "Since you left Canterbury Court, I have also learned that you knew of Monique's subterfuge all along."

Gregory cast her a lingering glance. "I saw her play Suzanne in *The Marriage of Figaro*." He smiled warmly. "I never forgot her. Hard to forget a woman of her talent and beauty."

She eyed him skeptically. "I seem to recall

your not being quite so complimentary then, my lord."

"I was a fool. Fortunately, I've had three years to regret that."

The count narrowed his gaze. "Very touching, sir. That does not mean, however, that I shall let you blithely marry my great-niece without a number of meetings between my solicitor and yours to hammer out a suitable settlement."

"*Uncle*," she chided under her breath, shocked and embarrassed that he meant to step in on such a thing after all these years.

"I would think less of you if you did," Gregory told him. "Bring the solicitors on, old man, though I'm not sure you need them. I will agree to anything as long as it means that your great-niece can be my wife."

Monique swallowed, especially when Gregory followed that pronouncement with a wink at her.

"Very well," the count said. "Then I will consider giving my consent to the match."

She stifled the urge to tell him what he could do with his consent. He was being very magnanimous about everything, after all, especially considering the surprise her cousin had dropped into his lap.

Gregory stared him down. "There is *one* thing more I need from you. In the weeks to come, a number of news accounts concerning my courtship of Monique will appear. I ask that you stand behind whatever I'm quoted as saying in those accounts." His gaze hardened. "If you can do *that*, then *I* will consider consenting to your being 'friendly' with my mother."

To her surprise, her uncle chuckled. "Touché, my lord. Say what you please. I will support it."

Monique rolled her eyes. Men! They always had to brandish their spears and thump their chests as they laid claim to their women. Though she suspected that Lady Fulkham would have something to say about all this. Gregory's mother would lead the count a merry chase, no doubt. Monique looked forward to seeing it.

"And speaking of Lady Fulkham," the count went on, "shall we adjourn to the reception? Your mother had promised to attend."

"An excellent idea," Gregory said. "A carriage is outside to take you and Lady Ursula and Princess Aurore—the real one. Monique will be riding in my equipage." When her uncle bristled, Gregory added, "Suitably chaperoned, I assure you. Flora is waiting in the carriage."

That soothed her uncle's sudden chivalric impulses, though she wanted to tell him how hypocritical they were in light of the way he'd been behaving for the last two weeks. It seemed that having a baron want to marry her had altered his feelings considerably.

The group walked out together, and she and Gregory watched as their companions drove off in one coach. Then his carriage arrived and they climbed in. They had scarcely settled into their seats, and Monique had just registered that they were alone, before Gregory pulled her into his arms and gave her a long, heartfelt kiss that sent her pulse racing and her knees melting.

As it dawned on her what he was doing, she pushed away. "You told my uncle we'd be suitably chaperoned!"

"We will be . . . as soon as we fetch Flora from the park where she is indeed waiting in the carriage. Just not this one." His eyes gleamed at her. "And if we happen to take an hour or so touring the park beforehand, who will know? Certainly, Flora won't say anything. She works for *me*, after all."

When he reached for her again, she pressed her hand against his chest. "*You* said we had to behave above reproach until the official announcement of our betrothal!"

"We do. And when we arrive at the reception, you will be perfectly presentable, with your maid following right behind you." His voice lowered to a husky rasp. "But it's been three days, *mon amour*. If I don't have you to myself for at least an hour, I will die."

She eyed him askance. "A rather extravagant claim for a man who only last week couldn't bring himself to say the words 'I love you.'"

He grinned. "People change."

"Forever?" she asked, wanting to be sure. "Once all the furor is over, there will still be people who remember I was once a 'whore of an actress,' who will refuse to invite us, who will—"

"I don't care." Taking her hand, he stripped the glove from it with clear intent. "And I believe I told you never again to call yourself that." He tongued her wrist, reminding her of the last time he'd done so.

When a thrill shot through her, she caught her breath and had trouble remembering what she'd been saying. "O-other people may still . . . call me that."

"Not if they want to keep their teeth," he said, nipping at her tender skin as if to emphasize the *teeth* part. "Because I will tolerate no insult to my wife."

"You might not be able to . . . to stop them. If it costs you your career—"

"Enough." He cupped her chin in his hand. "I am going to say this only once. Unless you don't *wish* to marry me—and if that's the case, please tell me immediately—we are getting married. Because I love you, now and always. And nothing short of an act of Parliament will prevent me from making you my wife. So there will be no more worrying about the future or my career. Understood, *ma fiancée?*"

Fiancée. Oh, she *did* like the sound of that. And if he was mad enough to risk all to marry her, who was she to protest? "Whatever you say, *mon coeur.*"

He arched one eyebrow. "Why do I get the feeling that this will be the last time I ever hear those words again?"

She blinked. "*Mon coeur?*"

"No. 'Whatever you say.'"

"Oh, monsieur." She reached up to untie his cravat. "I can think of quite a few things you might tell me where I would respond with that phrase."

Need flared in his face. "Ah. Things like 'Take off your stockings, my love.' 'Lift your skirts, my love.'" He bent to whisper in her ear, "'Come to bed, my love.'"

"Whatever you say, *mon coeur.*" She lifted her skirts enough to unfasten her garters. "Whatever you say, *mon coeur.* And . . . I see no bed here, *mon coeur.*"

A chuckle escaped him. "I knew it. You could never be entirely biddable."

She smirked at him. "If you wanted 'biddable,' sir, you would have married long before now."

He laughed outright. "True. Then I suppose I must put this in terms you will accept. *Voulez-vous coucher avec moi, mon amour?*"

"Whatever you say, *mon coeur.*" Then, pulling his head down to hers, she showed him precisely how biddable she could be for the man she loved.

Epilogue

January 1831

In the ballroom of Canterbury Court, Gregory drank punch and watched his new wife dance with her great-uncle, who, true to his word, had been on an extended visit to England for the past two months. Rumors were already swirling that an offer of marriage from him to Gregory's mother was imminent. That made Gregory scowl.

"It's only been three hours since the wedding. Surely you are not already regretting the marriage," Hart said as he approached.

"Hardly. The only part I regret is having to call Beaumonde my relation."

"Twice over, if I'm to believe the rumors."

Gregory's scowl deepened. "Don't believe everything you hear."

"You do realize that your mother has a right to be happy, too."

He sighed. "I just worry that Beaumonde isn't the sort to make her happy."

"No one can decide that for someone else." Hart nudged him. "Though, honestly, you landed in clover, old fellow, getting to have Monique Servais as a wife."

Gregory's scowl vanished. "Don't I know it. No man was ever so lucky."

"You got an actress and a princess all in one. Who could ask for more?"

"Well, I doubt the princess part will ever come to fruition, with Princess Aurore still young and healthy." He shot Hart a sly glance. "Though a royal title could come to pass for our child."

Hart stared hard at him. "My God, don't tell me that you two are expecting."

With a smug smile, Gregory lifted his glass. "Keep this under your hat, but why do you think we married so quickly?"

"Quickly! You courted her for two months! And that was after you had clearly secured her affections."

"The plan was to court her for six." He grinned at Hart. "Not that I'm complaining. You have no idea how hard it is to court a woman respectably when all you want to do is marry her."

"I have no idea, indeed," Hart said, "since I have *never* wanted to marry. Or at least not in a very long time." Just as Gregory was going to press him further on that, Hart released a heavy sigh. "And now I owe damned Jeremy a hundred pounds."

"What for?" Gregory asked.

"*He* said that you were marrying to cover up the fact that you'd got Monique with child. Idiot that I am, *I* insisted that you would never be so reckless as to allow such a thing to happen, if you know what I mean."

Gregory chuckled. "I do, actually." The dance had ended, and his wife was heading toward him. His heart sped up, as it always did at the prospect of spending time with her. "But when I see something I want, I don't stop to think about consequences. It's my one failing."

"Huh. Better you than me. When it comes to women, I *always* think about consequences."

"You do *now*. That may change."

Hart frowned. "Unlikely."

Monique had reached them. "Lord Hartley! It's so good to see you. Where have you been the past two months?"

"Nowhere he can tell you, my sweet," Gregory said as he drew her to him. "You know how that is."

"Ah. More schemes, I see." She cast Hart a fond glance. "Well, good luck to you, sir. I assume you'll need it, to follow any instructions my husband would give you."

"What I need is to stop betting against married men," he grumbled, and walked off.

She eyed Gregory quizzically. "What is he talking about?"

"No idea." Somehow he doubted that she would enjoy hearing about Hart and Jeremy making bets on her virtue. "So, how is the count?"

A snort escaped her. "Grumpy as usual. At present your mother refuses to consider the idea of marriage."

Thank God. "Well, he can't blame me. I said not one word against it. And at least he fulfilled his end of our bargain, too."

"He did, indeed. I was rather surprised that matters turned out so well. The papers have portrayed us most romantically, thanks to your grand play at the assembly hall."

"Surely you didn't think my plan would fail," he said smugly. "By this time next year, the actress Monique will be forgotten and the Princess Monique will be firmly entrenched in the public's mind."

"And you will be foreign secretary. Or so say the rumors."

More and more, it looked as if he would. His machinations at the vote had impressed many in the new government. He could only pray no one ever found out what a near thing it had been.

"So why is Mother balking at accepting the count's offer?" he asked, now curious.

"I take it she's had too many overbearing men in her life."

"I do hope you're not including me in that number."

She feigned a look of shock. "You? Overbearing? Never!"

"Watch it, *mon amour*," he teased. "As of tonight, you will be permanently in my bed, and

I might have a mind to show you exactly what overbearing is."

Her eyes sparkled. "I can't wait."

His cock twitched, and he lowered his voice. "Neither can I."

Then they were surrounded by his fellow members of St. George's. *And* their wives.

"So the bachelor has finally fallen," Warren announced. "I never thought to see the day when a master conniver like Fulkham married for love." He paused. "You *did* marry for love, old chap, didn't you?"

"Of course he did," his wife, Delia, put in. "I knew he was in trouble the first time I saw him gazing with such . . . enthusiasm . . . at Princess Aurore." She shot the newlyweds a sheepish smile. "I mean *Monique*. Forgive me, I keep forgetting. And I'm so very happy for you both."

With his wife, Yvette, hanging on his arm, Jeremy Keane moved into the fore. "I'm still not entirely sure that the marriage isn't one of Fulkham's schemes." He eyed Gregory. "I'll believe it's a real marriage when I see their first child."

"Jeremy!" Lady Yvette chided.

"What? Don't tell me you didn't think the same."

"I did not!"

If Gregory hadn't already heard about Jeremy's bet with Hart, he might have taken offense, but he could tell the man was fishing for information. "You'll see my first child, Keane, only when you agree to paint his portrait."

"Or *her* portrait," Monique said with a sniff. "You never know."

Brilliana rubbed her belly before she caught herself and dropped her hand. "No, you never do," she said brightly. Her husband, Niall, took her hand with a secretive smile.

Gregory's eyes narrowed on the couple. It seemed that he and Monique were not the only ones who had jumped the gun, so to speak. And since Niall and Brilliana had been married scarcely a month, the two babies might very well be born close together. That ought to make Monique happy, since she and Brilliana had already become fast friends.

Niall's sister, Clarissa, gazed up at her husband, Edwin. "Mama was *certain* I was having a girl after some fortune-teller told her that I would, wasn't she?"

Edwin rolled his eyes. "A fortune-teller who can't predict the future. What a shock." He patted Clarissa's hand affectionately. "When your mother told us that, I knew it would be a boy. You could set a clock by the inerrancy of her fortune-teller's predictions."

"Well, it's a little early yet for us to be talking about children," Gregory said blithely. Not for the world would he have Monique embarrassed, as she was liable to be if people found out she'd conceived on the wrong side of the blanket.

"Is it?" Jeremy said with a suspicious gaze.

"You are incorrigible!" his wife cried. "Stop teasing Fulkham or he'll wonder why he puts up with us."

"He puts up with us because we're jolly good fun," Warren replied.

"You are, indeed," Gregory said, and raised his glass of punch.

The others raised their glasses and made a toast to the happy couple.

When they were done, Clarissa sighed and glanced around at her friends. "Well, ladies, now that Lord Fulkham gained himself a wife all on his own, we need a new bachelor to help."

Hart had the misfortune to walk up just in time to overhear his cousin's remark. When all the ladies turned their gazes on him, he held up his hands. "No. No, no, *no*. Not me. Set your sights elsewhere, ladies."

Gregory laughed. "You'd better run, then, Hart. Otherwise . . ."

That was all the warning Hart needed to make a quick about-face and head in the opposite direction. The gentlemen laughed.

"With these ladies nipping at his heels, he's as good as married already," Jeremy said.

"His goose is cooked," Niall said in agreement.

"Might as well put the shackles on his legs himself," Warren said.

His wife eyed him askance. "You don't consider *yourself* shackled, do you?"

Warren blinked. "No, not me. Certainly not." He glanced toward the orchestra in a panic. "They're starting up a waltz. Shall we, my dear?"

That seemed to mollify Delia, for she let him lead her away. The others drifted off, too, obviously drawn by the chance to dance entirely alone with their spouses instead of in the usual country dances.

Only Gregory and Monique remained. She leaned up to kiss his cheek. "I like your friends."

Friends. He actually had real friends, who came around not because they needed his help in some scheme, but because they liked him. How gratifying.

He finished his punch and set the glass on a nearby tray. "I think they're all quite mad."

"Yes," she agreed. "But a little madness never hurt anyone." Then she sobered, and her gaze went to where her grandmother was now dancing with the count.

Gregory took her hand. "Your grandmother seems to be settling in here very well. My mother is growing quite fond of her."

A frown crossed Monique's brow. "I still wonder sometimes if she would be happier in Chanay."

"Without you there? I doubt it." He squeezed her hand. "But if you wish, we could take her there. Now that Danworth's trial is over and he's been sentenced to hang for conspiracy to commit murder, I daresay I could get away for a few weeks. And I'm sure Princess Aurore and Lady Ursula would be delighted to have you for a visit."

"I would love to see them, too." She gazed up at him. "You wouldn't mind going? To be honest, I don't know how much longer Grand-maman has. Lately she's been talking about Grandpapa as if he is right there with her."

A lump stuck in his throat. "Perhaps he is. When you love someone, being apart is the worst punishment of all. I know that if I were here and you had gone on to the great beyond, I would pray to see your ghost every day, even if it meant I was insane."

Her eyes filled with a love that swelled his own heart. "That's the sweetest thing you've ever said to me." Then she broke into a teasing smile. "Although this talk of ghosts makes me wonder if you haven't been reading a bit too much of *Hamlet* lately."

He lifted an eyebrow. "You do realize it's the greatest play ever written by Shakespeare."

She laughed. "Forgive me, sir, but the greatest play ever written by Shakespeare is *Much Ado about Nothing*. And to quote his finest male character, Benedick, who can be almost as somber a fellow as you at times, 'Come, come, we are friends: Let's have a dance now we are married, that we may lighten our own hearts and our wives' heels.'"

"Wait a minute, I thought the line was, 'Let's have a dance *ere* we are married.'"

Striking her bosom in mock surprise, she said, "Why, Lord Fulkham, you *have* read a comedy or two."

He smirked at her as he quoted, "'Ask me no questions, and I'll tell you no fibs.'"

It was rather satisfying to watch her jaw drop. "You said you'd never seen or read *She Stoops to Conquer*!"

"Three years ago, no. But after a certain female handed me my pride on a platter, I thought it might be prudent to give it a go." He bent to whisper, "Just in case I ever happened to see her again."

"And you waited until now to tell me this astonishing tidbit?" she cried.

"The secret of flirting, my dear, is never to let on how much you like someone until you've secured them. Everyone knows that."

Then, while she was laughing, he led her to the floor.

Author's Note

The British politics in the book is relatively accurate, although some of the characters are invented (of course, since this is a fictional romance). Also, Guy Fawkes Day *had* become problematic at this time because it was celebrated *so* enthusiastically. I figured that made it safe to use in my book.

The London Conference of 1830 did exist and did come on the heels of the fight for Belgium's independence, although I fudged the dates by a few weeks to make it fit with Guy Fawkes Day and I telescoped the action. Most of the real events in the book took place over a span of months (not the conference itself, but the completion of the negotiations). But since I could find no information on what social gatherings were connected with the London Conference, I made some up.

Also, while the delegates *did* decide who was

going to be ruler of Belgium (and it did end up being Prince Leopold), there was no big vote and no structured group of delegates versus candidates. As far as I know, the candidates were never involved in the actual conference.

Prince Leopold, however, *was* second choice. First choice was a French prince, the Duke of Nemours, who turned it down because his father, King Louis-Philippe of France, saw what a political minefield it would be and cautioned against it. No woman was ever considered as a candidate. But the princes and princesses of Chanay *were* based in history, on the princes and princesses of Chimay, an actual Belgian principality. While none of them were candidates, the princely line stretches from 1486 until today and did include both male and female heirs, so I figured they *could* have been considered. Why not?

And after reading about the line of Chimay, I thought, *What if one of the princesses ran away with an actor and became exiled from the family?* That and the events surrounding Belgium's independence were the basis for my story.

*At St. George's Club, guardians conspire
to keep their unattached sisters and wards
out of the clutches of sinful suitors.
Which works fine...*

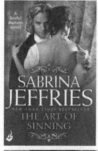
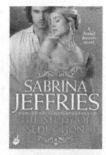
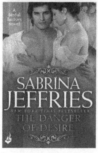

...except when the sinful suitors are members.

Don't be shy.
Meet the Sinful Suitors.

Available now from

HEADLINE
ETERNAL

Do you dare to encounter the
Hellions of Halstead Hall?

They're the scandalous Sharpes,
five hell-raising siblings tainted by a shocking family legacy.

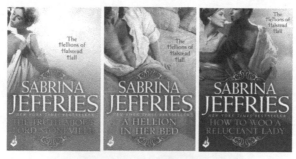

Meet Lord Oliver, Lord Jarret, Lady Minerva,
Lord Gabriel and Lady Celia.

Expect secrets, shenanigans and sensuous romance.

Available now from

HEADLINE
ETERNAL

HEADLINE
ETERNAL

FIND YOUR HEART'S DESIRE...

VISIT OUR WEBSITE: www.headlineeternal.com
FIND US ON FACEBOOK: facebook.com/eternalromance
CONNECT WITH US ON TWITTER: @eternal_books
FOLLOW US ON INSTAGRAM: @headlineeternal
EMAIL US: eternalromance@headline.co.uk